The Night Olivia Fell

Christina McDonald

ONE PLACE. MANY STORIES

HQ
An imprint of HarperCollins*Publishers* Ltd
1 London Bridge Street
London SE1 9GF

This edition 2019

1
First published in Great Britain by
HQ, an imprint of HarperCollins*Publishers* Ltd 2019

Copyright © Christina McDonald 2019

Christina McDonald asserts the moral right to be
identified as the author of this work.
A catalogue record for this book is
available from the British Library.

ISBN: 978-0-00-830766-0

MIX
Paper from
responsible sources
FSC™ C007454

This book is produced from independently certified FSC™ paper
to ensure responsible forest management.

For more information visit: www.harpercollins.co.uk/green

Printed and bound in Great Britain by
CPI Group (UK) Ltd, Croydon, CR0 4YY

For Richard, always and forever

*Also for every single parent out there doing the most difficult job
alone; but especially for my mom, the strongest and most inspiring
single mother I know. Thank you.*

PROLOGUE

'You want the truth? I'm –' My admission was cut off by a streak of blazing hot pain as something exploded against the side of my head. My brain barely registered the blow, my vision a dusky blur of red, pain searing into my skull and down my jaw. I felt my body spin with the force of it.

I reeled backward until my legs whacked against the low cement wall and I tumbled over, my body hurtling sideways across the ledge. A dark fog pressed against my outer vision, and before I knew it I was falling, plunging into empty space.

I hit the river on my back, my eyes fastened on the bridge's soaring spires illuminated by a flickering streetlamp.

Then the shadowy water tipped me under.

1

ABI

october

I woke abruptly, dreams tumbling from me in cottony wisps. I couldn't remember falling asleep, but the lamp on my bedside table had been switched off, the only light a full, glowing moon outside my window.

The phone was ringing.

'Olivia?' I murmured, hoping she'd get it so I wouldn't have to. My daughter was one of those people who could wake up and fall asleep as if flipping a switch.

I rolled over and peered at my alarm clock. The red lights blinked 4:48 a.m. Nobody called at this time of night with good news.

I bolted upright and grabbed the phone, the feather duvet sliding from my body, leaving my bed-warmed arms cold and exposed.

'Hello?'

'Hello, is this Abigail Knight?' The voice – a man's – was low and tight, coiled like a viper about to strike.

'Yes.'

'This is Portage Point Hospital. It's about your daughter, Olivia. I'm afraid there's been an accident.'

× × ×

I ran down the hall to Olivia's room, cold wings of fear fluttering in my stomach.

Her door was shut and I threw it open thinking, irrationally, that she'd sit up in bed blinking her eyes at me sleepily. I imagined, hoped, that she'd be angry at me for invading her teenage space. She'd throw a pillow at me, and I'd laugh weakly, clutching my chest with one hand as my heart rate returned to normal.

'I had a terrible dream,' I'd say.

'I'm fine, Mom,' she'd reply, looking at me with all the scorn a seventeen-year-old could muster. 'You worry too much.'

But her room was silent and empty, her bed a jumble of blankets. Dirty clothes spilled from the laundry basket in her half-open closet. Sheaves of paper were scattered in a disorganized jumble on her dresser.

I lurched out of the room, down the stairs, and into my car.

Last night, at the Stokeses' barbecue, she'd been fine.

But, no. I shook my head, really remembering. No, she *wasn't* fine. She hadn't been fine for a while.

Maybe it was just the typical moodiness of a teenager, but this felt different. Olivia was usually sunny and sweet. She was an easy teenager. The girl who never partied, got straight As, helped all her friends with their homework.

Lately she seemed distracted and temperamental, irritable whenever I asked what was wrong. And then there were the questions about her father.

She wants the truth.

The thought came fast, an ugly surprise. I set my teeth against it. I'd worried for so long that all the lies I kept hidden on the dark side of my heart would one day be washed into the open. These lies, my past, kept me always on guard.

× × ×

October drizzle coated the car, and a handful of brown leaves covered the windshield. The acidic feeling in my stomach clawed its way up toward my throat as I wrenched the car door open and threw myself inside. For once my old beater car started without any hesitation, as if it too knew we had to hurry.

I tore out of the driveway, my tires spinning in the gravel. I flicked the wipers on, but a single dead leaf was caught, wiping a jagged, wet arc across the windshield, back and forth, back and forth.

I thought of the last time I'd gone to the hospital with Olivia – she'd broken her arm falling out of the ancient willow tree in the backyard when she was ten. My guilt had been overwhelming. I'd failed at the most important job I would ever have: keeping her safe.

I gripped the leather steering wheel hard, securing myself to the

11

present while the past threatened to overtake me. My car squealed as I whipped around a corner too sharply. I was being reckless, I needed to slow down, but Olivia . . .

I couldn't even finish the thought. My daughter was my center of gravity, the only thing tying me to this earth. Without her, I'd surely float into space, a kite with its string severed by glass.

I pressed my foot hard against the accelerator as my knees began to shake. The decaying leaf was still stuck to the wiper but it had been ripped in half now, leaving the shape of a broken heart behind.

I braked sharply as I rounded the last corner and skidded into the hospital parking lot. It was nearly empty, one ambulance parked at the front, a handful of cars scattered across the lot. Streetlamps glinted against the wet pavement. I slammed on my brakes in a spot near the entrance just as the last half of the leaf in my windscreen was mercilessly ripped away.

×　×　×

I staggered into the hospital, cracking my elbow hard on the sliding door. Pain seethed toward my fingertips but didn't slow me down. I needed to find Olivia.

Please, please be okay.

A doctor appeared suddenly from a set of swinging doors. His steps were brisk, the swift, resolute walk of a man who knew what he was doing. Behind wire-rimmed glasses, his eyes were bloodshot when they landed on me.

'Abigail Knight?' I could just make out the clipped voice I'd heard on the phone. He had thinning white hair and a close-shaven face. Around his neck hung a stethoscope. His white coat had a rust-colored smear across the front.

He stepped closer and held one hand out to me. His eyebrows, thick as caterpillars, were pinched together.

'Where's Olivia?' I gasped, feeling like I would hyperventilate. People were staring, but I didn't care. 'Where's my daughter?'

I tried to sidestep him, but he moved his body to block me.

'I'm Dr Griffith.' He took a step closer. I could see the flecks of gold in his brown eyes. 'Will you come with me?'

'Why?' My voice sounded too high, the words crushed on my tongue. 'Where's Olivia?'

'I'm going to take you to her, but first we need to talk. Perhaps somewhere a bit more private.' The doctor's tone conveyed the gravity of what he had to say. The weight of it kept the frantic questions in my throat from vomiting out.

I looked around at the busy waiting room. A handful of people openly stared at us, while the rest fiddled with cell phones or pretended to read newspapers.

I nodded, a small jerk of my chin.

Dr Griffith led me through the swinging doors and down a brightly lit corridor to a private meeting room. The room smelled of floral potpourri and was decorated in pale pastels. The floor was shiny, the color of cinnamon, the walls a washed-out cream.

'Please. Sit.' Dr Griffith motioned toward a cushioned taupe chair. I sat stiffly on the edge.

He crossed to a water cooler in the corner of the room. A hulking tower of plastic cups, white, like vertebrae, leaned on a low black table next to it. He swiped one and filled it with water. The cooler gurgled and belched as air drifted to the top.

He thrust the cup toward me, but I just stared at it. I couldn't seem to get my hand to take it. Eventually he set it on the table.

Dr Griffith dragged a plastic chair from the wall and placed it across from me. The scraping of its feet against the floor set my teeth on edge. He sat, planted both feet on the ground, pressed his elbows against his knees, and steepled his fingers, as if in prayer.

'There's been an accident –' he said, repeating his earlier words.

'Is Olivia okay?' I interrupted.

But the way he was looking at me. With pity. I knew.

An intense desire to run hit me. My shins still burned from my run yesterday morning, my thigh muscles ached, but I felt the pang hit my body hard.

I jumped up, looking around wildly. The doctor stood, eyeing me as if I were a wild animal. But the urge to know kept me rooted to my spot.

'Tell me. . .' I rasped.

'Your daughter . . .' Dr Griffith touched my forearm. His hand was heavy, cool against my clammy skin.

He said something about an accident.

Somebody finding Olivia at the bottom of an embankment near the ZigZag Bridge.

Something about a grand mal seizure, corneal reflexes, and a Glasgow score of four.

He said something about a head wound, about fixed and dilated pupils and a CAT scan.

That they'd taken her in for surgery as soon as she'd arrived.

I couldn't make sense of any of it.

I collapsed on the chair, bending forward until my head was between my knees, as if preparing for a crash landing. I could hear my heart throbbing in my chest, the blood roaring in my ears, the harsh hiss of my breath as it rushed in and out of me in sharp, hollow gasps. My elbow throbbed painfully where I'd banged it.

'No . . . no . . .' I pleaded over and over, clenching and unclenching my sweat-soaked hands.

The doctor sat next to me, his voice breaking through the heavy, viscous bubble surrounding me.

'—sustained severe head trauma. I'm really sorry, Mrs Knight, but your daughter has suffered permanent and irreversible brain damage.'

My mind reeled, trying to assimilate these facts into something that made sense. Shards of his words assaulted me through a roar of panic.

'Is there someone we can call . . . ?'

Who was there? My mom was dead. I never knew my dad. There was no husband, no boyfriend. I was too busy being a mother to date, too busy to have friends. There was only . . .

'My sister.' My voice sounded very far away, as if it came from down the hall rather than my own mouth.

I wrote Sarah's number on a scrap of paper. He took it and opened the door, handed it to somebody, then sat back down across from me.

'I'm so sorry, Mrs Knight, we did everything we could to save her, but Olivia won't wake up. Right now she's attached to life support that's keeping her body alive.' He licked his lips, on the verge of saying something else. 'But she . . .'

'She's an organ donor,' I whispered numbly.

It was what they wanted, wasn't it? The day she got her driver's license Olivia had signed up to save another's life. 'You know,' she'd said, shrugging with the confidence the young have that they're impervious to death. 'If it ever came to that.' My kind, gentle girl.

'No, that's not – What I mean to say is, we can't legally turn Olivia's life support off in her condition.'

I didn't understand. It was as if he had suddenly started speaking Urdu. A throb began pulsing under my eyes.

He cleared his throat, his eyes scurrying momentarily away from mine. 'We can't turn life support off from a pregnant woman. Not in Washington State.'

'Wh –?' I breathed. My body went limp, boneless, my head spinning.

'Olivia was – is – Olivia's pregnant.'

2

OLIVIA

april, 6 months earlier

The yellow school bus swayed slowly past the glimmering sea that fringed Portage Point and headed toward Seattle: our day-trip destination.

'Ughh, the bus is so bo-o-oring.' My best friend, Madison, flopped back in her seat next to me. She took a compact from her purse and started sweeping powder across her already-matte nose.

We were heading to the University of Washington for the start of our two-day college tour. I didn't know why she was complaining. Being away from school was like a vacation.

Madison tossed her long dark hair and peeked over her shoulder. I knew she was looking at Peter and barely resisted rolling my eyes. Madison could be totally ADD when it came to guys.

I slid the cool metal of my charm bracelet through my fingers. 'At least we're out of school,' I said.

'Too bad we can't do something fun.' She applied a shiny layer of cotton-candy-pink gloss to her lips and smacked them loudly. 'Filling out college applications is totally lame.'

I bit my cheeks so I wouldn't say anything. Madison's parents were rich. She didn't really feel the same pressure I did about college.

My mom, on the other hand, scrimped and saved every penny so I could go to college after I graduated next year. Four years of tuition was totally going to break her. I kept offering to get a part-time job, but she'd just say my job was to study hard and do well in school.

I stared past Madison out the bus window and chewed a lock of hair. Sunlight slid through the window, interrupted every so often by the shade of passing trees.

'Did you see Zitty Zara's new zit this morning?' Madison stage-whispered. 'I think there's a science experiment happening on her forehead.'

'Don't be mean!' I smacked her softly, trying not to laugh. Zara *did* have gross skin, but I felt bad for her.

'Don't they have Accutane now?' Madison continued. 'Why doesn't she take it?'

She'd dropped all pretense of whispering, so I shot her a warning look. Zara was only a few rows in front of us. I didn't want her hearing.

But Madison ignored me. She could be mean. Like, hurtfully mean. Once in fourth grade we got in a fight, and Madison got all the girls in our class to stop talking to me. Girls who'd been my friends just 'forgot' to save me a seat on the bus or invite me to their sleepovers. I'd never forgotten that feeling of not belonging, like wearing someone else's shoes and feeling the pain all over. Since then I'd made sure never, ever to get on Madison's bad side.

'What's in a zit anyway?' she asked.

I snickered. 'It's pus, you idiot.'

'Eww. God, even the word is gross. *Puh, puh, puh*-sss.' She leaned hard on the *p* sound. I laughed out loud. '*Puh*-ss,' she enunciated. 'It's like an ejection from your mouth. A voiding of *puh-ss* from a *puh-stule*.'

'Oh God! Gross!' I gasped, breathless from concealing my laughter.

A few rows ahead, Zara turned around. We both ducked below the seat in front of us, laughing hysterically.

My phone beeped, and I pulled it from my backpack. It was my mom.

Knock knock

Who's there? I texted back.

Mom: *Olive*

Me: *Olive who?*

Mom: *Olive ya Olivia!*

I laughed and sent her a row of *x*'s and *o*'s just as Tyler's head popped up over the back of our seat.

'Hey, babe.' His amber-flecked hazel eyes crinkled in a smile.

My boyfriend was your typical high school athlete. He was captain of the football team, had lettered in every sport he did, and was working toward a football scholarship to UW. He was way popular, and he knew it. Like, in a confident way, not in a dickhead way.

He leaned down and licked my earlobe, trying to be seductive. I giggled and lurched away from him. He frowned, looking slightly put out.

'God, you guys! Get a room!' Madison huffed loudly.

Heat spread up my neck and into my cheeks. Madison could be such a bitch sometimes. Mom told me I should stand up to her. Tyler said I always saw the best in people.

The truth was, neither of them was right. I was just scared of not being liked.

Just then Tyler's friend Peter leaned over the seat next to Tyler. 'Jesus, you're the color of a tomato, Liv!' he hooted.

He reached out to touch my flaming cheek, but Tyler smacked his hand away, eyes blazing. 'Don't touch her, man.'

My cheeks burned even hotter, but Peter just laughed.

'You're such a lunatic.' Madison rolled her eyes flirtatiously.

Tyler's eyes tightened and his jaw clenched. 'Shut up, Madison. You're just salty 'cause you can't get a boyfriend.'

I forced a loud laugh. 'At least my face isn't as red as your hair, Peter,' I joked, trying to defuse the situation.

'Whatever, asshole.' Madison twisted in her seat so she could scowl out the bus's window. She popped the earbuds to her iPhone in her ears and turned the volume up until I could hear the tinny beat of pop music.

'Ignore her.' Tyler tugged me from my seat and sat in my place, pulling me onto his lap and nuzzling my cheek. Tyler and Madison had never really gotten along. She thought he was way too needy.

With his wavy blond hair and hazel eyes, Tyler was the hottest guy in school. I'd worked hard for my seat at the popular table, but that seat had only been firmly cemented when Tyler and I started dating. And it felt nice being his girlfriend. But it was still mortifying when he tried to make out with me in front of everybody.

'I've been thinking about yesterday,' Tyler whispered in my ear.

I blushed again, blood pulsing in my ears. I looked around, hoping nobody could hear him.

Yesterday we'd had a heavy make-out session in my room before my mom got home from work. He got a little too excited, and I'd felt so pressured I burst into tears. He could be like that sometimes: too insistent and intense. But weren't all boys?

He leaned away from me and cracked his neck. I shuddered, grossed out by the sound of his bones popping.

'I'm sorry about . . . you know,' he said. 'It's just, I love you. I think we've been together long enough to show it that way.'

'Soon, okay? I'm just not ready yet.'

'I was thinking. . .' He leaned closer and kissed my cheek wetly. 'Maybe one of these weekends we could make it extra special? Go somewhere, just us? You could tell your mom you're spending the night at Madison's.'

I wanted to laugh at how ridiculous he sounded. What would we do, rent a hotel room for the night? Besides, I didn't want to have sex yet. I wasn't going to be one of those stupid knocked-up teenagers – like my mom was.

But I didn't say that. Instead I smiled and said: 'Sure, yeah, maybe.' I didn't want to hurt his feelings, and if it would make him happy, I'd let him think we could go away for a night.

The bus lurched to a stop, and I realized we'd arrived at the University of Washington.

21

'We're here!' somebody shouted from the front of the bus.

Madison pulled her earbuds out and pointed out the window. 'There's everybody else!'

I followed her gaze. A group of about forty teenagers was gathered at the end of the parking lot. Half of them were wearing casual clothes, but the other half were dressed in matching uniforms: the girls in green tartan skirts with green blazers and knee-high stockings, the boys in gray pants and green ties.

'Preppy dicks!' Peter shouted. A slice of sunlight shone on his red hair and lit the smattering of freckles across his face. He was watching Madison, waiting for a reaction. For his sake, I hoped he stayed away from her. She would eat him alive, and Peter was actually a pretty nice guy. Tyler called her a thot behind her back. If she weren't my best friend, I'd probably agree. She'd go out with a different guy every weekend, then dump him the next day.

'Fuckheads!' Tyler's friend Dan shouted.

Bold and bullish, Dan was a fat little tryhard, but his overconfidence and arrogance meant nobody stood up to him. Tyler thought Dan was hilarious. I thought he was a jerk.

'Watch your mouth, guys!' Mr Parks, our PE teacher who was running this little field trip, yelled from the front of the bus. 'Come on, off the bus.'

We stepped out into the glorious spring sunshine. It was one of those pristine Seattle days when the rain has finally stopped, leaving behind a scrubbed blue sky. The air had just a hint of warmth in it, a promise that more days like this would soon follow.

Cherry trees coated in frothy pink and white blossoms peeked from between towering evergreens. In the distance I could see the start of Greek Row, a collection of Tudor, Gothic, and Georgian fraternity and sorority houses.

'Over here, guys!' Mr Parks waved his arms to us, his beefy biceps rippling under his white polo shirt. We shuffled over, and Mr Parks made introductions: Portage Point High, Ballard High, and Seattle Catholic Academy, the Catholic kids in the uniforms.

Somehow we'd faced off so we were separated into three groups, but once we'd been introduced, everybody started talking to each other.

Tyler had an arm draped around my shoulder, tucking me tightly against his body. Madison was just to the right of me. I felt comfortable, safe, secure in my world.

And then I saw her.

Just steps from me was a girl wearing the green school uniform of Seattle Catholic Academy. She had long, pale blonde hair, sharp Slavic cheekbones, a pointed nose, and a slightly off-center dimple in her chin.

As she swung her eyes toward me, I felt my world slipping toward the edge of a cliff I didn't even know existed.

She looked like she could be my sister.

The girl's eyes widened when she saw me, emphasizing the unusual shade of forest green: just like mine.

In that instant, as I looked at the face I'd known my entire life, I felt myself tumble over that cliff. I didn't know how far I would fall or how hard I would crash, only that nothing would ever be the same.

3

ABI

october

'Do you understand what I'm saying, Mrs Knight?'

I blinked at Dr Griffith, not sure I'd heard him right.

'Your daughter is pregnant.' He spoke slowly, as if I were a child unable to grasp his words. 'Olivia's suffered irreversible brain damage and she won't wake up, but Washington State law prohibits us from turning off life support. We have to give the fetus the best chance at surviving. Do you understand?'

I nodded and shook my head at the same time. I *did* understand, but it made no sense, as if he'd grabbed random words from a dictionary and pasted them into a sentence.

'Wha –?'

A knock at the door interrupted me, and a pink-scrub-clad nurse with the sad, droopy face and flabby jowls of a Saint Bernard entered.

'Mrs Knight, your sister –'

Sarah burst past the nurse, elbowing her way into the room. Her blue eyes were laced with red, the translucent skin of her lids as raw and puffy as mine. She grabbed my hand, and I stared at her fingers. Her nails were smooth and perfectly oval, shining red, the color of fresh blood. Even now in the middle of the night, her long, perfectly highlighted hair swung and shone under the anemic hospital lights.

She pulled me in for a hug so hard it hurt my ribs. I stiffened and she dropped her arms, a shadow of hurt crossing her face. It had always been there, this slight distance between us. My fault, admittedly, but I no longer knew how to stop it.

'Where's Olivia? Is she okay? What happened? Why was she out in the middle of the night?'

The questions were rapid as a machine gun, asked in Sarah's most demanding mom voice. The one she'd been practicing since I was ten and she was twenty, when our mother left me on Sarah's front step with nothing but a backpack of dirty clothes. She'd gone home and killed herself that very day, leaving Sarah to raise me.

I shook my head, tears rising in my throat.

'She . . . she . . .'

I didn't know why Olivia was out in the middle of the night.

After my bath, I'd had some wine and then gone to bed with a book. I was asleep while my daughter was out doing . . . what?

The dark fog of anxiety swirled violently around me.

Panic: my old friend.

'Mrs Knight?' I heard from somewhere far away.

My vision blurred and a high-pitched whining droned in my ears. I couldn't hold it away anymore. I crashed to the ground.

'Abi!' People rushed around me, hands lifted me up, pushed me into a chair.

I was sweating heavily. The air was like molasses, weighted like water.

Somebody pressed a paper bag into my hands, and I heard Sarah's soothing voice speaking to me from a great distance.

'Breathe. There you go. In, then out. In, then out.'

I used to have panic attacks all the time as a kid. But I'd learned to control my emotions, stamping them out like the flames of a fire. Sarah always said I should talk about my feelings, get them out there, but I knew it was better to push them away, pretend everything was okay. It was better not to feel anything.

Somehow, without me even wanting to, my breathing evened, my heart rate slowed. And then my hearing came back. Dr Griffith and Sarah were talking.

'What happened?' Sarah asked.

Sarah was good at being composed in tough situations. She never seemed desperate or panicky. I felt a stab of anger that she could manage this. I couldn't even ask the right questions.

'A retired paramedic found Olivia on the banks of the ZigZag River, next to the bridge. We don't know if she fell from the bridge or – well, the police will investigate,' Dr Griffith replied. He was crouched in front of me, holding one of my hands tightly in his. His skin felt dry and cool against my sweaty palm.

Sarah shifted in her seat next to me, her hand holding the paper bag to my mouth. 'People come out of comas all the time –' she began.

'Olivia isn't in a coma,' he interrupted gently. 'Comas are usually from a localized injury. Olivia's suffered a massive bleed, which has damaged almost every part of her brain. I'm so sorry, I know this is hard to understand and even harder to accept, but Olivia isn't going to wake up.'

Grief hurtled toward me, crashing into me and beating inside my chest like a giant, furious animal.

'And she's pregnant?' I whispered.

'Yes,' Dr Griffith replied.

I looked at Sarah. Her jaw worked, as if she were chewing leather.

'How far along?' I asked.

'We'll do an ultrasound to find out for sure, but the HCG hormone indicates about thirteen or fourteen weeks.'

I thought back to what we were doing three months ago. It would've been July. Olivia was out of school. She was studying for her driver's test, taking practice SAT tests, swimming, hanging out with her friends.

We hadn't done anything special. Money was always tight, and I was saving for the tuition I knew I'd have to pay when Olivia went to college. I couldn't put my finger on when something might've changed, when she would've gotten pregnant. She must not have known. She would've told me if she'd known.

'Surely the baby's been exposed to radiation, chemicals . . . ?' Sarah trailed off.

Dr Griffith winced. 'Yes. Possibly. Probably. We do a standard pregnancy test when female patients are admitted, but it was delayed by the surgery.'

A dusty vent blew stale air into the room, the noise an obnoxious whine. Sarah and Dr Griffith had lapsed into silence.

'I want to see her. Right now.' My voice was hollow and flat.

'Of course,' Dr Griffith said immediately.

Sarah helped me to my feet, and we followed the doctor down the corridor, toward the ICU.

Despite the harsh reality of the stark white hallway, a part of me still clung to the faint hope that Olivia wasn't here – that this was all some horrible mistake, some silly clerical error. Not my daughter.

Dr Griffith walked briskly to the end of the hallway and turned left, then waved a security badge at a locked door. Inside the ICU Jen Stokes, Olivia's best friend's mother, hovered over a bed that was surrounded by beeping, clunking machines. A stethoscope dangled from her neck.

'Dr Stokes,' Dr Griffith greeted her.

'Jen?' I stared at my neighbor. Just a few hours ago, I'd been at a barbecue at her house, and now we were standing in the ICU. She was wearing faded jeans and an old Seahawks jersey under a lab coat. Her eyes were red, her dark curls a messy halo around a pale face. Her hands were clasped into tight fists and pressed into her belly.

'What are you doing here?' I asked.

'I called her,' Sarah explained; then I remembered that Jen was the senior doctor in the emergency room here.

'Abi, I'm so sorry.' Her mouth worked as if she wanted to say more, but nothing else came. She broke eye contact and looked down.

I followed her gaze, but it took me a moment to realize that the person she was staring at was Olivia. My daughter was as white as the sheet she lay on. Her body was too still, as if all her dynamic energy had been trapped beneath the sheet draped over her.

A tangle of IV bags and pumps surrounded the hospital bed. So many tubes and lines I couldn't count them: down her throat, breathing for her, up her nose, keeping her stomach empty, flowering from her chest, recording her heartbeat. The ventilator next to the bed made rhythmic *blip, shhhh* noises.

Her head was swathed in white bandages, stark against her face. She had a deep cut above her right eyebrow, a sickening black and purple bruise blooming across her left temple, and a spray of scratches across her nose and cheekbones.

I stared at my daughter, and the agony I felt wasn't just emotional but physical. A sharp pain wrenched in my chest so it seemed my heart must've stopped, but I could feel it, I could hear it; it betrayed me by continuing to beat when it should have frozen in my chest. The pain and impotence were white lightning searing through me.

My gaze drifted to Olivia's abdomen, still flat and smooth, no hint of the baby tucked within.

Somewhere in the back of my mind I registered Jen leaving the room. The emotions piled up, threatening to crack me open, splintering me into a billion little pieces. I reached for Olivia's hand, wanting – no, *needing* – to be connected to her.

Her wrist lay limply in my hand, but something was missing. The silver charm bracelet Olivia always wore was gone.

In its place was a string of black and purple bruises.

4

OLIVIA

april

'That girl. Jesus. That was creepy,' Tyler said the Monday after our field trip to the University of Washington. We were eating lunch at our usual table in the cafeteria, the one next to the neatly stacked towers of orange chairs used for pep assemblies.

'I know, right!' Peter said. His carrot-red head bobbed in agreement. 'What was that about? Do you have a sister we don't know about, Liv?'

I shook my head emphatically. 'No way.'

Next to me, Tyler shoved a handful of fries into his mouth. 'She was totally your doppelgänger,' he said. 'My dad says everybody has one somewhere.'

'I guess.' I set my peanut butter and jelly sandwich down, my appetite suddenly gone. I didn't want to talk about this. Why wouldn't they just shut up?

'She had the same butt chin, too,' Peter added. 'She looked *just* like you.'

Tyler frowned at Peter. I ground my teeth together, waiting for Tyler to make some snappy clapback. Tyler always called my chin dimple a butt chin. Not in a mean way, just in a Tyler way. But I knew he wouldn't like anybody else saying it.

But Tyler went back to his fries. I let out a breath I didn't know I was holding.

Madison laughed and bit into a carrot stick. 'Having a chin dimple doesn't mean you're related to somebody, you idiot.'

'She's not my sister, *all right*?' I snapped. 'I've never even met her before.'

Everybody went quiet. My heart pulsed in my neck and I looked down. I felt them all exchanging looks. I was the peace-maker. I never lashed out or got involved in arguments.

I picked at the edge of my sandwich until it was as bare as a stone. I hated the dry feel of crust in my mouth. When I was a kid my mom would cut the crusts off my sandwich, snip away the square edges, and cut a little bite-size hole in the middle so it looked like an O. I suddenly wished she were here to reassure me.

Madison abruptly changed the subject. 'Sooooo, my brother's coming home next week.'

My head snapped up and blood rushed to my cheeks. I let my hair swing in front of my face to hide it, chewing hard on a strand of hair.

Tyler snorted and dropped an arm around my shoulders, pull-ing me closer to him. 'Can he score us some pot?'

'Tyler!' I shushed him.

'Shut up, fuck-face.' Madison's dark eyes flashed. 'It was only one time. He was just stupid enough to get caught.'

'Wait. I thought he was in New York. Isn't that where your parents sent him after he got caught dealing?' Peter's freckled face creased with confusion.

Madison scowled. '*Once!* And it was only pot.'

She was mortified that everybody knew Derek had been sent to a private East Coast school to 'reform' him. We all drank sometimes and a few of our friends smoked pot, but only stoners and losers actually dealt it.

Peter's eyes darted between Madison and Tyler, sensing the tension.

'Olivia,' he said, changing the subject quickly. 'You don't have swimming practice tomorrow, right? Could you help me with some chemistry shit later? I'm on that homework grind, trying to catch up again.'

'Sure.' I darted a look at Tyler. His brows folded down. I could tell he wasn't happy with me studying alone with Peter.

He could be a little possessive sometimes. It wasn't like I'd ever cheated on him or anything. He was just like that: all macho on the outside but sort of insecure on the inside. I knew it was just because he loved me, though.

'Thanks, dude.' Peter grinned at me.

I scraped myself out of the hard metal chair. 'I'm going outside for some fresh air. Wanna come, Mad?'

Madison unfolded her slender frame and stood, brushing off her black leggings and black sleeveless sweater. She tossed a hard glare at Tyler and Peter and huffed toward the door.

We stepped into the cool belly of April and headed for the quad, huddling on a bench near the fountain. We were the only students around, the air still too crisp to sit outside.

Clouds raced overhead as if they were on a conveyor belt; one minute it was sunny, the next threatening rain. Squinting at Madison, I tried to judge her mood.

I fiddled with the bracelet on my left wrist, pulling the cool metal through my fingers, back and forth.

'Sorry about Derek,' I offered.

''S okay. Sorry about that girl.' She picked a hangnail. 'I'm sure she isn't, like, your sister or anything.'

I appreciated her saying it. No matter how moody Madison could be, I knew I could always count on her. It's probably why we were still best friends all these years later.

We'd met in kindergarten and became friends when it turned out we both hated playing dress-up. I didn't want anyone knowing my mom made me wear long underwear under my clothes all winter. Madison just wanted to play outside.

'Do you think you'll, you know, look her up?' Madison asked.

I shrugged. I didn't want to admit I'd talked to her in the bathroom at the University of Washington.

Up close she didn't look quite as much like me as I'd thought. Even though her eyes were the exact same shade of green as mine, hers were slightly wider spaced. The dimple in her chin wasn't as pronounced as mine, her cheekbones not as sharp, her nose a little smaller. Still, she made me uncomfortable.

She'd dried her hands, then leaned casually against the sink.

'I'm Kendall Montgomery,' she said. She flipped her long blonde hair over one shoulder in that way bitchy rich girls did.

'I'm Olivia,' I replied.

There was an awkward pause. 'My dad's dead,' I blurted, afraid she was going to say something about how alike we looked. 'Just in case you thought we might be related. And there's no way we have the same mom.'

'That's too bad.' She smirked. 'My parents are assholes. It'd be awesome if I could replace them.'

I laughed, a rush of surprised air bursting out of me. At least I was always glad my mom was my mom. Her entire life was dedicated to me. Sometimes a bit too much.

'Where do you live?' she asked.

'Portage Point. It's this tiny town just south of –'

'I know Portage Point. That's where my mom's from.'

There was a heavy silence as we both realized what she'd said.

'Your mom?' My palms suddenly felt hot and damp.

'Well, not from. . .' She hesitated. 'That's where she lived when she was in high school, I guess.'

I didn't know what to say.

'Anyway,' Kendall said, heading for the door, 'it was nice meeting you, Olivia.'

'Yeah, you too. See you around.'

She'd waved, a little flick of her fingers, and left.

On the bench, I turned to Madison and shook my head. 'Naww. I don't think I'll look her up. What would be the point? I already know she isn't related to me.'

'You don't *know know* that,' Madison countered.

34

I stared at her. 'What do you mean?'

'Well, what if you have a long-lost dad out there and a whole other family? What if your mom had, like, some illicit affair or something?'

The idea was so ridiculous I laughed out loud. I couldn't imagine my mom having some passionate affair. She was like a study in self control – she frowned but never yelled; she smiled but never laughed too loud; her makeup was always lightly done, her clothes neatly ironed.

Mom was as steady as a statue. There was none of that flighty, hyper-gossipy vibe that some of my friends' moms had. She was the type of mom who was always there for me, ready with a tissue if I needed to cry or sitting in the stands cheering me on at swim meets.

'Yeah, right!' I snorted. 'She wouldn't know how to flirt, let alone have an affair. Plus, she'd be all worried she'd get an STD or something.'

Madison laughed too. 'Okay, maybe that girl's your dad's daughter.'

'My dad's dead, Mad.'

'I know, but maybe he had another family before he died? Or he was cheating on your mom? Or'– she widened her eyes dramatically –'maybe he *isn't* dead.'

I rolled my eyes. 'You really need to lay off the soap operas.'

'Get woke, Olivia. You're so naïve. Sometimes people lie, and you don't even know why,' Madison replied.

I flinched as the insult hit me. 'I really don't think my mom would lie to me about my dad.'

'How do you know? Sometimes the truth hurts.'

'So do lies,' I said under my breath.

× × ×

That night, Mom came home with an armful of groceries and announced she was going to cook. I cringed. Martha Stewart she was not. Usually her cooking experiments ended in disaster.

Once she tried to bake these Cornish game hens with this gross, gloopy sauce, but she turned the oven on broil instead of bake. Within a half hour the whole house was filled with a smoke so thick you could almost chew it.

I wished we could just order pizza.

'So, what're we making?' I put my game face on and started unpacking ingredients from the paper bags. I didn't want to hurt her feelings or anything.

'Spaghetti bolognese.' She reached for the other bag and pulled out fresh basil, a bulb of garlic, an onion, one carrot.

I smiled. Mom hated carrots, but I loved them. She always got one and cooked it up to put on the side for me.

'Okay, I've got a good one,' she said, peeling the skin from an onion. 'Knock knock.'

'Who's there?'

'Puma.'

'Puma who?'

'Hurry up or I'll puma pants.'

'Eww, yuck, Mom!' I laughed. 'That's totally gross!'

She chuckled. 'Thought you'd enjoy that.'

'So. What's the occasion?' I waved at the ingredients.

'Oh, I don't know.' She shrugged and laughed. 'I'm off work early, and you're going to be a senior in high school pretty soon, and I'm just so proud of my girl.' She pulled me in for a hug and kissed me on the forehead.

My mom was a toucher. She patted my shoulders, stroked my hair, kissed my cheek, hugged me. She held my hand when we crossed the road until I was ten and started getting teased about it. Once I asked her why she always touched me and she said, 'I guess it makes me feel more connected to you.'

Sometimes it felt weird hugging my mom, like I was too old for hugs, but it was nice, too.

'How was your day?' she asked as I minced garlic.

'Good. I got an A on my history test, and we finished the layout for the yearbook.'

She'd stopped chopping onion and looked at me intently. She had this way about her where she really listened, even to the most trivial things.

Soon the scent of garlic and onion sizzling in butter mingled with the rich smell of hamburger. The diced carrot was boiling in a small pot on the stove. Mom popped the french stick in the oven to warm, and we piled our plates high with pasta and took them to the dining room table.

'Mom.' I dumped my carrots over my sauce and stirred them in, trying to seem casual. 'Can I ask you some stuff about my dad?'

A noodle slid off the edge of Mom's fork and landed with a soft plop on her plate. She stabbed at it and cleared her voice.

'Sure, sweetie. What do you want to know?'

'Well . . .' My mind whirled.

Usually she didn't want to talk. Not that I asked often. She'd always get this funny frozen half-smile on her face, like she was in pain. But since seeing that girl Kendall, I don't know, I guess it got me thinking more about him.

'How far along with me were you when he died?'

Mom took another bite of her pasta and screwed up her face into her thinky look – lips twisted to one side, eyebrows down, eyes up.

'Only a few weeks. I never got the chance to tell him.'

'Was he hot?' I smiled slyly. 'You know, when you first met him, did you get all fluttery inside?'

'Very!' She fanned her face with her hand and laughed. 'He made my knees weak. All that blond hair and those brown eyes. I could just fall into them.'

I paused, my brain jamming on that one word. 'Brown?'

'Yeah.'

I stared at her hard. She'd told me before that his eyes were green, just like mine. I remembered the day, the very moment, she said it. I'd held that nugget of information in my heart since I was thirteen, proof that I was connected to the father I never met in some tangible way.

I waited for her to retract it, to assure me she wasn't lying. But she didn't.

I stared at her, scrambling to untangle the threads overloading my brain.

'Did he have, like, another family?' I asked finally.

Late-afternoon sunlight flooded in through the open curtains and beamed across the dining room table. The light fell on Mom's face, landing in lines carved so deep she suddenly looked twenty years older.

Mom burst out laughing. 'No, of course not! What on earth gave you that idea?'

I watched her carefully, looking for any cracks.

'Well, like, maybe I have brothers or sisters out there I don't know about.'

For a moment the prospect of her reply opened under me like a gaping hole. What she said now, I knew, could change everything.

Suddenly she jumped up, eyes wide. 'Oh my goodness! The bread!'

She threw the oven open and a cloud of black, acrid smoke billowed out. I slipped the oven mitts on and grabbed the charred french stick, tossing it in the garbage while Mom threw open the sliding glass door and started fanning the air with a kitchen towel. Chilly spring air blew through the house, dissipating the smoke. But the bitter smell of something burning remained.

Mom pushed at a lock of blonde hair stuck to her forehead with sweat. 'I'm sorry, sweetie. I guess we won't be having bread with our pasta.'

'It's okay. It wouldn't be a homemade dinner if we didn't burn something,' I joked.

She laughed sheepishly. 'Why don't you tell me about school? Not too long and you'll be a senior. How does that feel?'

Her words tumbled out too fast, her voice edgy as a serrated knife.

'Mom, you haven't answered my question. Did my dad have other kids?'

A puff of clouds rolled over the sun, shifting the light and casting sporadic shadows over Mom's face. I felt a quiver in the air, a vibration like electricity that weaved its way through the burnt toast smell.

Mom met my gaze, her blue eyes innocent. 'Nope,' she said. 'Your dad died before he even knew about you and he most certainly didn't have any other children.'

I stared at her smooth face, trying to get a handle on the emotions rolling through me: fear, panic, confusion, anger. Mostly anger, because something told me she was lying.

A dark horror slid into my heart. I'd always trusted my mom. Trusted everything she said, obeyed everything she told me to do. I'd never thought twice about questioning her.

But now I felt that trust disappearing like evaporating mist. If she could lie to me about something as fundamental as this, what else had she kept from me?

5

ABI

october

As the hours bled into each other, I alternated between numbness and sorrow, each as intense and debilitating as the other.

'I need to know what happened,' I said to Sarah.

She was so still, barely moving since we'd settled in the family waiting room the doctors gave us. I couldn't hold still, pacing the floor, counting the ceiling tiles, pouring water from one cup to another. I needed to move, to do something. My analytical brain needed to make sense of things, to question the facts and frame the story, to make the columns align, the numbers add up.

'You should go home. Get some rest,' she replied.

I glared at her. 'I'm not going anywhere.' Olivia and I were linked by birth, by life. I wouldn't leave her in death.

More time passed. 'Why does she have bruises on her arms?' I asked Sarah, slamming an empty cup to the ground. I sucked my lips over my teeth, trying to steady myself. 'Do you think some-body hurt her?'

Sarah looked startled. 'I don't know. The police – they'll inves-tigate.'

Tears tumbled down my cheeks, sliding into the hollow of my neck. I could barely breathe, whimpers racking my body as I sank into a chair. Sarah came to me, slid her arms around my shoulders. We held each other like that for a long time, our bodies shaking.

'I wanted to keep her safe!' I sobbed.

'This isn't your fault, Abi,' she replied, her voice raw with pain.

I pulled away and looked into her reddened eyes.

'What if it is?'

× × ×

Night washed over Olivia's room. The hospital lights turned on one by one, and still I didn't move from my seat next to her bed, the intermittent bleeps and swooshes keeping Olivia connected to this world a bizarre lullaby to my pain. Despair swirled inside me, a relentless fog that made me incapable of anything: eating, drink-ing, moving.

I stared, lost, at the bruises circling Olivia's wrists. They were ringed with blue and purple, as if someone had grabbed her, stain-ing her beautiful skin with the color of anger.

I laid my forehead on the edge of her bed, grateful to be alone with her. All day the doctors had encouraged me to go home, get some rest. Sarah had brought me a ham sandwich, left untouched and eventually tipped into the garbage, and then relentless cups of coffee. But it just made me need to pee, and I didn't want to leave Olivia. So I stopped drinking altogether.

My head pounded from tears and dehydration, but I couldn't leave. Not yet. I felt like I was living inside a tear in the fabric of time, the real world outside on pause.

Two days had passed since my dash to Olivia's broken body, time shuffling past with excruciating slowness. More doctors trundled in, more reports, another CT scan, an ultrasound showing a fetal heartbeat. Cautionary whispers that she might miscarry and more whispers that if her heart held up long enough, they could save the baby.

Save the baby? I wanted them to save *my* baby.

I slept in fits and spurts, my forehead pressed against Olivia's stomach. Night inched by. Alarm bells rang intermittently, and I imagined the people being told their loved one hadn't made it. I imagined what would happen when it was Olivia's turn.

I awoke with a start when somebody shook my shoulder.

'Mrs Knight?' Dr Griffith held a cup of water out to me. 'Why don't you have a drink?'

'It's Miss,' I corrected him. 'I'm not married.' My voice rasped, my throat barren of any moisture. But still I refused the water.

He slid a chair across the room and sat next to me, the cup clasped between both hands. 'Miss Knight. You need to take care of yourself. You need to eat, drink, get some rest.'

'Why does everyone keep saying that?' I burst out. Pain ripped through me, undiminished by the passing hours, and I pressed my fingers hard into my temples.

'You have a long road ahead of you.' He glanced at Olivia. 'All three of you.'

I stared at him for a long moment, tried to lick my cracked lips.

'Olivia isn't coming back,' he said gently. 'But there's a chance your grandchild could survive.' It hurt him to say this, I could tell by the tightening of his eyes, and it made me like him. Or at least respect him.

'How long?' I finally said.

'How long what?'

'How long does Olivia have to be on life support for the baby –' I broke off, the words skewering my heart.

'We'd aim to get her to thirty-two weeks' gestation.'

I did the math quickly. Eighteen more weeks on life support.

'Is it possible?'

Dr Griffith hesitated. 'As far as I'm aware, it's never happened before. But I think it's possible.'

I tried to breathe, but a solid lump had formed in my chest, squeezing all the oxygen out. I clenched my eyes shut, then opened them.

'Why haven't the police come? Where are they?'

Dr Griffith looked surprised. He took his glasses off and polished them on his lab coat.

'The hospital doesn't report . . . accidents.'

'Accidents? This wasn't an accident!' My voice pitched high, anger and pain surging through my body. 'You've seen the bruises on her wrists!'

'My apologies.' Dr Griffith shook his head vigorously. 'I just mean that the hospital isn't legally required to report anything other than gunshot or stab wounds, and this is likely why you haven't heard anything from them.'

I pressed my palm to my forehead, a tingle of panic buzzing in my fingertips. But this time I won, pushing the anxiety away. I would report it myself.

'Olivia's a good girl. What happened?' I asked.

I heard myself using the present tense, but I couldn't help it. I didn't want her to slide into the past yet. She was still here.

His eyes were kind but calculating, the eyes of a lawyer rather than a doctor.

'I don't know. But I promise you this' – he held the cup of water out to me – 'you'll need your strength to find out.'

I took the water and gulped down every drop.

× × ×

It started raining as soon as I left the hospital. It was almost night, black clouds edging over the horizon.

I turned onto my street, slowly rolling toward my Victorian-style three-bedroom. Mine was the smallest house on the street, perched at the end of a row of grander ones.

My neighbors were middle-class professionals, lawyers, doctors. Their wives stayed home and raised chubby-cheeked toddlers. They had playdates and did hot yoga and went for coffee dates. I, a single working mother, pregnant at eighteen, stuck out like a sore thumb.

I never would've been able to afford the house on my own. But everything I did was for Olivia, to give her a better chance in life: middle-class neighbors, a good school, low crime rate, and right by the beach. I wanted her to have all the things I'd never had. So I couldn't regret any of it. Not now, not ever.

I imagined Olivia on our last morning together. I'd watched her swaying to silent music in the living room, her eyes closed, the earbuds of her iPhone pressed deep into her ears. A scarf I'd never seen before was draped around her neck. It was silk, scarlet, like a flame around her throat. She was wearing a baggy sweatshirt, loose-fitting sweats. Dark circles were smudged like half-moons beneath her eyes, her face pale as a tissue.

'Are you feeling okay?' I'd pressed the back of my hand to her forehead, concern washing over me. It was smooth and cool. I wrapped my arm around her shoulders and drew her close for a hug.

'I'm fine. Just studying.' She pulled away sharply, her brow crinkling.

I caught the undercurrent of her words: *Would you ever just stop asking?* My mom used to tell me that I never let things go. Sarah said that too.

I almost started questioning Olivia. Everything was something to be worried about. She was sick, she had cancer, she was being bullied. My stomach gave a panicky spasm. I did that sometimes: worried and questioned and analyzed until I found a rational reason. I needed the whole picture to understand the details. The problem was that it never changed anything. Like when my mom died.

Get a grip, Abi, I said to myself. *She's just being a teenager.*

I busied myself with my laptop bag, the cold slice of her rejection smarting.

'I know it's Saturday, but I have to go into work for a bit.' I hated leaving her alone, but as a single mom sometimes I had no choice. 'You know the rules. No riding in your friends' cars. Don't walk on the main road.'

I waited for her to point out that I never worked on the weekend. I wanted to tell someone about a new case I was working on at my CPA firm, Brown Thomas and Associates.

It was the first time I'd felt excited about work in years. Accounting wasn't what I was supposed to do with my life. Once upon a time, I'd been a journalist. I'd had fire, ambition, ideas. I loved the buzz of investigating, seeing my byline under a headline.

But the antisocial hours of a journalist didn't work for a single mom with a baby who battled severe ear infections. I was a mother first. I would never abandon my daughter the way my mom had abandoned me – loving me, then turning away; being there, then . . .

So I'd switched to accounting. It allowed me regular hours and more time with my daughter. I'd come to accept the trade-off years ago.

'Do you want me to stay?' My smile slipped a notch. 'You know you come first.'

'No, honestly, it's fine, Mom.' She'd already dismissed me. 'I have to study for this calculus test anyway.'

I looked at her, feeling strangely lost. I wondered suddenly when the last time was that we'd talked properly. I opened my mouth to find out what was going on. We were closer than other mothers and daughters; we told each other everything. But Olivia stood abruptly and stretched, yawning big.

'I'm gonna take a shower, Mom. See you at the barbecue later.'

She'd plucked up the red scarf from where it lay on the table, turned, and walked away, the slip of silk dragging like a discarded teddy bear across the floor.

Within seconds, she'd disappeared into the shadows at the top of the stairs.

× × ×

The memory sliced through me. It seemed so obvious now. Of course she was pregnant. I hated myself for not seeing it, for walking away when I should've stayed. Guilt suffocated me, pressing down on me like a crippling fog.

I slowed outside my driveway as lights flashed around me. Cars and vans overflowed along the street outside my house. A microphone was shoved in my face as soon as I opened my car door, and people started shouting my name.

'Abi! Rob Krane, KOMO-TV. Can you tell us more about Olivia's condition? Will her doctors try to keep her on life support? Will they be able to save the baby?'

'I-I-,' I stammered, edging toward my front porch. How did they know? My elderly neighbor, Mrs Nelson, stared at me from across the road, her mouth hanging open, the evening newspaper in her hand.

'No comment,' I said, my voice wobbly and unsteady.

I raced up the steps and let myself inside, black dots dancing across my vision from the flashbulbs. Exhaustion swept over me and I leaned against the door, the voices now muted to a dull mumble.

Finally I staggered to my feet. I needed a distraction from the creeping anxiety threatening to overwhelm me. I went into the kitchen and pulled a bottle of vodka from the freezer. I poured a finger into a glass and swallowed it fast. It burned, but I poured another and took it upstairs to Olivia's room.

I snapped on the light. It was still messy, like an explosion in a clothes factory. It smelled of lemony shampoo and dirty socks. Her blankets trailed off the bed.

I set the glass of vodka on Olivia's dresser and draped the blankets neatly over the bed, then sat on the edge. Something on her bedside table caught the afternoon light. Olivia's cell phone. It was attached to a charging cord, but when I picked it up, the plug dropped out. The battery was dead.

The sound of a knock at the front door startled me. I slipped Olivia's phone into my hoodie pocket as I went downstairs. I looked through the peephole, expecting it to be a reporter, but instead it was a tall, broad-shouldered teenager wearing a wrinkled blue shirt halfway untucked from his jeans. His fair hair was disheveled, his hazel eyes so raw and swollen I almost didn't recognize him.

The football build of Olivia's boyfriend looked like it had been put through the washing machine and shrunk. I took in his red eyes – the dark circles, the tear tracks trailing his putty-colored cheeks – and felt a swell of compassion. This inexorable tide of grief was his as well. It was something we shared.

I opened the door and flashbulbs instantly started popping, reporters shouting questions. I ignored them, pulling Tyler inside. Word traveled fast in a town as small as Portage Point, and it looked like every major Seattle media outlet was on this story.

'Is it true what they're saying about Olivia?' he asked.

'Yes.' I pressed my fists into my eyes. 'There was an accident.'

Tyler swayed on his feet. I grabbed his elbow and directed him to a chair at the kitchen table, pressed a glass of water into his hands. He gulped it down.

'An accident?' he echoed.

'I don't know. The police . . . I have to report it . . .'

'What happened?' he asked thickly.

'Nobody knows. She might've fallen off the bridge. But . . .' I hesitated, unsure if I should share my suspicions. 'Did she leave the barbecue with anyone?'

'No. She was by herself.'

'Madison didn't drive her?'

'I'm pretty sure she walked.'

Olivia knew she wasn't allowed to walk home alone in the dark. It was a firm rule of mine – one she'd never broken before.

'What time was that?'

'Like, ten thirty? Maybe more like ten forty-five?'

'Tyler, there's something I need to tell you.'

He stared at me. Waited.

'Olivia's pregnant.'

His arms dropped to the sides of the chair, heavy and limp. He looked like I'd punched him in the stomach.

'Did you know?' I needed information. Anything he could tell me mattered intensely.

He swallowed, then balled his hands into fists and stood. He turned away from me and hunched his shoulders.

'Tyler?' I walked to him, touched his back with my fingertips. 'I promise I won't be mad. Did you know she was pregnant?'

The muscles under his shirt jumped, and he pulled away from my touch. When he finally looked at me, his eyes were wide, the whites dominating his face.

'I'm sorry, Miss Knight. There's no way that baby's mine.'

6

ABI

october

'I don't understand,' I said.

Fear crept over me, sliding along every muscle and bone as a new realization settled over me: maybe I didn't know my daughter at all.

'How?' I asked Tyler. 'How could – how do you – ?'

'I know it's not mine,' he cut me off, his voice rough. 'Because Olivia and I never . . .' He looked away.

I pressed my fingers hard into my eyeballs, stars exploding on the undersides of my lids. The vodka I'd gulped earlier burned bitterly in my empty stomach. 'You never had sex.'

'Right.'

Olivia was cheating on her boyfriend. It explained so much. She'd been so different lately. Distant. I had a sudden memory of her at the Stokeses' annual neighborhood barbecue. I'd arrived late, work a handy excuse.

It wasn't that I didn't like people, just that I didn't really have anything interesting to talk about. Once I'd ticked off Olivia's achievements, the conversation went stale. Besides, I was really more of an observer than a participator. I was better at standing on the sidelines.

Jen Stokes had opened the door, a glass of champagne in each hand and a wide smile on her lips. Her dark corkscrew curls bounced around a heart-shaped face.

'Hi, Jen.' I smiled hard, the muscles in my jaw twinging painfully.

Jen and I had known each other since the girls were five. Even after all this time, we were friendly but not friends. Truth be told, Jen intimidated the hell out of me. Standing next to her made any bravado I had disappear, as if it had been sucked into the black hole of her self-confidence. She reminded me of what it was like being in junior high and high school.

Back then I was an outcast. The Girl Whose Mom Committed Suicide. Nobody knew what to say to me, nor I to them. I never wore the right clothes or had the right hair or makeup. I spent lunch alone in a corner of the cafeteria, was never picked for teams in PE, was the last to get a partner for school projects. My teenage years were even worse, lonely until I developed breasts and learned to use my looks to get guys to like me.

As I got older, I learned I was perfectly fine on my own. In fact, I preferred it that way. I didn't need any better friend than my daughter.

'Abi, so glad you could make it!' Jen leaned in and kissed me on the cheek, then handed me a glass of champagne.

I took a tiny sip. It was sweet and crisp, obviously expensive.

'How are you?' I asked. My voice was too quiet, lost in the chatter of people inside, so I said it again. 'How've you been?'

'Oh, you know, kids, work, life.' She rolled her eyes and laughed drily, but I knew she loved it. Jen was an ER doctor; she thrived under pressure.

I followed Jen through her tastefully decorated living room, my feet sinking into thick, oatmeal-colored carpet. We exited the back door to a sprawling deck that overlooked a shade-dappled yard. A shimmering rectangular swimming pool glinted in the waning light. The rich scent of barbecued ribs and burgers wafted up toward me.

'Have you seen Olivia?' Jen asked. Something in her voice made me look up sharply. I felt my face freeze, determined not to show that her words sent a gush of worry flooding through my veins.

'No,' I said slowly. 'Why?'

'Oh, no reason.' Her eyes skated sideways, and she set her glass on a table. 'I'm gonna grab you a plate of food. Then we can catch up. Here –' She turned to a leggy blonde woman wearing a short sunset-colored caftan and high canvas wedges and pulled her over to me.

'Marie, this is Abi. Abi, Marie Corbin.'

Before I had a chance to reply, Jen had headed down the stairs and disappeared into the crowd. I frowned, feeling inexplicably abandoned. I tidied a few loose strands of hair behind my ears.

Marie was gorgeous, and I felt my shoulders round as nerves pinched my stomach. She smiled at me, her sapphire eyes crinkling, her blonde hair a sleek mane perfectly framing an angular face. 'Oh, Abi, yes. I remember you. You're –'

'Olivia's mom.' I forced a smile.

'I was going to say an accountant at Brown Thomas and Associates. You did the books for my new interior design company, and I was so pleased at how quickly you got them done.'

'Oh,' I said, startled. Usually people only knew me as Olivia's mom, the mother of the rising star of the swim team. I tried to think of the last time I was anything else, and couldn't. 'I'm glad to hear it.'

Across the yard, Jen's husband, Mark, raised a hand in greeting. Mark was a square-jawed business type, handsome in an aging frat-boy sort of way. I waved back.

'I'll just go say hi.' I pointed at Mark, glad for an excuse to leave. 'Nice to meet you.'

I went downstairs, grabbed a Coke from an ice bucket, and huddled next to a tall shrub in the corner of the backyard. If Sarah were here, she'd push me to go talk to people. She said I used work and Olivia as bricks in a wall I'd built around myself.

Sarah was always right and she did everything in the proper order. She'd finished college with a degree in psychology, then got a job, then a husband, a kid, and so on. Now she was a counselor for victims of traumatic cases. Most of her clients were referred from the Seattle Police Department. I was a wrecking ball in comparison: a single mom with a job I'd settled for and no real friends.

Just then something cold splashed against my arm.

'Hi, Abi!'

'Derek. Hi.' Mark and Jen's son used to call me Miss Knight. I remembered when he was a chubby-cheeked second-grader with perpetually grass-stained knees, and now here he was, calling me by my first name. I suddenly felt rather old.

He grinned sheepishly. 'Sorry about that.'

I brushed the liquid from my arm. 'When did you get old enough to drink?' I teased.

'I'm nineteen now,' Derek said, proud in that way teenagers get when they think they're all grown-up.

I smiled fondly at him. 'Have you seen Olivia?'

His smile faded. 'No. Why? Is she in some sort of trouble?'

'No!' I laughed at the thought. Olivia never got in trouble. 'Nothing like that. We were planning to meet here.'

'Oh. . .' He ran a hand over his jaw and I noticed how much he looked like his mother. He had the same intense beauty: shaggy, dark curls; a narrow, heart-shaped face. His dark-blue eyes were piercing and intelligent. He was a good-looking kid. Probably already breaking hearts.

Somebody – a young woman – came up next to him then, touched his shoulder. He glanced at her, then at me, then stepped back. The entire exchange probably only lasted seconds, but it took me all that time to realize that the young woman next to him was Olivia.

My brain felt like it was spinning in mud. Her long, silky blonde locks were gone, cropped into a pink-streaked pixie cut. Gone also were her usual T-shirt and jeans, replaced with black leggings and a low-cut peasant top that plunged into her cleavage.

I remember looking at Olivia in the fading evening light and feeling like I didn't know her anymore. I knew then that something had been shaken loose, something I had no power to put back together. . .

'Whose baby is it?' I asked Tyler now, my insides tight as a fist.

He didn't answer. He looked very far away.

'Tyler. Whose baby is it?'

He didn't look at me. Didn't answer. Instead he said: 'I wish I could've saved her.'

'Saved her from what?'

His eyes crashed into mine.

'From everything.'

7

OLIVIA

april

After dinner, Mom went upstairs to take a shower. The house still smelled of burned bread even though all the windows were cracked open. It clawed at my throat and seared my nose, making me feel sick.

As soon as I heard the shower turn on, I ran to the desk in the corner of the living room and shuffled through the neatly organized paperwork and alphabetized, color-coded files. Nothing there. I took the stairs two at a time to Mom's bedroom. I pushed through electric cords and notebooks in her bedside table drawers. I dropped to my knees and checked under her bed. Just a scattering of dusty, mismatched hand weights, random books that didn't fit on the bookshelf downstairs, a box with cards and notes I'd given her.

Obviously I'd been in Mom's room loads of times, but I wasn't a weirdo. I'd never searched through her personal things. It felt gross. Disgust slithered up my throat, but then I remembered her lie: . . . *those brown eyes.*

There must be some proof somewhere about who my father was. The minutes crawled by. I was running out of time.

In her closet, I shuffled through clothes and shoes, ran my hand along the top shelf. Suddenly my fingers knocked against something. I stood on my tiptoes and pulled it out. It was an old shoebox, a thick layer of dust across the top. I sat cross-legged on the floor with it on my lap. My heart pounded wildly in my chest. The shower was still going but I knew I didn't have much time.

The box was light. I almost thought it was empty. But when I took the lid off and pushed a layer of tissue paper aside, I saw a thick piece of paper. It was my birth certificate. I looked at the spot where my parents' names were listed, but only my mom's was there.

I put it down and lifted out the tissue paper. Underneath was a hospital ID bracelet with my name in pale blue letters.

And then I saw it: a small square piece of plain white card, the type you might find in a bunch of flowers delivered to your doorstep. On one side it was blank. On the other, in thick capital letters, it said:

SORRY.
G

× × ×

The next day I stayed after school to help Peter with our chemistry homework. Tyler gave me the silent treatment all day, but I just pretended everything was fine. It was the best way to deal with Tyler. Pretend everything was all right, and pretty soon it would be.

I didn't really want to go home after that, so I texted Mom and told her I was still studying, then grabbed the late bus to Madison's. I wanted to tell her about the card I'd found and the lies my mom had told.

I pulled the hood of my coat up over my head as the mist thickened into rain. Storming down the quiet suburban road toward Madison's house, I passed elegant mock Tudors and Pacific Northwest timber homes and dove into the dripping green pines spread out lush and thick above the ZigZag Bridge.

The ZigZag Bridge wasn't really a zigzag – it was only called that because the river that ran underneath it twisted back and forth until it reached Puget Sound. When I was a kid, we used to call it the Cinderella Bridge because it looked like something out of a fairy tale. The suspension cables were hung from four silver towers, two at either end, crowned by soaring spires, while the gleaming metal framework was decorated with lacy arches and ornamental railings.

I hunched my backpack higher on my shoulders and headed over the bridge, my feet echoing loudly against the wooden slats of the pedestrian walkway. Usually I took the shortcut from my house through the woods to Madison's instead of looping up and around, walking over a mile along the ZigZag Road. Mom had made me promise never to take the shortcut – she thought the woods were full of murderers or something – but the paved road took way too long.

For her peace of mind, I told her I always went the long way to Madison's. I didn't want to lie to her or anything, but I didn't want her worrying either. Sometimes she could be a bit overprotective. Besides, it wasn't exactly lying. It just wasn't the whole truth.

I leaned on the doorbell at Madison's house, my breath coming in short bursts until the door flew open.

Madison's brother, Derek, looked like he'd been facedown in a pillow for a really long time. His face was crinkled with sleep, and he blinked his eyes fast, as if the late afternoon light burned his retinas.

'Olivia? What are you doing here?' His voice was raspy, and he raked one hand through his dark, tousled curls.

I stared at Derek, totally speechless. I hadn't seen him in almost three years. He looked so different. And by different, I mean really, really hot.

Gone was the lanky, awkward teenager I'd known. His chest had filled out, his face slimmed down. He'd grown a few inches and now towered over me. He was wearing skinny black jeans and a fitted black T-shirt that was tight at the biceps. A silver chain necklace was coiled twice around his neck.

'Derek, hey.' My voice squeaked, and I coughed to cover it. 'I forgot you were back from New York. Sorry about pushing on the doorbell. I thought Madison would answer.' The words rushed out of me too fast, and I knew I sounded like a dumb little kid.

I was desperate to know whether he'd thought about me while he was away the way I'd thought about him. Last time I'd seen him, I'd declared my undying fourteen-year-old love. He'd kissed me gently on the cheek and said, 'See you later.' The next day he'd left for New York.

I never told Madison about my crush on her brother. She'd hate it. She could be jealous and nasty when it came to Derek. Once I was at their house and I didn't feel well, so I played Nintendo with Derek instead of hide-and-go-seek with her. She went to his room and took all his certificates he'd glued into a scrapbook and shredded every one of them.

'You want to come in?' Derek asked.

I followed him through the dining room into the designer kitchen. The stainless steel shimmered in the afternoon light. An expensive watercolor of trees hung above the mahogany dinner table.

I shrugged out of my wet jacket, draping it over a chair. He pulled two bottles of water out of the refrigerator, tossing one to me.

'So.' I took a sip of my water. 'You back for good?'

'Yep.'

'Did you like it?'

He shrugged.

'Well, what was it like?' I had so many questions, but this new Derek wasn't like the one I'd known three years ago. Plus, all the things Madison had told me about him . . . maybe I was a little bit scared of him.

'It was fine, it's a big city, so it's pretty busy, but yeah, I liked it.' He sounded bored. Or maybe annoyed. 'Madison isn't here,' he added.

'Where is she?'

'Auditioning for some play or something.'

I hit my forehead with my hand. 'Oh yeah. Shoot. I forgot about that.'

He set his water on the counter. 'So, what's up?'

'Nothing much. Just school and finals, getting ready for senior year and stuff.'

'No.' He looked exasperated, like I was the dumbest person ever. 'I meant, why'd you come storming over here?'

I hesitated, not sure I wanted to tell Derek about my mom.

'Did you get in a fight with your boyfriend?' He smirked.

Anger boiled in me, and I clenched my fists. I wasn't used to feeling angry. But I felt like it was leaking from me, set free by the acid of my mom's lies. I couldn't control it, and suddenly it took a new direction.

How dare he? The last time I was with him, I'd thought – well, it didn't matter now, but I'd thought we shared something special. It was silly, just the slight brush of our arms against each other while watching a movie. A long gaze. It was stupid.

I didn't even recognize this new Derek.

'I'll come back later. Sorry I bothered you.' I put my water bottle on the counter and spun around, heading for the door.

Derek stopped me with a hand on my shoulder.

'No, I'm sorry.' The smirk fell off his face, and for the first time since I'd arrived he looked like the Derek I used to know. 'Honestly, you're not bothering me.'

He was so earnest, it reminded me of when we were little kids and I got stuck in the washing machine trying to hide from him during hide-and-seek.

'So. Boyfriend problems?'

'No,' I snapped. 'For your information, my mom lied to me and I'm really pissed off about it.'

Derek leaned away, as if blown back by the force of my anger. 'Shit. Sorry. What about?'

When I didn't reply, he headed toward the stairs. 'Come on,' he said. 'Let's go downstairs.'

I hesitated, confused by his quick change of personalities. Maybe he was more like Madison than I'd thought. I followed him to the far side of the kitchen, across the hall, and down the stairs to the basement.

'My mom and dad gave me the downstairs. I think they're just hoping I'll disappear down here.' He chuckled, but the laugh didn't quite reach his eyes.

Downstairs was more welcoming than upstairs, all blond wood and worn brown leather. A grunge band blasted on a massive surround-sound stereo system. A huge entertainment center and two leather chairs took up one side of the basement, while the other side had an unmade king-size bed. At the back of the room, a hallway led to darkness.

He shoved clothes off a leather chair. 'Here, sit down.'

He picked up a set of remote controls and turned off the stereo, then pressed a button. The ornately carved walnut doors of the entertainment center opened slowly, revealing a huge plasma-screen television. He flopped onto the other chair and flicked through the channels until he found a rerun of *Family Guy*.

He looked up at me. 'You gonna sit?'

'Um, sure.' If Madison came home and found me hanging with her brother, she'd totally flip. I perched on the arm of the chair and tugged on the tail of the silver bracelet at my wrist.

'So, what'd your mom lie about?' he asked.

'Well, last week some kids from my school and I were at U-Dub at this thing to get juniors ready for college. We saw this girl – Kendall – and she looked *just* like me. I'm not even kidding. Everybody said it. Like sisters.'

'That's weird.'

'Yeah. So yesterday I asked my mom about my dad. Like what was he like and did he have any other family and she mentioned that he had brown eyes.'

'So?'

'First of all, I'm in advanced biology. My mom has blue eyes, so if my dad had brown eyes, it's pretty unlikely I'd have green eyes. Not impossible, but genetically unlikely.'

'And second?'

'Second of all, I asked her when I was *thirteen* what color eyes he had, and she said green. And now she said brown.'

'But why would she tell you two different colors?'

I threw my hands up and slid into the chair. 'She's getting confused with her lies.'

'And this girl, Kendall. She has green eyes too?'

'Yeah. And this same chin dimple.' I pointed at the cleft in my chin. 'I Googled it. It's genetic. But my mom doesn't have it.'

'So Kendall looks a lot like you, she has a chin dimple, she has the same color eyes as you, and now your mom lied about what color your dad's eyes were – and you think, what? That you're related to this girl?'

'Well, yeah.' Saying it that way made it sound really stupid.

'It seems a bit, you know, Hollywood.'

'I know,' I admitted. 'But my mom lied to me. We never lie to each other. . .'

I chewed my lip.

'At least, I thought we didn't,' I amended. 'But now I'm wondering what else she's lied about. And . . .' I pulled the piece of white card out of my back pocket. 'I found this in her room. It was in a shoebox in her closet.'

I held it out to Derek, and he read the text. '*Sorry*. Sorry for what?'

'I don't know. But it was with my birth certificate. It must have something to do with me.'

'Have you looked her up on Facebook?'

'My mom?'

'No. Kendall.'

I shook my head. The thought hadn't even crossed my mind.

'Well, did you ask her who her father is? Find out his name?'

'I didn't think of any of that stuff when I met her.'

Derek grabbed a shiny silver MacBook from his bedside table. He brought it back to the chair, flipped the lid up, and opened Facebook.

'Do you want to look?' Derek asked.

Madison said I was a doormat. Mom said I let Madison walk all over me. Maybe they were both right. Maybe it was time I stood up and did something for myself.

I nodded. 'Yeah, okay.'

I leaned over his shoulder and typed in my log-in details, aware of how close we were. He smelled just faintly of pine trees and the clean, soapy smell of shaving cream.

Kendall Montgomery's page popped up right away. In her profile picture she was pouting, her eyes creased as if she was about to smile. I didn't want to know her. And yet I did.

'Holy shit.' Derek's eyes popped open wide. 'She does look just like you.'

'I know. It's creepy. What should I do?'

'What do you want to do?'

I was surprised. People never asked me what I wanted. I usually just went along for the ride.

I looked into Derek's midnight-blue eyes. Something in them made me feel safe enough to find out things I should probably leave alone.

I leaned over him and pressed Add Friend.

'I want to talk to her,' I said.

8

ABI

october

The sound of Tyler's feet thumping down the front steps jolted me out of my stunned trance.

'Wait!' I flung myself out the open front door and into the rain, crashing into the driver's door of his Jeep as the engine vroomed to life.

A flash went off from my front yard, but I ignored it.

'Wait!' I smacked my open palm against Tyler's door.

Tyler rolled the window down, his eyebrows drawn together. His eyes flicked up to the reporters watching our exchange.

'What do you mean?' I hissed so only he could hear. 'Saved her from everything?'

He glared at me, but kept his voice down also. 'You had all these *rules*. You *controlled* her. She said you were writing the script for her life and she was *sick* of it. If you weren't trying to run her life, maybe she wouldn't have done stupid things.'

My fingers slipped off the edge of the window, and I stumbled backward, propelled by the vitriol of his words. Tyler reversed out of the driveway quickly, his wheels skidding in the gravel.

Another flash went off near me. I turned my face to my shoulder and raised my hand as if I could ward it off.

God only knew what the reporters would write about this. I looked like a lunatic, my blonde hair a nest of damp tangles sticking up in every direction, the scent of alcohol on my breath.

I looked up as I heard the crunch of tires on the gravel. Two police detectives, badges clipped to their belts, got out of the car.

'All right, guys, get out of here. You know the rules. Get off her property now,' the male detective said.

He was squarely built with short legs and a squat body. Dark circles were etched beneath watery blue eyes that appraised me from under thick eyebrows. His wrinkled black suit covered an equally wrinkled blue shirt and tie. His thinning hair was a mess, as if he'd only just woken.

Just behind him, the female detective waved a reporter edging closer to my house back to the road. She was a complete contrast to him: crisp black business suit, starched white collar. She was tall as an Amazon with cropped, pale blonde hair, a chiseled jaw, and ice-blue eyes. Her face was completely blank: the picture of professional detachment.

Once the reporters were a safe distance away, they crossed the grass to me.

'Abigail Knight?' the man said, extending his hand to shake mine.

'Yes?'

'I'm Detective Phillip McNally, and this is Detective Jane Samson.' He jerked a thumb over his shoulder. Samson gave me a brief, firm handshake. Her hands were warm and large, making mine feel small and childish in comparison.

'We'd like to speak with you about your daughter's accident. Can we come inside?' McNally asked.

I stared at them, blinking. Accident? Why did they think they were here if it was an accident?

'Yes . . . come in.'

I led them inside and shut the door, then stood awkwardly in the living room for a minute. I couldn't immediately recall what I was supposed to do.

'Would you like a drink?' I finally asked.

'No, we're good,' Detective McNally said. 'Can we sit?'

'Of course.' I showed them to the couch and sank onto the recliner.

'We're very sorry for what's happened to your daughter,' Detective McNally said. He blinked slowly, as if trying to wake himself up. 'Also for the delay. We've only just been alerted to what happened by a' – he glanced down at his notepad – 'Dr Griffith. I know this must be a difficult time for you, but we'd like to take an official statement. Is now okay?'

'Yes. Of course.'

He pulled a pen from a pocket on the inside of his coat.

'Let's start with that last night you saw Olivia. Can you tell me what happened?'

My eyes flicked to Detective Samson's face, but she didn't say a word.

My hands shook, and I pressed them under my thighs. I wanted my daughter. I missed her so much it was physical, like scraping cotton wool over an acid burn.

I started at the beginning, telling them about our Saturday: work, homework, the barbecue.

'Did everything seem normal?' Detective McNally asked.

'Yes. I mean, except – well, she got a haircut.'

'A haircut?' McNally echoed. I could see he thought grief had driven me a little bit crazy.

'Yes. It was unusual.'

'Unusual how?'

'Olivia's sensible. She doesn't drink, she's on the swim team, and she gets straight As. She never does stupid teenager stuff like walk home alone in the dark or sneak out at night to go drinking. It was just weird that she suddenly cut all her hair off. But teenagers do these things, right?'

'Sometimes.' He didn't look at me, just kept staring at his notepad. 'Is there anybody who didn't like her or had a grudge against her?'

'No,' I said, shocked. 'Everybody likes Olivia. I'm not just saying that. Last year at school, she was voted 'most likable.' She was homecoming queen. She's happy and popular and, and –' My voice broke, and for a second I couldn't continue.

Both detectives nodded, their heads moving up and down like bobble-head dolls.

'Do you think –?'

'We don't think anything yet,' Detective Samson cut me off. It was the first time she'd spoken, and it startled me. 'We're just building a picture, gathering evidence.'

'Something happened! She has bruises!'

'Do you have any reason to think anybody would hurt Olivia?' McNally asked, his eyebrows raised.

I stared at him, dismayed. They'd been here ten minutes, and already they didn't believe me.

McNally continued asking me questions: Who were her friends? Her boyfriend? Had they had any problems? Had she ever tried to harm herself? Had anybody ever tried to hurt her? Had she been having problems at home? At school?

Occasionally he'd jot something down. The longer we sat there, the more unsettled I felt. Samson barely said a word, and McNally was the picture of a frazzled, overworked cop. How would these two find out what had happened to my daughter?

I showed them upstairs, and the detectives searched Olivia's room, put random items into little plastic bags. They took her laptop and some of her school notebooks, asked me more questions.

By the end, my neck ached from carrying the weight of my pounding head. I wanted everything to go back to the way it was. I wanted my daughter back.

'Did you find her bracelet?' I asked Detective Samson.

Her brow creased.

'A silver charm bracelet. Olivia always wore it. Always. But it wasn't on her wrist.' I brushed a hand over my eyes.

'No, we didn't find it, but I'll check again.'

'Was Olivia with anyone that night? Drinking with friends?' Detective McNally asked. Neither of them had bothered to sit down after searching Olivia's room. They towered over me in the living room, and my toes curled at the invasion of my personal space.

'What? No!' I replied, startled. Olivia wasn't a drinker. 'All her friends were at the barbecue. And she doesn't –' Then I remembered the scarf, her haircut, her pregnancy.

Bile, thick and acidic, rose in my throat.

I jumped up and raced to the bathroom, slamming open the toilet lid just in time to heave up every last drop of vodka, retching again and again into the white porcelain bowl.

Afterward, I shut the toilet seat and rested my head on the lid. I closed my eyes and breathed deeply. The insides of my eyelids were red. I was sweating, hot moisture covering my entire body. I shoved Olivia's phone into the back pocket of my jeans and stripped off my hoodie, tossing it on the floor.

When I opened my eyes, I saw a slip of white plastic sticking up from the mess of tissues in the trash can. I sat up slowly, reaching for it. It was a pregnancy test. A pink plus sign practically glowed on the end.

Olivia knew she was pregnant. And she hadn't told me.

The knowledge was raw inside me, jagged as a broken windowpane. As scared as I was when I found out I was pregnant, at least I'd had Sarah.

Memories of the day I'd told Sarah I was pregnant bubbled in my mind, like a pot of water boiling over.

'Do you know who the father is?' Sarah had asked.

The old mattress sagged under her weight as she sat next to me on the edge of my bed.

'Yes,' I snapped. Okay, maybe I used to sleep around a bit.

I used sex as a way to get guys to like me. I drank and dabbled in drugs and stayed out late smoking and partying. But it wasn't going to be like that anymore.

'Have you told him?'

'Of course!'

'And?'

I looked away, and Sarah sighed heavily.

'He doesn't want to be in the picture,' she stated.

I didn't answer. The worst part was that he'd cemented everything I felt all over again – that everybody eventually left me.

Sarah slapped her hands on her legs and stood. 'I'll come with you to sort it out.'

I stared at her, horrified. 'Are you telling me to get an abortion?'

Sarah looked confused. 'Of course not. I just –'

'This is my baby. I won't abandon it. I'm nothing like . . .'

I didn't have to finish the sentence. We both knew the ending. Mom had abandoned me, and I had been powerless to stop her.

Sarah's face softened, and she sat back down. 'Abs, of course you're nothing like her. But a baby? You can't . . .' Her voice trailed away and she searched my face.

That was exactly what *he* had said, right before he threatened to hurt my baby and me if anybody found out it was his. So I'd gone to the abortion clinic and was going to do it. But I couldn't go through with it. Being abandoned was my life's greatest fear. I couldn't do it to my own baby.

I looked around at the tiny storeroom I'd used as a bedroom in Sarah's apartment since I was ten. A baby wouldn't fit here. But I had a way to get out now. Maybe I shouldn't have taken it, but I wanted my baby to have everything I never did, a stable home, a solid middle-class upbringing, good opportunities.

'I've registered at Valley,' I said, referring to the local community college. 'I'll get a certificate in journalism. I like writing and I'm good at it. I can get a job at a newspaper.'

Sarah looked surprised. I was usually more of a joiner than a planner. She struggled with words for a minute, but I knew she'd give in. She was the only parent figure I'd had for most of my life, and she was nothing if not supportive.

Finally she said, 'You know I'm here for you whatever you decide.'

'Thanks, Sar.' I leaned into my big sister, and she put her arms around me.

She brushed my hair off my forehead, and I pulled away, getting up and crossing to look out the window at the Christmas lights stringing the neighborhood. I hated it when she did things my mom used to do.

I'd looked down at my stomach, the first hint of a bump pushing out from my sweater, and imagined my baby curled under my heart. I would have someone to be with me no matter what. I'd love her more than I'd ever been loved. . .

In the bathroom, I stood shakily and splashed cold water on my face to help the memories fade. I grabbed Olivia's pregnancy test and took it to Detective Samson in the living room. For a second, her professional mask slipped, and I thought I saw compassion flare in her eyes, but it was gone as quickly as it had appeared. She pulled a plastic bag from her pocket, then zipped the proof of my grandchild away inside.

'I don't know if Olivia was with anyone that last night,' I said, sinking back into the recliner. 'I didn't know she was pregnant. She didn't tell me.' The admission scraped like razor blades across my raw, aching throat.

Neither detective spoke for a minute, but when I looked up I saw them exchange a look.

'Well.' McNally stood and moved toward the door. 'That's all we need for now. We'll be in touch if we have any other questions.'

'Wait.' I sprang to my feet and put a hand out. 'The bruises, her bracelet – are you going to investigate?'

McNally sighed, and I wanted to scream. 'We're still in the early stages,' he said, but he wasn't looking at me anymore. 'We'll speak to witnesses, process the scene, analyze the bruises. . .'

Both detectives moved toward the door, but at the last second Samson turned and spoke. 'We're very sorry for your loss. We'll be in touch, keep you up-to-date if we find anything new.' She slid a business card into my palm. 'Call me anytime. And, Miss Knight, just ignore the reporters. They'll go away in a few days.'

I stood frozen in place, the front door flapping in the increasing wind, and watched as they got in their unmarked police car and drove slowly away. I hunched my shoulders against the cold and shoved my hands into the back pockets of my jeans. My fingers knocked against something hard.

They hadn't asked for Olivia's phone.

9

ABI

november

November arrived abruptly in Portage Point. The sky was gray and wet; the wind tossed leaves across the ground in angry flurries. I scurried across the parking lot toward the hospital. By the time I reached the front, my hair clung to my forehead in damp tendrils.

Inside I headed for the elevators while dialing the numbers on the business card Samson had left me. It was the third time that day, but still it went to voicemail. I knew there were budget cuts; I knew other cases were important too, that the investigative process took time; but surely, surely Olivia's case would take priority.

Even on the rare occasion when a detective answered, they just told me to be patient, they'd let me know if anything new came up. They were always fobbing me off like that. And I didn't have time for it. Four weeks had passed since Olivia's fall. Only fourteen weeks until the baby would be born. And that was if we were lucky. I needed answers sooner, not later.

I took the elevator to the floor Olivia had been moved to last week. Now that she was out of the ICU, the baby had a better chance at surviving; but seeing the ventilator and feeding tube was no less of a shock each time I arrived.

I steeled myself against the pain and pushed open the door. Sarah was slumped over the edge of Olivia's bed, her mouth hung open in sleep, a deep crease denting the middle of her forehead.

'Sarah,' I whispered. My sister jumped when I touched her shoulder. 'You should go home. Go see Dylan and Brad.'

She rubbed her arm over her eyes. 'I couldn't sleep. What time is it?'

'Six.'

'They're sleeping. You should be too.'

I put my purse down and slipped out of my coat, sitting in the chair next to her as the pale light edged the darkness from the room. I picked up Olivia's hand and inspected her wrist. The bruises had faded, the broken skin mostly healed; her skin renewed itself, even though her brain never would.

'I'm thinking of going back to work,' I told Sarah.

I realized with some surprise that I missed the rhythm of my job. The predictability. At least I knew what I was doing in accounting, what to expect. There was no guesswork, only right or wrong. Right now I was just waiting through my days, but for what? The police rarely responded to my calls. Olivia's case was still open, but it felt like they weren't really investigating.

The last four weeks had passed in a slow, nauseating spin. I slept and ate little, sobbed a lot. I shoved fistfuls of sedatives in my mouth, washing them down with red wine and vodka until I'd drunk everything in my house and had no pills left to take.

The dull lethargy that had plagued me immediately after Olivia fell was being replaced by a crazed adrenaline and an urge to know the truth. People throughout Portage Point had heard the news. They wanted to ask questions, to know what had happened, but I had no answers and no energy to explain that the police had yet to piece together any intelligible reason for Olivia's fall.

At least Samson had been right about the reporters – they'd eventually trickled away, in search of more urgent stories.

The cost of caring for Olivia was mounting. My insurance was already balking and I knew I'd have to find a way to pay for everything for another three months at least. And then there was the baby. . .

'I can't lose my insurance,' I said.

Sarah nodded. She, of all people, knew that the weight of unexpected responsibility could be as heavy as water.

I looked at Olivia in the hospital bed, a pale, shriveled version of herself. Eyes closed. Intubated. The incessant mechanized hush of the machines keeping her alive.

'I don't understand why the police aren't working harder on this,' I said, anger and frustration simmering inside me.

'I'm sure they are,' Sarah reassured me. She stood and rolled her neck in slow circles. 'Investigations take time.'

'They said the bruises were probably from the fall. But you saw them, right? They were fingerprints. Somebody did this to her.'

Sarah looked away, and I could tell she didn't really agree.

I didn't like everything I said second-guessed, my emotions and my sanity questioned. I knew what I'd seen. I just had no way to prove it meant what I thought it did.

'They're still investigating,' she repeated. 'We have to let them do their job.'

I glared at her. 'I know you don't understand, but I need to know what happened.'

Flames of anger curled in my stomach, and the air between us tightened. After our mother died, it was me who acted out and raged. Sarah had stayed calm and composed. She'd organized the funeral, taken care of the will, boxed up all my things and moved me in with her.

I was a basket case in comparison. I wailed and wept, wanted to know why Mom was dead, who I could blame. When I didn't get answers I wallowed, sinking into the grief and letting it hold me like a warm bath. That's what losing your only parent when you're ten does – it makes it so you can't ever let go.

Sarah didn't want to talk about Mom at all. She wasn't interested in remembering and certainly didn't want me talking about that day. Her emotionless, brisk efficiency made me doubt my feelings. I wondered why I cared so much, but she didn't.

Over time I'd learned to hide my emotions. But on the inside I was still just a wreck, barely keeping it together.

'Of course I understand,' Sarah said, her forehead creasing with hurt. 'I get it. I want to help. I know people at the Seattle Police Department through work. I'll call around. See if anybody there can help.'

'I don't need a shrink picking my brain apart.' I gritted my teeth. 'I *need* to know what happened to Olivia. Besides, I can't pay for it.'

'I don't mean a counselor. And I don't mean in an official capacity, just as a favor. Maybe they can ask around, get some insight into what the Portage Point police are doing, what they're thinking.'

My pulse raced through my clenched muscles. I looked away, wanting her to stop talking.

'The baby's doing well,' she said, changing the subject.

She reached over and touched Olivia's stomach. Somehow, despite so many tests, drugs, and X-rays, the baby was healthy. It was growing at a normal rate, swimming in the space beneath where my daughter's heart pumped blood around her body.

I dug my fingernails into the skin of my upper arms until they left pale, moon-shaped dents, then raked them across my upper arms, scratching at the invisible itch. The pain was sharp, intense, but in a way that felt good.

'Abi, stop!' Sarah exclaimed, her voice sharp as a ragged hangnail.

'Then stop talking about the baby!'

'Why?' Her brow puckered.

'Don't you get it?' I exploded. The spark of anger lit and consumed my insides, suddenly so bulky that I couldn't sit still. I launched out of my chair and crossed the room to stare out the window. The maple trees that lined the park across the street were nearly bare, slowly losing the last of their crimson and gold leaves.

'Get what?'

I whirled to face her. 'When the baby's born, Olivia will die! So stop harping on about the baby, because that deadline means my daughter fucking dies!'

I didn't wait for her reply. I pushed past her and ran out the door, down the stairs, back into the driving rain.

× × ×

Back at home, I felt a deep, dark self-loathing stealing over me. I shouldn't have blown up at Sarah.

Whatever problems I'd had with my sister, whatever resentment I'd held in my heart, Sarah had always been my rock. Even when my mom was alive, it was Sarah my teachers called if I was sick, Sarah who helped me with my homework. When I was five and got lost when we were picnicking at the beach, it was Sarah I howled for under the hot white sun. I was alone and she ran to me, shouting my name, and I knew I was safe. I never felt that way with my mom.

A sudden, vivid memory of my mother the day she died flashed through me: the blood, the screaming – was it Sarah or me? – the gun still hanging from her finger. I'd lost my mother and my childhood in one cruel day. I guess being angry and blaming Sarah was easier than moving on.

Fuck. I scrubbed my hands over my eyes. I was such a mess.

I crossed the living room to the small oak desk in the corner next to the fireplace and sat down. Once my old laptop had booted up, I opened my e-mail, prepared to send a request for another leave of absence to my boss.

I had thirty-four new e-mails: a mix of junk mail, persistent interview requests, well-wishers at work, friends and acquaintances in the community who were too scared to talk to me face-to-face. And then my eye fell on something else.

Your invoice from Apple – Invoice APPLE ID
olivialouiseknight@gmail.com.

Tears sprang to my eyes. It was yet another reminder that Olivia wasn't here anymore. I didn't need to pay this bill anymore, but I didn't want to stop because that would be an admission that my daughter wasn't coming back.

I wanted to drop my head to the desk and let my broken heart overwhelm me. Instead I took a deep breath and typed *iCloud.com* into the browser. I logged in with her e-mail and password, which I'd insisted she give me when I bought us both the iPhones, and a number of brightly colored icons filled my screen: e-mail, contacts, calendar, photos. The guts of Olivia's life were here.

I clicked the Mail icon, but the mailbox was empty except for a welcome e-mail. I shut it and moved on to Contacts. There were hundreds of people listed. Some I knew, but a lot I didn't. I scrolled slowly down the page, staring hard at each name. Who were they? Had one of these people hurt Olivia? Next I opened Photos.

At first I didn't understand what I was seeing. Horror stole over me like a mist, uncurling deep within. And then a fiery knot began to burn in my stomach.

I squeezed my eyes tightly shut, then opened them again. The pictures were still there. The first one was slightly blurry, as if it had been zoomed in from far away. Olivia was standing outside her school staring at something in the distance. Somebody had drawn devil horns over her head and a red line across her throat with what looked like drops of blood below.

Die bitch! was written across the bottom.

In the second one, Olivia's face was colored over in hard, angry scribbles, a red noose twisted around her throat. But I could tell it was Olivia by the clothes she wore, her favorite swim-team shirt. I leaned closer to read the red text.

Kill!

And another: a knife drawn plunged into Olivia's heart, blood dripping down her chest. The words *U die!* were scrawled on the picture.

Shock rippled through me.

There were a handful more, all variations of the first three: pictures of Olivia with her neck slit, blood dripping down the image, her eyes whited out, bloody intestines vomiting from her mouth. All with *die*, *kill*, and *fuck you* scribbled across them.

'Oh my God,' I whispered. A rush of adrenaline thumped hot and silent in my blood.

Someone had been cyberbullying Olivia.

10

ABI

november

I started to shake all over, a shocked and angry vibration that started at the very core of me and radiated out.

Why would somebody send these to Olivia? And who?

I scrolled down through the rest of the photos, but there was nothing else there. Nothing threatening, anyway.

I rested my head on the desk and thumped it softly against the edge, as if that would knock loose rational thoughts that might solve this puzzle.

'Think, Abi. Think!'

Her phone. I bolted upright. Maybe there were more on her actual phone. I racked my mind, trying to think where I'd put it. I barely remembered what had happened since Olivia fell. It felt like I'd been sleepwalking since then.

I ran to the kitchen and grabbed Olivia's phone from the counter I'd thrown it on after the detectives left. The fact that the police hadn't even asked for or looked for Olivia's cell was further proof they weren't taking the investigation seriously.

I plugged the phone in to charge, and after a few seconds it chimed and burst to life.

There were two unread text messages.

The most recent was from someone Olivia had saved as K at 10:42 a.m. later the same morning Olivia was found: *You ok? I'm so sorry. I seriously didn't know. Anyway, he's a dick. If you're like me you'll cut him out for good!*

I brushed a hand over my face, more baffled than ever. I scrolled down and read the other text.

It was from Tyler at 11:20 p.m. the night Olivia fell.

I scrolled up to read the whole thread.

Olivia: *You're right. We need to talk. You still at bbq? Meet in 15?*

Tyler: *Yep. See you in a few.*

I paused, letting the part of my brain that allowed me to analyze numbers so well take over. I latched on to something as my mind anchored and examined it. The thought crystallized into something cold and hard.

'Fuck,' I whispered out loud. Tyler had told me Olivia left at 10:45 p.m. and he hadn't seen her after that. But according to this text, they'd met up at around 11:30 p.m. 'Tyler lied to me.'

I scrolled back through some of Olivia's old texts. The most recent ones were from K and a string of texts from somebody called only D. As I read, I realized they were sweet, some rather romantic, and I remembered Tyler telling me the baby wasn't his. Perhaps this D was the baby's father.

The shock of finding the disturbing images in Olivia's iCloud account and the texts from Tyler had begun to dissipate, leaving behind a completely clear view.

This was the proof I needed. Somebody had hurt Olivia on purpose. I had to go to the police.

× × ×

The Portage Point Police Department was situated in a miniature antebellum-style brick building on the far side of town, nestled under tall pine trees and fronted by a series of low boxwood shrubs.

I drove too quickly up Main Street, flying past the white, steepled church, a handful of indie coffee shops, a yoga studio, and the small town square, then turned right past a children's playground and baseball diamond. I parked outside the station, between a police SUV and an American flag flapping aggressively in the wind.

Carol-Ann, the police station receptionist, recognized me as soon as I walked in.

'Abi!' She came around the desk and reached for me, folding me against her massive, doughy bosom. She smelled of lavender and soap, which made me suddenly aware of how long it had been since I'd showered. When Carol-Ann pulled away, her soft brown eyes sparkled with tears.

Carol-Ann was like the police department's built-in grandma, complete with thick glasses and permed graying hair that poufed around her face. She'd run the front office as long as I could remember, helping the town's four police officers and two detectives organize legal paperwork, answer the phones, and comfort victims.

'Carol-Ann, I need to see Detective Samson or McNally. Are they here?'

I took a step toward the half-open inner door and caught a glimpse of Samson sitting in a small kitchen, a sandwich in front of her as she stared at her cell phone. The murmur of police radios floated out to me.

Carol-Ann stepped in front of me and put her hand on my elbow, gently guiding me to a chair by her desk. 'Let me see if they're free. I'll be right back.'

A few minutes later she returned with Detective Samson.

I jumped up, anger flaring in me. 'Where have you been?' I snapped. 'I've left a thousand messages for you guys, and nothing! No wonder you haven't solved Olivia's case if you're sitting here eating lunch and checking your phone all day!'

Samson's ice-blue eyes flashed something I couldn't immediately recognize. Not anger, exactly. Surprise.

She nodded at Carol-Ann, then jerked her head toward the door. 'Please come with me.'

I followed her down the hallway past the kitchen to a characterless room painted a cold gray. There were no pictures on the walls, no decorations, nothing except a window to the hallway with half-closed blinds and a table like the kind you'd find in a cafeteria with a handful of folding chairs around it.

I pulled Olivia's phone out of my purse, set it on the table with a loud *thunk*, then glared at her as she sat down.

'You didn't take Olivia's phone.'

Samson crossed one leg over her knee and studied me for a long minute. 'Didn't Detective McNally ask you for it?'

'No.' I started to shake my head, then stopped. I couldn't actually remember. 'I don't think so.'

'We are pursuing a number of leads, Miss Knight.'

I gritted my teeth, knowing that was code for *We haven't found anything*.

'Olivia's boyfriend, Tyler, he lied to me. He told me they didn't see each other after she left the barbecue, but there's a text here.' I clicked into the text thread and handed the phone to her. 'See? She says she's going back to the barbecue. She would've met him at eleven thirty. And . . .' I dug in my purse for the threatening pictures I'd printed from Olivia's iCloud account and laid them on the table. 'Somebody sent her these.'

Samson scrolled through the phone for a moment, then picked up the pictures, her face a cold, hard mask. She studied them for a long moment. 'Were these on her phone?'

I shook my head. 'No, they were in her iCloud account, which was synced with her phone. They must've been deleted from her phone.'

'Any idea who sent these?'

'No. None at all.'

Samson leaned forward and handed me her notebook and a pen. 'Can you write down her log-in details for me?'

I did, then started to ask if she believed me now, but a knock at the door interrupted me. McNally's head poked in, his flabby jowls stretched into what I assumed was meant to be a smile. He looked as exhausted and unkempt as usual, but this time there was something else I hadn't noticed before: an unmistakable edge of animosity.

'If I could just borrow Detective Samson for a minute.'

Samson carefully folded the printed pages and slipped them into her blazer pocket, along with Olivia's phone and her notebook. The door closed with a sharp snap behind her.

I sat on one of the metal chairs and watched them through the slats of the cheap metal blinds. I couldn't hear what they were saying. McNally was speaking forcefully to Samson. He looked angry. Samson gestured with both hands, more animated than normal. She lifted Olivia's phone, but he shook his head and batted it away. Samson glanced at me, gave me a small tight smile, but something tilted inside of me when I saw it. I felt a sense of foreboding. Of time running out.

And right then I knew, with a dark certainty, that if I left it to them, I would never know the truth about what had happened to Olivia.

I'd spent my whole life hiding, just existing behind the walls I'd built around myself. I never got the answers I needed when my mother died. I was powerless to stop my mom killing herself. Powerless to make Olivia's father choose me. Powerless to stop my daughter from – the pain of reality hit me in the stomach.

But I couldn't afford to feel that way now. Self-pity was fine when you were ten, but in a few months I'd have Olivia's baby to take care of. Wallowing was an indulgence I didn't have. I needed answers now.

What do you do when you know something and nobody will listen? When you need answers and nobody will provide them? When you can't trust anybody to help you?

I stood at a crossroads, half aware that my choice now would send me down a path from which there would be no turning back. The decision wasn't a hard one. I didn't want to be powerless anymore. I wanted answers.

I slammed the interview room door open, and Samson and McNally turned to me, eyes wide with surprise.

'Something's wrong,' I said, a crazed fury surging through my body. Rage had hijacked the rational part of my brain, the part that never stood up to people, that sat back while others told me what to do. 'I know something's wrong. And you both know it. Whether you help me or not, I'm going to find out what happened to my daughter.'

11

OLIVIA

may

'D'you guys wanna go to Java Café?' Madison raised her voice to be heard over the racket of teenagers spilling into the hall. With its exposed brick walls and mismatched array of cushy couches, Java Café was our usual hangout.

It was one of the first really hot days of the year and everybody was either going there or heading for the beach. 'I'm *dying* for a smoothie.' She slammed her locker door next to mine and faced Tyler and me.

'Can't. It's "Dad's night with me."' Tyler air-quoted, his words laced with sarcasm. His parents had announced their divorce just a few weeks ago, and he already had to split his time between them. He didn't talk about it much; but I could tell he was super pissed. I was trying to be nice. Honestly. But he was so grumpy I mostly just stayed away from him.

'Umm . . .' I thought fast, scrambling for a believable lie. Derek was taking me to Seattle after school so we could look up Kendall, who still hadn't responded to my Facebook friend request.

Since I'd met Kendall a few weeks ago, I'd spent a ridiculous amount of time Googling her. I felt kinda stalkerish. She played tennis for her private Catholic school, was on the debate team, volunteered in the community.

Half of her pictures showed her with an older man – her dad, I presumed – but the weird thing was, I recognized him. At first I couldn't figure out how I knew him. It was only when Derek saw his picture that he reminded me he was Gavin Montgomery, our state senator.

Duh! An election was coming up in a few months. His billboards were posted all over the place; his political ads ran constantly on TV. And then a thought had crashed into me: if I looked like Kendall and this Gavin guy was her dad, maybe he was my dad too.

Then I totally started tripping. Maybe my dad *wasn't* dead. Maybe he was happily living in Seattle with his other family.

So I'd decided to talk to Kendall and see if I could find out anything else.

'Ugh, I have to get an hour of swim practice in and then study for a math test. I can't even.' I rolled my eyes. 'Plus I promised Mom I'd fill out some applications for volunteering tonight.'

'What?' she exclaimed. 'Volunteering's such a waste of time!'

'Mom says it'll help me get into college or whatever.' I defended her half-heartedly, but made a face. 'Anyway, if it makes my mom happy –'

'—it'll keep her off your back.'

I laughed. 'Exactly.'

It was a weird thing we'd started doing lately. Madison would make fun of some stupid rule my mom had, and I'd say at least it kept her off my back.

Madison and my mom had never really gotten along. It wasn't like they fought, exactly. My mom was way too nice for that. She was a worrier, overprotective, but she wasn't a hater. But Madison was always throwing shade.

I shut my locker and gave Tyler a quick peck on the cheek. 'See you tomorrow.'

Outside the sun was splitting the sky, cheerful puffs of cotton clouds wafting overhead. The air had that sharp, grassy smell to it, like somebody had just mowed the lawn. I walked around the side of the school, cut across the track and into a residential neighborhood, then ducked into Derek's car.

His black leather biker jacket creaked as he turned toward me.

'Hey,' he said, a molasses-slow smile creeping over his face.

I was being a stupid girl. Of course my insides weren't melting. Okay, my heart sped up a little, but that didn't have to mean anything. I loved my boyfriend. I did. Derek was just a friend.

Anyway, it wasn't like I could tell Madison we were friends. She'd told me some crazy shit. Like, that he'd threatened a guy in New York with a knife. She'd majorly freak if she found out I was hanging with him.

'Hey yourself,' I replied, grinning at him like an idiot.

'Where to?'

'I thought we could find the Starbucks in Mercer Island. If her friends are anything like mine, that's where they'll go after school.'

'Good thinking.' Derek nodded like he was impressed. 'Here, do you want to drive?'

'What?'

'Drive.' He waved at the car. 'Do you want to?'

'Uh, no. I don't know how,' I admitted. I was the only one in my class who didn't have a license. Considering I'd be seventeen next month, it was totally mortifying. 'You think my mom would let me do something as normal as drive? She made me wear a helmet in T-ball. I'm surprised she doesn't make me take a snorkel to swim meets.'

He snorted a laugh. 'D'you wanna learn? I can teach you.'

I hesitated. I *did* want to, but I also wanted to talk to Kendall Montgomery.

Derek made the decision for me. 'Drive it is.' He got out, walked around to my side of the car, and opened the door.

'What about Kendall?' I asked.

'We'll talk to her another time.'

'Okay,' I agreed uncertainly. 'But don't let me forget to text my mom at four. Otherwise she'll freak.'

'Why?'

'She just worries.' I couldn't help the note of defensiveness that crept into my voice.

He didn't say anything, which I liked. It was pretty annoying when Madison and Tyler made fun of me for still having to call or text my mom.

I got into the driver's seat and clicked my seat belt on.

'Let's do this!' Derek said, trying to pump me up. 'Ready?'

I inhaled, already aware that he could probably get me to do just about anything. 'Ready.'

I put my hand on the stick shift, and he put his hand over mine. It was warm and rough.

'A bit of enthusiasm, please,' he joked.

'Woo-hoo!' I shouted.

Derek threw his head back and laughed. The afternoon sunlight spilled like melted butter across his face, lighting his dark-blue eyes. They penetrated deep inside of me, promising something different than the safe, sheltered life I'd lived so far.

I drove a few laps around the neighborhood, lurching the car from start to stop more often than I wanted to. I couldn't believe Derek was letting me maim his poor car. His dad had helped him do it up when he'd first bought it: a spoiler, aftermarket headlights and taillights, expensive-looking rims, banging subwoofers. I knew it was special to him.

I got the feeling those were the only days his dad had ever shown him any sort of attention. Derek and Madison's parents weren't really involved in their lives that much, which was sort of sad. My mom was totally up in my business. But in a good way. She'd do anything for me.

I ground the gears and paled as the Mustang jerked out of my control and careened toward a mailbox. Luckily, I slammed my foot on the brake and stopped just in time.

'I think I'm done for now,' I said quietly. Thinking about my mom had upset me, uncertainty wedging in my gut. I wasn't sure if I was okay with defying her like this. She'd told me I couldn't drive yet, so I shouldn't have been doing it.

Derek looked at his watch. 'Do you want to go to the arcade in Laurelwood? I'll drive.'

I nodded, relieved. We switched places, and he drove us to Laurelwood, parking in front of a big metal-and-stone warehouse that housed the town's popular arcade. I sent my mom a quick text checking in, then followed him into the arcade.

Bright lights flashed everywhere. Teenagers out of school for the afternoon battled over games of pool or aimed plastic guns at flickering screens. It smelled like popcorn and a little bit like feet. My own feet squelched in something brown and sticky, then stuck to the gummy tile floor.

Derek barreled across the arcade, and I followed, darting looks left and right, worried I'd see someone I knew. How would I explain being here with Derek? Especially since I'd told Madison and Tyler I was working on applications today. But I blinked, and it was just a sea of unfamiliar teenage faces.

'So you don't know how to drive, but do you at least know how to play air hockey?' A teasing smile played across Derek's mouth.

'Play it? I'm the queen of air hockey,' I joked, tossing my pony-tail over my shoulder.

'Oh-hoo! Is that so? Because I've won championships, so don't make things up around me, missy!'

'Please! You couldn't hold a candle to my awesomeness.' I grinned. Was I *flirting* with him?

'You're on!'

Derek put some coins in the table's slot and grabbed the puck.

'You ready?'

'I was born ready!'

He cracked up. 'You're too much, Olivia.'

'Bring it!'

Derek hit the puck, sending it sliding across the table so fast I almost didn't see it. I flailed but managed to hit a glancing blow. It ricocheted off his side of the table and bounced back to me. I slammed the puck, this time making proper contact. The puck launched off the table, sailing right toward his head.

Derek ducked, throwing his arms up to protect his face. The puck flew over his shoulder, landing on the ground beyond him and skittering a few feet away.

Derek popped back up, his eyes wide in surprise. Laughter spluttered from his lips. 'God! You said you were good, but I didn't know you actually took people out!'

I laughed so hard I could barely breathe.

'All right!' He grinned. 'No more mister nice guy. It's on!'

We battled it out for four games, finally calling it a draw when we noticed some younger kids lining up for a turn.

Derek punched me lightly on my shoulder as we left the arcade and headed toward the empty boardwalk. The islands in the distance bloomed emerald against the fading sunset. Below us the tide rolled in, the sound of the surf a gentle song.

'I had no idea you were so competitive!' He laughed.

'I compete in swim meets all the time. You'll see the real competitive Olivia come out again in September.'

'I know, I just never knew you were so, you know' – he looked sideways at me and laughed – 'aggressive about it.'

'I guess I'm not normally.'

'What's changed, then?'

'I don't know.' I lifted my shoulders. 'I feel like a lot of things are changing. Obviously, trying to find out about my dad, that's totally out of character. Then, you know, coming here with you.'

Derek's eyebrows lifted in surprise. 'How's that?'

'Well, like, I had to lie to Tyler and Madison. I told them I'm doing volunteer applications today. So don't let Madison know we were here, okay?'

'Would she be mad you're hanging out with me?'

'Yeah!' I laughed, surprised he even had to ask. 'She'd go mental!'

He shook his head; his jaw ticked an angry rhythm. 'She always has to be the center of attention. Even when it comes to you,' he said.

'No she doesn't.' My sense of loyalty flared up, and I jumped to her defense. 'She just worries about me.'

'What the hell does that mean?' He stopped walking and turned to me abruptly, the blue of his eyes suddenly edged out by darkness.

'I mean . . . I don't know . . .' I stuttered, flustered. I didn't want to tell him about all the things she'd told me. How scary she made him sound. 'You know, like when you pulled a knife on that guy in New York? And selling pot at school? She just thinks maybe you can be dangerous or something.'

'What the actual fuck!' he exploded. 'She's such a liar. I got *robbed* and the guy pulled a knife on *me*! Not the other way around.'

I shook my head, confused. 'Why would she lie to me?'

He shrugged and started walking. I had to hurry to catch up with him. 'Because that's what she does. She does it all the time with my parents. She's the one who told them I'd been selling pot at school.'

'Weren't you?'

'No. Jesus! I smoked pot at home *once*. She caught me, so she went to my dad and said I'd been selling it. She did it because he'd been spending time with me, redoing the car. She can't stand anybody else being the center of attention.'

'Didn't you tell them the truth?' I asked.

'Of course! But Madison's their princess. They believe everything she says.'

Wanting, no *needing*, to be the center of attention was Madison's biggest flaw. He had that right. I twisted the tail of my bracelet, looping the linked silver inside, then outside the bracelet's circle. I thought back to how pissed off she was that everybody thought her brother was a drug dealer. If she'd lied about it, her plan had backfired.

I blew out a harsh breath. 'I'm sick of being lied to. My mom, Madison. Can't people just tell the truth?'

'Hey.' Derek stopped walking. He put his finger under my chin, lifted it so I had to meet his eyes. 'I'm sorry I upset you. Look, don't even let Madison get you down. She has some issues because she's, you know, her. But you're her best friend, and I know she cares about you. Don't let what I've said get in the way of that.

'And if it's any comfort' – he slung an arm around my shoulders – 'I will never lie to you.'

I held his gaze. Suddenly I realized that not once during the entire afternoon had I thought about Kendall or who my dad was or my mom's lies. He'd done that for me. Helped me forget.

I swept my eyes across his face, so familiar but so new. His eyes looked even bluer against the black of his clothes. He had a tiny strawberry-shaped scar above his right eyebrow. I imagined pressing my lips against it. I wanted so fiercely to touch him that I was taken aback.

My eyes drifted shut. I thought for a moment we would kiss but something pinged, startling me. I moved away from him.

I fumbled awkwardly in my pocket for my phone. It was a Facebook message. I clicked into it.

'It's Kendall,' I said. I read out loud: '*Hi Olivia. Great to meet you! My dad said he owned a vacation house in Portage Point until he sold it in 1999. That's where your mom's from, right?*'

My eyes shot up to Derek's. 'That's the year I was born,' I said flatly. 'He sold the house he owned in the town where I was born, in the year I was born.'

Derek sucked his breath in sharply. 'That's a lot of coincidences.'

'Yep.'

He looked at my face, which suddenly felt like it was made of stone. 'I think maybe it's time you talk to your mom.'

12

ABI

november

A bitter wind flapped at the awning of the Piece of Cake Café. I stared at it from my parking space outside the police station. Across the street, the postman leaned into the wind as he delivered the mail, his body bent as he reached for a mailbox, reminding me that the world continued to turn with insulting haste.

I don't know how long passed as I sat there. My mind felt as if it were stuck inside a tumble dryer. My life was so messed up, my heart so broken, my head so muddled that I couldn't even think straight.

I rested my head on the steering wheel and squeezed my eyes closed. I needed to organize what I knew, arrange all the clues into straight columns that added up to a logical answer.

The detectives had proof, indisputable proof, and still they weren't going to investigate. But why? What wasn't I seeing?

My phone rang inside my purse, and I grabbed it. An unidentified number. My heart thumped hard in my chest. I'd found that, like a Pavlovian dog, I now reacted to the sound of my phone with intense fear, as if every call would bring bad news.

'Hello?'

'Is this Abigail Knight?' The voice was male, gentle and soft-spoken.

'Yes.'

'This is Anthony Bryant. I'm a victim advocate with the Seattle Police Department.'

I flashed back to Sarah telling me this morning she knew people with the SPD who might help me.

'Oh, right. Hi.' I looked at the police station, distracted, my mind still on what had just happened. 'That was fast.'

'Excuse me?'

'Sarah told me you'd call.'

'Who?'

'My sister, Sarah. Sarah Cassidy.'

'Oh, yes. Sarah.' There was a slight pause. 'Well, as a victim advocate, my job is to support those affected by crime. What I can do is help provide clarity and answer any questions you have about your daughter's case. I can also arrange access to a counselor.'

Rage hit me hard and fast, filling my organs and pulsing along my nerve endings. I'd told Sarah I didn't want a counselor. I wanted answers!

'I don't need a shoulder to cry on,' I said tightly. 'I need somebody to help me find out what happened to my daughter. There were bruises on her wrists!'

'Bruises?'

'Yes!'

He paused for a long moment, and I heard papers shuffling. 'I'm looking at the police report for your daughter now. Would you be free to meet today to discuss it?'

My heart leapt and I looked at my watch. He had access to Olivia's police report. Maybe he could help me after all.

'I can meet you now,' I said.

× × ×

I pulled my scarf tighter around my neck and headed toward the café. Decorated with vintage lamps and deep-seated couches, it was one of those indie joints serving organic coffee, homemade sandwiches, vegan muffins, and gluten-free brownies. Although new in town, it had become popular with the yummy-mummy crowd. As I pushed open the door, the scent of cinnamon and sugar, and the hiss of a coffee machine assaulted me.

The sound of indistinct chatter faded as I entered. Two moms with strollers stopped ordering and exchanged glances. The barista frothing milk stared at me, her mouth open. A girl who'd graduated from Olivia's school last year was in the corner with her mother. Their eyes landed like hot wax against my face, then slid away.

A prickly flush crawled up my neck, but I forced myself to the counter and ordered a grilled-cheese sandwich and a black coffee. I suddenly wished I carried a flask of whiskey with me. A shot would go a long way right now.

I sat beside a window near the door and stared outside as I

waited for Anthony, the coffee warming my hands while the cheese in my sandwich cooled and hardened. The hard lines of the maple trees that lined the road stood out like charcoal drawings against the gunmetal-gray sky. Between lingering brown leaves, I could just make out the horizontal expanse of the sea.

I took the opportunity to e-mail my boss, Malcolm, requesting another two-week leave. He replied almost immediately, saying to take as much time as I needed. I assured him it would just be the two weeks.

About a half hour later, the door opened, letting in a rush of cold air. The man who entered with it was tall and broad-shouldered, handsome in a rugged, outdoorsy way, with a thatch of dark hair that flopped over his eyes, and the early workings of a beard on his face. He wore comfortable-looking brown leather shoes, a beige canvas coat. His eyes, when he turned to me, were a wide, earnest green.

'Miss Knight?' His voice was the same gentle tone I'd heard on the phone.

'Yes.' I stood and shoved a hand out to shake his. When he clasped mine, his grip was firm and rough with calluses. 'Abi. It's just Abi.'

He nodded as he settled a black laptop bag on his chair. Then he peeled off his coat and draped it over the back. Underneath he wore navy wool trousers and a long-sleeved white shirt.

'I'm Anthony. Let me grab a coffee, and I'll be right back. Can I get you anything?'

'No, I'm good, thanks.'

I watched him as he ordered. His skin was tan for this time of year, weathered, as if he spent a lot of time outdoors. It made the winter green of his eyes even brighter. He looked like a man who'd seen things, done things. There was something about him that seemed inherently kindhearted, and something else . . . fractured.

Anthony smiled widely at something the barista said. He had deep creases around his mouth, smile lines. He tipped two dollars, which seemed excessive, and waited patiently while the girl talked over the steamer. He listened intently, his body still and calm, until his coffee was ready.

He took a long sip as he sat down across from me. 'Pumpkin latte,' he said. 'I'm counting the days till the peppermint mocha comes out. I live on those things all winter.'

I cringed. Yuck.

'Thanks for meeting me,' I said.

'It's no trouble.'

'So. You've worked with Sarah?' I asked.

'Sarah? Oh, your sister.' He took a big gulp of his coffee, his Adam's apple bobbing above the collar of his shirt. 'I've referred a number of victims and their families to Sarah for counseling. A few years back, my mother – she has Alzheimer's – went missing. It was terrifying. Sarah stayed out most of the night helping me look for her. She's great that way.'

I was taken aback. 'Sarah never said.'

Anthony smiled. 'No, she'd never brag. She's a good egg.'

He reached for his laptop bag and pulled out a sheaf of papers. It was the police report and a copy of McNally's notes. 'You mentioned that there were bruises on Olivia's wrists. I wanted to speak to you about that because it isn't in the police report.'

He pushed the papers toward me, and I scanned them.

'I don't understand.' I shook my head, feeling dizzy and confused. 'They saw them – they said the bruises were from the fall. She had bruises on her wrists. Finger-shaped bruises.'

'It isn't here. Did an investigator measure the depth of the bruises?' he asked. 'Determine if they were defensive wounds or not?'

I shook my head. 'I don't think so. But Olivia's doctor told me Detective Samson took pictures of the bruises on her wrists. Why wouldn't she include that?'

'It could just be an accidental oversight. It could be . . .' Anthony looked like he was floundering, groping for a reason. 'I don't know, to be honest. I'll have a word with one of my contacts and see what I can find out about the detectives. Maybe they're newbies and need some direction.'

I told him about the texts from Tyler and the hideous images in her iCloud account.

'Any idea who might have sent them?' he asked.

'No. None. Like I told the police, everybody likes Olivia.'

'Have you asked Tyler why he lied?'

'No. I haven't seen him in weeks. But I'm sure it's just miscommunication. Tyler adores Olivia. He's broken up about her.'

Anthony handed me a sheet of paper and a pen.

'Can you list the names of all the people she knew? It'll help us know who to talk to.'

I noticed immediately he'd said 'us,' and a wave of relief rushed over me. For the first time, it felt like somebody was on my side in all this. Somebody believed me. I wasn't alone.

I wrote down every name I could think of in a neat list. Everybody was a suspect now. But it was a start.

My phone rang then, and I reached for it. It was Sarah.

'Abi,' she said in a rush. 'I have to leave the hospital – something's happened at Dylan's school. He threw a book or something. But my car battery's dead. Any way you can give me a jump? Brad isn't answering his phone.'

I told her I'd be there in a few minutes and hung up. I stood and pulled my coat on.

'I'm really sorry,' I said to Anthony. 'I need to go.'

'No problem.' He swept the papers into a neat pile. 'I'll be in touch soon.'

× × ×

Night was settling onto the gray horizon over Puget Sound as I drove home from the hospital. Rain pattered against my car, and I clenched the steering wheel tightly, my wipers clattering as they shoved at the rain. Beyond my windshield, the rain hammered the sea grass into submission. The churning white surf battered the sand along the beach road, foam fanning out from the waves as they crashed into the shore.

At home, I slammed my car door shut and plodded up the front steps, the freezing air slapping me in the face. Inside I stood motionless in the entryway. The overwhelming anguish I'd been fighting all day climbed up the knobs of my spine.

I'd tried so hard to keep my daughter safe. I had so many rules: you're not allowed in a car with friends after dark; never walk on the road. We talked about stranger danger; I signed her up for self-defense classes when she was thirteen. All these rules I'd created for our life, I thought they'd keep her safe.

I grabbed a bottle of red wine and poured a hefty glass, draining it faster than I should have. I refilled the glass and took it to my living room, setting it on the coffee table just as my house phone rang.

'Hello, Miss Knight. Kaycee Bright, KOMO News,' came the overly sparkly voice of an eager young reporter. 'We'd like to –'

'No comment!' I roared, and slammed the phone down. The inexorable tide of tears crashed into me, and I crawled onto the couch, grasping my chest as if my heart would break.

I missed Olivia, her smile, her laughter, her lighthearted chatter. I missed the inside jokes we used to crack, the sound of her voice, the twinkle in her eyes. I felt a giant, all-encompassing yearning guzzling me whole.

It reminded me of the yearning I'd felt when my mom died.

I took another long slurp of wine and refilled the glass, anxiety curling inside my body. I drank heavily and deeply as night crashed around the house, dark memories rolling over me. Eventually I slid into a strange, disjointed sleep, my dreams chaotic and colorful, as if my mind were having a lunatic's house party. I swam toward consciousness, floating in the space between thoughts and dreams.

I looked down at my pajamas, and they were the purple princess ones I had when I was six. An icy wind blew up the bottom, chilling my legs as I stood on the roof next to my mom.

The air smelled electric. The clouds frothed angry and gray, and a fork of lightning illuminated the sky in the distance. I counted the way Sarah had taught me, reaching five before a violent clap of thunder vibrated along the gutters.

Mom wrapped her arms around me, her eyes glinting like wet pebbles. I could feel the warmth of her skin through her thin shirt.

'If you jump you'll be able to fly!' she hissed, her breath hot against my ear.

She tugged me toward the edge, and I peered down to the front yard, where dead leaves cartwheeled across our patch of grass.

Something horrible and scary scratched at the back of my throat and my tummy felt like I'd been whirling too fast on the merry-go-round. It was so far down. I didn't think I could actually fly. But I really wanted Mom to be happy.

The first drops of rain splattered against my bare arms, and my pajamas swirled around my ankles.

Over the edge of the gutter, I could see Sarah pulling up in her battered old green Gremlin. She jumped out and started waving her arms like crazy windmills. Her words were ripped away by the wind.

'Fly, Abi!' Mom screamed. 'Fly!'

I took a tiny step closer to the edge, and then another, but suddenly Sarah was there, wrenching me backward.

I jolted awake, my mouth wine-dry, my neck aching from sleeping on the couch. A feeling huddled in my chest, something like fear but also a deep longing and a desperate sadness, all at the same time. The dream was still hanging around me, caught in the damp blanket tangled around my body.

A rustling sound startled me and I froze, listening to the noises of the darkened living room – the ticking of the clock, the hum of heat through the vents – my whole body tense and tingling.

Eventually I sat up and threw the blanket off, looking to where the sound had come from. A white piece of paper had been pushed under my front door. I padded across the room in my bare feet, my neck aching and my head thumping. I picked it up and read the small, printed words:

They were told to stop investigating.

13

ABI

november

I didn't fall asleep the rest of the night. Instead, I stayed up making lists: of people Olivia knew, of who the baby's father might be, of who might want to hurt her. I wanted answers. Clarity. But there was none. As dawn broke over the horizon, the feelings inside me felt too big to turn off.

I paced the kitchen floor, the note clutched in my hand.

They were told to stop investigating.

I walked past the mirror in the living room and caught sight of my reflection. I looked terrible, blonde hair stringy and dark with oil, skin yellow and jaundiced, my eyes bloodshot, from lack of sleep or too much alcohol, I wasn't sure. My clavicles jutted out of my chest like little elbows. I looked disgusting.

Why had the detectives been told to stop investigating? And by whom? And who'd left me that note? I glanced at the clock, but it was only 6 a.m. I couldn't call Anthony yet.

I dropped the note on the dining room table, my hands shaking, and headed for the shower. Stripping off my clothes and turning the temperature up as high as I could stand, I stepped into the water, directing the spray onto the knots along my shoulders. I let the water scald my skin until I felt faint and had to get out.

After that, I forced myself to eat breakfast. The stale Cheerios slid down my throat and plopped into the wine that still pooled in my stomach. I nearly retched but managed to hold it down. I needed my strength.

If the detectives thought I would walk away meekly, they had another think coming. I would make them see me, take me seriously. I wouldn't let them close Olivia's case without finding out what had really happened.

I stared at my cell phone. For the first time in a long time, I found myself in the position of needing someone. I'd become very good at being self-reliant, pushing people away. Losing Olivia had made me realize that. I supposed in a way I'd hidden behind my daughter, not only living for her, but also living through her. And I was fine with that. But now I needed help. If only it didn't make me so uncomfortable.

At seven on the dot, I dialed Anthony's number.

'Good morning, Abi.' He sounded pleased to hear from me, not at all surprised by the early morning call.

I rubbed my neck and told him about the note from last night, what it said and what it might mean. He listened intently in that way some people have of listening like there's nothing else in the world but you.

'Did you see anybody around?' he asked.

'No. I mean, I didn't exactly look. It was the middle of the night.' *And I was terrified*, I finished silently.

'Was there anything else left?'

'No, just the note.'

'Do you have a security camera? Anything to see who it was?'

I almost laughed. 'No. Just a regular old floodlight.'

'Hey, I was thinking, do you mind if I swing by your house and look at those picture files you were telling me about? Maybe I can see something in them. I'm meeting a friend near you today. If you don't mind printing them out, I could stop by and grab them afterward?'

It was Saturday, and I had nothing planned. If Olivia were here, we'd lounge in our pajamas until noon, have bacon and eggs for breakfast, and put on a movie. Pain ripped through me, and I squeezed my eyes shut.

'Yes, of course.' My voice sounded ragged, the words like chips of ice scraping past my throat.

'Great. I'll swing by around lunchtime.'

× × ×

I slammed the front door of my house so hard it rattled and launched myself across the road toward the beach, my tennis shoes thudding hard on the pavement. The morning was brittle and bright. The cold air hissed in and out of my lungs like a serrated knife, turning my breath to an icy fog. The pain felt good.

I pounded along the boardwalk, the sound of my feet hitting the old boards echoing in the early morning mist.

I'd abandoned my daily run since Olivia's fall, and now my muscles felt like they were filled with sludge. But I pulled my beanie tight over my scalp and pushed on.

The rhythm of my feet, the staccato beat of my heart, the yelp of the seagulls became a melody, and soon I'd drifted into that zoned-out trance runners go into. Before I knew it, I'd run the four-mile half loop along the beach into town and back.

One of my neighbors, a chubby, overly friendly woman pushing a toddler in a stroller, waved as I passed. I waved back but didn't slow. I still couldn't bear talking to anybody, answering questions that had no answers.

Just before home, I slowed and veered off the path, picking my way across the huge boulders toward the water. The tide was all the way out, driftwood and seaweed marking the sand in a patchwork of art.

I stopped just before the water's edge and sat on a huge boulder jutting out of the sand. I closed my eyes as wind whipped tendrils of hair around my face and deafened my ears. I let the spray of Puget Sound dampen my face as I listened to the sound of my heart beating. Suddenly something wet slapped against my face.

I gasped and leapt up. It was a dog. A beautiful golden retriever, her tongue lolling happily out of the side of her mouth. She tried to lick me again, and I smiled and stroked the dog's head.

'Hey, you,' I murmured. Olivia had always begged to get a dog. I'd always said no, with the excuse that we didn't have time to take care of it. I wished now I'd said yes. I wished I'd always said yes.

'Sorry!' I heard somebody shout. I looked over my shoulder, and two women were running toward me. One was model-thin and blonde, the other a tall, athletic brunette. Both were dressed head-to-toe in running gear. They had the tight, toned bodies of women who had too much time on their hands and spent most of it at the gym.

'It's okay.'

The blonde grabbed the dog's collar. 'She likes you,' she said with a smile. She bent to the dog and gave her an affectionate nuzzle. 'Sadie, you funny thing!'

I patted Sadie's head. 'I like her, too.'

'You're Abi Knight, right?' the blonde said as she straightened.

I nodded, startled. On second glance, I recognized them both.

Petite and pale, with hair pulled back dramatically from a narrow face, the blonde was Lizzie. I couldn't remember the brunette's name. She was strong and masculine-looking, with cheekbones like arrows and almond-shaped eyes.

They were both PTA moms: organizing fund-raising events for the school, chaperoning class field trips, setting up coffee mornings for the other mothers. I avoided them like the plague.

I knew the other moms thought I was aloof, reserved. I didn't go for coffee or indulge in school-gate gossip. But being cool and detached were learned traits. Loss and life had taught me to contain my emotions, to stay away from things that could hurt.

And anyway, I was a single mom. I didn't have time to manage these things.

'We were really sorry to hear about Olivia,' Lizzie said, her eyes shining like wet glass.

'Thanks,' I said. The word felt sharp in my mouth. The dog licked my hand, and I patted her again, then turned to go. 'It was nice seeing you.'

They waved good-bye and walked away, the dog loping off ahead of them. I jogged a ways, then stopped and looked back. Their bodies leaned toward each other, as if they were a united force against the wind. I felt a stab of jealousy. When was the last time I'd felt I was part of a united force like that?

When was the last time I'd cared?

× × ×

When I returned home, Sarah's car was idling in the driveway, the exhaust making white puffs in the chilly air.

Sarah cut the engine and got out as soon as she saw me. Her husband, Brad, climbed out of the passenger side and came around to hug me. I leaned against his massive chest. Brad was like a giant teddy bear.

Big and broad-shouldered, he wasn't conventionally handsome. He had a neck thick as a football player's, hands as large as my head, a receding hairline, and a nose too large for his face. But his brown eyes were warm and kind and he exuded an aura of safety and security. He was the exact right match for my sister.

When I pulled out of Brad's embrace, I noticed his eyes were glittering. He swiped at his eyes and turned away as Sarah reached out to hug me.

She looked horrible. The purple smudges under her eyes, the gray cast to her skin, the deep creases etched like quotation marks around her mouth, all showed the toll the last month had taken. I was sure I looked like a mirror image.

'What's up?' I asked.

Brad cleared his throat. 'We're taking Dylan to a movie. Do you want to come?'

I bent down and waved at Dylan in the backseat. Eight years old, blond and honey-sweet, Dylan waved back, then held up the iPad to show me a game he was playing. I gave him a thumbs-up and a weak smile.

I knew they were putting on the charade for me, to help me move on, accept. But I didn't want to. The idea of sitting in a theater like a normal person made me want to scream.

'Thanks, but no.'

The sweat was drying on my skin, and I shivered in the sharp breeze. I needed to go inside.

'Please,' Brad said simply.

My sister reached for his hand and shot a smile at him. The way she looked at him made my heart hurt. They adored each other. There was none of that fighting or resentment some marriages had; only love and respect. A complete family. I couldn't be around them.

'Honestly, I can't.' I took a step back toward my house. 'Anthony's coming over.'

Sarah looked startled. 'Wh –?'

'Mom, I'm hungry!' Dylan shouted out the open window.

Sarah leaned into the car's open passenger window, rummaged in the glove compartment, and tossed him a small box of raisins. Sarah was an excellent mother. She was relentlessly competent, infinitely patient. I wished I had an ounce of her confidence.

Sarah turned to me. 'Anthony who?'

'Anthony Bryant. I want to show him some pictures I found in Olivia's iCloud account.'

Her face tightened, and I thought she was going to argue.

'At least somebody's helping,' I said pointedly.

Sarah lifted her shoulders resignedly. 'If it'll help, I'm all for it, Abi,' she said.

Irritation sneaked up along my insides. I scraped my fingernails across the Lycra of my running pants so I wouldn't say something mean. 'He believes me.'

Sarah closed her eyes. She breathed deeply and slowly, drawing on her inner reserves of patience. I hated it when she did her yoga breathing. It meant she was at the end of her rope. It meant she'd stopped really listening.

'I just don't want you to get your hopes up.'

'You don't think anybody hurt Olivia,' I accused, stunned by this realization. 'You think the police were right!'

'I just think . . .' She looked up. 'Why do you always think you know better?'

'Because this time I do!' I exclaimed. 'And it seems like the only way I'm going to find out what really happened to Olivia is if I do it myself. The police aren't investigating.'

'Yes they are!'

'No they –'

'Sarah!' Brad interjected, sliding a hand between us and looking pointedly at his wife. He turned to me. 'What she means to say is, we just want to . . . manage expectations.'

I stared at them, incredulous. As grotesque as it was, the urge to find out what had happened to Olivia had stirred a small part of me, long buried beneath the rubble of what my life had become. Finding the truth was the right thing to do: for Olivia and for me.

'I didn't come here to fight,' Sarah said wearily. 'Actually, there's something I wanted to talk to you about.'

Just then there was a crunch of wheels on gravel. An unfamiliar silver BMW parked behind Sarah's, and a second later Anthony got out. He looked freshly showered, his hair slightly damp. He seemed like the most normal person in the world with his scuffed tennis shoes and beige canvas coat.

'Hi, Sarah,' he said, walking toward her with a pleased smile.

'Hi, Anthony. Long time, no see.' Sarah hugged him, then introduced him to Brad. 'How's your mom?'

'She's doing okay, thanks for asking. Her memory's getting worse, but physically she's still really healthy. Small blessings.'

'You still teach rowing at the boat club?'

'I've just come from there.' Anthony grinned.

'Mo-om! Da-ad!' Dylan shouted from the car.

Sarah rolled her eyes and laughed. 'He calls,' she joked. 'We better get going.'

Sarah and Brad slid into their car, but at the last minute Sarah stuck her head out the window. 'Call me later, okay, Abi? We need to talk.'

I waved good-bye, and a minute later Anthony and I were alone in my front yard.

14

OLIVIA

june

I sucked furiously on the end of a lock of hair and glared at my mom across the living room. There had been a huge shift in our relationship in the last few weeks. On the surface, she probably didn't even notice. But underneath, deep down, I felt it. I didn't trust her. And I was mad.

'Why do I have to study *all* day? It's *Saturday*!' I burst out. I was starting to hate how she always wanted to see my work, looking over my shoulder, making sure I was still getting As.

It felt like she had my whole life mapped out for me. I would go to U-Dub, then move back to Portage Point, get a job, get married, have kids. Sometimes I just wanted to be my own person. Maybe I'd backpack through Europe, study abroad, live in exciting places like Paris or Moscow or London. I liked history and political science. I could totally study international relations.

I knew I'd never do it, though. I worried how Mom would cope when I left for college, let alone if I left the country. The guilt would be awful. I mean, I knew I was lucky. Not everybody had a mom who cared so much – like, Madison sometimes joked she'd have to get admitted to the ER for her mom to notice what she was doing. I guess it was just hard to explain what it felt like having a mother whose love comforted and smothered me at the same time.

Mom's expression was pinched, her lips drawn tight as she wiped the kitchen counters with a wet cloth. The house smelled like Windex and bleach.

I knew fighting with her was the wrong tactic; it would only make her dig her heels in. She seemed all sweet on the surface, but she could be seriously stubborn when she'd made her mind up about something. If I pushed too hard, she'd never back down.

'It doesn't matter,' I finally said, feeling suddenly exhausted.

I'd been so busy all week: sneaking in time with Derek, hanging out with Madison, and squeezing in swimming before meets started again in the fall. Studying for finals had slipped to the bottom of my priority list, which meant I'd come home with a B rather than an A on my chemistry final yesterday. Thus Mom totally flipping out. Like I'd intentionally tried to do worse than usual.

'If you don't pull it together, you won't get into a good university, Liv,' she said, exasperated.

I clenched my jaw. I'd wanted to talk to her about Gavin and Kendall Montgomery, but now I didn't want to talk to her at all. All I wanted was to be in charge of my own life, my own future. Good grades weren't everything.

It was only going to get worse when I started competing again. Mom came to every swim meet she could, coordinated with my coach to get me on the best training routine, made sure I went to every practice session. It suddenly seemed like such a waste of time. It wasn't like I was going to be a professional swimmer after high school.

'It's like living in a prison here.' I scowled at her.

'That's completely unfair,' Mom said, her face flaming red. 'I just want what's best for you!'

'Maybe you don't know what's best for me! Maybe *I'm* the one who knows what's best.'

Mom took a deep breath. 'I'm just trying to make sure you have a good future ahead of you.'

'Why can't you just give me some freedom? You don't have to keep me under lock and key, you know!'

Mom looked at me for a long moment, her blue eyes serious. 'I didn't know you felt that way. You're not under lock and key –'

'I always have to tell you where I am,' I cut her off. 'You make me come home at nine o'clock. That's, like, the lamest curfew in the world. And I have to call you at four. And you always check my homework. It's like I'm twelve!'

'Only to make sure you're doing well!'

'I don't need you to check my work, Mom. If I get a B, it isn't the end of the world. It doesn't mean I'm slacking, okay? It just means I'm not as good at chemistry as I am at history.'

Mom finished wiping down a counter and rinsed the cloth in the sink. Silence expanded between us like a rubber band, something that would eventually break.

Finally she sighed deeply. 'Fine, I won't check your work anymore. But you have to be responsible and get good grades. You know how important college is. And as far as today, you can finish studying and go over to Madison's house at three. Is that fair?'

I huffed out a loud sigh, hoping she knew how much this sucked. Suck fest. Suckopolis. Majorly sucketh.

I crossed the room and flicked on the TV to fill the silence, then flopped back into my chair. I opened my AP history book and hunched over it, irritation and fury warring inside of me.

Mom filled a glass with water from the sink and took a long drink. She put the glass in the dishwasher, then sat at the table across from me.

'I'm sorry if I've been making you hit the books too hard.' She touched my hand with her fingertips and smiled, but it was that fake, forced smile she used on people who didn't know her that well.

'It's okay,' I said grumpily. 'But could we at least talk about me getting my driver's license? And a car?'

'A car? Why would you need a car?'

'Because I'm almost seventeen. I'll be the only seventeen-year-old in the world who doesn't drive!'

'That's a bit of an exaggeration, Olivia.'

'It would be nice to have some freedom, is all.'

For a moment Mom looked conflicted. But then she shook her head.

'No. It's too dangerous. Do you know how many teenagers die in road accidents every year? You're not going to be one of them.'

'People die in terrorist attacks, too! And you still let me go to shopping centers.'

'Well, fortunately we don't have to worry about that here.'

'That's not the point! Most of my friends have cars.'

'You don't need a car,' Mom said. 'You can walk pretty much anywhere here. Madison's right up the road from us. Or you can walk to Sarah's.'

That gave me an idea. Maybe my aunt would talk to me about my dad. Mom had lived with her until I was born; maybe she knew something.

'Can I at least go somewhere with Madison later? Like other than her house?'

'Like where? How long will you be gone? Who'll be with you? Who will drive?'

She fired off questions without even thinking about it. I winced and groaned inwardly. Rookie mistake. Mom always seemed to need specifics. Or maybe I was just noticing it more.

I thought fast. 'The arcade in Laurelwood.'

'With who?'

'Madison and Derek.'

'Oh, Derek's back?' Her eyebrows shot up in surprise.

'I guess.' I shrugged.

'Why don't we go somewhere tonight? We could catch a movie? Or maybe go ice skating in Laurelwood?'

I tried not to let my face show anything. It was sort of a trick question. As much as I loved her, I didn't want to spend Saturday night with my mother. But I couldn't say that. It would hurt her feelings.

'We're going out for my birthday, right?' I said instead.

'Yes, that's right. Shall I make reservations at Pagliacci's?'

Pagliacci's was where we always went for special occasions.

'Could we go somewhere else this time?' Even I heard the annoying whine in my voice. 'Like, somewhere out of town? Let's go into Seattle.'

I don't know why I said it. Mom hated going to Seattle. She got overwhelmed with the traffic and irritated by the constant press of people. The one time she took me to an orthodontist appointment in Seattle when I was fourteen, she was totally freaked out the whole time. She spent most of the appointment looking over her shoulder and checking her watch. The next day she'd switched me to an orthodontist in Lynnwood.

'Of course. If that's what you want,' Mom said. She stood and came around to my side of the table and rubbed her hand over my hair.

I ducked away from her hand and walked to the couch, flopping down and reaching for the remote.

She trailed after me. 'Come on, Olivia . . .'

But I'd stopped listening. On the TV was a political ad for Gavin Montgomery. I couldn't believe I hadn't recognized him before.

'Mom.' I pointed at the TV. This was my chance. 'Do you know him?'

We watched as Gavin Montgomery's smiling face flashed across the screen. The ad started with him standing tall and broad-shouldered in front of a crowd of people at what looked like a factory, then faded to stills of him speaking in front of a crowd.

Mom stared at the TV, her fair eyebrows scrunched into tiny knots over her jewel-blue eyes. The blood had drained completely from her face, leaving her pale and stark.

'Mom?' I said. A fizz of worry settled in my stomach.

She shook her head hard. 'No. Of course I don't know him.' Her face was suddenly completely blank, like a shutter had fallen. Perhaps I'd mistaken her reaction just a moment before. 'How on earth would I know him?'

'He just . . .' I hesitated, searching her face. *Had* I imagined it?

I stared at her, feeling like I wanted to crack her open and see what was inside. But Mom's face was pale as chalk. Maybe I didn't want to talk to her about it. Not if it upset her this much.

'He's running for reelection to state senate,' I said carefully. 'We were talking about the elections at school, and I wondered who you were going to vote for.'

'I honestly hadn't thought about it.' She breezed over to the remote and turned the TV off. 'I'm going for a run,' she said, heading for the stairs to change.

I knew right then that she was hiding something about Gavin Montgomery. Part of me was terrified to find out what, but the other, bigger part of me wasn't terrified at all. That other part was pretty pissed off.

So I decided then and there that I needed to talk to Kendall, sooner rather than later.

I was going to find out what my mom was hiding.

15

ABI

november

I watched Sarah and Brad's car disappear around the corner and felt loneliness mingle with the chill creeping over my skin.

Maybe I should've gone with them. Anything would be better than the feeling of emptiness pressing down on me.

But I cleared my throat and turned to Anthony. 'I have those pictures printed out for you. Do you want to come inside? I'll grab them.'

'Sure.' He shoved his shaggy locks out of his eyes and looked at me earnestly, falling in step with me as we crunched toward my house. 'Have the police closed Olivia's case?' he asked.

'No, I don't think so. They just aren't investigating it. Is that unusual?'

Anthony hesitated. 'To be honest, not really,' he said. 'Budget cuts mean there are fewer detectives investigating crimes these days. There simply aren't enough resources, so detectives prioritize what they think are the most important or solvable cases.'

I opened the door and gestured him in, then gathered the pictures I'd printed from the kitchen table and handed them to him.

He glanced at them, then folded them into neat squares and continued, 'What is unusual is that Portage Point is one of the biggest tourist destinations in Washington. A potential homicide here should be as irresistible as crack. The police should be all over this. I also find it curious that the detectives didn't examine Olivia's skin for trace evidence or embedded fragments, although the police report did note there was no sign of a struggle or blood spatter at the scene.'

I winced, and Anthony abruptly stopped talking. 'I'm sorry,' he said, touching my hand. 'That was insensitive of me.'

'No.' I shook my head and shoved aside a throb of emotion rising like vomit in my throat. 'I need to know everything. What does it mean, then? If Olivia's case should be an important one, but they've been told to stop investigating it?'

'I really don't know. It's an election year. Maybe the police chief wants to keep his crime stats down.'

'But as you said, closing a homicide should be a big deal here.'

'Not if you hide that it was a homicide.'

I breathed out hard, shock rippling through me. 'You think they're hiding it?'

'No.' He shook his head vigorously and ran a hand through his shaggy hair. 'That came out wrong. I'm sure nobody's hiding anything. Honestly. It's probably just shoddy detective work.'

I nodded, but my mind was whirling.

'Anyway' – he held the printed pictures up, then slid them into an inner pocket in his coat – 'thanks for these. I'll have a look and let you know if I see anything in them.'

'Thank *you*. Actually . . .' I dug a toe in the tile, hating how awkward I was. 'I owe you a couple of thank-yous.'

'For what?'

'For looking at the police report. And those pictures. I really appreciate it.'

'It's no problem.' Anthony smiled. He did that a lot, I noticed. His face seemed made for it, wide cheekbones, a high forehead, upturned eyebrows. It was a face you could trust. 'I know how hard it is. I'm happy to help any way I can.'

'Do you want a coffee?' I asked.

It was an impulse, an unfamiliar one. I never sat down with people over coffee. I wasn't good at small talk. But I found I didn't want him to go. I wanted somebody to talk to.

'I, uh, don't have any pumpkin spice syrup, but I have lots of sugar.'

Anthony laughed, and it was a nice sound. Warm, like a blanket. 'Sure, yeah, I'd love one. I probably shouldn't stay too long, though. I have a sitter.'

'Sitter?' I echoed.

'For my mom. I have a health-care assistant who watches her for a few hours on the weekends.'

'It must be hard,' I said as I scooped ground coffee into the french press. 'Losing her by inches.'

'I suppose I could look at it that way,' Anthony said. 'Really I'm just grateful I have her at all.'

It was a funny answer, so different from how I would look at it. But he was right.

'How much sugar do you want?' I asked Anthony.

'Three spoons, please. No milk.' I made a face and he saw it, smiling sheepishly. 'I have a horrible sweet tooth.'

'And yet you're so slim.' I handed him his coffee, and we went to the couch, sitting on opposite ends. 'Guys are always like that. All I have to do is look at sugar and I gain five pounds.'

He laughed. 'I highly doubt that.'

He sipped his coffee without speaking, seeming completely comfortable with long silences. I liked that about him.

I pushed a handful of papers across the coffee table toward him. 'I know I gave you a list of everybody Olivia knows, but I've also written down how each of them knows her. And I've made a timeline of Olivia's day. Or at least what I know of it. Tyler said Olivia left the barbecue at ten forty-five, and she was found at three in the morning.'

It helped, these lists. To have a purpose, a plan; to move with it. For the first time in more than a month, I had a reason to get up in the morning beyond sitting vigil at the hospital. I felt more in control of my world.

First, I needed to find out who the baby's father was. He could be the one who'd pushed her, or, at the very least, he might have some idea who had. Second, I needed to talk to Olivia's friends, her teachers, the people she knew.

Anthony set his coffee down and picked up my notes.

'This is incredibly organized,' he said, looking surprised. 'You'd make a good investigator.'

I ducked my head, embarrassed. 'Thanks.'

Outside, wind clattered against the house and a draft sneaked under the front door, licking at my ankles with an icy tongue. I pulled the knitted blanket from the back of the couch over my legs and tucked my feet under my body.

'If the detectives didn't initially take Olivia's phone, maybe there's something else in her room they left.' Anthony set his coffee down. 'Do you mind if I have a look?'

'I guess not,' I said doubtfully. 'But they probably took anything important.'

'Maybe. I just want to look around.'

I showed him to Olivia's room, opening the door slowly. It physically hurt to go in, to see the bed where she'd last slept, the vanity mirror she'd looked in only a month ago.

I hovered in the doorway as Anthony entered her private space. Dirty jeans lay inside out on the floor. One tennis shoe had been kicked across the room and lay upside down near the bookshelf; the other peeked from under the side of her bed.

Anthony shuffled through Olivia's drawers, systematically pushing aside balls of crumpled clothing. He opened her closet, rifled through her clothes. I turned away. It seemed too intimate. I wanted to tell him to stop. But I would do anything to find out the truth. I'd sell my soul to the devil if I had to.

Anthony knelt next to the bed, pushed a stray shoe aside, and lifted up the duvet. His dark head moved left and right, like a typewriter. He thrust an arm under and pulled out a small white plate – one from the kitchen set downstairs. It had been used as an ashtray, a cigarette crushed in the middle of a pile of cement-gray ash.

Anthony held the plate up for me to see. 'Did Olivia smoke?'

'No.' I shook my head vigorously. 'No way. That's one thing I know she wouldn't do. She was completely against smoking. Always yelled at me if I did.'

'Whose is it, then?'

'I don't know. Maybe one of her friends'?'

Anthony bent closer and squinted. 'There's lipstick on the end.'

I leaned in to inspect the cigarette butt. Sure enough, coral-colored lipstick marked the end.

'It's definitely not Olivia's, then. She hated lipstick. Said it made her lips feel 'icky.' She is – was – a bit of a tomboy like that.' I worked hard to keep my voice from wobbling.

Anthony plucked thoughtfully at the stubble on his chin. I noticed for the first time a speckling of gray threading through the dark.

'We need to find out whose this is. It could lead us to one of the last people who was with Olivia. Maybe she knows something.'

'But how?'

'One step at a time,' he said. 'We'll start at the beginning and keep picking apart the threads until we find what connects. In a way, we're lucky the detectives didn't look too hard and didn't have the CSIs come around. Now we have this to use as evidence.'

Anthony pulled a plastic bag from his back pocket and tilted the cigarette into the bag. 'I have a friend. If there's DNA on this, she'll find it.'

He knelt and reached under the bed again. 'There's something else.'

What he pulled out made my blood run cold.

It was a wooden photo frame with its glass shattered. The photo inside had been ripped out and torn to pieces.

'Oh no,' I whispered.

Dread throbbed in my chest, drawing my mind quickly down the stairs of my own murky subconscious.

'It's a picture of my dad, but – oh, it's complicated.'

'It could be important, Abi.'

I exhaled sharply. 'I never told Olivia who her father was. But one day when she was in first, maybe second grade, she came home from school crying because she didn't have a dad. I framed this picture of my dad and told her it was *her* dad. It seemed to help, and she's had it here ever since.'

I stopped abruptly, not wanting to tell him who Olivia's father was. I was a coward, hiding like a rabbit in the woods. But all the fear and worry I'd been holding back was rushing in. Memories of Olivia's father's threats reawakened my deepest fears. Nobody could know she was his.

I expected more questions, but Anthony didn't say a word. He slipped the contents of the broken frame and its torn picture in another plastic bag.

Anthony studied me. 'You look beat.'

'No, I'm fine,' I said, even though I felt dangerously close to passing out. My body ached from my run, and I was basically surviving on alcohol fumes and short bursts of nightmare-riddled sleep.

'Let me make you something to eat.'

'What?' I said, startled. 'No, I'm okay.'

'Come on.'

Anthony took my elbow and led me down the stairs to the couch, pressing me into its soft folds before he went to rummage around in the kitchen. I watched him, feeling disconnected from my old life. Like I'd split in two and was walking in parallel lines. It felt weird: somebody in my house, taking care of me. It had never happened before. I took care of Olivia, but there was nobody to care for me.

Anthony pulled a package of dried pasta from the cupboard, along with a jar of Classico. He made us a simple pasta dish, then cut the mold off the edge of a block of cheese he found in the fridge, and shredded it over plates piled high with steaming noodles and sauce.

He quietly moved Olivia's schoolbooks from the dining room table to the kitchen counter. I turned my face away, unable to contemplate what it meant that we were moving her things, rearranging our lives. It was unbearably, intolerably sad.

Anthony brought the plates to the dining room table and called me over. 'It isn't gourmet or anything, but here you go,' he said.

I sat across from him and mumbled an awkward thanks. Part of me resented the fact that I had to eat, that I had to carry on at all. But the other part knew he was right. I had to keep my strength up for everything that lay ahead.

We ate in silence for a few minutes, my first hot meal in weeks, the only sound the bloated rain beating against the windowpanes. Occasionally the wind howled, rattling the door; tree branches scraped against the side of the house.

'My sister was murdered when I was in my first year of college.' Anthony didn't meet my eyes, twirling the noodles on his fork.

I stopped chewing, surprised at his candor. So that was why he looked so fractured.

'I'm so sorry.'

'It was a long time ago.'

'Does it . . .' I swallowed hard, a balloon of sorrow swelling in my throat, '. . . get easier?'

'Yes. I know that sounds bad. I still miss her and I often find myself thinking about her, but yes, it does. I was in college working toward my law degree when it happened. It took fifteen years for the case to be solved. Every few years the papers would run an anniversary story, or a new detective would call and ask a few questions.' He exhaled heavily, blowing his floppy hair out of his eyes.

'Sometimes I think it's a blessing that my mom has Alzheimer's. That sounds horrible, too. But my mom was tormented by what happened. My dad died of a heart attack a few years after. I know how hard it is, having all those questions and no answers. There's nothing worse than not getting closure.'

The house phone rang, and Anthony offered to get it.

'No, it's okay,' I said. 'Probably just a reporter – they want their inside scoop.'

There had been a few other cases in Washington State where a pregnant woman in a coma had been kept alive until her baby was born, but never a teenager. Olivia's case had captured the attention of the media, but I didn't have the energy or head space to answer their questions.

I'd learned to be grateful I'd never become a journalist. I didn't care how much I loved a byline; I'd never have stalked someone in personal agony the way they stalked me. Fortunately, in the last couple weeks they'd eased off, heading in search of new stories.

'I'll tell them to stop.' Anthony scraped his chair back and picked up the phone.

'Hello?' He waited a beat. 'Hello?'

He set the phone down. 'There's nobody there.'

He sat down, and we lapsed into silence again. We'd both finished our pasta when he spoke again.

'We're going to find out what happened to your daughter, and one day, a few months from now, you'll have a beautiful baby to fill a piece of the hole that Olivia will leave. You can't stop living, Abi. You might as well be dead if you do.'

I understood now why he chose to work with those whose lives were tainted by tragedy. In some way, every time he helped somebody, every time he rescued them from their personal tragedy, he was recreating his own experience. He was mending the past.

Maybe that's what I was doing too. Giving myself – and Olivia – another chance.

16

OLIVIA

june

I swam lazy laps back and forth across the school swimming pool. I swept my arms up and then down, pulling my body slowly through the water. The smell of chlorine was strong in my nose, the cool water slipping like satin around me.

At the end of the lane I crunched my body, lifted my feet, and spun underwater. My feet connected with the wall. I pushed off, arrowing my arms ahead of me. I pulled my right arm back and kicked. Then *bam*, head up for my first breath, and back down.

This was what I liked about swimming: the rhythm of it, the consistency, the freedom. At its core, swimming was about me being free to be me. I didn't have to worry about all the shit outside. I knew this feeling would be ruined once I started competing again in the fall. Sometimes I thought about quitting. I just didn't want to let anybody down. My coach, my teammates, my mom.

When I pulled myself out of the pool and draped my towel around my shoulders, I heard my text message indicator going off from my bag. I dried my hands and rummaged around for my phone.

It was Aunt Sarah replying to my earlier text. *Hi sweetie! What a lovely offer from my favorite niece! ☺ Yes, let's meet up today for a girly chat. What time are you free?*

I typed a quick response. *Just finished swimming. How about now? I'll be home in fifteen.*

She replied right away. *Ok, see you then.*

I put my phone away and pulled my bracelet out of the safety compartment in my backpack, securing it around my wrist. Swimming was the only time I took my bracelet off. I didn't want the chlorine to ruin it.

Then I headed toward the showers. I knew Mom would be gone for a couple hours – she ran the eight-mile beachfront loop every Saturday – so I had lots of time to get some answers from Sarah.

I'd only just gotten home when I heard the crunch of tires outside. I threw open the door and stepped onto the front porch. The gravel in the driveway was pitted with dirty puddles. My aunt stepped carefully around them, trying to keep her white ballet flats clean. Her cropped tan pants and pink, lace-edged Banana Republic top shouted suburban mom.

'Hi!' She waved enthusiastically.

I waved back. Sarah was always overly cheerful and friendly; she was sort of the opposite of my mom. My mom's nice – it's just she's pretty shy. I always feel like I need to protect her a little bit.

Sarah and I went to the kitchen and I sat in the breakfast nook, which looked out over our backyard. It was slightly overgrown: a square of lawn bookended by rosebushes and lavender. The lonely weeping willow at the back sent tattered fronds chasing the air.

'Your mom out for a run?' she asked.

'Every Saturday.' I smiled.

'So, what's up, sweetie? Is it a boy?'

I almost rolled my eyes. Like I'd talk to her if I had boy problems.

'No,' I said. 'That's not it.'

She set her massive mom purse on the kitchen island and leaned forward to smooth my hair behind my ears. Irritation sparked in me. Could nobody see I was sixteen, not six?

I took a deep breath and clasped my hands together on my lap, hoping Aunt Sarah would answer my questions. I didn't want to hurt Mom's feelings. There was just so much I wanted to know. Like, if my dad was actually alive.

Growing up without a father had been hard. At Christmas it was just Mom and me hovering around the corners of Sarah's house. And Father's Day was just code for Fake Day. Mom was always extra smiley, trying to make up for what I was missing.

Madison said you couldn't miss someone you'd never met, but she was wrong. There was a giant dad-shaped piece of me missing. I would never be whole if I didn't find out who he was.

'I can't get Mom to tell me anything,' I began. 'That's why I'm asking you. I have a right to know, and I've found out some weird things, so I really want the truth now.'

'Okaaay.'

'This is going to sound totally random, but . . .'

'Olivia, out with it.'

'Is my father Gavin Montgomery?'

Sarah's eyes widened. Her upper body moved backward, as if blown by a sudden wind.

'Wow.' She laughed nervously, her eyes darting around the room. 'Where is that coming from?'

'Will you just answer me?'

'Olivia, you know it's not my place –'

'Mom won't talk to me about it! We saw him on TV the other day, and I asked her about him and she looked like she was gonna faint, and then she told me she's never heard of him. He's a politician. Of course she's heard of him! She's lying about something.'

'Well, maybe there's a reason for that.'

'No good reason! I mean, all it does is make my imagination go crazy. Like, did he rape her? Am I that kid that came out of rape? Or is he you guys' long-lost brother and he molested her? Or did she, like, kidnap me? Or . . .'

Suddenly I was so angry that this had been kept from me. I jumped to my feet, eyes blazing.

Sarah shook her head and stood slowly. 'Olivia, you're right, you're letting your imagination get away from you. Of course she didn't –'

'Stop!' I cut her off. 'I don't want to talk to you until you're honest with me. I'm sick of being lied to!'

And with those last hurtful words, I raced up the stairs and slammed the door to my room.

I flopped on my bed, heart pounding wildly in my chest. I

felt like it would crack open or burst into flame or explode into a thousand pieces.

Only a couple minutes had passed when Sarah knocked softly on my door. She peeked her head in without waiting for me to answer.

'Sweetie?'

I sat up and pulled my knees to my chest and glared at her, stubbornly refusing to speak.

She slid into the room, leaned her back against the wall. Her hair was in a ponytail and she stretched both hands back to tighten it.

'Listen.' She pulled a packet of cinnamon gum from her back pocket, popped a piece in her mouth, then offered me one. Sarah always had cinnamon gum with her. She'd been smuggling me pieces since I was a kid. My mom hated it, thought I'd choke or something. But I'd beg and beg and eventually Sarah would give in.

I ignored the gum. 'I'm already pretty sure he's my dad, so you might as well tell me the truth. I just want to know why Mom said he was dead.'

'I don't know.'

I glared at her.

'That's the truth. Your mom never told me. In fact, she'd kill me if she knew I was talking to you about this.'

She let her legs fold and slid down the wall until she was sitting cross-legged on the floor. 'Look, your mom was no angel in high school. I mean, she had a tough childhood, you know?'

I nodded. Mom had told me how her mother left her on Sarah's doorstep, then went home and killed herself. It was, like, movie horrible.

'Well, your mom had a bit of a . . . reputation with guys. She went from one to the next and was a bit, you know . . .' She looked away, not wanting to say it out loud.

'Easy?' I asked, shocked.

'Yeah.'

I shook my head, speechless. That didn't sound like Mom at all. She'd never even gone on a date in the whole time I'd been alive.

'Don't judge her too much. She was extremely insecure and very, very vulnerable, and things were really tough for her. She was looking in the wrong place, but all she wanted was to be loved. Just after she graduated, she started seeing someone. She stopped hanging out with her friends and partying. I didn't know who he was because she kept it really quiet.'

Sarah looked out the window and nibbled the edge of a fingernail. Finally she dropped her hand into her lap and looked at me.

'Listen, Olivia, are you sure you want to know this? Sometimes the truth isn't what you expect. You know, when I was in college there was this experiment we did in one of my psychology classes where our teacher asked us what we'd prefer: happiness or truth. Most people chose happiness.'

'Not me,' I said stubbornly. 'Besides, that's stupid. Truth brings happiness.'

She shook her head. 'Not necessarily. In fact, sometimes it brings the exact opposite. Or the truth isn't even what you thought it would be. It just opens up a whole can of worms you wish you could shove back inside.'

I clenched my jaw and wrapped my hands around my knees. 'I don't care,' I said. 'I still want to know.'

Sarah sighed, resigned.

'Well, like I said, your mom started secretly seeing this guy the summer after she graduated. One night I stopped by her work to give her a ride home and saw her get into someone's car. When they drove past me, I saw it was Gavin Montgomery.'

Sarah unfolded her legs and crossed her ankles. 'She dated him two, maybe three months. Then, as suddenly as it began, it was over. He left Portage Point and never returned.

'What I *do* know, Olivia' – she fixed me with a flinty gaze – 'is that your mom loves you and would do *anything* for you. If she hid who your dad is from you, she must have a good reason for it. You should keep that in mind.'

× × ×

After Aunt Sarah left, I lay on my bed staring at the ceiling for a long time. A tiny spider was busy knitting a new web in a corner of the ceiling. After a minute, it disappeared into a crevice.

So many emotions jostled in me that I felt a bit sick.

Gavin Montgomery was my dad.

My mom had lied to me my entire life. Who cared why. My dad was alive. I'd been robbed of the chance to know him.

I flopped onto my stomach and my eyes landed on a photo of my dad that Mom gave me when I was little. I picked up the picture from my bedside table, ran my fingers across the smooth wooden frame.

I looked at the face of the man in the picture. He was in his thirties with blond, thinning hair and light eyes, deep dimples in both cheeks. He was looking just off camera, smiling at whoever was taking the picture.

This was not Gavin Montgomery. The picture had probably come in the frame.

An overwhelming sadness washed over me and tears welled in my eyes, tumbling out of me like broken promises. I'd never physically had a father in my life, but I'd always thought I had this man, whoever he was. I felt like I was losing that now.

I wiped my eyes, a sudden, rising anger burning away the sadness. I sat up and lifted the picture and smashed it hard against my bed frame. The glass cracked but didn't shatter, so I flipped up the metal flaps at the back and lifted out the picture. Then I meticulously tore it into tiny pieces and stuffed it under my bed.

Now I understood what Sarah had been telling me. Sometimes even the truth was a lie.

17

ABI

november

Olivia's hospital room was absolutely boiling. Her body no longer regulated her core temperature, so the heating was kept high, warming blankets tucked around her shrinking frame.

Sarah and I shrugged out of our coats and hung them on the back of the door.

One of the nurses peeked her head in the door. Her name tag said Katie. She was very young, almost a girl, with round, flushed cheeks, clear brown eyes, and mousy brown hair pulled into a tight bun. Everything about her screamed wholesome and sweet.

'Dr Maddox will be in to do the ultrasound in just a moment.' She smiled, a dimple flashing in her right cheek, then disappeared.

Thirteen and a half weeks left until the baby would be born. I ticked every day off the calendar. One more day the baby was alive. And Olivia.

146

Today we'd find out the sex.

Sarah flopped in a chair and flicked the TV on, finally settling on a rerun of *Judge Judy*. We watched as Judy berated a fat, bald man while a woman who looked like a truck-stop hooker smirked at him.

'You all right?' I asked Sarah.

She sighed. 'We're having some problems with Dylan. I met his teacher this morning. He's having a hard time reading and writing. She thinks he's dyslexic.'

'Surely they can't tell that at eight!'

'Not definitively. She's giving me a heads-up, though.'

Sarah glanced at the TV. *Judge Judy* had finished and the news was on. Senator Gavin Montgomery was speaking at a political rally in Seattle. He gestured wildly to a cheering crowd: just another politician on the campaign trail.

'Abi,' she said, rubbing her eyes. The skin on her hands was covered with angry red patches. Her eczema was back. 'There's something I need to –'

'Afternoon, ladies.' Dr Maddox entered the room pushing a portable ultrasound machine. She flashed a warm, grandmotherly smile, her gray curls bobbing around a round face. 'Look at you two,' she scolded gently. Her accent dripped with the honey of the South. 'You both need a square meal on your bones. Promise me you'll go get a muffin after this. You need to keep up your strength.'

Sarah and I exchanged smiles and promised.

'Now then. Are you ready to see your grandchild?'

I nodded.

Dr Maddox positioned the machine next to Olivia's stomach, then pulled back the white sheet to expose the bump underneath. She squirted clear gel onto Olivia's belly. It made a hollow *pftt pftt* sound.

I watched the static on the screen blur in and out as Dr Maddox looked for the best angle. My throat ached and my eyes burned, and I realized I hadn't blinked in a long time.

Finally a black-and-white picture emerged. The rapid *thud, thud, thud, thud* of a baby's heartbeat filled the room. And then I could see it, the pixels merging to show the life blossoming inside Olivia: a round head, a tiny nose, the silhouette of a face. A baby. There was a baby inside my baby.

I gasped and tears sprang to my eyes. An emotion I couldn't identify filled the hollow cavity of my chest, something with enough power to push the anvil of grief aside.

The baby jerked, then rolled over, its tiny hands waving, as if it knew we were watching.

'Look!' I whirled to Sarah, who'd come around the foot of the bed to stand behind me.

Sarah's eyes glistened like washed stones. 'It's beautiful.'

For a moment it felt wrong, this happiness. But I knew Olivia would be happy too. So I let myself stand on that cliff and peer over the edge into the future, at the happiness that I could have one day if I would only allow it.

'See, she's sucking her thumb.' Dr Maddox pointed at the screen.

'She?' I asked.

'It's a girl.'

I grasped Olivia's hand tightly. 'Look, Liv. Your baby's a girl.'

Dr Maddox did some measurements and printed a picture for both Sarah and me, then wiped the gel from Olivia's stomach.

'Everything looks great.' She pushed her wire-frame glasses up her nose. 'We'll ultrasound her every week or so, but right now the baby's healthy and growing well.'

She stood and shook my hand, then Sarah's.

'Thanks, Dr Maddox,' I said.

'Now then.' She folded us into a cushiony embrace, smelling of apples and rain. 'You go get that muffin, all right now?'

'We will,' Sarah promised.

Dr Maddox waved good-bye and pushed the portable machine out of the room.

'You okay?' Sarah asked after a minute.

'I'm scared,' I admitted.

Letting myself love Olivia's child when there was no real guarantee that she would live was a massive risk. Loss, death, a broken heart, no matter how figurative, was unbearable. There was never a guarantee you wouldn't lose those you loved.

But I knew it was a risk I had to take.

'What if the baby dies?' I said.

Sarah touched my hand. 'What if she doesn't?'

Just then, my phone rang, interrupting the moment. 'I have to get this,' I said. 'I'll meet you outside, okay?'

I grabbed my coat and left before she could ask any questions.

Night was creeping across the horizon. The rain had eased, leaving the air heavy and damp. I sat on a bench just kitty-corner to the hospital entrance and returned Anthony's call.

'Hi, Abi,' he greeted me. 'I got the DNA results back from the cigarette in Olivia's room. It's from Kendall Montgomery, date of birth May 1999.'

I flashed back to seeing the text from K on Olivia's phone. Was K short for Kendall? And Montgomery: could it be?

I squeezed my eyes shut. 'Please don't tell me she's related to Gavin Montgomery.'

'I'm afraid so. How did you know?'

'Gavin Montgomery is Olivia's father.' Fear tangled on my tongue. 'He told me to get an abortion but I didn't. I never told him I kept Olivia. I think he has something to do with what happened to her.'

Anthony blew out a low whistle.

'She must be about the same age as Olivia. Why would a minor's DNA be in the system?' I asked. My heart raced at all the possibilities.

'I didn't exactly look in any criminal database,' he admitted.

'Then where?'

'All newborns in the US are screened for genetic diseases by the National Newborn Screening and Genetics Resource Center. Washington State keeps DNA on file for twenty-one years. I gambled that the cigarette was either Olivia's or a friend's.'

I pressed my fingers into my eyes until I saw white stars. 'So, Olivia knew Gavin's daughter? What if she pushed Olivia?'

'We have no evidence of that – only that they knew each other.'

'If Gavin's daughter knew Olivia, then he probably knew her too!'

Dread churned in me. I bent my head, my throat tightening

like a fist. I had been weak. I hadn't spared Olivia the pain she didn't deserve, but had robbed her of a truth she did deserve. However hard it would've been to tell her about her father – to admit my own mistakes – I should've been honest. The truth had been mine to give.

'What's next?' I asked, swiping at a tear.

'We talk to Kendall. Find out how she knew Olivia, if she knew Olivia was her sister, if they were together that night.'

A dark, oily fear slithered over me at the possibility of seeing Gavin. I'd watched his meteoric rise in politics. At thirty-four he'd become the youngest-ever senator in the Washington State Legislature. He was a darling of the Republican Party, much admired and well liked. He had that effect on people: swept them up in his charm and convictions.

But Gavin's cleverness and charisma went hand in hand with a darker side, one that only appeared in private. Those who crossed him were treated to intimidation, tirades, and, when he was pushed hard enough, violence.

I swallowed, hard bubbles of anxiety rising in my throat. But I couldn't hide anymore. The more I found out about Olivia's last months, the more certain I was that he had something to do with what had happened to her.

'Okay. When?'

'I'm in court tomorrow supporting one of my clients and then at a support group I run in the afternoon, so tomorrow's difficult. We could talk to her together on Friday?'

'Oh.' Impatience and fear mingled in my throat. Anthony mistook my hesitation for disappointment.

'We could meet tomorrow night to figure out who we need to interview,' he offered. 'I just won't be home until about nine. Why don't you come over? I'm in Queen Anne. I order a mean takeout.'

I could hear the smile in his voice, but my body stiffened with terror. I couldn't go to Seattle.

But I could, I reminded myself. The reason I'd stayed away from Seattle was to protect Olivia from Gavin. But that wasn't necessary anymore. The revelation hit me, vivid, intense, terrifying.

'We can always just meet on Friday, it's no prob –' Anthony began.

'It's okay,' I interrupted. 'I don't mind coming to you.'

'Okay, great!'

He gave me his address and I said, 'See you tomorrow,' then hung up.

'See who tomorrow?' Sarah's voice made me jump.

'Jesus, Sarah. You scared me.'

'See who?'

'Anthony.'

'But why?' She looked angry. Or sad. Sometimes it was hard to tell the difference with Sarah.

'I'm going to find out what happened to Olivia,' I said.

'But the police – they're investigating,' she said weakly.

I rummaged in a hidden pocket of my purse for a long-forgotten pack of cigarettes and a lighter. I rarely smoked. Hadn't for years because Olivia hated it so much.

I lit the cigarette, the flame blazing brightly against the sky. I took a long drag, then exhaled slowly. Smoke twisted lazily up through the tree's stark branches, hanging momentarily with the last shriveled leaves of autumn.

'No. They aren't,' I said.

'It'll just take some time.'

I sighed, irritation sparking in me, and told her about Tyler lying, the threatening picture texts, the note slipped under my door.

She didn't speak for a long time, but when she did, it wasn't what I expected. 'I get that you think somebody pushed Olivia. Okay? But do you have to prove who? Looking for answers like this, it only distorts the truth. The truth about what happened and the truth about who Olivia was. It tricks you into thinking you have some control when you don't.'

'I have to do this, Sarah.'

'Why?'

I sucked on the cigarette, letting the smoke sear my lungs. Finally I answered: 'I never knew why Mom killed herself.'

Sarah looked like I'd hit her.

'There was no note. No good-bye. Nothing!' I slashed my hand through the air. 'She killed herself and I found her and she didn't even say why. I've wondered my whole life, and I've never gotten any closure. I can't spend the rest of my life wondering what happened to Olivia. I need to know. For me. For Olivia's baby.'

A chill wind whipped off the water, and I pulled my scarf higher on my neck. Sarah zipped her coat up to her chin and sat heavily on the bench next to me.

'Here, give me one of those.' She pointed at the cigarettes.

I held the pack out and she took one, bending forward so I

could light it. We'd both struggled with the addiction off and on throughout our lives, but this was the first time we'd ever had a cigarette together.

Sarah tucked her hair behind her ears. Even though she was ten years older than me, my sister still had that natural, girl-next-door look: full lips, pale-blonde hair, good skin. Only now was a lifetime of responsibility starting to show, her skin puckering slightly at the corners of her mouth, her eyes drooping at the corners.

Sarah held the smoke in her lungs for a second, then released it into the frosty air.

'God, that feels good!' she exclaimed. 'It's pretty fucking cruel they don't let you smoke in the hospital. Don't they know that's exactly where you want to smoke the most?' She examined her cigarette. 'I haven't had one in years.'

'Me neither. Last time was when Olivia was twelve. She'd just started her period, and I decided it was time to have The Talk. I sneaked outside to have a smoke first, but she caught me and man did she lose it.' I laughed at the memory. 'She said maybe I didn't care about my life, but she did, and she wanted me in hers.'

The bittersweet aftertaste of the memory filled my mouth, and I wrapped my hands around my stomach.

'I want her back.' My voice strangled in my throat.

Sarah put an arm around me. 'I know,' she whispered. 'Me too.'

For just a moment I allowed myself the luxury of closing my eyes and soaking up my sister's comfort. Then I imagined what it would be like if it were my mother comforting me. I pulled abruptly away from Sarah, wiping my eyes.

Sarah stubbed her cigarette out on the ground, then set it on the bench between us.

'I have to tell you something,' she started again. Sarah picked something off her lip. 'Olivia called me a few months back and asked me to come over. Said she wanted to talk about her father. She said you'd been lying to her.'

'What'd you say?' I whispered, dread leaching into my heart.

Her eyes dipped away from mine. 'I'm sorry. I've been trying to find a way to tell you. . .'

'What – did – you – say?' I bit off each word.

Sarah finally met my eyes. 'She already knew.'

'How?'

'She wouldn't tell me how. She just said she already knew Gavin Montgomery was her father, and she wanted to know why you told her he was dead.'

I gasped. I had the sudden dizzying sensation that things were unraveling. I pressed my fingernails hard into my palms until they left deep half-moons in my skin, trying to control my shaking hands.

'Why didn't she ask me?'

'Are you kidding? She *did* ask you. Like, hundreds of times. But you wouldn't tell her the truth.'

My head fell into my hands. The thought knotted and spun in my mind, making me dizzy.

'No, no, no,' I moaned. A pale gray desperation hurtled through me.

'I'm sorry, Abi! I know you didn't want her to find out, but she had a right to know! You should've heard the things she was thinking!'

I whirled on her and hissed: 'You stupid fucking bitch. You have no idea what you've done!'

Sarah recoiled, her face blanching white. I'd never sworn at her before. Not even when I was a teenager. I wasn't the type who lashed out. I held everything in, kept it inside.

'I never told Gavin that I didn't get an abortion. If Olivia confronted him, if he saw her . . .' I wrapped my hands around my throat, panic clawing at me. Gavin wasn't somebody to mess with. 'If he knew she was his daughter, there's no telling what he might've done.'

18

ABI

november

It was a monumental battle of willpower over fatigue to pull my running shoes on, but I knew I needed to do it. It was the best way to rejoin the living.

It was still dark when I slammed the door shut behind me and headed into the chill of the early morning fog. My shoes thumped heavily along the pavement, my arms pumping, and I let my mind drift.

Olivia had known who her father was.

Fury at my sister ground inside of me. Blame lay heavy as a brick on my heart, festering, ready to be propelled at somebody at the first provocation.

Maybe she'd confronted him. Maybe he'd been the one sending her those pictures. Maybe he'd hurt Olivia, followed through on the threat he'd made eighteen years ago.

I couldn't push aside the niggling seed of worry that he had something to do with her fall. Nor could I stop blaming Sarah for handing Olivia the tools to find him.

I'd first met Gavin Montgomery at the ice cream shop where I worked the summer I graduated. I knew his girlfriend, Cassandra Winters. She was a few years ahead of me in school, the bubbly, popular prom queen, rich parents, a giant McMansion home. Everyone knew she was dating a hot college boy from Seattle.

I'd seen them together around town, so the first time he came into the ice cream shop and asked for a scoop of vanilla in a cup, I knew who he was. When he started coming in regularly, I couldn't help but feel special. I was savvy enough to know he wasn't just there for the ice cream.

The memory was bitter, like vomit in my mouth, but I let it sweep over me.

× × ×

The bell above the door of the ice cream shop jangled.

'We're closed!' I shouted, not looking up from mopping the sticky floors.

'Glad to hear it.' The voice was deep, throaty, obviously older.

I jerked my head up. It was Gavin.

'Back for another scoop of the world's most boring ice cream?' I teased.

Gavin threw his head back and laughed. 'You're funny, Abi. And no. I didn't come for ice cream.'

He crossed to stand in front of me. He was so tall, I felt like a child in comparison. There was something inherently powerful about him. He filled the room. It was a little intimidating. But the way he was looking at me . . .

I set the mop against the wall and cocked one hip, smirking. 'You really need to try something besides vanilla.'

He quirked an eyebrow. 'Maybe I will,' he said, moving closer still. 'I couldn't get you out of my mind.'

'You must not have much going on in there then. Even less than I have in mine. I'm just a boring teenager from Portage Point.'

'You don't give yourself enough credit. You're gorgeous, and I'm sure very clever.'

'You sound like my big sister. "You're so clever, Abi. Why don't you study law?"' I imitated her voice, and he laughed.

'Do you want to be a lawyer?'

'No, not really. My sister just wants me to because it's a steady job.'

'And what do you want?'

I shrugged and reached for the mop, continued swooshing it across the floor. I wanted what most girls wanted. To be loved.

He closed the distance between us, his mouth landing hard on mine. It surprised me, sending the mop clattering to the ground. But I didn't push him away. His hot hands circled my waist, burning the skin under my shirt.

'Wait.' I grabbed his hand and tugged him out of sight into the back office, where the coins and bills from the till were still scattered across the desk.

His fingers tangled in my hair as we kissed, then dipped under the elastic of my skirt. He was rock hard against me. I undid his belt and lifted my skirt to rub against him.

Suddenly he flipped me over so I was bent over the desk. I pulled my panties down and reached between my legs, guiding him inside of me. I felt a secret thrill. I was having sex with Cassandra Winters's boyfriend! Money and security weren't everything after all. I had power, too.

After that we met maybe once a week, sometimes after I'd closed the shop, sometimes at the beach. The only rule was that I wasn't allowed to contact him. He promised to break up with Cassandra, but he had to wait because her grandfather had just died.

One night after I locked up the shop he was there, leaning against his car and smiling that devilish smile.

'Picnic on the beach?' He lifted the wicker basket he was holding.

We drove to the far end of the beach, then hiked to a secluded spot where the sand dove into a tiny tree-lined cove. He spread a pale-yellow blanket on the ground and kissed me as he laid me down. Shivers dusted my head, splashed between my thighs. A full moon lit a silver path across the dancing waves and the water caressed the shore at our feet.

I knew then I was in love with him. But by the time I found out I was pregnant, everything had fallen apart. I knew things about him, what he was capable of, how far into the darkness he'd go for his career.

Still, I waited outside the golf club, catching his eye from the edge of the parking lot as he walked to his car. Despite everything, I hoped he'd do the right thing.

At his car, he grabbed my arm roughly and pushed me inside.

'What are you doing here, Abi?' he growled. 'I told you: *I* contact *you*.'

'I had to talk to you,' I said urgently.

'Why?'

'Gavin, I'm pregnant.'

Gavin looked shocked; then panic rolled across his handsome features. He looked like a cornered animal. 'I thought you were on the pill!'

'I am!'

'Fuck.' He clenched and unclenched his fists, his face hard. 'Take care of it.' He leaned over me and pushed the door open.

'I can't get an abortion!' I exclaimed, ignoring the door.

'What kind of mother do you think you'd be?' he sneered. 'You're anxious and unstable. You serve ice cream for a living and you still live in your sister's house. You can't take care of a baby. You're a pathetic mess!'

I stared at him, stunned. It was everything I'd ever thought about myself, right out there in the open. But an abortion? I opened my mouth to argue, but Gavin grabbed my face in one hand, pinching it so hard that tears filled my eyes.

'Do you understand how much this could fuck everything up?' he snarled. 'I could be senator one day. Maybe even governor. And I won't let a bitch like you ruin it. Not now. Not ever!'

He shoved my face away and pulled a checkbook out of his blazer's inner pocket. He wrote a check and handed it to me. I took it, unsure what else to do.

'I'm not kidding, Abi. I will kill you and that baby if you ruin this for me.'

He leaned over me and opened the door, and this time I got out.

I went to the abortion clinic like I was told. But I looked at the other girls around me and didn't see myself in them, and I couldn't go through with it. I'd lived with my mom's abandonment since I was ten. This was my chance to do better than she did.

But I also couldn't have Gavin find out. I'd seen what his threats did to others. I knew what happened when you crossed him.

So I cashed that massive check.

It was completely dishonest, but I took his money and let him think I'd gotten an abortion. Instead I used it to go to college, buy a house. I raised my daughter – *my* daughter – to be a good girl, because bad things didn't happen to good girls.

And that was the truth I'd hidden from Olivia. At least part of it. I'd taken blood money to get rid of my baby, and then lied about it.

Gavin had paid me to eliminate my daughter, and then he'd disappeared from our lives. He'd abandoned me and he'd abandoned her, and it rankled on a deep level. Maybe because I knew the pain of being abandoned by a parent. I knew what it felt like to be deserted by the person you should be able to count on no matter what. I knew better than most.

Which was why what I did to Olivia was far worse than what he did.

× × ×

When I got home from my run, a massive box was sitting on my porch. It was about three feet by three feet, my name and address typed neatly on the label. I maneuvered the bulk awkwardly through the door and set it next to the dining table, bewildered. I slit the top and peered inside.

Nestled in white Styrofoam was an exquisite pure-white orchid. The delicate fragrance – light and sweet – floated up to me. I carefully pulled the pot out of the box, and a small white envelope fell out. The card inside read:

> *Wishing you courage and strength. Please know that we are here anytime you need us.*
>
> Lizzie and Kelly

I stroked the velvety leaves of the orchid, the unexpected kindness causing a sharp stinging in my chest. I thought of how I'd kept myself apart from these women for so long. In fact, when I analyzed my own behavior, I realized I'd denied myself everything: the anticipation of a date, laughter over coffee, the blur of a shot of tequila on a night out.

And for what? Olivia would've wanted me to have a life. She wouldn't have begrudged me that.

I did it because I was scared. Of rejection. Of loss. Of hurt. Of being anything other than Olivia's mom. It shocked me to realize that was all I thought of myself as. Olivia's mom. I'd gotten pregnant so young that I never had a chance to find out who Abigail Knight was. I'd been thrust without warning into a very adult world without ever finishing being a kid.

Everybody around me had sharply forged personalities. But I didn't even know who I was without my daughter. Somewhere along the way, I'd lost myself.

I looked at my watch. I'd seen Lizzie picking up her daughters from the high school. Maybe I could catch her and say thank you. It wasn't too late for that.

And maybe I'd see Tyler as well.

× × ×

I parked across the street from the high school and slammed the car door just as the tinny sound of a bell jangled from the school building. It was a beautiful day, a cloudless turquoise sky shimmering above me, but the wind was sharp, gusting across the parking lot and slicing through my wool coat. Chills chased across my skin, and I tucked my chin deeper into my scarf.

Students flooded onto the manicured lawn that circled the front of the school. I scanned the crowd for Tyler, then Lizzie, then Kelly, but didn't see any of them.

After a few minutes the parking lot was mostly empty. Disappointed, I turned to go, but just then I spotted Tyler halfway across the parking lot.

Poor kid. Agony was stamped indelibly on his body, weighted across the miserable hunch of his shoulders. He looked smaller somehow, shrunken, the way a grape shrivels into a raisin.

I jogged toward him, but he must not have heard me calling his name because he jumped when I touched his shoulder, his eyes wide, keys held out as if fending off an attacker.

'Tyler. Hi,' I said, breathless from my sprint.

'Oh. Miss Knight. Hi.' He wiped a hand over his face, then darted a glance back at the school.

'Do you have a second?'

'I guess.'

I fell into step beside him, our shoes crunching on the gravel.

'You said you didn't see Olivia after the barbecue,' I said. The words came out sounding like an accusation, and Tyler's eyes immediately went flat and defensive.

'Yeah. So?'

'Well, um.' I loosened my scarf. 'It's just, I found Olivia's phone the other day, and there was a text on it from you. It said you were going to meet later that night. Did you?'

'No.'

We'd reached his car, a flashy red Jeep Renegade. Olivia'd gushed about that car when they first started going out together. The alarm chirped twice as Tyler unlocked it and opened the driver's door.

My hand shot out to stop him. I grasped his arm, my nails digging into his bicep.

'Her text said you did.'

'I didn't see her, Miss Knight.' Tyler's voice was sharp as a paper cut. He wrenched his arm away from me, his eyes hot and red. 'She texted me about meeting up, all right? She said she was coming back to the barbecue, but she never showed up. I thought she'd fallen asleep or something.'

'What time did you leave?'

'Like, midnight. That's what I told the police, too.'

Tyler wiped a forearm across his eyes. His face was haggard, the freckles spattering the bridge of his nose standing out starkly against the paleness.

I stepped away from Tyler, and he climbed into his Jeep, slamming the door. He rolled his window down and looked at me for a long moment. I held his gaze, waiting for whatever it was he wanted to say.

'The police said it was an accident,' he said finally. 'That she slipped. That's what happened, right?'

'Yes, of course.' My voice sounded anemic, pitiful. 'I just, you know, I wanted to see if you knew anything else.'

'I don't,' he said. He wiped a hand across his nose. A thin trail of snot still hung off it.

'Did she really say I was too strict? That she felt like I was writing the script for her life?' I asked.

He looked away. 'I'm sorry. I shouldn't have told you that.'

'Did she say it?'

'Yeah.'

I backed away from him, wanting more than anything to be in the comforting solitary confinement of my car. 'Bye, Tyler.' I spun around, walked away, my legs leaden.

'Wait, Miss Knight,' Tyler called after me. 'Have you talked to Madison?'

I turned around.

'Not yet,' I said slowly. 'Why?'

'Madison and Olivia weren't talking. They had a big fight, like, a couple months ago. Madison was *such* a bitch to Olivia. She's the one you should be talking to.'

Tyler started up his car and pulled away. I don't know how long I stood there in that spot, the parking lot as empty as a promise.

× × ×

Back in my car, my mind raced, trying to catalogue everything I'd learned: Olivia knew she was pregnant; she knew Gavin was her father; she'd met Gavin's daughter; she and Madison weren't speaking.

I couldn't find any logical connection between these strands. How did they lead to my daughter's fall?

I drove slowly through town, hugging the beach as I wound along the road that led to my house. It was low tide, Puget Sound pulling away into the distance. The water was gunmetal gray, dappled with boulders and chunks of seaweed. Cotton-wool clouds hung low in the sky, threatening to burst at any moment.

My cell phone rang and I glanced at it: it was Sarah. I pressed End, unable to talk to her just yet. I was still furious with her for keeping the fact that Olivia knew about Gavin from me.

Instead I called Anthony.

'I just talked to Tyler,' I said when he answered. 'He said Madison and Olivia had fought and weren't talking.'

'Interesting. Did he say why?'

'No.'

'We need to talk to Madison, see what happened. If the fight was motive enough for her to hurt Olivia.'

I could easily imagine Madison getting angry and freezing Olivia out for some perceived wrong, but hurting her? I wasn't so sure, and I said as much to Anthony.

'You could be right, but we should talk to her anyway,' he replied. 'If there's one thing I've learned in my job, it's that everybody – no matter how harmless they seem – has the capacity to veer outside the lines. It's just a matter of how far they go.'

19

OLIVIA

june

Diiiiinnnnnggg!!!

The end-of-school bell rang shrilly.

Everybody in history class leapt up and started talking, an excited hum of teenage chatter. Finally! No school for three months. I slammed papers and books into my backpack and slung it over my shoulder.

'Hurry up, Liv!' Tyler urged. 'Let's get outta here! I want to go to the beach.'

'About that . . .' I began but didn't get a chance to finish.

Dan appeared in the classroom doorway and pointed at Tyler with both hands. 'Duuude!!!' he shouted. 'I have a volleyball with your name on it. Let's get to the beach. We're gonna kick some ass!'

Tyler gave him a high five, and they walked down the hall together. Dan didn't even look at me. I trailed after them in the direction of our lockers feeling inexplicably snubbed. Tyler used to stick next to me like glue. He'd open doors for me and sling my backpack over one shoulder while his was over the other. Dan was such an asshole. I was sure this was his fault somehow.

All anybody was talking about was the annual after-school beach party. Usually we'd all play volleyball and laze about on the beach, waiting to see who was brave enough to go in the water first. Then someone would spark up the barbecue, and we'd eat ribs and chicken before starting the bonfire and making s'mores. Mom always hated it when I stayed out after dark – like all the bad things in the world only happened after the sun went down – but just so she didn't worry, Madison and I usually headed to my house around sunset for movies and a sleepover.

But this year I had a handful of lies ready to get out of the beach party.

What I was really doing was going to see Kendall. We'd been messaging each other on Facebook lately.

I opened my locker and shoved loose papers, plastic bags, a few apple cores, a hairbrush, my locker mirror, and a pair of tennis shoes into my backpack. By the time I finished, Dan had disappeared and Tyler was waiting for me at the other end of the hall. When I reached him, he put an arm around my shoulders and pulled me against him. I wanted to shrug him off. It felt like we were about to run a three-legged race or something.

Outside, the sun was shining brightly, making everything look sparkly and beautiful. June was the best month in the Pacific Northwest. The weather was just warming up, new shoots pressed through the ground, and vibrant green leaves unfurled on the trees. The scent of spring roses mingled with the salty sea air.

In the next few weeks Portage Point would fill with tourists, the ice cream shops heaving with people, the beach thronged with sun worshippers. Traffic through town would become a nightmare, with horns blaring and sunburned people jostling for space on the sidewalks. But for now, it was still peaceful, the sky scrubbed clean by occasional showers.

'You all right?' I asked Tyler as we headed toward the front of the school. He'd been really weird lately. Not that I could blame him. Rumors were flying about exactly why his parents broke up and he was totally pissed about it. Madison had told me that Peter told her that Tyler's dad had walked in on his mom and the mailman having sex in their bed. Eww! I was too scared to ask Tyler if it was true, though. He'd go totally ape-shit.

'Actually, I, uh . . .' He lowered his voice and leaned closer. 'I wanted to tell you something.'

Tyler dropped his backpack on the ground, and I sat on a bench in front of the school. Tyler turned to face me. He had a weird look in his eyes. He reached down to pick a long piece of grass, which he started tying in knots that kept breaking.

'I'm not going to be around for the summer,' he said finally.

'What?' I blinked. 'Why not?'

'My stupid parents.' The amber flecks in Tyler's eyes sparked with anger. His hands curled into fists. 'My dad's moving to Seattle, and apparently I have to go with him.'

'But . . .' I couldn't think of anything to say. 'Why?'

'Dad said he mostly works there, so he might as well move

there. And apparently he got summers with me in the custody agreement. I'm not sure who's more pissed off about it, me or him.' Tyler's nostrils flared.

'Are you coming back?'

'Yeah, I'll be back at the end of August for football. Mom gets me during the school year. Dad gets me one weekend a month and summers.'

Tyler's dad was some senior, high-up manager at an IT firm in Seattle, but he'd worked from Portage Point as long as I could remember. I didn't know him very well. He seemed nice enough: a quiet, bookish type, shaped like a turnip, with a shy, lopsided smile.

'When do you go?'

'Monday.' His jaw worked furiously, but he shrugged. 'Whatever. At least I don't have to be with *her* all summer. This is all her fault for cheating.'

'Hey!' Madison appeared suddenly from behind me.

She flopped onto the bench with a loud huff, throwing her bag on the ground dramatically.

'Hey,' I replied. I turned back to Tyler, but he obviously didn't want to talk about it anymore because he quickly changed the subject.

'Do you want to get something to eat at Bagel Barn before we head to the beach?' he asked.

'Oh, shoot, I forgot to tell you,' I said, smacking my forehead. 'I have a dentist appointment in just a bit, so I'm gonna miss the beach party. I'm sorry.'

'What?' Madison exclaimed, her eyes wide and horrified. 'Since when?'

'Um, like, yesterday? My tooth has been bothering me.' I poked at a molar and made a face. 'I have to get a filling, I think. Today was the only time they could fit me in.'

It amazed me how easily the lies flowed off my tongue. The easiest way to tell a lie, I was learning, was to add in a drop of truth. My tooth *did* hurt, and I *would* make a dentist appointment. Adding that to the lie made it even more believable.

'Well, that's shit,' she huffed. 'The barbecue's gonna be lit!'

Peter arrived then, and she was instantly distracted. She gazed up at him adoringly, then stretched a foot out to touch his. He smiled and sat next to her, looping an arm around her shoulders and pulling her close. She leaned in to kiss him and murmured something in his ear with a girlish giggle.

I watched them for a moment, realizing that I'd never seen Madison like a guy for this long before. Maybe she was actually serious about Peter.

'When am I going to see you, then?' Tyler asked, throwing down the frayed and tattered piece of grass. For just a moment he looked vulnerable and needy. But then he shifted his body and the sun slid away, turning his eyes dark and shadowy.

'How about Sunday? My mom will be home, but we could go somewhere if you want?'

'What, you think she'll let you?' he asked sarcastically. He reached down and picked up another piece of grass and blew into it, making a high, sharp sound.

I ground my teeth. 'She just worries,' I said stiffly.

'Whatever,' he muttered. He ripped the grass in half and tossed it on the ground at my feet before turning and storming toward his car.

I said good-bye to Madison and Peter and sneaked around the back of the school to a neighborhood side street. Derek was waiting in his Mustang and I slipped in, throwing one last look behind me. Madison and Tyler would kill me if they saw me now, after all my lies. Derek gunned the engine, and we headed toward Seattle.

I slouched low in the car so nobody could see me and didn't say anything until we reached the freeway.

'How come you don't go to U-Dub?' I asked Derek. I'd been wondering it for weeks now.

He blew a lock of hair off his forehead and looked like he was debating saying something. 'It's complicated,' he finally said.

'Try me.'

'Well . . . I want to go to art school.' He glanced at me.

'Why don't you, then?'

'Mom and Dad won't pay for it.'

'But why not?' I asked, baffled. 'Don't they want you to be happy?'

'I guess. It's just they want me to do something that I'm guaranteed to get a job in, like finance. Dad says art is a waste of money. Mom, I mean . . .' He downshifted the Mustang to exit the highway. 'You know her. She's in her own world. But I'd rather die than waste away in some office and become a middle-class dillhole like my parents.'

'What kind of art would you study?'

'I like drawing.'

I pondered that. I hadn't pegged Derek as the creative type.

But now that he mentioned it, I remembered loads of times when he'd sat around doodling while Madison and I played. 'Would you draw me?'

He glanced sideways at me, his eyebrows high.

'Sure.' He grinned. 'One day I'll draw you.'

We pulled into Kendall's Mercer Island neighborhood and parked in a slot across the street from Starbucks, where I'd organized to meet Kendall. This little alcove of Seattle was home to the wealthy and affluent. Behind the ironwork fences and guarded gates, another world existed that even Derek hadn't been exposed to. Here in Kendall's world, Mercedes Benzes and Lexuses parked in cavernous garages; paid staff maintained swimming pools and hot tubs. It was a world I knew nothing about, and it made me extremely uncomfortable.

'Nice.' Derek whistled softly as a Ferrari rolled by.

'Look, there she is!' I pointed across the street to where Kendall was chatting to a teenage girl who looked vaguely familiar. They were with a man and woman I'd never seen before, all of them holding venti iced coffees. Derek and I got out of the car and jogged across the street.

'Hi.' I smiled at Kendall as we approached.

Kendall jumped and whirled to face us. 'Oh, uh . . .' she stammered.

'Oh my God!' the girl next to her shrieked, grabbing Kendall's arm. She gaped at me. I couldn't tell if she was grinning or leering. 'It's your twin!'

I suddenly knew where I recognized her from. She'd been with Kendall the day we met at the University of Washington. She was one of those spoiled-looking rich girls, long bottle-blonde hair, a boob-clinging top, thick layers of mascara, skinny jeans, and too-high heels.

The girl noticed Kendall's shocked gaze. 'Wait.' She turned to me. 'Are you *stalking* Kendall?' She turned to the older couple next to her. 'We saw this girl, like, *months* ago at U-Dub. Do you know each other?'

Kendall's face froze. 'No. Of course not.'

She offered me her hand. I shook it dumbly.

'It's nice to see you again,' she said primly. A politician, just like her dad. 'I hope you enjoyed U-Dub.'

And before I knew what was happening, she was gone, whisked away by the rich girl and her parents.

× × ×

I cried the whole way home, sniffling as I stared out the window. The rejection was like acid in my stomach. I didn't know what I'd done wrong.

Derek obviously didn't know what to say, so he didn't say anything. He handed me a napkin from the glove compartment to wipe my nose. Every once in a while he patted my arm.

'I don't want to go home,' I said just before we reached our exit. 'Can we go somewhere else?'

'Sure. Of course.' He veered across traffic and took the exit for Laurelwood.

He parked near the arcade, and we got out of the car. Derek shed his black leather jacket and threw it in the backseat. Underneath, he was wearing his usual black T-shirt and black jeans. We crossed the street to the boardwalk, walking the length of it until it stopped. Then we kept going, shuffling along the sandy shore to the jetty, where it pointed into Puget Sound.

The water whispered as it glided across the sand under our feet, sloshing as it slid between the jagged rocks that framed the edges of the beach. The sharp scent of salt and something softer, like honeysuckle, painted the air. A chorus of birds chirped, their song rising with the roll of the surf.

'I'm sorry about Kendall,' Derek said. His eyes were a deep shade of blue, like a midnight sky. The wind tousled his chocolate curls. 'Is there anything I can do?'

He looked so worried that I forced a small smile and touched his cheek. He was the steadiest person in my life. He'd promised never to lie to me, and I knew beyond a shadow of a doubt that he never would. And now here he was, offering me comfort when I needed it most.

'Thank you,' I said. 'For . . . everything.'

When I was with him, I wasn't scared of the truth. I wasn't scared of the future. I wasn't angry at my mom's lies or how neurotic she could be. Everything seemed as pure and shiny as a diamond. Even Kendall's rejection hadn't tainted that.

Derek held my eyes for a long time, and that spark between us flared, the heat that drew us together like magnets. Inevitably, we fell into each other, my mouth moving eagerly on his. He brushed my hair away from my face; his breath fanned my lips.

His mouth parted and the kiss deepened. I willed my heart to stop beating so fast. It knocked hard against my chest. This was nothing like with Tyler.

I'd loved him since we were kids, I realized. Madison's lies, his absence, the fact that I had a boyfriend – none of it mattered. I'd loved him from the first time I sat across the dinner table from him when I was five to the time he'd carried me home after I sprained my ankle rollerblading when I was eleven, to now, this very moment.

It amazed me that the words didn't come tumbling out of me. I could feel them like three small pearls in my mouth: *I love you*.

I slid my fingers into his hair as we gasped for air, consumed by each other.

'Olivia.' His mouth, pressed against mine, went suddenly flat. 'Olivia.' Both his hands pushed against my shoulders, and suddenly I stood a few feet away from him, my head spinning.

'I'm sorry.' He shook his head. 'I shouldn't have. . .'

He walked a few steps away, his shoes denting the sand.

'You don't like me?' I asked softly. It sounded childish, and it wasn't how I meant it. I just meant he didn't feel the same about me that I did about him. Now that I knew I loved him, how could I ever go back to pretending I didn't?

Derek took two long strides back to me, looking almost angry.

'That's not true. Don't be silly. I *do* care about you, but you have a boyfriend.'

'You care about me?'

Derek smiled, put a hand on my cheek. 'Of course I do. I've cared about you for as long as I can remember. It's torture knowing you have a boyfriend. Why do you think I was so pissed off when I first got back from New York?'

A delicious warmth unfurled in me, a loosening of happiness in my chest. I'd never felt this way with Tyler, this deep connection on a visceral level.

'I'll see Tyler on Sunday. I'll break up with him then.'

My phone rang then, jangling in the space between us. The screen flashed with Kendall's information.

I held the phone up for Derek to see.

'What do I do?' I asked.

'I think you already know the answer to that.'

20

ABI

november

Later that evening I pulled up to Anthony's house. I peered at it through the thickening twilight. Nestled amidst a row of Cape Cods, painted a bright robin's-egg blue that was cracked and peeling, it looked like it was in desperate need of a lick of paint, and maybe a bit of gardening. The grass was short and waterlogged; a handful of scraggly rhododendron bushes clung to the front steps.

I stepped out of my car and tugged at the soft pink cashmere sweater I'd pulled on over my skinny jeans. I smoothed my hair, wondering fleetingly if I looked okay, then hating myself for caring.

It wasn't like this was a date. But what if he thought it was a date? Shit. I dove back into my car, breathing hard. What was I thinking? The urge to ask Olivia if this was okay swelled inside of me, and I realized that not only had I lost my daughter, I'd lost my best friend. I clawed a tissue from my purse and swiped fresh tears from my eyes.

I just wanted my girl to come home.

I was already fifteen minutes late, so I took a shaky breath and got out of the car. At the door I inhaled deeply and knocked. It swung open right away.

'Abi! Come inside!' Anthony looked delighted to see me. He pulled me into a warm and beautiful living room. Light-stained hardwoods glistened under my feet; small oil paintings were hung through the room, indistinct splashes of color. To the left was a homey sitting area with an L-shaped couch and wide-screen TV. To the right was an open-plan country-style kitchen with a breakfast nook and french doors leading to a deck. It had the cozy feel of a much-loved home, a stark contrast to the exterior of the house.

'Sorry I'm late,' I mumbled.

'No problem,' he said easily. He was probably the most laidback person I'd ever met. He pulled a chain across the door behind me and ran a hand over the thick stubble on his chin.

'Sorry, I have to lock my mom in so she doesn't wander.' Anthony crossed the room to an elderly woman who sat on the overstuffed couch. Her eyes were glued to an episode of *Jeopardy!* on the TV. Anthony set a large hand gently on her shoulder. 'Mom, this is Abi.'

The old woman looked up at me, her blue eyes clouded with confusion. 'Laura?'

'Not Laura, Mom. Abi.'

'Hello, dear.' Her gaze traveled back to the TV.

Anthony tilted his head toward the kitchen, and I followed him.

'Who's Laura?' I asked.

'That was my sister.'

'Oh. I'm sorry.'

'That's okay.'

'How's your mom doing?' I asked tentatively. It felt like prying but right to ask.

Anthony ran a hand through his hair. He looked exhausted, smudges of purple stark beneath his eyes.

'Last night she went ballistic because I wouldn't give her the car keys. I couldn't get her to go to bed. But today she's been really calm. So, you know, good days and bad.'

'It must be hard.'

'I don't get it right all the time,' he admitted. 'But I love her. You don't have to be right one hundred percent of the time to show you love someone. And she doesn't have to be perfect to be well loved.'

A sleety rain started to fall, pattering against the skylight in the kitchen. I sat at the kitchen table and Anthony slid a piece of pizza from a Domino's box onto a plate and handed it to me. I stood and reached for it, but my fingers missed and I fumbled the plate. Anthony moved to catch it, but accidentally grabbed my hand instead. I felt a jolt of electricity in my fingertips and stepped back as the pizza plopped, facedown, onto the floor.

'Oh God, I'm sorry! Let me clean it up!' My face warmed with embarrassment.

Anthony smiled and waved me away. 'Honestly, don't worry about it. At least the plate didn't break. I think I've broken about five this year. I only have three left!'

He wiped up the mess and handed me a fresh slice of pizza, then started cutting a wedge into small, precise pieces.

I sat down and looked around. There were plants and paintings everywhere, a large fern in one corner and spider plants hanging from a shelf above the sink. A copy of Barack Obama's memoir sat on the table next to me.

'I called a friend of mine who works in Portage Point,' he said as he got to work dicing the second slice. 'He said both Samson and McNally are strong detectives with a solid solve rate.'

'Then why wouldn't they investigate Olivia's fall?' I asked.

'I guess if they were told not to, they'd focus their energy elsewhere.'

'But why would they be?'

Anthony ate a quick bite of pizza, chewing as he thought.

'I don't know,' he admitted. 'Let's think about what we do know. One, Madison wasn't talking to Olivia. Two, Olivia knew that her father was Gavin Montgomery, and she'd met her half sister, Kendall. And three, Tyler lied about meeting up with Olivia after the barbecue.'

'Actually,' I interjected, 'Tyler told me he got that text from Olivia saying to meet him at the barbecue, but she never showed up.'

'What else do we know?'

'She had some texts on her phone from somebody listed as D. They were romantic, signed with kisses. I think the father of Olivia's baby has a name that starts with *d*.'

'Can you think of any friends Olivia had with names starting with *d*?'

'Not in her group, but I'm sure somebody at school does.'

My phone rang from my purse on the island, and I stood to get it.

'Hello?' There was no reply. A few seconds later the *beep-beep-beep* of an empty line echoed in my ear.

'Another hang-up?' Anthony asked.

The phone rang again before I had a chance to answer him. 'Hello?'

'Abi!' Sarah's anxious voice filled the line. 'Don't hang up!'

'Sorry,' I murmured to Anthony. 'I just need to . . .'

'No worries. I'll take this to my mom.' Anthony grabbed the plate of diced pizza and headed toward the living room.

I turned toward the wall. 'What do you want?' I murmured.

'Abi! Thank God you answered. Look, we need to talk, I want to –'

'I can't do this right now. I'm at Anthony's house.'

'Abi, listen –'

'Not right now!' I pressed 'end' and stared at my phone. *If only she'd told me the truth. . .* I shut the thought down.

I felt shaky all over, my body swaying as a wave of emotion fizzed in my bloodstream. My earlier urge to speak to Olivia, to see her one last time, rushed over me again.

'Are you okay?' Anthony's voice from behind me made me jump.

'Yes. No. I mean, I need to get going. Thanks for . . .' I waved at my untouched pizza. 'This.'

I felt suddenly as if I were trapped inside an hourglass, the sand trickling onto me, the weight bearing down on me. Thirteen weeks until the baby was born. Thirteen weeks, and I was sitting here eating pizza, being all buddy-buddy with a virtual stranger.

I was running out of time.

I grabbed my bag and brushed past Anthony. My hands fumbled with the lock on the front door. A surge of emotion heaved through me. I had to get away before I fell apart.

The rain had eased and a full moon gleamed through racing, white-rimmed clouds. My shoes clipped harshly against the sidewalk.

'Abi!' I wanted to get in my car, but Anthony was suddenly in front of me.

'Are you okay?' Soft moonlight slid over him, turning his eyes a silvery green. In his face was nothing but honesty and kindness.

'I'm fine. I just need to go home.'

I tried to move past him, but he didn't budge.

'You aren't in any condition to drive,' Anthony said. 'Let me drive you.'

I stared at him in shock. He'd been in court all day, then in a support group helping other victims of crime, and then he'd come home and cared for his ailing mother. It was what he did, I was noticing. Tried to fix all the wounds of the world.

'Are you kidding?' I snapped, suddenly, inexplicably angry. 'You look like you haven't slept in weeks.'

'I'm not as emotionally strung out as you. You've had a difficult time. Let me drive. I can get a taxi back.'

'Your mom.'

'She's safe. I've locked the door, and her night nurse is on the way.'

I huffed out a harsh breath. 'I didn't ask for this.'

I meant his concern, but he misunderstood. 'No one does.'

I tried again to move past him. I was just another problem to fix. I didn't want to be some fucking damsel in distress. I didn't need him.

'Abi. Let me help you.'

'Why? Why do you even want to?'

He looked surprised, a shadow crossing his face. 'I know what it's like to lose someone you love, to feel powerless to know why. My sister was killed, and most of my life I didn't have any answers. Her case was only solved four years ago. The detective . . .'

He swallowed hard and looked like he wanted to say something, but he shook his head.

'I can't tell you how much the detective helped me. Laura was just another cold case. A file in a box. When they solved her murder, I felt years of anxiety slip away. It didn't bring her back, but it mattered to me how the pieces fit together. So I know what you're going through.'

A current of understanding cut through my resistance. He saw it and moved toward me.

'Come on.' He held his hand out for my keys. 'Let me drive you home.'

I wavered, then finally gave him my keys and climbed into the passenger side. Suddenly I was tired to my very core. I felt like a stuffed animal that had been cut open and had all its insides scooped out.

'Fine.'

I told myself I was agreeing because I was too exhausted to argue. But the truth was, deep inside, I didn't want to be alone.

Outside my house Anthony turned the engine off. He got out, the car dipping to release his weight, and came around to open my side. He guided me up the stairs, took my keys from my numb fingers, and opened the front door. He turned on a lamp and pulled a cover over me as I sank into the pillowy softness of my couch. Then he headed for the door.

'Thanks,' I whispered. My voice stretched with tiredness and sadness and so many other things.

'It won't always be this hard, Abi. Get some sleep.' He smiled gently, then locked the handle, and pulled the door shut behind him.

As I drifted off, I realized something: as much as I liked to think that I was better off on my own, maybe it wasn't true. There were people who wanted to help me, people who cared about me without any agenda. Like Anthony. Like Lizzie and Kelly. And Sarah.

21

OLIVIA

july

Derek's and my footsteps echoed in the mist as we crossed the ZigZag Bridge, heading from his house to mine. The air smelled of damp soil after last night's rain, and I inhaled the rich scent.

'What time's Kendall going to be there?' Derek asked, tucking me tighter under his arm. When he did it, I felt treasured, not trapped.

'She said noon.'

'Do you think she'll show?'

I thought back to last week when she'd bailed on me at Starbucks. I was totally ready to write her off, but then she'd called me in tears. She said she was scared of her dad finding out about me during an election year when the media could find out. She'd offered to drive out to meet me. It sort of made sense, plus, if she didn't show up, at least I'd already be home.

'I hope so, but who knows?' I shrugged.

My phone pinged.

Kendall: *We still on for today?*

'Hold on,' I murmured to Derek. I hefted myself up so I was sitting on the bridge's low concrete barrier wall and typed a reply: *Yeah. My house. You still have address?*

Kendall: *Yeah. Driving to you. Be there 12ish.*

Kendall: *Soz again about last week.*

Me: *It's ok. See you later.*

I put the phone away and looked at Derek. His face had gone pale as an envelope. 'What's wrong?' I asked.

'You ready to come down from there now?'

I leaned back and peered over the edge of the bridge to where the ZigZag River gurgled below.

'Derek, are you scared of heights?' I couldn't imagine Derek afraid of anything.

'No!' he denied emphatically. But his face was pinched tight. I knew I was right.

'Oooh,' I teased. 'I'm sooo close to the edge.'

I laughed and stood up on top of the concrete barrier, walking like a gymnast, arms flung out for balance. Heights had never bothered me, and anyway, if I fell in the river below, I was a great swimmer.

'Come down from there, Olivia!' Derek's voice was laced with anxiety, and I realized the joke had gone too far.

'Okay, I'm sorry.' I hopped down and wrapped my arms around his waist, smiling up at him. 'I was just teasing you a bit.'

He brushed my hair back from my face and blew out a shaky breath. 'Fuck's sake. That wall is too low.'

'I was safe. Sheesh, I didn't know you were so afraid of heights.'

'I'm not afraid. It just makes me a bit nervous when the girl I like is perched on the edge of a fifty-foot drop. I'd prefer you stay safe.'

I stiffened in his arms. 'You sound just like my mom.'

Derek stepped away from me, scraped a hand through his hair. 'Look, I'm sorry. I don't want to sound like your mom or anything. I'm scared of heights, but that doesn't mean you have to be, okay?'

I moved closer to him, instantly forgiving him. The warmth of his body radiated out toward mine, and I pressed myself along the length of him. I wrapped my arms around him and kissed his jaw.

'I thought we were going to wait until you broke up with Tyler to be all couple-y?' Derek said. I could hear a smile on his lips as they pressed against mine.

I'd planned to break up with Tyler when he came over before leaving for Seattle, but he'd canceled, saying he was too busy packing. Technically, that meant we were still together. I didn't care.

'I know.' I slid my tongue along his teeth and deepened the kiss anyway.

'We should stop, then,' Derek murmured.

'Yep.'

But we didn't. Instead, I lifted his shirt to touch the hot skin on his back. He cupped my butt and pulled me closer, our thighs pressed together. I wanted him like I'd never wanted anything in my life.

The sound of a car approaching finally tore us apart. I ran my fingertips across my lips, the imprint of his mouth still burning.

'We should go,' I said.

Derek nodded, and we dove into the woods that separated my house from his, holding hands.

'So, when are you going to talk to Tyler?' Derek asked, holding up a tree branch so I could pass.

I ducked under his arm and climbed over a downed tree.

'I should probably do it in person, right? Wouldn't that be, like, more respectful?' Tyler was already going through so much. I didn't want to hurt him more than I had to.

'Hmmm . . .' Derek replied noncommittally.

'I was going to when he was here. He just left so suddenly.'

'What a weirdo.' Derek shook his head. 'If I were moving away from my girlfriend for the summer, I'd make sure I said good-bye first.'

'Yeah, but his parents are going through this intense divorce, and it's really shit for him right now.'

We emerged from the woods into the sunlight and crossed the street to my house. I could hear the crash of the surf in the distance and smell the sea salt in the hazy summer air.

Just as I was opening the front door, my phone rang from my back pocket.

'Hi, Mom,' I answered cheerfully.

'Hi, sweetie. Just calling to make sure you're okay.'

I rolled my eyes at Derek and mouthed that it was my mom. 'I'm not a baby, Mom.'

She laughed and gave me her standard answer. 'I know, but you'll always be my baby.'

I chuckled a little, but it was kind of getting old.

'Anyway,' she said, 'you forgot to call me at noon, so I was getting a bit worried.'

'Woops.' I glanced at the clock. It was 12:11 p.m. 'Guess I lost track of time. Sorry.'

'That's okay. What do you think about Safeway roast chicken for dinner?'

'Is it okay if I eat at Madison's?' I asked.

'Sure, sweetie.' She sounded disappointed, and guilt made my stomach spasm. 'Just be home by dark.'

'That's, like, nine o'clock! How about ten?'

'Okay, but I'll come pick you up. I don't want you walking home in the dark.'

'How about I get Derek to drive me?'

She thought about that for a minute and agreed. He flashed me that slow grin just as there was a knock on the door.

'Okay, Mom, gotta go. I'm heading to Madison's. Byeeee!'

I hung up before she could reply and rushed to the door.

Kendall had cut her hair into a sleek, shoulder-length bob. Gone was the schoolgirl Catholic uniform. Instead she wore trendy skinny black jeans, black high-top Converses, and a form-fitting pink tank top under a black leather jacket. She looked very biker chic.

She air-kissed me in a way that felt overly familiar, then breezed past me into the living room.

'I like your hair,' I said awkwardly, still clutching the door handle.

'Thanks.' She spotted Derek and extended a hand. 'I'm Kendall.'

Her heavily mascaraed eyelashes fluttered, and jealousy stabbed at me. She was so like me, but like me on some performance-enhancing drug. The way she looked, acted, dressed, everything just slightly . . . better. Derek had to see it too.

Derek shook her hand and introduced himself. I shut the door and stood awkwardly, unsure what to do or say.

Kendall tossed her expensive black leather bag onto the couch and flopped down next to it, looking around. For the first time, I saw my house through somebody else's eyes.

The old overstuffed tan sofas were rubbed raw. The river-rock fireplace at the far side of the living room looked dreary. The sunny breakfast nook at the back of the kitchen was in need of a fresh coat of paint.

'Your house is super cute,' Kendall said. I couldn't help but take it patronizingly.

Derek cleared his throat and came to take my hand. He led me to the couch and we sat next to Kendall.

'You said your dad owned a house here in 1999,' he said. 'Do you have any other information to, I don't know, show he's related to Olivia?'

Kendall lifted her shoulders and reached up to twirl a massive diamond earring in her right ear. 'Sorry. I really don't. I mean, how do we even know he is?'

'My aunt told me my mom and your dad had an affair right before your parents got married,' I said. 'They were together a few months, she got pregnant, and he disappeared.'

Her eyes flashed with interest. 'Shit, really?'

I nodded.

Kendall chewed her cheek. 'I can ask, but I don't think he's gonna admit anything. Like I said, it's an election year. Plus, our money comes from my mom's side. I doubt he'd give that up.' She gave a harsh, metallic laugh that made my stomach clench angrily. She might resent him, but at least he'd stuck around for her.

She stood and paced the living room, tapping her chin, deep in thought. Suddenly she spun to face me.

'I know! Why don't you come meet him? You could ask him yourself.'

I laughed, skeptical. 'Why would he talk to me?'

'I mean, sometimes I hate him because he, like, *mortifies* me, but he's not a bad guy. I bet he doesn't even know about you. Did your mom even tell him she was pregnant?'

I'd wondered that myself. *Had* she told him? Had she even given him a chance to know me?

I was about to answer when she caught sight of the book sitting on the dining room table. She picked it up.

'Hey, I love Gayle Forman!' she exclaimed. 'Have you read *Just One Day*?'

I nodded, my head dizzy at the sudden change of subject. 'Yeah, I own all her books. I have all of John Green's books too. I get, like, the whole set and read them all in a row.'

'No way! Can I see them?'

'Yeah, they're in my room.'

'I'll leave you girls to it,' Derek said. He kissed me on the cheek and gave a funny little salute to Kendall.

Once the door shut behind him, she lifted one eyebrow at me and smirked.

'Hot friend or older boyfriend?'

'Uh, neither.' I blushed. 'I mean, it's complicated.'

'I see.' She winked at me. 'I get the hint.'

But I didn't think she did. She had that look about her that girls get when they think the chase is on.

Kendall's eyes widened when we entered my room. 'Holy shit!' she exclaimed.

I swept dirty clothes from the floor into the laundry hamper, totally mortified. But Kendall wasn't looking at the mess. She was staring at the medals, ribbons, and trophies displayed in a glass case attached to the wall.

Mom had found it at a garage sale and meticulously took it apart, brought it home, then reassembled it in my room shortly after I started competing in swimming when I was ten. I think she built it to remind me how awesome it was to win, which worked for a while.

Lately, though, I didn't care as much about winning. It wasn't like I was going to swim in the Olympics or anything. I probably wouldn't even swim once I went to college. I'd been thinking lately maybe I'd study history. I liked the way you could almost predict what was going to happen in the future based on the past.

'I don't think I have any medals for anything,' Kendall said.

'Do you do sports?' I asked, feigning innocence. I knew she did, but I didn't want her knowing I'd Googled her like some total creeper.

'Yeah. Tennis. And I'm on the debate team, but we don't get medals. And' – she laughed – 'I'm crap at tennis. I only do it 'cause my dad makes me.' She stared again at my trophies and medals. 'What's it like?'

'What's what like?'

'Winning.'

I thought about it. 'It's great at first, but then you have to keep doing better every time. It's exhausting.'

'Why don't you quit?' she asked, as if it were so simple.

'I don't want to let anybody down.'

She sat on the edge of my bed. I thought she'd say how stupid that was, but she didn't. She got it. Even though I didn't really know her that well, I could tell she knew exactly how it felt to be stuck in something that defined you, even though you didn't want it to.

She pulled a crumpled pack of cigarettes out of her back pocket.

'Mind if I smoke?' she asked, but she said it that way some people have of asking, but not really asking. I hated cigarettes, but I knew I couldn't stop her.

'Uh, sure, but hold on a sec.'

I opened my window all the way, then raced downstairs and grabbed a small plate from the kitchen.

'Here.' I handed her the plate. 'I don't want my mom to know.'

She took a long drag on the cigarette, then blew the smoke out the window. She held it weird: between her pointer finger and her thumb.

We talked about school, how bitchy the girls could be, what colleges we wanted to go to. I decided I liked Kendall. She seemed a bit spoiled – maybe *entitled* was a better word – but I was glad we'd finally met up. And it was cool that she might be my sister.

I'd always wanted siblings. Growing up with just my mom was a bit lonely. When I was little and hanging out at Madison and

Derek's house, I'd pretend they were my brother and sister. I knew Madison and Derek annoyed the shit out of each other, but when it really came right down to it, they'd do anything for each other. I wished I had that.

My iPhone pinged, and I pulled it out of my back pocket. It was a text with a picture attached. Somebody had snapped me outside the chemistry lab. They'd drawn devil horns on my head and a red line across my throat, drops of blood dripping down the picture.

Something in the background caught my eye, a reflection in one of the chem lab's windows. I zoomed in. The reflection had caught someone taking a picture of me. But a glint of light blurred the picture too much. I couldn't tell who it was. But I could read the message.

Die bitch!

22

ABI

november

Night was slowly falling around Mercer Island, the big-leaf maples lining the road barely visible against the inky sky as Anthony drove us to the Montgomerys' house. I stared out the passenger-side window, silently quaking, terrified that Gavin would be there too.

The last time I'd seen him, he told me he'd kill me and my baby if anybody found out about us. I knew it wasn't an idle threat.

The summer I met Gavin, he was interning in Senator George Winters's office, dating the boss's daughter. Obviously he didn't want Winters finding out about us, so our relationship was clandestine. Usually we met for a quickie on the beach or in the back of his car.

I fell in love with him hard and fast, but only in hindsight did

I realize that to him I was just a bit of illicit sex on the side. The kind that men with a superiority complex engage in because they think they're entitled to it.

One evening, as the summer was drawing to a close, we were walking back to town from our secret spot on the beach. I saw the silhouette of a man coming toward us. The moon outlined him, revealing a narrow, wolfish, pockmarked face. I tripped on a ridge in the pavement, knocking into him just as he passed.

'Watch it!' he cried.

Gavin stopped walking and stared at the man, who was now hurrying away. Something slid over his face then, something like calculation. 'Wait here,' he said, his voice hard and cold.

He crossed the road and was quickly swallowed up by the weighted darkness and the whispering pines along the beach. Time ticked by at an excruciating pace.

Finally Gavin reappeared, but his hair was mussed, his blazer crumpled, something dark – dirt? – on his pants.

'Let's get out of here.' He walked quickly toward town.

I hurried after him. 'What's going on?' A giant pulse inside my chest beat hot, then cold with fear. 'Did he hurt you?'

Gavin's eyes glistened in the yellow glow of a streetlight. 'Of course not. I just had a talk with him.'

'Why? Who –?'

'*Shut up!*' Gavin whirled to me, his face a menacing mask. 'Stop with your incessant questions!'

I let it go then because, honestly, I didn't want to know the truth. I loved him. I didn't want to see anything negative in him.

The next day I saw on the news that a man accusing George

Winters of misconduct was in the hospital after a 'robbery' gone wrong. A quick snap of his face showed a bloodied, misshapen nose and deep bruising around his neck, as if somebody had tried to strangle him. A few days later, the man withdrew the lawsuit. At the end of the summer, Gavin was given a permanent position in Winters's office and quickly rocketed through the political establishment.

That was when I knew Gavin was capable of doing just about anything for his career. So when he threatened to kill my baby and me, I knew, unequivocally, he meant it.

I loosened the scarf around my neck as Anthony buzzed the intercom at a set of ornate black iron gates. Fear was an invisible rope tightening around my throat.

Anthony asked for Kendall, and a minute later the gates rolled open. We drove along an expansive driveway that fringed a palatial, three-story limestone house. Giant windows, a wrought-iron patio, and an elaborately designed stone chimney decorated the façade.

To the left, the driveway swept to a four-car garage. In front of us, a set of stairs led to two oversize arches framing a solid oak door.

Kendall met us at the door, and I knew her instantly. She bore such a striking resemblance to Olivia it took my breath away. But then our eyes met, and I could see immediately she was nothing like my daughter. Olivia was gentle and innocent. She was all soft edges and sweet smiles. This girl was hard and worldly. Insolence hung about her like a cloud of fruit flies around day-old watermelon.

Kendall wore a crisply starched, white-collared shirt topped with a navy blazer she'd pushed up to the elbows. Tight black leggings rolled down to knee-high brown boots.

'You're Olivia's mom,' Kendall said softly. The sneer had dropped from her face.

I nodded, my tongue stuck fast in my mouth.

'I was really sorry to hear about Olivia.'

I dipped my head. 'Thanks. Do you mind if we ask you a few questions?'

She lifted her shoulders and flicked her expensive streaky bob behind her ear. 'Whatevs. Come in.'

We followed her into the foyer, a high-ceilinged affair with large, blurry Impressionist paintings of flowers, then down a long hallway to an elegant living room. A colossal stone fireplace stood at one end, accented by two cream leather couches. On the other side of the room was an antique wooden table holding a bowl of fresh flowers and an impressive floor-to-ceiling mahogany bookshelf.

Kendall sat on one of the couches while Anthony and I sat on the other.

'You already know I'm Abi,' I said. 'This is Anthony. He works for the Seattle Police Department.' I was careful not to say what he did for the SPD. It was only partly a lie.

Kendall settled back against the cream of the sofa and crossed her ankles. 'What did you want to know?'

'Well, how did you meet Olivia?'

'It was totally random, actually.' She laughed, a polished, bell-like laugh, and reached up to twirl a diamond earring in her right ear. Her fingernails were painted black. 'Our high schools were both at a college tour in April. We saw each other, and obviously we look a lot alike, so we got to talking.'

'About what?' Anthony asked.

She pursed her lips, like she was trying to think. 'She said she was from Portage Point, and I told her that's where my mom's from too. And that was it, really. Later we became Facebook friends and started hanging. She told me she thought my dad might be her dad and she wanted to meet.'

'And did you?' Anthony asked.

'Well, yeah. I mean, she seemed cool and all, so I wanted to help.'

'Where'd you meet?'

'At her house.'

'What did you talk about?'

'She told me her aunt said you had, um . . .' She glanced at me and cleared her throat, '. . . an affair with my dad and she thought he was her dad too. I told her she should come here and meet him, but I doubted if he'd admit anything.' Her face turned nasty, an ugly sneer marring her delicate features. 'It's an election year, and he wouldn't want anything to ruin that.

'There was one weird thing,' she continued. 'She got this really creepy text. It was totally effed up.'

'What did it say?' I asked.

'It said' – she hesitated briefly – 'it said, "Die bitch!"'

My brain struggled to sweep through the cobwebs of information. So Kendall had been there when Olivia received one of the texts. I opened my mouth to ask if Olivia had any idea who'd sent it, but a loud shout cut me off.

'Kendall!' The angry voice was deep and masculine, coming from right outside the living room door. 'Kendall, whose car is that? I told you no press right now!'

I jumped up, heart slamming in my chest at the familiar voice. Gavin. Fear, metallic as a penny, vibrated against my tongue. A tight ball lodged in my throat, and the room felt suddenly airless.

Anthony stood and touched my arm. His presence brought me comfort, but my fears were deeper than simply physical. I was scared of what I'd find out.

'In here, Dad,' Kendall called. She leaned back against the couch and crossed her ankles, showing off her knee-high boots.

'What are you up to, Kendall?' Gavin's face was creased with irritation as he entered the room, but as soon as he saw us a charming smile smoothed his handsome features.

Just like when we were younger, Gavin's presence filled the room. He was, if possible, even more handsome now. The years melted away as he recognized me. His face momentarily dropped in shock.

Dressed in a navy-blue suit with a crisp white shirt and a blue pin-striped tie, he had just enough silver at his temples to look distinguished. His broad shoulders and confident frame gave off an aura that said 'trust me.' His square jaw indicated strength and power.

He looked every bit the power player I'd met all those years ago. It was no wonder Washington State voters were beguiled by him. You just looked at him and felt compelled to follow.

'Abi?' he said, his eyebrows high on his forehead.

I flinched at the sound of my name, but kept my face blank.

He kissed me on the cheek in greeting. He smelled expensive, faintly of citrus, like Acqua di Parma. 'It's been a long time. How are you?'

'Hello, Gavin.' My mouth felt full of cotton. I tried to keep my voice even, but I heard it: I sounded pathetic and weak.

Kendall watched her father, her head tilted to one side – and, my God, she had a smile on her lips. She was enjoying his discomfort.

'So you know Abigail Knight, Dad?'

Gavin turned to Kendall, looking somewhat uncomfortable. 'Abi and I were . . . friends . . . a long time ago.'

'And this is Anthony, with the Seattle Police Department,' Kendall said, her eyebrows raised in a mocking gesture. 'They're here to talk to us about Olivia Knight. You know the tragic accident that happened last month in Portage Point? It's been all over the news. Abi is Olivia's mom.'

'I'm sorry for your loss,' Gavin said immediately. He blew his mouth out and tilted his chin down in a calculated conveyance of sympathy. He looked like a blowfish with neck pain. 'I'm not sure how we can help. We didn't know your daughter.'

'Actually, Kendall did know Olivia. We were just discussing how they met,' Anthony said.

Gavin's smile dropped just a hair. 'Oh.' He arranged the smile back on his face, as easily as if he were draping clothes on a clothesline. 'Is my daughter being questioned?' He crossed to Kendall and put a hand on her shoulder. Jesus. They looked so much alike – so much like Olivia. All of them with their blonde hair and forest-green eyes, their sharp Slavic cheekbones, and the slightly off-center cleft in their chins.

'No, not at all.' The laid-back smile didn't match the steel in Anthony's eyes.

The tension in the air tightened a notch. Nothing tangible. Nothing concrete. In fact, on the surface everybody looked polite and pleasant. But it was there, snaking around us like a noxious gas.

The men sized each other up, and I couldn't help but compare them. Gavin with his clean-shaven face, his perfectly pressed suit, his athletic body; Anthony with his tousled curls, his three-day stubble, his casual canvas coat. He was so decent, so accepting of people and of life. Gavin had none of that quiet kindness in him. He was all bluster, no substance.

'Well, I have complete confidence the police know what they're doing. If you have any further questions, you'll need to address them to my lawyer.' He had the air of someone who imagines he can negotiate with gravity. I hated him fiercely.

'I invited them here, Dad.' The lie fell smoothly off Kendall's tongue. She flipped her hair behind her ear. 'I wanted to talk to them about Olivia. You know, Olivia's brain-dead, and I want to help find out what happened to her. Do you know anything about that?'

She batted her eyes innocently, and I realized she was baiting him. An undercurrent flowed between father and daughter that I didn't entirely understand.

Gavin clenched and unclenched his fists. It was the only indication he was pissed off.

'Of course I heard about Olivia's accident on the news. Absolutely tragic.'

'Did you know Olivia?' I asked.

'No, of course not.' He spoke too quickly. He was lying. He did it as easily as water flowing over a waterfall.

Hot waves of anger washed over me; a high-pitched buzzing rang in my ears. He was involved in this. Somehow. I just didn't know how to prove it. The police wouldn't believe me – a grieving mother – over Gavin Montgomery, a successful, well-respected politician.

Gavin shed his navy suit jacket and meticulously folded it in half, then draped it across the back of the couch.

'Now.' He turned to face us. He was still smiling, but his eyes had gone wintry cold. 'I presume you don't have a warrant, so I suggest you rethink this line of questioning.'

'No problem,' Anthony said easily. 'But this isn't going away. We'll be back.'

'Bring a warrant next time. And take it to my lawyer,' Gavin tossed over his shoulder as he left the room, as confident as any man who knew he was untouchable.

× × ×

Outside, rain had started to fall, fat drops pinging against my scalp as Anthony and I walked to his car. A wet leaf smacked against my shoe and I kicked it free.

My phone rang.

'Abi, it's Brad. Have you seen Sarah?' My sister's husband sounded stressed.

'No. Not for a few days.' I cringed at the admission. 'Everything okay?'

'I don't know. She texted earlier asking me to get Dylan from school, but I haven't heard from her since. She still isn't home, but Dylan's sleeping and I can't leave him to go look for her.'

'Oh God.'

'What's wrong?' Anthony asked sharply.

'Sarah's missing.'

'We'll find her. Where would she go?'

I thought hard, panic spinning in my chest. 'To Olivia in the hospital. Or to her office.'

'Let's go.'

I told Brad we'd call him back, and got in the car.

Just then a shout sounded. 'Wait!'

Kendall was running from the house. She fell dramatically against my door, her face streaked with tears. I rolled my window down, and she thrust a crumpled piece of paper at me.

'Olivia had this DNA test done on my dad. She asked me if she could have the results sent to me so nobody would find out. I got it right before . . . you know.' A tear rolled down her face. It hovered on the corner of her jaw, then splashed onto my hand, which gripped the car door where the window was rolled down.

I took the paper and read it. It was unnecessary, really. I already knew Gavin was her father. 'Did Olivia see this? Did she know for sure?' I asked urgently.

'Yeah.' Her voice cracked like a piece of old leather. 'I called her that day. She said she was going to talk to him about it. I think she confronted him. If the media found out about Olivia, or if my mom did . . .' Kendall snorted a laugh, even though she clearly didn't think it was funny. 'She'd leave him in a heartbeat, and take her money with her.'

23

ABI

november

Anthony pulled up at the hospital, and I dashed inside, up the stairs to Olivia's room. But Sarah wasn't there. I gave my girl a quick kiss on the cheek and told her we were looking for her aunt, but I'd be back soon.

We drove to the strip mall where Sarah rented space for her counseling sessions. But as soon as we got there, I knew she wasn't there. The lights were dark and the doors locked tight.

I banged my hand against my forehead.

'We'll find her,' Anthony reassured me.

'This is my fault,' I moaned.

'Of course it isn't.'

But I knew he was wrong. The closer I got to the truth about Olivia, the more I'd pushed Sarah away. The one person who'd always been there for me, no matter what. I didn't want to deal with how I'd feel if she left me too. Maybe that was why I isolated myself – not just from her, but from everyone. It was easier to hide.

And suddenly, I knew where Sarah was.

× × ×

After our mother died, Sarah had spent a lot of time at her grave. We never talked about it – Sarah didn't want to talk, which was ironic, considering she'd chosen counseling as a career. I only found out years later, when she admitted to me she went nearly every day after dropping me off at school.

She said it was where she went to hide.

When we pulled up to the cemetery, it was pitch black. Anthony grabbed a flashlight from the trunk and swept it along the pathway in front of us as I led him to my mother's grave.

After a few minutes, the flashlight illuminated Sarah's face. She was sitting on the ground, her back against our mother's headstone.

'Sarah!' I rushed toward my sister and knelt in the grass next to her, the knees of my jeans immediately soaking through.

Sarah started crying when she saw me, great, heaving sobs. She looked like she'd been crying all day. Her eyes were so puffy she peered at me through slits. An open fifth of whiskey was propped against the marble headstone.

Anthony took my phone and texted Brad while I turned to Sarah, suddenly furious.

'Jesus, Sarah! You scared me! Brad's been worried sick! What were you thinking?'

'Abi,' she sobbed. 'I've fucked up. I've really fucked up.'

'I doubt that.'

Sarah never fucked up. She was perfect, selfless as a saint. When our mother died, she'd boxed up all my things and moved me in with her. She sat with me as I did my homework every night, papers spread across the wobbly veneered kitchen table, the smell of cardboard pizza and cheap TV dinners thick in the air. She'd worked evenings so she could watch Olivia during the days while I finished college. Sarah was relentlessly competent and infinitely proficient. She never made mistakes.

'I didn't know it would hurt you your whole life. I would've done it differently.' Sarah pushed the heels of her hands against her eyes, her mouth contorting on a sob.

I glanced at Anthony. 'What are you talking about?'

'You said you never got any closure after Mom died. You said it broke you.'

'Yeah, but –'

'Mom left a note!'

I let go of Sarah and swayed backward as memories of that day rushed at me. . . .

The day my mom had killed herself dawned bright and blue, but with a sharp chill to the air. Halloween was just a few days away, and pumpkins sat on the front porches of most of the houses in the neighborhood, their sinister mouths and jagged teeth grinning at me.

I woke to the sound of her vacuuming her office, where she only went when something was wrong. I huddled under my covers longer than normal, just to avoid her.

She could be like that: happy one day, withdrawing into a shell the next.

I got dressed, ate some cereal, brushed my teeth. But when it was time for her to drive me to school, she was still cleaning. I opened the door to her office, and she was on her hands and knees, scrubbing the floor.

'Mom, I'm late for school.'

'You're not going.'

'What? Why?'

She didn't answer. Just kept scrubbing.

'Mom, why?'

She looked at me for a long moment, her expression unreadable. Her blue eyes were wide, veined with red. Suddenly she scrambled to her feet and shoved past me. In my room, she grabbed my backpack and filled it with dirty clothes from my hamper in my closet.

'Get in the car,' she said. 'I'll take you to Sarah's.'

Her face looked weird, pale and stressed. She was sweating – not just a bit of moisture but actual drops that trickled down the side of her face and filled the dip of her throat.

At Sarah's apartment, she dragged me up the stairs, her hand like a shackle around my wrist. She pushed me down until I sat on the muddy mat, then leaned into my face.

'You stay *right here*,' she hissed. Her eyes were dilated, the blue edged out by a darkness so great I almost didn't recognize her.

'Mo-ooom!!!' I whined, angry and feeling the first whispers of panic at the thought of being left alone. 'Where are you going? I don't want to wait here!'

'Sarah will be home soon.'

'What if she isn't?'

'Trust me.' She started to walk away.

'You are such a *freak*!' I scrambled to my feet. 'You can't just leave me here all by myself!'

Mom came back fast. For a second I thought she'd hit me, but instead she hugged me so tight it hurt my ribcage.

'What does Mommy always say?' she asked, kneeling in front of me.

I rolled my eyes. I hadn't called her Mommy in years. ' "Whenever, whatever. I'm here forever," ' I recited.

'That's my girl.' She touched her fingertips lightly to my chest, her eyes glistening. 'Forever.'

Then she straightened and walked away.

'Mooom!!! Mo-om?' I stomped the ground furiously. I waited a minute, and when she didn't reply I yelled: 'Fine! Go then! I don't care if you leave!'

The only sound was the screech of the car wheels as she gunned it out of the parking lot.

I waited more than an hour, my emotions veering between fear and anger. Finally Sarah appeared at the end of the hallway, home from college.

'What are you – where's Mom?' she asked, her eyebrows crumpling.

'She left.' I scowled.

'She left you here? *When?*' Sarah's voice pitched high.

'I don't know. An hour ago?'

Sarah's fingers dug into my shoulders; her face had turned the color of old putty. 'Think, Abi. Where was Mom going?'

'I don't know. She didn't say!'

Sarah grabbed my hand, and we ran to her car. When we pulled up to our faded, two-story clapboard house, I burst out of the car, an acidic sensation wheeling in my stomach.

I could hear the leaves we'd raked just yesterday crunch under my feet as I pounded across the yard to the front door.

'Mom?' I shouted, flinging the front door open.

'Abi! Come here!' Sarah was right behind me, but I darted out of her reach. She was always telling me what to do.

I ran up the stairs to Mom's office and pushed open the door. The first thing that hit me was the smell – as if somebody had lit off a firework.

Mom was slumped over her desk, the wall behind her sprayed with something dark. Her fingers still clutched a gun. I'd never seen a gun in real life before.

Sarah crashed into me, shouting my name, but I couldn't hear anything anymore. Nothing registered. All I could do was wonder where that gun came from.

I shoved Sarah away and turned to vomit all over my mom's nice clean carpet.

× × ×

The peculiar numbness of psychological shock was settling over me.

Suicide of a parent, that type of abandonment, it did things to a person. It didn't take a shrink to tell me that I didn't trust people to stay because my mom had promised she'd be there and then wasn't.

I was terrified that there was some deep flaw inside of me that had made her leave, that made everybody leave. That worry had clawed its way into me, cemented by life's hairpin turns and sudden drop-offs.

'Mom left a note?' I said, my voice a ragged whisper.

Sarah nodded. 'I hid it from you. I'm sorry.'

'Where is it?'

'You won't get any closure from it,' she said. 'Words on paper won't make what she did logical.'

I held my hand out.

Sarah pulled a crumpled piece of paper from her coat pocket, smoothed it against her thigh, and handed it to me. When I opened it, I noticed dark flecks sprayed across it. There wasn't really much to read.

I don't want this world. I don't want to be your mother. I can't handle it. I don't want

The note ended abruptly in the middle of her sentence. No final stop, no resolution, as if she'd realized midnote what she was going to do.

I let go of the note. It floated like a feather through the air and landed gently in the mud at Sarah's feet.

I don't want to be your mother.

'Mom had bipolar disorder, Abi. She wasn't well.'

My mind flashed back to my recurring dream of my mother and me on the roof. And I knew. It wasn't a dream.

Other memories assaulted me. Mom screaming at Sarah

because she'd shrunk a sweater in a hot wash; waking after a bad dream and finding her furiously painting the bathroom after a 3 a.m. run to Walmart.

'That night, on the roof.' My voice was weak with shock. 'You saved me.'

Sarah nodded. 'Yes. Mom told you that you could fly.'

'Why didn't you call social services?'

'I was a teenager. I couldn't take care of you. And I was scared. I didn't want you to go into foster care. Then she got better. She got some counseling. Took her meds every day. But then I started noticing little things. She'd forget to pick you up from school, or she'd go on manic spending sprees. I should've known she was spiraling.'

Anthony had been listening to us talk, but now he turned off the flashlight and handed it to me.

'I'll be in the car when you need me,' he said quietly.

I watched him walk away, then moved the bottle of whiskey and sat next to Sarah, our backs against our mother's headstone.

'I thought it was my fault,' I said, scrubbing a hand over my eyes. 'That last day . . . God, I've never told anybody this. When she dropped me off at your place, I called her a freak. I said I didn't care if she left. Next thing I knew, she was dead. I thought it was my fault.'

'No, Abi. Mom was sick. I saw all the signs. I shouldn't have let you go in there first. . .' Her voice strangled, but she kept going. 'When I saw her note, I put it in my pocket so you wouldn't think it was your fault. I was selfish, thinking I could fix it for you. I wanted to protect you. And Olivia. God, I've been so arrogant! Maybe if I'd told you she knew about Gavin –'

Sarah started crying again.

'No. It isn't your fault. None of it. I'm sorry I said it was. I hope you know I didn't mean it.'

Suddenly it made perfect sense. Mom hadn't left me because she didn't want me. She'd withdrawn, pushed me away, because she was more damaged than I ever knew.

I didn't understand her mental illness, but I knew one thing. Being a mother wasn't something you just 'handled.' Olivia had saved me, and if Mom had been mentally stable, I would've been enough to save her. Her death didn't have anything to do with me at all.

I grabbed the fifth of whiskey and took a swig. Sarah had barely touched it. The liquor stung, but I swallowed it anyway.

I didn't want to be like my mom, hiding from the world, pushing the people who cared for me away. I wanted to connect and experience my life.

'You have the truth about Mom. Now can you say good-bye?' Sarah said, her voice husky from crying.

'I'm gonna try,' I replied honestly.

'Once you get the truth about Olivia, you'll still have to say good-bye to her. Nothing's going to change that.'

'I know.' I leaned my head against my sister's shoulder and she put an arm around me. 'I know.'

Sarah brushed my hair off my face and kissed my forehead. And for the first time in a long time, I didn't pull away.

24

OLIVIA

july

A loud knocking on the front door shook me awake. I blinked against the sun beaming brightly through my window, disoriented and half-asleep. The knock came again, and I jolted out of bed. I pulled a pair of shorts on over my underwear and hurried down the stairs.

'Tyler!' I gasped when I opened the door. I hadn't seen him since right after school got out, and other than a few texts we hadn't even spoken.

'Hi, babe,' Tyler said with a grin. He swept past me into the room as I stood speechless, the doorknob still clutched in my hand. He held his arms open.

I hesitated. My still half-asleep brain reeled. I'd have to hug him, of course. But I didn't move.

His arms dropped to his sides and his face crumpled into that dejected, heartbroken look I'd seen so often since his parents' breakup. 'What's wrong?' he asked.

'Nothing.' I hugged him quickly, then sat on the couch and pulled my knees to my chest, suddenly feeling underdressed. 'I'm just still waking up. What are you doing here?'

'What do you mean? I told you I was coming this week.'

'You said the weekend.'

'Oh. Well, I meant this week. It's not a problem, right? You don't have plans with your secret other boyfriend?'

His words were casual, teasing, but there was a weird look in his eyes I'd never seen before. It was time to tell him the truth, I decided.

I swallowed hard, working out the right words to say. I'd never broken up with someone before. I didn't want to hurt Tyler's feelings, especially with all he'd been through lately.

Tyler dropped onto the couch and reached for me. 'Come here. I haven't seen you in weeks, and we've barely even spoken lately. Why are you so far away?'

I scooted a few inches closer, a sickening lump pulsing in my stomach. It felt like I was betraying Derek, even though technically I was betraying Tyler by being with Derek. God, I'd made such a mess of things!

'How's your dad?' I asked, hoping to distract him from holding me. 'And Seattle? Do you like living there?'

Tyler scowled and shook his head. He pressed his knuckles against his knees until they cracked loudly. I cringed.

'I hate it. I'd stay at my mom's, but I can't stand being around her. She's sucking up so hard-core, like that'll make it any better. She bought me some golf clubs and said she's taking me to Barbados for Christmas this year, but I hate her. She's the one who cheated, fucking bitch.' His eyes blazed with anger. I'd never heard him speak that way about his mom and I pulled away, feeling uncomfortable.

'Every day I just sit in my dad's apartment,' he complained. 'I have nothing to do, nowhere to go, nobody to talk to. And when my dad comes home, he goes straight to his computer, so it's not like we even talk.'

He sagged against the couch, the anger seeping out of him. 'I'm alone *all* the time. I don't have anybody to hang out with. It's fucking boring.' And to my utter horror and embarrassment, Tyler suddenly started crying.

I'd never seen Tyler cry before. Hugging him seemed like the only option, so I put my arms around his shoulders and patted his back.

I laid my head on his shoulder and turned my face so he wouldn't see me. He smelled of mint and evergreen trees, the Axe body wash I knew he used. It was simultaneously familiar and also super annoying. A pocket of irritation gathered in my belly.

'You're the only person I want to be with, Liv.' Tyler dashed at his eyes with the heels of his hands. 'Everything's so shitty right now. Being with you again when school starts is the only thing getting me through. I don't think I'd be able to live if I didn't have you.'

'I'm so sorry,' I murmured, squeezing my eyes shut. He didn't know how much.

A secret surge of selfishness churned in me. I couldn't break up with him now.

Tyler left after a while to go golfing with his mom.

I worked in the garden the rest of the morning, weeding and planting new vegetables, until my mom called at noon, then I headed over to Derek's. I sneaked in the back way – through the gate and into the backyard – and was about to tap on his door when I felt the fine hairs on the back of my neck stand up. The hot, prickly sensation of somebody's eyes blistered against my back. I looked over my shoulder, but there was nobody there. The yard was completely empty. Just behind the fence a forest of evergreens waved lazily in the breeze.

I tried to shake off the feeling. I peered around the edge of the house at the gate. It was open about three inches. I couldn't remember if I'd shut it when I came in. My heart leapt to a gallop in my chest.

A text message pinged loudly from my back pocket, and I nearly jumped out of my skin.

When I opened it, it was a picture of my face, bloody intestines vomiting from my mouth. My eyes had been whited out.

Fuck you! was scrawled across it.

Goose bumps prickled along my skin, and my mouth went dry and dusty, terror clawing at the back of my throat. I looked behind me, suddenly terrified that someone was watching me.

I crept up the yard's slight incline, breathing heavily. I stuffed my phone in my pocket and pressed my back against the bushes that lined the fence, letting the shadows swallow me as I moved toward the gate.

Once there, I counted in my head, wiggling my fingers tensely against the smooth wooden handle: *One, two, THREE!* I threw open the gate and looked around, out the front yard, up and down the road.

There was nobody there. The suburban neighborhood was as quiet as you'd expect in the middle of a weekday. A lawnmower buzzed somewhere down the street; a sprinkler threw staccato arcs on the neighbor's front yard; the sound of children laughing came from across the street. A bird called from somewhere above me.

My hands shook and my heart banged painfully in my chest. I sucked in deep breaths of soupy summer air and bent over, pushing my head between my knees. It took me a few minutes to stop trembling. This was ridiculous. Of course I wasn't being watched.

Get a grip, Olivia.

These stupid fucking picture messages. They were really freaking me out. I didn't have enemies. Not that I knew of, anyway. The only person who disliked me was Tyler's friend Dan. But sending anonymous messages wasn't Dan's style. If he had anything on me, he'd confront me in front of Tyler just to humiliate me as much as possible.

I stood straight and rolled my shoulders, my body tingly with adrenaline. I pulled the gate closed, making sure it was latched this time, and retraced my steps down the yard to Derek's door.

Once I was safely inside Derek's room and sitting next to him on the edge of the bed, I felt better. I decided I'd blown the weird, creepy feeling of being followed out of proportion.

Derek grabbed two Cokes from his mini fridge, handing me one as he sat next to me on the edge of his bed.

'I saw Tyler this morning,' I said. Our feet were entwined, and I could feel the warmth of his body stretching along the side of my leg.

Derek froze, the hand that held his Coke halfway to his mouth. 'Really? Where?'

'He showed up at my house. He woke me up. It was weird. He's never done that before.'

'Did you break up with him?' he asked.

'Well . . .' I slid my fingers back and forth along the slippery metal of my bracelet, fumbling over the truth.

Derek set his Coke down on his bedside table. 'You didn't.' It was a statement, not a question.

'I'm sorry!' I defended myself. 'He started crying and I didn't know what to do! I just thought I should wait until he's a little . . . better.'

'Shit, Liv.' Derek ran a hand through his dark curls, pulled away from me, and stood. I felt cold where his body had been. 'We can't keep hiding this. I don't even like hiding it from Madison, but at least I get it. Why are you having such a hard time breaking up with him?'

'He's fragile right now. Besides, he made it sound like the only reason he isn't throwing himself off a bridge is because of me. I don't want him to hurt himself.'

'He's not going to hurt himself, Liv. He's manipulating you!'

Derek crossed the room to stare out the window. He was silent for a long moment, his back to me.

'I can't be with someone who's embarrassed to be with me. I get enough of that from my family.'

I stared at him, feeling lost. He was less than an arm's length away, but it might as well have been miles. The sadness in his voice made me ache.

'Derek –' I began, but just then the door upstairs crashed shut. Derek's and my eyes collided.

Madison was home.

25

OLIVIA

july

'Hello?' Madison shouted from upstairs.

Shit, shit, shit! How would I explain my presence in Derek's bedroom?

What do we do? Derek mouthed.

I lifted my hands, palms up. *I don't know.*

I heard Madison's footsteps in the kitchen above us and held perfectly still, hoping she wouldn't hear us. My heart smashed wildly into the walls of my chest cavity. Maybe I could sneak out the back. But just then my phone beeped loudly. There was no way she hadn't heard that.

I pulled my phone out of my pocket just as Madison barreled down the stairs. It was another picture message. This time in front of Madison's house. I was wearing the same clothes I had on now. My mouth went suddenly, sickeningly dry.

I was right. Someone had been following me.

In the picture a knife was drawn sticking out of my heart, blood dripping down my chest. The words *U die!* were written on it.

'What are you doing down here?' Madison's dark eyes met mine, hot with suspicion and anger. Her eyebrows were bunched into tight knots above her eyes, her cotton-candy-pink lips pursed.

'Oh, hey, Mad.' I forced a breezy laugh. 'I was just showing Derek this crazy picture message.'

I held the phone out to her and she grabbed it, her face crinkling with shock. 'Oh my God! Who sent that?'

I shrugged, twin emotions of relief and terror surging through me.

'It must be a really mean joke,' Madison said, handing the phone back to me.

'Yeah, probably,' I agreed.

Derek reached for my phone. His mouth contorted, twisted around words he couldn't quite say. I tried to catch his eye, to apologize for not telling him.

'But who? And why?' Madison said, her eyebrows scrunched up. 'I can't imagine anyone hating you. You're so, you know . . . *nice*.' She smirked. 'But, like, in a good way, of course.'

'Of course,' I replied drily.

It was so like her to wrap up a compliment in a cutting remark. But at least I'd completely distracted her from the fact I was in Derek's bedroom. She'd kill us both if she found out about us. Once when we were kids we were playing capture the flag and I chose Derek for my team. She bit her arm until it bled and told her dad Derek did it.

'You should tell the police,' she said.

If I told the police, they'd tell my mom. And I couldn't have that. I'd lose every drop of freedom she'd finally given me. Besides, maybe it was Dan or some weirdo at school pulling a sick prank.

I laughed. 'And tell them what? Somebody's sending me mean pictures?'

Madison laughed too.

I changed the subject. 'Do you want to go into town and get lunch?'

She shook her head. 'Sorry, can't. Have to get back to rehearsal. I only came home to grab a sandwich.'

I pretended to be disappointed as I followed her up the stairs. 'Bummer. Okay, soon, though, right?' I threw a look at Derek over my shoulder, begging him with my eyes to understand. He wouldn't meet my gaze.

I walked with Madison down the driveway. I waved as she turned to go into town, then I ducked down a side street and circled back. Derek opened the door without a word, his mouth in a thin, grim line.

I followed him meekly inside, ready to apologize, say whatever he wanted so he would stop being mad at me. I couldn't bear that I'd upset him.

'Derek,' I began.

'Please.' He held up a hand. 'Can I go first?'

I nodded.

'I get that you don't want to hurt Tyler's feelings, and I get that you don't want to upset Madison by letting her know we're together. I even get that you don't want your mom finding out you're looking for your dad. But don't you think lying to every-body will just make it worse?'

I stared at him, shocked. 'I'm not lying,' I denied emphatically. 'I'm protecting the people I love.'

Derek shook his head. 'You're not protecting anybody, Olivia. You want to know the truth, but you're not willing to be honest. Like with me. You didn't even tell me you've been getting those messages.'

'I thought they would stop. And then I was going to tell you but, I don't know, I just didn't want to worry you!'

'But I love you!' he exclaimed, throwing his arms up in frustra-tion. 'I *want* to worry about you.'

'You love me?' I stepped closer to him. A smile played across my lips.

'Of course I do.' He stroked a finger down my jaw. 'I promised never to lie to you, and I hope you'll promise me the same.'

I leaned against him, nuzzled my neck into the soft, warm spot where his throat met his chest.

'I will,' I promised. 'I'll tell everybody the truth. I'll break up with Tyler and I'll tell Madison about us. I'll even tell my mom I'm trying to find my dad. I just need some time, okay? This is the first time in my life I've been able to do things on my own, without my mom telling me what to do. I need to do this my way. Please.'

I searched his eyes, begging him to understand.

Derek leaned down and kissed me. His chest warmed mine, and I felt his pulse thrumming through me. I opened my mouth to him, pressed my body along his. I felt his resistance melt as he folded me in his kiss.

'Promise me,' he murmured against my lips.

'I promise.'

His hands slid under my shirt, and as he traced each nipple with his fingers I gasped at the unexpected pleasure. We'd messed around a bit, but there was always this unspoken line we didn't cross.

I ran my hands over his back, his hips, down his belly. He moaned, a deep thrum in the base of his throat. His hands dove into my hair and under my clothes, and my breath became his.

'Olivia,' he whispered urgently.

'Please,' I murmured. 'Don't stop.'

That was all it took to break his last barriers. He lifted me up, hitching me against him, and carried me to his bed, laying me down ever so gently. I trembled as he undid the button on my jeans, pulled my zipper low. I'd never felt this way before, as if my skin would burst into flames.

'Derek,' I breathed. My skin was hot where his hands touched me.

He lowered his mouth to rain kisses from my ear to my jaw, down to the hollow of my throat.

The fire between my legs spread throughout my body. He moved his hands slowly down my stomach. His fingers caressed me, stroked inside of me, memorizing my body until I felt I would scream from the ecstasy. I curled my fingers into his back and thrust my hips up, wanting more of him.

He slipped my jeans off my ankles, then kicked his off, and we were side by side, naked as our need for each other. I felt vulnerable suddenly, laid bare by this need.

But Derek knew my thoughts before I did.

He bent over me and covered my face in butterfly-soft kisses, every one of them showing me how much he loved me, how vast that love was.

'You,' he whispered. 'I love you.'

With him, I knew I would always find my way home. For the first time in a long time, I was clean, stripped of all the lies I was weaving, the lies that tangled me in a web of my own making.

'I love you too.'

× × ×

We lay pressed together for a long time after that, his hand stroking my hair until I fell into that warm, velvety place between sleeping and awake.

My phone beeped the arrival of a text from my jeans on the floor, jolting me back to consciousness.

I slid off the bed and reached for my phone. If my mom messaged or called and I didn't answer, she'd freak.

But the text wasn't from my mom. It was from Kendall, saying that her dad was working at home, and did I want to meet him?

I showed Derek the text and looked at the time. One o'clock.

'Do you think we could get there and back before your mom gets home from work?' he asked doubtfully.

'Yeah, let's go. I want to find out what he's like. I can always tell her I'm having dinner with Madison.'

He held my gaze for a second, his face looking unhinged. I saw right there what I'd done: my blasé disregard for lying was now obvious to both of us. I turned away from him and dressed quickly.

It was fine. It was just a tiny white lie. It almost didn't count. And if it took lying to get the truth, that's what I'd do.

26

ABI

november

I woke with a jolt, my bedroom stuffy and dark, the sheets soaked with sweat. A hangover thudded in my brain, a gift from the fifth of whiskey Sarah and I had finished at our mother's grave last night.

A graveyard was an odd place to start living again, but I'd found healing in Sarah's words. And when you start to heal you can start living again. Not just existing, but actually living in the present moment, looking toward the future rather than looking back, wishing you could change what couldn't be changed.

The tones on my phone chimed, reminding me I had a meeting at the hospital at noon today. A handful of administrators, ob-gyns, and surgeons were meeting to discuss Olivia's case.

My stomach knotted into a bitter lump and emotion corded my chest. My health insurance had refused to pay any more and the cost of Olivia's care was mounting at an incredible pace. Added to that, I was coming up to the end of my leave of absence and my boss was now sending me daily e-mails, oh-so-politely asking me to come back to work. And with only twelve weeks until the baby was born, I was running out of time to find the truth.

I stumbled out of bed and changed into my running clothes. A few minutes later I pounded along the boardwalk. Fresh air hissed in and out of my lungs.

On the way home I saw Sadie, Lizzie's dog, nipping at the waves. Impulsively I jogged down the sloping dunes along the rock-studded beach toward Lizzie, who was huddled in a polka-dotted raincoat near the water. She picked up a bit of driftwood and tossed it; Sadie ran after it, splashing into the water, tongue lolling.

'Hi, Abi!' Lizzie called as I approached.

'Hi, Lizzie.' I had to raise my voice to be heard over the roar of the waves. 'I just wanted to say thank you. For the orchid. And the note.'

She pushed a wet lock of hair under her hood, water dripping into her eyes. 'Oh, Abi. I wish I could do more than just send flowers. It must be dreadful.'

'It is,' I replied honestly. 'But the flowers mean a lot.'

I turned to go, but Lizzie stopped me. 'You want to get a coffee one of these days?' She looked down, blinking fast.

'I'd like that,' I said, surprising myself.

Lizzie smiled, her eyes warm. 'Okay. Enjoy your run.'

I waved and continued toward home. By the time I unlocked my door I felt better, the alcohol evaporated from my blood, the groggy thud in my head gone.

An hour later, I'd showered and dressed and was waiting outside the hospital boardroom when my phone rang.

'Hello, Miss Knight, this is Detective Samson.'

'Detective Samson.' My heart sped up, hammering against my ribs so hard I felt they would crack. 'Have you found anything?'

'No, I'm sorry, I didn't mean to get your hopes up. I just wanted to let you know I looked through our evidence and spoke to Detective McNally, and we didn't find a silver bracelet. I'm really sorry.'

'Did you look at the pictures on Olivia's iCloud account?'

'We're pursuing a number of leads, Miss Knight.'

I gritted my teeth, knowing that meant they'd done nothing.

'Can't you subpoena her phone records?'

'I know this is frustrating, but it takes time. How are you doing?'

I frowned, picturing Samson's icy demeanor, her impassive face, her professional detachment.

'I don't . . . I'm not sure . . .'

'Of course,' she said. 'I understand.'

'Do you?' I replied bitterly.

Samson didn't answer for a beat.

'Some of us never get hardened to other people's suffering,' she said finally. 'Killing, murder, death, it isn't an easy business. People kill for so many reasons – usually to do with control and power. The one constant we know is that the killer usually knew the victim. That's where I always start looking: the people the victim knew.'

My palm felt slick against the phone. I opened my mouth to ask her more about this, but Dr Griffith appeared around the corner, followed closely by Sarah. I said good-bye to Samson and hugged my sister as Dr Griffith unlocked the boardroom door.

Inside, we chose chairs set neatly around a long, oval table that dominated the room. Dr Griffith sat across from us and laid a handful of skin-toned folders in front of him.

Soon men and women in business suits and white doctor's coats began to trickle into the room, quickly filling up the other seats.

Dr Griffith started the meeting and the others spoke in turn, reciting the work being done to care for Olivia and her baby. I let my mind drift until a tall man the shape of a cucumber stood and started speaking. He pulled at his pale pink tie as if it was too tight and adjusted his glasses.

Suddenly my mind snagged on something the administrator had said, and I glanced at Sarah. She looked confused, too.

'Wait,' I burst out.

'Yes?' The man seemed startled.

'What'd you just say? About a donation?'

His gray head bobbed. 'We've received a substantial donation toward the costs of intrauterine support and hope you won't worry at all about the length of time, nor the level of care Olivia will receive.'

'A donor?' Sarah interjected. 'Who?'

He fumbled through his notes and straightened his glasses. 'An anonymous donation.'

'Anonymous?' I repeated.

'Yes. The person or persons who made this donation have asked not to have their identity revealed.'

I clenched my icy fingers together on the table. Sarah reached over and squeezed my hand. Her fingernails were round ovals, smooth and pink against my tattered, torn ones.

'Who would pay for this?' Sarah asked. 'How do they even know about it?'

'Well, Olivia's story was initially all over the news,' he said. 'There's a continued interest, and we've issued numerous statements to the press, as I'm sure you know.'

'Will we ever find out who's donated this money?' I asked, thinking of the mysterious silent phone calls I'd been getting.

The administrator in the pink tie shook his head. 'I'm afraid not. Anonymous is anonymous. All I can say is, if he ever decides to go public with it, you'll be the first to know.'

Sarah's hand tightened on mine; the frown line between her eyebrows sharpened. She'd caught the slip as well.

The administrator had referred to the anonymous donor as 'he.'

× × ×

Later that afternoon Anthony arrived with two large paper bags that smelled intoxicatingly of Chinese food.

'I didn't know what you liked, so I got options,' he said, unpacking little white boxes of food. I pulled plates from the cupboard, and he dished out egg foo yong, kung pao chicken, egg rolls, and fried rice. It smelled delicious, and we headed to the living room to eat.

'How's your mom doing?' I asked.

'Really well. Physically, at least. But mentally . . .' He blew out a breath. 'I think it might be time to put her in a home.'

He looked so sad at this realization. I touched his arm.

'I'm sorry, Anthony.'

I knew that saying good-bye, even just to what you thought you knew, was a difficult thing.

'Thanks,' he said. He took a bite of fried rice with his chopsticks. 'Tell me about your meeting today. How's the baby?'

'Really good.' I smiled. 'Growing fast.'

I showed Anthony the ultrasound picture and told him about the mysterious donation and how it had relieved some of the pressure of paying for Olivia's medical care.

'No idea who the donor is?' he asked.

'No. I wish I did so I could thank them.'

Anthony scooped up some egg foo yong. 'I was thinking, maybe tonight we could talk to Madison?'

I thought about it for a minute. 'Madison wouldn't have hurt Olivia. They were best friends. Kendall thinks Gavin had something to do with this, and so do I.'

'We can't talk to Kendall again just yet. Gavin would have us in jail for trespassing so fast we wouldn't know what hit us. Besides, I wouldn't trust that girl as far as I could throw her. And we need to talk to Madison about what Tyler told us. If she and Olivia weren't talking, we need to know why.'

27

OLIVIA

july

When Derek and I arrived at the address Kendall had given me, I texted her that we were there. A set of ornate black gates clanged open and we drove slowly up the driveway, past a manicured lawn hedged with shrubs to a ginormous three-story limestone house.

Panic licked at my throat. I was out of my depth. I didn't belong here. It didn't matter who my father was – I didn't need him to complete my family. I already had my mom and Aunt Sarah. I should turn around, go home, forget about all of this.

But suddenly Derek was opening my door and it was too late to change my mind. We skirted around a white van with some sort of writing scrawled across the far side and walked up the stairs.

Before I even lifted my hand to knock, Kendall flung open the door. Her eyes were weirdly bright, the pupils sharp and black, and she had a huge smile on her face, like she had a secret she didn't want to say out loud.

'Hi! Come in! Welcome! Welcome!' She was talking in exclamation points, her voice high-pitched and creepy. I narrowed my eyes and looked at her, but she wouldn't meet my eyes.

She pulled us into a massive foyer accented with mahogany wood and expensive-looking rugs. A tall ceiling soared high above us. The house looked like it belonged in a movie.

Derek's eyes widened, and I tightened every muscle in my face. I didn't want to show how intimidating it was. Fake it till you make it, right?

'We'll just wait for your wife to arrive,' I heard a woman's voice say from behind a set of double doors just across the entrance foyer. Kendall slammed the front door hard behind us. I whirled around, startled, and the same polished voice said, 'Is that her now?'

'I'll check. Wait here, please,' a deeper voice replied.

A moment later a man came out of the double doors. His thick blond hair gleamed in the afternoon sun. He had a high forehead and very tan skin. He wore chinos and a baby-blue polo shirt with a cream-colored sweater draped casually over broad shoulders.

'Kendall?' He looked puzzled, but then his eyes landed on me. And that's when I knew he was my father. His eyes were the same dark green as mine, but the giveaway was the off-center cleft in his chin – just like Kendall's and mine. And a million other little things: the sharpness of his cheekbones, the curve of his nose. He was like a masculine version of me.

I think he knew it too. The blood drained right out of his face.

He looked totally rattled, but he forced a smile and stuck out a hand to shake mine, and then Derek's.

'Oh, hello. I didn't know Kendall had friends over.' He turned to Kendall. 'Honey, I have KOMO-TV in there waiting to do an interview with me. Why don't you take your friends to the game room?'

'Don't you want me to introduce you?' Kendall said, her face bright with deceit.

Gavin looked taken aback.

She introduced us with an exaggerated gesture. 'Olivia, this is my dad, Gavin Montgomery. Dad, these are my friends Olivia and Derek. Olivia and I saw each other at the University of Washington a few months ago and we were like, "Oh my God, we look so much alike. What are the chances of that?" So I invited her over.'

Kendall tossed an arm around me like we were best friends. I looked at her, totally confused. What the *hell* was going on?

'I thought *you* especially would want to meet her,' Kendall added, pinning Gavin with a mocking look.

His smile faded for the first time since he'd walked into the room, and a muscle in his jaw started to tick. He clenched and unclenched his hands rapidly.

Right then I realized two things.

One: Kendall had lied to me. Her dad didn't know anything about this meeting.

And two: I'd been set up. The blue of the KOMO logo on the van outside should've been my first clue. If I'd been paying more attention instead of being so focused on meeting Gavin, I would've figured it out sooner.

Even I knew that if a story about a politician's illegitimate kid got out when reporters were there, it would hit the news hard and fast.

Kendall is using me to ruin her father's career.

Gavin grasped Kendall's elbow roughly and dragged her down the hall. The mask was gone and any pretense of being nice with it.

'Come with me,' he growled over his shoulder.

We obeyed, following Gavin and Kendall down a long hallway into a grand kitchen filled with stainless steel appliances and state-of-the-art cooking technology. Skylights lined the ceiling, and floor-to-ceiling windows showed a perfectly manicured emerald lawn sloping gently to sparkling Lake Washington. A dock jutted out from the private beach, bumped gently by a luxury speedboat.

Gavin let go of Kendall's arm and whirled to face us.

'Don't you want to know who she is, Dad?' Kendall smirked at him.

'I don't really c –'

'This is Olivia *Knight*,' she interrupted, emphasizing my last name, and his eyes swung to mine.

Derek edged closer to me, grasped my hand tightly in his. I swallowed hard and looked down. I couldn't meet Gavin's eyes because I knew if I did I'd feel smaller. I'd feel so small I'd disappear and never finish this mission I was on.

Gavin was silent. When I finally glanced at him, his face was pinched, as if he were working out a very hard math problem in his head.

'I'm sorry. I didn't know KOMO would be here, I swear,' I burst out. I didn't want him to hate me. 'I'm not trying to get you in any trouble. I just wanted to meet you.'

My voice wobbled and my throat closed. I was dangerously close to tears.

Kendall gave me a dirty look, as if I'd just tattled on her.

Gavin took a step closer, his nostrils flaring. Derek's hand tightened in mine, his body rigid. An icy claw of fear scraped the back of my neck as I remembered Mom's reaction to seeing him on TV.

'Why did you want to meet me?' he asked tightly.

'Duh, Dad.' Kendall rolled her eyes like the whole exchange was boring. 'Because she thinks you're her daddy dearest.'

My face blazed with humiliation, and a sudden hurtling anger expanded inside me. I wanted to punch Kendall in the face.

'Let's go, Olivia,' Derek said quietly.

He tugged on my hand, but I refused to budge. I hadn't done anything wrong. This guy had nothing on me. Maybe he frightened Mom with his size and his wealth and his steely glare, but he didn't intimidate me. That was the old Olivia, the Olivia who let people get away with murder just to be nice.

I lifted my eyes and glared at Gavin, trapped his gaze in mine. The air tightened between us, the balance of power wavering just slightly before Gavin burst out laughing.

The sound startled me.

'Is that what Kendall told you?' he asked. 'That I'm your *father*?' His voice was filled with such consternation and, worse, pity, that I actually doubted myself for a minute.

He crossed the kitchen and opened the fridge, pulled out a can of Coke, snapped it open, and took a long sip. He didn't offer anybody else one. He set the can on the kitchen island next to Kendall and shook his head, tsking.

'How old are you?' he asked, arching an eyebrow at me.

'I'll be seventeen next week.'

'Well, there you go.' Gavin's grin widened. 'I wasn't even in America then. My wife and I were in Italy.'

He took a long pull of Coke and then shook his head. 'I'm sorry you've been dragged into my daughter's little game – Olivia, is it? She tends to enjoy playing out her fantasies. Her latest is a desire to have a sister. It looks like we might need to put her back in therapy.'

Back in therapy?

'What the fuck!' Kendall leapt up from where she was leaning against the kitchen island. 'That's such a lie! You were only in Italy later. This girl genuinely wants to find her dad, and you just might be him. You obviously fucked her mom in Portage Point.'

'Watch your mouth, Kendall,' Gavin said sharply.

'All you care about is your career!' she shouted, her face mottled red with anger. '*Look* at her!' She gestured at me. 'Look at me. We look the same. *All* of us do!'

'Stop it, Kendall!' Gavin snapped, his nostrils flaring. 'I have an interview to do, and you will *not* ruin it for me.'

He took a deep breath and seemed to compose himself. The pleasant, unruffled smile returned to his face, and he looked at me with unmistakable pity in his eyes.

'I'm truly sorry if you're trying to find your dad,' he said. 'I'm sure Kendall hasn't helped with all this. But I'm not your father. Now, I think it's best you go.'

× × ×

242

I didn't realize I was shaking until we were back in the car and driving toward the freeway.

Thoughts scuttled around my brain, too fast to focus on. I couldn't figure out what exactly had just happened. And why. Only that Kendall had set me up. I felt sick and betrayed.

'I'm done,' I finally said. 'You're totally right. I'm going to tell my mom the truth. She'll freak out, but whatever. What's the point of this anyway? I don't want to waste another second on that man.'

Derek glanced at me. 'You sure?' Something mischievous glinted in his eye.

'I think so. Why?'

Derek pulled an empty Coke can from his coat.

'I took this from the kitchen.' He darted another glance at me. 'Gavin was drinking from it. You can send this in to a lab and get DNA evidence. You'll know for sure whether he's your dad or not. And once you know that, once you have actual evidence, he'll have to tell you the truth. About everything.'

28

ABI

november

It had started raining so Anthony and I decided to drive to the Stokeses' rather than walk. By the time we pulled up, night had fallen in earnest, a cool velvety mist blanketing the suburban road.

Anthony parked across the street and turned off the engine. He scraped one hand over his beard uncertainly, then said, 'Do you mind if I do the talking with Madison? I know you've known her practically her whole life, but I've done a lot of interviews. I know how to get information out of people. Will you trust me?'

I looked at him, traced with my eyes the lines that life had left on him. Like my own, they were the scars, the residue of loss.

Hadn't Anthony proved I could trust him? And anyway, maybe you could never know all someone's hidden sides – like an apeirogon, a polygon that looked, on the surface, like a circle, but with an infinite number of sides.

I touched his hand, skimmed the warmth with my fingertips, and raised my eyes to his. I felt the connection between us tighten a notch.

'I trust you,' I said.

Anthony smiled, an ironic quirk of his lips. 'My wife used to say that.'

'You're married?' I drew back, shock rippling through me. There had been no sign of a wife at his house, no picture of domestic bliss. I'd assumed he was a confirmed bachelor and caretaker.

'Sorry, my ex-wife,' he clarified with a wry grin. 'She's somebody else's wife now.' He chuckled, but it sounded forced. 'She couldn't deal with my job. Said I was too invested in my clients. And when my mom moved in . . .' He lifted his shoulders. 'She wanted me to put her in a home. Maybe it would've been better to do it back then.'

He looked sad for a second, his eyes haunted.

'You did what was right for your mom at that point in time. You'll never regret the time you've had with her.'

Anthony smiled at me then, a wide smile. It lit up his whole face, turning his pale eyes an arresting shade of bottle green, like the color that budded on the stems of a winter tree. He pushed a hand through his hair and blew out a breath.

'Thanks, Abi.'

We got out of the car and crossed the soggy front lawn to the porch. It was colder than usual for this time of year. Jen opened the door, her face pale and drawn. She was wearing black yoga pants and a form-fitting pink T-shirt. She looked surprised, but hid it well – the poker face of a doctor.

'Abi!' Her eyes darted between Anthony and me, and she gave me a quick, one-armed hug. She smelled like baby-powder deodorant and something sharper, the stale stink of cigarette smoke.

'Why don't you come in out of the rain?' she said.

She was trying to sound glad to see me, but I knew she wasn't. I'd brought my tragedy to her door. An acerbic anger sliced through me, burning away my ability to be intimidated. In its place was a brazen sort of courage, the sense that for the first time in my life, I didn't give a fuck what Jen Stokes thought of me.

'Good evening, Mrs Stokes,' Anthony said. 'I'm Anthony Bryant. I work with the Seattle Police Department. We'd like to ask your children a few questions.'

Jen paled. 'The Seattle Police Department?' Her eyebrows scrunched.

'Yes, we're looking into Olivia's case.'

'Olivia's case?' she asked faintly.

'We're following up on a few things,' Anthony replied.

'Mom?' I heard Madison's voice. 'Who is it?'

Jen exhaled loudly. 'Derek isn't here, but Madison's watching TV.'

She fixed me with a look that told me then and there our friendship would never be the same. 'I know things are really difficult for you, Abi, but please don't drag my children into this. They don't need to suffer too.'

I drew back, stung. I hadn't spoken to Madison or Derek since –

My mind tripped and froze.

Derek.

Could the mysterious D on Olivia's phone be Derek?

My stomach tightened. Before I could reply, Jen turned on her heel, heading through the living room to the den, where Madison was slumped on the couch watching a rerun of *Game of Thrones*. Madison's eyes were bloodshot, as if she hadn't stopped crying in weeks. Her dark hair was a bird's nest of tangles. She bit a corner of her mouth that was already ragged and bloody and stared at me, her eyes fathomless pits of despair.

Anthony moved past Jen to sit on the couch next to Madison, while I leaned against the wall by the TV and watched them.

'Hello, Madison,' he said. 'I'd like to talk to you about Olivia.'

'Sure.' Madison looked at her mother, but picked up the remote and turned the TV off.

'Did Olivia seem different at all, upset about anything, before she fell?'

'No. She seemed fine.'

'Okay. Did she tell you about the picture messages she was getting?'

'Messages? I saw one psycho one, that's it.'

'When was that?'

'Dunno. June?'

'Did she say who she thought it was from?'

Madison shook her head. 'No. It was more like, you know, a joke. It wasn't a big deal. Just somebody at school messing around. She never said anything about it again. . . .' Her voice trailed off.

'What about Tyler? Where was he the night Olivia fell?'

'At the barbecue.'

'The whole night?'

'Yeah. I mean, he didn't get here till, like, ten. But, yeah, he was there.'

'Why weren't you and Olivia speaking?'

Madison pressed her lips together and picked at a tiny piece of skin on her thumb. After a second the bit of skin broke loose from her thumb, and I watched as a drop of blood oozed from the nail. She brought her finger to her mouth, sucked the blood away.

'This is important, Madison. Not telling us makes it look like you're hiding something.'

Something played across her face, a pull of regret, maybe sadness, but she didn't answer. She just kept pulling at that hangnail, watching as more and more blood rolled along the crease of her fingers, pooling in the palm of her hand.

Anthony narrowed his eyes at her and changed tactics. 'What is your relationship with Olivia?'

Her chin jerked up and her eyes widened. She looked startled by the question. 'What do you mean? We're friends. Best friends.'

'More than friends?'

'Jesus Christ!' Jen exclaimed. She pushed herself away from the door and crossed in two angry strides to stand like an enraged bull next to Anthony. 'I've had just about enough.'

Madison started to shake. 'No,' she breathed. 'No way! It wasn't like that with us.'

Anthony ignored Jen. 'Okay.' He changed direction fast. 'But your brother, now, he was maybe more than friends with her. How did you feel about that?'

Madison stared at him defiantly, her jaw thrust out, her lip quivering slightly.

Anthony leaned toward her so he was directly in Madison's face.

'Did you push Olivia off that bridge?' His eyes blazed, his voice harsh.

'That's enough!' Jen roared. 'You need to go. Now!'

Anthony ignored her. He kept his eyes fixed on Madison, whose face crumpled as she started to sob.

'No!' Madison cried, ignoring her mother. 'No, I would *never* hurt Olivia. She's my best friend, okay? Fine, yes, we had a fight and we weren't talking, but it wasn't forever or anything. We would've made up!'

'Stop this now!' Jen shouted. 'Or I'll call my lawyer.'

'No, Mom, it's okay,' Madison said. She sniffed and shook her head. 'If somebody hurt Olivia, I want to help.'

'Why did you and Olivia fight?' I took over, playing good cop.

'Because.' Madison's eyes were shiny with tears, little drops of agony pouring from her eyes. 'Because she lied to me about Derek. She never told me she was with him. I mean, she lied to everybody about everything. Even you.'

She pinned me with a look that somehow conveyed both her disgust and her pity. 'You thought she was such a good little girl, going to school, going to swimming, then straight home to do her homework. But she fooled you. Every day, right under your nose, she was here fucking my brother.'

'What are you talking about?' I whispered.

Madison laughed harshly. 'She hated your rules. She just didn't have the guts to tell you. She was tired of being a good girl. Did you know she quit swimming? And she quit her job volunteering at the nursing home before she even started? It was easier to lie. And I thought it was fine until she lied to me too. That was the last straw.'

'Did you know she was pregnant?' Anthony asked.

'No.' Madison shook her head, her lank, unwashed hair swinging around her face. 'I swear I didn't. All I knew was she chose Derek over me, and I hated it. I felt . . . betrayed by her. But I didn't hurt her. I swear. Last time I saw her, she was walking home.'

Anthony's phone rang just then and he stood quickly.

'Excuse me. I have to take this.'

He stepped into the hallway, and Madison eyed me warily.

'Did she tell you about Gavin?' I asked.

'Who?' Madison looked confused.

'Her dad.'

'No. What are you talking about?'

I struggled to process that. Olivia hadn't even told her best friend about finding her dad. Maybe it wasn't just me she'd closed herself off to in her final months.

'If there's anything you can remember –'

Jen interrupted again; her cold tone matched the look in her eyes. 'She's already told you everything she knows, Abi. I think it's time you left.'

'Abi?' Anthony said from the door. His eyes looked tense, strained. 'Ready to go?'

In the car Anthony buckled his seat belt, his mouth pinched angrily.

'That was the Seattle chief of police,' he said. 'He's just asked me to meet him in his office tomorrow.'

'Why?' I asked.

Anthony pulled onto the street, the tires spinning against the loose gravel as he punched the gas a little too hard. I glanced in the wing mirror. The downstairs light was on at the Stokeses' house, and a dark shadow moved across the curtains.

Derek was home.

Anthony's voice, coiled tight as a wire, cut through my disbelief. 'He wants to discuss allegations that I've been impersonating a police officer.'

I huffed out the name as if it were a cuss word: 'Gavin.'

'That was my first thought, too.'

29

OLIVIA

july

'Hello?' I pushed open the Stokeses' front door. I knew Madison was at the beach with Peter – I was meeting them there in a bit – but just in case, I thought I'd better be careful.

'Down here,' Derek called from his room.

I walked down the steps, and as I turned the corner, there was Derek holding a pink cake with blazing candles, a party hat tipped at an angle on his head. A goofy smile lit his handsome face.

'Happy birthday to you, happy birthday to you, happy birthday dear Olivia, happy birthday to you!' he sang.

I clapped my hands in delight and ran to him. 'You remembered!' I threw myself at him, and he deftly moved the cake out of the way, setting it on the edge of his dresser before I managed to dump it onto the ground.

'Wait, blow out the candles!' he said, laughing.

I made a wish – obviously for Derek to be in my life forever – then blew them out in two breaths, which was fine; everybody knew those wishes weren't real ones.

Derek leaned down and trapped my lips in a delicious kiss. 'How could I forget your birthday?' he murmured against my mouth.

His breath lifted the hairs of my neck as he trailed kisses from my ear to the hollow of my throat.

'Here.' He handed me a small, wrapped present. 'Open it.'

I unwrapped the pink paper and lifted the lid on the box. Inside was a tiny silver heart charm with our initials etched on either side.

'I know you always wear the bracelet your mom got you, so I thought you could add this charm to it.'

'I love it!'

I slipped the charm on the bracelet and threw myself at him so we went crashing backward onto the bed. He covered my face with tiny, gentle kisses, his breath warm against my skin. I looked in his eyes and felt like I was dreaming. But I was awake, and he was all I could see.

He made me feel whole, like there was nothing else I needed.

He pulled me close, tucked me tight against his chest. I knew I needed to meet Madison at the beach, but I didn't want to leave yet.

'I love you,' I whispered, tilting my head to look into his eyes.

He leaned down and kissed me on the nose. 'I love you more.'

We lay like that for a moment, and something passed between us that I would never forget.

My future.

For all my lack of attention to it earlier, the cake was beautiful. It had layers of chocolate cake and a pale pink frosting decorated with pastel balloons. Derek grabbed a wad of toilet paper from the bathroom and we used it as napkins as we ate giant wedges of cake with our bare hands.

'Toilet paper as a plate,' I joked. 'Classy.'

'Hey.' He laughed, bumping me with his shoulder. 'If it means I don't have to leave your sexy body to run upstairs and get plates and forks, I'm all for it.'

He swallowed and licked the frosting from his lips. 'So, what are your birthday plans today?'

'Well, I'm meeting Madison and Peter at the beach pretty soon, and then later my mom's taking me out to dinner at this fancy French restaurant in Seattle.'

'That's good. You said you wanted to go somewhere new, right?'

'Yeah, I'm just surprised 'cause she's always afraid to go into Seattle. Like it's this vortex of evil.'

'What made her change her mind?'

I shrugged. 'Dunno. But the really good news is she finally said I can get my license, so I've made an appointment to take my test next week. Yay!' I was so excited I accidentally squealed a little. 'Can I practice in your car?'

'Sure, as long as you don't crash it!' He elbowed me playfully.

I threw a pillow at him. 'I'm not that bad!'

Derek ducked and laughed just as my phone rang.

'Olivia?'

It was a strong, masculine voice. One I almost recognized but not quite.

'Yes?'

'This is Gavin Montgomery.'

'Oh, hi, Mr Montgomery.' I looked at Derek, stunned. He moved closer, and I held the phone away from my ear so he could listen too.

'I wanted to invite you to have lunch with Kendall and me today. I'm sorry I was short with you last week, and I thought lunch would be a perfect opportunity for the three of us to get to know each other a little better.'

My mind raced. Mom and I wouldn't go out for my birthday dinner until after she was off work. I'd have to come up with a good lie for why I couldn't go to the beach, but this was too perfect to miss.

'Works for me,' I said.

We arranged to meet at the Black Cat Diner in Laurelwood, and I hung up.

'Did you hear that?' I squealed. 'He wants to meet me! Maybe he'll tell me the truth now.'

Derek nodded and chewed a mouthful of cake, his eyes never leaving mine.

'What?' I wiped at my mouth self-consciously.

'Nothing.' He shook his head, his eyes gleaming hungrily.

'Did you hear what I said?'

'Yeah. We have another hour before we have to go.'

He reached and pulled me to him, and I smiled.

30

OLIVIA

july

Derek turned the Mustang into the Black Cat's parking lot and parked at the very back.

'Should I come in with you?' he asked.

I hesitated. 'If you don't mind, I'd like to talk to him on my own.'

Derek bit his cheek, and I could see the struggle playing out across his face. 'All right,' he said. 'But if you need anything, call me. I'll wait right here.'

I nodded, leaned across the console for a kiss, then got out and slammed the car door.

Inside, the diner was decorated in 1950s décor with black-and-white-checked linoleum and shiny chrome fittings. Candy-red booths lined the perimeter, while high-seated chrome tables filled the center. Pictures of Elvis, Marilyn Monroe, Clark Gable, and a series of other famous '50s actors dotted the walls. 'I Get Around' by the Beach Boys sang dimly on the speakers. I wanted to laugh out loud.

A handful of customers were eating burgers dripping with grease and thick, yellow fries. Gavin was already there, sitting in a back corner booth hunched over a steaming cup of coffee. He was wearing a black trench coat with the collar flipped up and a blue Mariners hat pulled low over his forehead. He looked ridiculous.

Kendall was nowhere to be seen.

I stopped in the entrance, a sinking feeling twisting in my gut. Suddenly I understood. Kendall wasn't here, and I'd bet every one of my swim trophies she didn't even know we were meeting.

I tossed my bag onto the seat and scooted into the booth so I was facing Gavin. He looked at me, that creepy, wide smile stretched across his mouth. Before he could speak, the waitress came over. She had zits and braces, lanky black hair, and black, loose-fitting clothes under a dirty black work apron. A shadow of disgust passed over Gavin's face, but he looked away quickly.

'Just a Coke,' I said, catching her eye and smiling. I hoped she hadn't seen Gavin's look. She disappeared and returned with a frothy glass of Coke a minute later.

'So –' Gavin began.

'Kendall isn't here, is she?' I interrupted.

Gavin looked at me over the rim of his coffee cup as if every person he dealt with was so dumb, and he was so superior, he couldn't help but be surprised when somebody actually had half a brain cell.

'No.'

'You lied to me.'

He laughed, a dry, horsy sound. 'Get used to it. Everybody lies. It's just a question of degree.'

'Lies are for cowards and thieves. I'm neither, so let's cut the bullshit. Are you my dad?'

I was done being little miss nice girl. It hadn't worked so far, and all I wanted was the truth so I could move on with my life. I needed to know why Mom had lied about him.

Gavin choked on a gulp of coffee and dabbed daintily at his chin.

'Okay.' He recovered smoothly. 'No, of course not. And if we're dispensing with formalities, I'll just say I want you to stay away from my daughter. She's in a very fragile state of recovery right now and I don't want you upsetting her.'

'Recovery?'

Gavin tilted his head and studied me. 'Kendall's a very troubled girl. She had a complete meltdown last year and tried to swallow a bottle of oxycodone. We had to have her committed for her own safety. I'm guessing she never told you?'

I struggled to keep my face blank. Was he telling the truth? I couldn't imagine sassy, confident Kendall in a mental hospital, but there was something just slightly . . . unbalanced about her. She was the kind of girl you'd worry would stab you in the back if you took your eye off her for too long.

'Well, it's true,' he said. 'And then it was rehab and then months of therapy. So all this drama isn't good for her. I'm afraid it'll set her off again and she'll end up right back in the hospital.'

He pulled a checkbook and a pen out of his coat pocket and started writing.

'Kendall's on a mission to destroy me,' he continued. He shook his head. 'Maybe she's not getting enough attention, or maybe I spoil her, I don't know. But right now her mother and I need to take care of her.'

He pushed the check toward me, but I refused to look at it.

'You want to *pay* me to stay away from Kendall?' I said, stunned.

'If you want to look at it that way, then yes. It's for Kendall's own good. And yours.'

I exhaled, then reached up and pulled my hair back into a messy knot, then crossed my arms over my chest and assessed Gavin.

'So actually, you're paying me to disappear so nobody finds out I might be your daughter.'

Gavin didn't answer. He pushed the check toward me. I peered at it. The zeros at the end made my spit stick in my throat. It was enough for college. Enough so my mom wouldn't have to scrimp and save so much, always worrying about my future.

'Go on, take it,' he encouraged me. 'I know you'll be smart about it. You seem like you have a good head on your shoulders.'

I scowled at him. If I had a good head on my shoulders, it was because of my mom.

And right then I realized that whatever had happened between her and Gavin must've been really bad. She must've hidden the truth to protect me.

I ignored the check and leaned back against the cherry-red vinyl. It was cold against my bare neck.

'Is this what you did to my mom when she got pregnant?' I asked. 'Did you pay her to "take care of it"?'

'You don't know what you're talking about. Take the check and leave this alone.'

'Fuck you,' I spat, leaning forward sharply. The words felt foreign on my tongue, poisonous, fizzing like a chemical that belonged under the sink.

Gavin looked surprised, but covered it well.

'You know when I met you last week,' I said, 'you were drinking a can of Coke. Well, I took that can, and do you want to know where it is now?'

Gavin looked confused, so I barreled on: 'It's at a DNA lab along with a swab from my mouth. So you might as well tell me the truth now. Otherwise, when I get the results back saying you're my father – and they will say you are – I'll take them straight to KOMO-TV. I wonder how that would look for your precious image? Especially since it's an election year.'

Gavin's lips tightened.

'Or is it your wife you're really worried about?' I taunted him cruelly. Somewhere inside my brain I was wondering who this new person was. She didn't sound like me at all. 'That's what Kendall thinks. She said you're scared of losing her money. Either way, she'll find out too. So why don't you just cut the bullshit and tell me the truth.'

Gavin's nostrils flared and his eyes narrowed. The smarmy smile he'd had on his face since I first arrived dropped and I realized it was a mask, a façade disguising the real Gavin Montgomery, who wasn't as charming or as powerful as he liked to think.

'Fine. You want to know the truth?' His lip curled slightly. 'Yes, you're my daughter. But it doesn't change anything.'

I sagged back in my seat. Suddenly, surprisingly, I wished he'd said no. It was much easier to love the father of my imagination. There was nothing to love about the man in front of me.

'Look,' he continued, as if he hadn't just cast my childish hopes and dreams into a pile of nuclear waste. 'I had an affair with your mom right before I got married and I didn't want my fiancée to find out. So I gave your mom some money to get an abortion.'

I looked at him and felt empty inside. I'd wanted to find my dad, to fill this dad-shaped hole in me. And instead I'd found him. He'd ruined the image of a dad I'd built over the years: a hero who might be capable of loving me. In reality, he was much smaller, more imperfect than what I'd created in my head.

'What happened then?' I asked. 'What'd you do?'

He shrugged. 'Nothing. She told me it was done. She said she'd gotten the abortion, and I went back to Seattle. That was the last I heard of her until you showed up on my doorstep.'

The pieces slowly slotted into place. Mom must've told him she'd get an abortion and then, lucky for me, changed her mind.

He'd underestimated her. People did that a lot. But my mom was strong, stronger than people gave her credit for. And she *was* remarkable. Raising me all by herself was remarkable. She gave me everything she never had just because she loved me. Every single day of my life I'd always known that she was proud of me and that I could do whatever I wanted with my life.

'You sent her a card,' I said. '"*Sorry.*" Why'd you send her that?'

'I sent her flowers after I thought she had the abortion. I knew she didn't want to do it, but I couldn't risk her having a baby. It could've messed everything up. My career, my future, my relationship with my fiancée. I did feel bad, but . . .' He shrugged, a dismissive 'what other choice did I have?' movement.

He was arrogant enough to believe a five-letter word could

make up for what he'd tried to force her to do. I made a sound of disgust in the back of my throat.

'You make me sick.'

'Look, I was sorry then, and I'm sorry now. I can't be your father. I'm offering you a lot of money, Olivia. Just take it and walk away.'

Gavin again pushed the check toward me, smiling that smile that I knew was supposed to charm me. His voice was kind, but it was as fake as the tan staining his cheeks.

I stared at him, repulsed.

'What did you say to make her lie to you about the abortion? You must've said something to make her *hide* from you,' I blurted. 'Did you say you'd take the money back? Did you tell her that you'd hurt her? That you'd hurt *me*?'

His eyes flashed, and I knew I was right.

'That's it, isn't it?!' I shook my head, horrified. 'You threatened to hurt me, *your* unborn baby, if your fiancée ever found out. So Mom told you she'd done it, and then she hid from you because she was scared of what you might do. She never told me about you, by the way. She said my dad died in a car accident when she was pregnant with me. I only started questioning it when I met Kendall. Mom was protecting me from *you*.'

I pressed the tip of my pointer finger onto the check and pushed it back to him, a bitter, metallic loathing rising in my throat.

'I don't want your money.'

I swallowed back an unexpected rush of emotion. I suddenly wanted to tell my mom everything. I'd tell her about the mess I'd caused and this useless, exasperating truth mission I'd been on to find this waste of space of a man. I never should have hidden it from her anyway.

'My mom is worth a million of you.' I scooted out of the booth and glared at him. He looked suddenly small and insignificant, disbelief creasing his face. I wondered how often people stood up to him. 'Don't worry, I won't tell your wife or the media. I'd be mortified if people found out we were related. Poor Kendall, having to grow up with you. No wonder she's so messed up; you're a monster.'

And with that parting shot, I grabbed my bag and speed-walked out of the diner.

× × ×

In the car I refused to talk about it with Derek. I needed to make sense of it in my own head first. I was angry, but also really, really sad. I would never have a relationship with my dad; not the one I wanted anyway. Real or imagined, I'd lost something today.

Fortunately, Derek seemed to understand and he didn't press me for more information. He dropped me off at home, and I promised to call him later.

I didn't have much time to think about Gavin before Mom came home, and we rushed to get ready so we wouldn't be late for our reservations for my birthday dinner.

Mom parked across the street from Marché Marché, Seattle's iconic French restaurant, so we wouldn't have to pay for valet parking. She made me stay in my seat while she opened the car door for me.

'M'lady.' She doffed a pretend top hat and bent in a grand sweeping bow.

I giggled. 'Why, thank you,' I joked with a little curtsy.

We crossed the road and climbed the sweeping steps to Marché Marché. The restaurant was housed in a stunning stone building just outside of Seattle. It overlooked Puget Sound, the lights of Bainbridge Island twinkling like a pearl necklace in the distance.

'Mom, this place is amazing!' I whispered.

She chuckled. 'So good they named it twice.'

Uniformed men in funny black berets held the front doors open, and a pencil-thin hostess with blonde hair pinned back in an elegant chignon greeted us. While Mom gave her our name, I looked around the restaurant.

Off to the right, a sign saying ComCore Tech Republican Fundraiser pointed toward a hallway that disappeared into what I presumed was a private dining room.

I swung my eyes to the left and gasped. The main dining room was absolutely gorgeous. A high, intricately coffered ceiling soared over a mosaic floor, detailed moldings, and floor-to-ceiling Renaissance-style murals. Elegant chandeliers dripping with hundreds of tiny crystals cast a soft light over the polished mahogany tables and cream linens. I felt like I'd walked into a painting from the nineteenth century.

We followed the hostess to a quiet corner table in the main dining room. Just a few feet away, a fire cheerfully sparked in the pale stone fireplace.

'Seriously, wow!' I said once we were seated.

'It is pretty spectacular,' Mom agreed, looking around.

'I didn't think we'd really come to Seattle,' I admitted.

'You said you wanted to go somewhere else for your birthday.'

'I know, but you're always, like, kinda scared of going to Seattle and all.'

'Is that what you think?' She looked dismayed.

'Well, yeah.' I bit my lip, afraid I'd hurt her feelings.

She put a hand to her throat, then her mouth. 'I'm so sorry.'

'For what?'

'For everything.' Her eyes were glossy and damp, her chin trembling ever so slightly. 'For all the wrong things I've done as a mother. Being a parent is one long process of daring yourself to let go. It's like I always have this instinct to never let you out of my sight, but I know I need to teach you to be confident and independent on your own. Sometimes it feels like an impossible tightrope to walk. I'm not very good at it.'

'Mom! Don't say that!' I reached across the table and grabbed her hand, as upset by her words as by her display of emotion.

I didn't think I'd ever seen Mom cry. She just wasn't a very emotional person. It was why I hadn't told her about this crazy, complicated thing with Derek and Tyler. I didn't think she'd understand.

'When you have a baby' – she swallowed hard and looked at our hands – 'you just want to do everything right.'

Her words looped around my heart, pulling so tight I could barely breathe.

'You did great, Mom. I promise. You've done everything right.' I tried to smile, but my throat was closing and a tear rolled down my cheek. She wiped away the moisture with the pad of her thumb.

She inhaled deeply and said, 'Okay, I've got a good one.'

I sniffed. 'Go on, then.'

'Knock knock.'

'Who's there?'

'Britney Spears.'

'Britney Spears who?'

'Oops, I did it again!'

'Ha!' I snorted loudly, and a handful of diners turned to look at us.

'Shhhh!' She giggled and squeezed my hand. 'My girl. I can't believe you're going to be a senior. Pretty soon you'll be leaving for college!'

'I'll still be around,' I said. 'You know you're going to be fine on your own without me, right?'

'I know. I'll miss you like crazy, though.'

'Maybe you'll start dating.'

'Ha!' She laughed. 'Not likely!'

'Why not? You could date. You're not old. You're pretty. Even Tyler thinks so.'

'Not MILF pretty. Just regular pretty,' she joked.

'Eww! Mo-om! How do you even know that word?'

'I'm hip with the lingo.'

'Oh God, make it stop,' I groaned, but laughed too. 'Well, at least the house'll be clean. You'll love that. No dirty tennis shoes in the living room, no milk rings on the counters. You'll be in OCD heaven.'

She laughed, and the clot of worry in my chest eased a bit. She'd be fine.

'You deserve your happy ending, Mom.'

'Thanks, sweetie.' She touched my hand. 'You too.'

Maybe it was because I'd met Gavin and learned the truth, but right then I felt ridiculously grateful that things had worked out the way they did. Knowing what I knew now just made me appreciate Mom even more. I didn't want to ruin our evening with talking about that jerk.

We talked about everything else late into the evening, the light gradually changing to an aubergine-pewter color that draped around the restaurant as we ate. Waiters scurried around, lighting candles in small crystal bowls, dropping off bottles of champagne with giant buckets of ice, and chatting easily with the customers.

'All right, one passionfruit crème brûlée with two spoons,' our waiter announced, placing the decadent-looking dessert in the middle of the table.

'Yum!' I exclaimed. 'Mom, look, there's a little flower on it!' I plucked the exotic purple flower up and held it out for her to see. But her gaze was fixed on a spot over my shoulder near the restaurant entrance. Her face had drained of all color.

'Mom?' I glanced over my shoulder. 'Are you okay?'

It took me a second, but then I saw what she was looking at.

Gavin.

He was with a tall, beautiful blonde woman wearing a tailored, fire-engine-red business suit, the skirt slim and knee-length. She had very white teeth, milk-pale skin, and almond-shaped eyes above a straight, Grecian nose. She looked like she could run companies, compete in triathlons, conquer nations. She had to be Gavin's wife.

The woman smiled and said something in Gavin's ear, then rested her arm on his as they followed the hostess past the fundraising sign to the private dining room at the back of the restaurant.

A sharp pain skewered my stomach. What were the chances of him being here? I wanted to laugh at the absurdity of it. Maybe he'd followed me. But I couldn't imagine why. Seattle wasn't that big of a city, and he was obviously going to a fundraiser. It must be just a weird coincidence.

Maybe this whole time that's what Mom was afraid of: not that Seattle was so dangerous, but that here she ran the very real risk of running into him. This was Gavin's turf, after all. If he saw her, she risked her lie being exposed, and coming here wasn't something Mom would ever have done if it weren't for me whining like a baby to get out of Portage Point for my birthday.

I felt desperately guilty, my mind a washing machine of muddled thoughts.

'So, I'm thinking about breaking up with Tyler,' I babbled, trying to distract her. 'I mean, what happens when we go to college? We might not even go to the same one. And he's being totally weird since his parents split up. He's, like, scary mad about it.'

That seemed to do the trick. Mom's eyes swung to mine, and she pinned me with her sternest look.

'Wait.' She held a hand up and shook her head. 'He scares you? Why?'

'Well, not scares exactly,' I backtracked. 'You know, just, he's not as fun or laid-back as he used to be.'

That was all the permission Mom needed. She chatted away

about the pros and cons, mostly cons, of being with Tyler at this point in my life, and how my future was the most important thing and tying myself down to a boyfriend would limit my options.

I'd heard it all before, but I pretended to listen as if it were the first time. It appeared to be working. She seemed to have completely forgotten about Gavin. But I certainly hadn't.

I suddenly realized I couldn't tell her about Gavin. She'd stuck around, no matter how real shit got. She cheered me on at swim meets and washed my dirty socks and made sure I did my homework, and she scrimped and saved so I could go to a good college. She drove me to my friends' houses so I'd stay safe, and she never, ever judged me about anything.

I'd rewarded her utter love and devotion by looking for my dad. I couldn't tell her. She might think she wasn't enough for me. It was my turn to protect her.

I looked at her face, as familiar as my own. *She* was my family. Family, I realized, was like a box of puzzle pieces. They filled all the holes of your life with little pieces that all together made you whole. I didn't need my dad to do that.

So I sealed the truth and kept it buried deep inside my heart. The truth, after all, only mattered as much as you allowed it to.

31

ABI

november

The tires of Anthony's car crunched on the gravel as he pulled up to my house. We hadn't said a word since he'd told me the Seattle police chief wanted to meet to discuss allegations he'd been impersonating a police officer. We were absorbed in our own worlds.

'I'm going back to the Stokeses',' I said as the car rolled to a stop.

'Why?' he asked.

'Jen lied to us. Derek's light was on, and I need to talk to him.'

Anthony blew out a breath and rubbed his forehead. 'I need to go home, check on my mom. Call the chief. Can it wait until tomorrow?'

I shook my head. 'I don't know what's going to happen now. Gavin's obviously gotten to everybody. I have to stop him.'

'It's gonna be okay. I can fix this.'

'You can't fix everything, Anthony.'

I moved to get out of the car, but Anthony touched my arm.

'Are you sure you don't want me to come with?' His eyes scanned my face, concerned.

'Absolutely. You need to call the police chief. I'll be fine.'

I shut the door and walked to my car. I'd gotten Anthony in enough trouble. I could do this on my own.

The inky cloak of night covered the sky as I drove. The road was clear. Only the odd car passed me, its headlights sweeping a path in the darkened sky. Jagged trees lined the road, pointing into the night and casting patchy shadows around the orange orbs of the streetlights.

I flicked my headlights off as I pulled onto the Stokeses' street, parking a few houses away. I shut the door quietly and ducked into the shadows along the perimeter of the house.

I felt in the dark for the gate latch, which lifted easily, then followed the curvature of the yard to the back, my shoes squelching in the sodden grass.

I tapped lightly on the back door. When Derek answered, he looked awful. His face was devoid of all color, unless you counted the black smudges under his red-rimmed eyes. His clothes hung off his already lanky form. A sour smell came from him, as if he hadn't showered in weeks.

'Abi,' he said dully.

He turned, and I followed him inside.

He was playing a video game on a massive wide-screen TV. It was one of those first-person-point-of-view games, someone carrying a sniper rifle. The sniper was perched on the edge of a cliff, the crosshairs fixed on a group of snarling zombies below.

'Derek,' I said. 'We need to talk about Olivia.'

He ignored me and kept playing.

'I know you're the baby's father.'

It was just a hunch, but Derek paused the game and sat utterly still for a moment, his head hanging heavy on his neck. His rapid breathing was the only sound in the deep silence.

'Why are you here?' he rasped harshly.

'Did you push Olivia?'

Derek spun to face me, his eyes wide. Now that he was looking at me, I could see they glistened with unshed tears. 'What?! No! I *love* her!' He shook his head and blinked furiously. '*Loved* her.'

'You *are* the baby's father, though, right?'

He nodded.

'Did you know she was pregnant?'

I sat on the matching brown leather chair next to him, wedging my body sideways so I was facing him.

He put the controller on the console between the two chairs. 'Yeah. She told me at the barbecue. I didn't know what to say. I'd had a few beers and I think it muddled my head. I was . . . in shock. We were careful, you know?'

'Did Tyler know?'

'I don't know. She never said. They'd already finished by then.'

'She broke up with him?'

'I guess.'

I froze. Tyler had never told me they'd broken up. Had he? I shook my head, unable to remember.

'Why didn't she tell anybody about the two of you?'

'First because of Tyler – she didn't want to hurt his feelings.

Then there was Madison. . . . I kept bugging her about it. I hated it being a secret, you know? When she told me she was pregnant, I –'

He dropped his head into his hands and started crying, his shoulders heaving soundlessly.

I watched him, feeling inexplicably disappointed. I wanted the culprit to be him. But could this broken, damaged person be to blame?

'You knew she was trying to find her father, right? Why didn't you stop her?'

He rubbed his eyes with the palms of his hands. 'It wasn't my call. It was hers. Besides, I would never tell her what to do.'

Whether it was intended as criticism or not, I felt his words slice like arrows through my heart. I held the pain inside, my body trembling.

'Why didn't you come forward when the police were investigating?' I said after a minute.

'I gave them my statement.'

'You didn't tell them the baby's yours!' I exclaimed.

'It wouldn't have changed anything!' Under the TV's garish lights, his skin looked gray. 'Anyway, I've seen *CSI*. I'm not stupid. They'd think I was the one who hurt her or something, and I didn't.'

I stared at the TV, the scope of an assault rifle frozen on the massive screen.

'How did she even find out about Gavin?' I asked.

'She met this girl on some school away day. Kendall. She looked just like her, only Kendall is crazy. Like, really just cuckoo. Ken-

273

dall invited Olivia over to meet Gavin, but it turned out Kendall had set us up. Or maybe she was just trying to set Gavin up. That's what I mean by crazy. She's always plotting and sneaking around. When we got to their house, there were all these reporters there. It was weird.'

I remembered the tension that had vibrated between Kendall and Gavin the day I met her. The girl had serious daddy issues.

'A week later, Gavin called Olivia and asked if she wanted to go to lunch. I drove her to Laurelwood, and they met at that diner there. I waited in the car, and while I was there I saw Kendall. She sneaked up to the diner windows and watched them talk, then she went back to her car and just sat there staring at the diner. And a few minutes later she drove off.'

'She followed Gavin there?'

Derek nodded.

'Did you tell Olivia?'

'Yeah. Later.'

'What did she say?'

'She told me Kendall was in the hospital for a while after trying to kill herself. And she'd gone through drug rehab. Like I said – cuckoo.'

'Did you tell the police?'

'Of course.' He seemed impatient with the question. 'I told them they should talk to Kendall. I thought maybe, you know, *she* pushed Olivia. The guy who took my statement said somebody would get in touch with me, but they never did.'

The thought slid into me like liquid mercury. Maybe Kendall had sent the pictures to Olivia. A mentally unstable teenager, jealous of her father paying attention to his other daughter. The child-ish scribblings on the pictures; the repeated threats: *die, kill, bitch!* It would make a disturbed sort of sense.

I stood, and Derek did too. His voice, when he spoke, sounded weary and hollow. 'Is she – will she really never wake up?'

I shook my head, my throat thickening.

'No. She doesn't have any brain activity.'

The words were like a million knives scraping across my throat. It was the first time I'd said it out loud. The first time, I think, that I'd really let the truth settle on me.

'The doctors have only kept her alive because of the baby. That's what they're focusing on now.'

I heard the sharp intake of breath, and I wrapped my arms around Derek as he sobbed.

'Is it . . . will it . . . ?'

'The baby's fine,' I assured him. 'It's a little girl. She's healthy and growing fast.'

Derek turned and walked to his chair, collapsing like a pile of laundry. His face was stark and angular, with none of the softness I remembered. He looked at me, his eyes sunken pools of anguish. 'Can I see her?'

'Derek, she's your daughter. You don't have to ask.'

Knowing I might lose Olivia's baby to Derek was a crushing realization: another loss to endure. But a child needed its father. I knew that better than most.

I turned to go, my hand on the door handle, when my eyes skated over something that made my heart stop. It winked at me from the edge of his dresser. Something silver and instantly familiar.

I stared at it, my mind scrambling to piece together its meaning.

Olivia's bracelet.

My mind flashed to that last day at the barbecue. It had sparkled on her wrist as she ran a hand through her newly cropped hair. Detective Samson had said they never found it. I'd thought it had gotten lost when she fell, the clasp perhaps snapping somehow.

I reached for the bracelet, my legs like jelly, and picked it up. I held the cool, slippery metal and fingered the clasp. It wasn't broken. That meant it had been taken off Olivia's wrist. A chill whispered over my skin and goose bumps sprang up along my arms.

I spun around to Derek.

'Where did you get this?' I said, something awful coiling in my brain, like a snake, tongue darting and ready to strike. 'Why is this in your room? Did you take it from her?'

Derek's eyes widened, horror filling the white spaces there.

'No!' He lifted his palms. 'No, I swear! I didn't take it. My mom gave it to me. The day after Olivia fell. She said it must've fallen off Olivia's wrist at the barbecue. She told me to keep it for her.'

'It didn't *fall* off! Look! The clasp isn't broken!' I shook it at him. 'And Olivia would *never* take it off!'

Olivia had been wearing the bracelet at the barbecue, but it was gone by the time I saw her in the hospital. I flashed back to that moment when Jen was in Olivia's room, her fists gripped tightly together, pressed against her stomach.

A spike of fury rose inside me, sharp as a knife stabbing into the soft skin of my stomach. It was weird, anger this intense. Maybe it was just my brain's way of coping with it. I couldn't handle it all at once, so instead it came in waves, swirling like a hurricane.

I lunged for the stairs and threw myself up them two at a time.

'Jen!' I roared. I barreled past the kitchen's gleaming hardwood floors, the neatly arranged dining room, to the den at the back of the house. Jen was curled into a corner of the pale leather couch, a book in hand. Mark had his legs out, eyes on the TV.

'You conniving bitch!' I shouted, rage filling every fiber of my being, making me feel suddenly huge and powerful. I was no longer the meek and timid woman intimidated by their wealth, their status, their self-assurance. A crazed sort of fury had burned that woman up, turned her into ashes that disappeared in the wind.

Jen and Mark jumped to their feet, confused by my sudden appearance.

'Abi –' Jen said, her eyes darting behind me.

'You took this from her, didn't you?' I crossed the room in giant strides until I was directly in front of Jen.

'Was it you? Did *you* push her? You couldn't stand the thought of a new woman in your son's life. Or maybe you just didn't want her ruining him. She was pregnant, after all. So you thought you'd get rid of her.'

I was pulsing with anger. Nobody knew what I was capable of, least of all myself.

Jen paled and shrank away from me. Mark put a protective arm around her and addressed me.

'What are you talking about, Abi?' he demanded. 'Jen had nothing to do with what happened to Olivia.'

I dangled the bracelet in the air between us. 'This is Olivia's bracelet. She's worn it every day since I got it for her, but when she was brought into the hospital, nobody knew where it had gone. And now I've found it in your house. Derek said Jen gave it to him after Olivia fell.'

I pointed at Derek, who'd trailed behind me and was now leaning, pale and shaken, against the arched entryway. Next to him Madison stood blinking sleepily, her hair in disarray.

'Jen?' Mark turned uncertainly to his wife.

Jen covered her face with her hands and started to cry. 'I'm sorry, Abi,' she wept. 'They took it off at the hospital when they gave Olivia an MRI. One of the doctors handed it to me and told me to give it to you. I know I should've, but I couldn't.'

'Why?'

'I saw that charm in Derek's room a few days before.'

I looked at the bracelet, wondering what she was talking about. But there it was, a small heart-shaped charm hanging from the bracelet. On either side were the initials: OK, DS.

'I knew as soon as I saw that charm on Olivia's bracelet that Derek had given it to her. But that meant the police would know too. They would think it was his fault. They'd blame him. You know my son. He's not a murderer! So I gave the bracelet to Derek and told him to hold on to it for her.'

'Mom!' Derek gasped.

Next to him, Madison's mouth fell open. Mark's arm dropped

from Jen's shoulders and he took a step away from her, as if she were now contaminated.

Sensations crawled up and down my skin: heat, as a furious flush crisped my cheeks; itchiness, as anxiety fluttered between my ribs. All the emotions I'd learned to hold in since I was a teenager were suddenly being laid bare, open and exposed as a nerve.

'You lied to me,' I hissed. 'You betrayed me.'

'No.' She shook her head, her curls swinging wildly around her pale face. 'I – I didn't betray you.'

'You think omission isn't a betrayal?'

'I was only trying to protect my child!'

'What do you think I'm trying to do?'

For a moment my rage was so huge I wanted to hurt her. I imagined putting my hands on her neck and squeezing. . .

And then the rage disappeared, as fast as it had come, and I felt nothing but an aching, hollow sadness that tightened like a fist, knuckles digging into my heart. I looked at them, this family I thought I could trust, and I had that feeling you get when you look at the rainy puddles on the ground and see the reflection of the sky above you, and for a second you can't tell what's real and what isn't.

I wanted to say something, but just then my cell phone rang, bleating into the stillness.

'Hello?' I answered sharply, holding my other hand in the air.

'Miss Knight?' Dr Maddox said. 'I need you to come to the hospital right away. The baby . . .'

32

ABI

november

I drove west from the Stokeses' house, cutting through the old part of town and emerging by the sea. I turned left, racing along the water's edge as waves pounded the rocks, reaching toward me like arthritic fingers.

I skidded into a parking spot and hurried to the hospital entrance. The line of trees that separated the hospital from the beach huddled shivering against the inky waves. Wind whistled noisily through their branches.

Sarah was already waiting for me inside; she'd beaten me to the hospital in the few minutes since I'd called her. Dr Maddox emerged as if by magic from the swinging white doors on the far side of reception. She was wearing jeans under her white scrub coat, a pair of white tennis shoes on her feet. She had a stethoscope draped over one arm, a chart in the other. She looked calm, serene, totally poised.

Dr Maddox took us through the swinging doors to a room behind reception – not the same one where they'd told me about Olivia, but similar. She shut the door, and the click was so absolute that a crashing familiarity rushed over me. I inhaled sharply.

'You should know right away that the baby is fine.' Her eyebrows crinkled inward, her eyes kind and comforting.

Sarah gasped and reached for my hand. Tears of relief bubbled in my throat, and I didn't bother to hold them back.

'What happened?' I asked.

'Olivia had a dramatic drop in blood pressure due to compression of the vena cava by her uterus. Basically, she was lying on her back and the weight of her uterus pressed on one of the main veins to her heart. As a result, the placenta and the baby suddenly weren't getting enough oxygenated blood. This usually doesn't happen until a bit later in pregnancy, so we weren't looking out for it just yet' – Dr Maddox touched my arm and smiled gently – 'but now that we know what the problem is, all we have to do is have her propped up or lying on her side and she'll be fine.'

I wiped my eyes. 'But the baby's okay?'

I noticed immediately the glaring emptiness in that sentence: I hadn't asked how Olivia was. Somewhere over the last few weeks, my priority had shifted from my daughter to her baby.

I closed my eyes as a crushing realization swept over me. I was already letting go of Olivia.

'The baby's fine,' Dr Maddox reassured me. 'In fact, we can do a scan, if you like?'

'Oh,' I breathed. 'Yes, please.'

We followed her down the labyrinth of halls to the private room Olivia's mysterious donor had provided. The room was warm, humid. Sarah and I stripped off our coats and hung them on the back of the door, then stood silently sweating as we looked at Olivia.

Olivia lay motionless. I crossed the room to touch her hair, a sudden memory hitting me.

Once when Olivia was about six or seven, she woke in the middle of the night crying. I ran to her room and held her tight, pressing my face into the dip of her neck and stroking the silk threads of her hair with my fingers.

Gradually her body relaxed and her sobs turned to snuffles. After a while she told me she'd dreamt that she died. She was buried under the Eiffel Tower looking up at all the people walking over her, continuing on their journeys as if it didn't even matter that she was just beneath the skin on their toes.

'It scared me,' Olivia said, 'because even though I was dead, everybody else just kept right on going, like it didn't even matter that I wasn't there anymore.' She nuzzled into me. 'Don't leave me, Mommy.'

'Oh, my darling.' I gathered her close so our hearts were pressed together, inhaling her strawberry scent.

And for some reason my mother's words had come back to me, floating on the breath of a long-broken promise:

'Whenever, whatever. I'm here forever.'

The memory was so vivid it was like a jolt to the heart when I opened my eyes and realized where I was. I wished I could go back to that moment and tell Olivia not to worry, that she wouldn't be forgotten. No matter what, she would still be here. I would feel her in the garden as it bloomed in the spring. I would see her in the crystal air as my breath fogged in winter. I'd smell her when I inhaled the soft, baby scent of her daughter.

She would *always* matter.

Dr Maddox positioned the bulky gray ultrasound machine next to Olivia. The head of the bed was elevated so her upper body was raised a bit. Under the white sheet a new roundness pushed out from her abdomen. A few seconds later I heard the rapid *thud, thud* of the baby's heartbeat. The map of the baby slowly took shape on the screen, and I felt a rush of pure love, a realization of the gift Olivia had given me.

'Look.' Dr Maddox traced the shape of the baby's spine as she spun around slowly. 'She's doing somersaults in there.'

Just then Dr Maddox was paged on the intercom.

'Excuse me a moment,' she said, standing and leaving quickly.

I stared after her for a minute before turning to Sarah. 'Derek, Jen's son, is the baby's father,' I told her. 'I talked to him before the doctor called.'

'What?' Sarah looked stunned. 'Are you kidding?'

'Not even a little bit.' I raked my hands through my hair and groaned, a low growl of pain and frustration. 'I don't know what's going to happen, if he'll want the baby or if I'll raise her. And, to be honest, I'm scared of having a baby again. Remember Olivia? Remember when . . .'

In a rush of emotion, I recalled those first difficult months after Olivia was born. Motherhood with its colossal responsibilities and weeks of little to no sleep with a colicky infant turned me into someone I didn't recognize. I loved my daughter with everything in me, but it was more complicated than that.

One morning I was running late dropping Olivia off at Sarah's so I could get to college. I pulled up to her house and leapt out, leaning into the backseat to unsnap Olivia from her car seat. A foul smell assaulted me and there was a thick, wet sucking sound as I tried to wrench her from the car seat.

I'd forgotten to put a diaper on Olivia. Her lower half was covered in poo. It squished over her chubby thighs, across the front of her tiny pink dress, up her back, and dripped over the edge of the car seat onto the floor.

For the first time – the only time – I wished I'd listened to Gavin. I regretted keeping my daughter – and how could any mother regret her own baby? I was as hopelessly inept at mothering as I was at everything else. In over my head.

When I was pregnant with Olivia, I'd sworn I'd be the type of mother who would never abandon her, the type I'd wanted my mom to be. I'd hold her against my chest, rub my nose against hers, brush my eyelashes along the curve of her cheek. I'd tell her that her DNA used to swim in my blood, that we were a part of each other, our heartbeats one.

But then she was born, and I was on my own and holding that tiny body, and it might as well have been the weight of the world right there in my arms. So I'd shoved my howling, poo-streaked baby at Sarah, got in my car, and drove away.

That was the shameful secret I didn't want Olivia to ever, ever know. Not only had her father abandoned her, so had her mother.

And of the two of us, really, I'm the one who should've known better.

I looked at Sarah, and knew she was remembering it too. 'I did so many things wrong,' I said. 'Maybe I'm just as bad as Mom was.'

'Abi,' Sarah said gently. 'You came back. That's the important thing. You didn't abandon Olivia; you took a much-needed break. And you were a better mother for it. You think everything is so black-and-white, but the world isn't like that. Maybe you weren't a perfect mother, but you were a *great* one. It doesn't mean you loved her any less.'

I stood abruptly and grabbed a small bottle of lotion from a drawer near Olivia's head. I took her hand in mine and worked the lotion into her cold, dry skin, gazing at the ultrasound screen.

I'd fallen headlong in love with this baby, and it might die, the way Olivia would die when we turned off her life support. The way my mom had. Or Derek could take her from me. It was a risk: the more I loved, the more I had to lose.

But I loved this baby with that crazy kind of love that reaches deep inside of you and changes you from the inside out. The kind of love that makes you say yes more than no. That makes you think you can wish on a shooting star and everything will magically be all right.

33

OLIVIA

The week before school started, Madison finally penciled me in for some girl time. I was torn between feeling resentful that I'd dropped to the bottom of her priority list and grateful so I could spend more time with Derek. Also, I was super aware that I'd been the one to cancel going to the beach with her on my birthday, so really I couldn't be that mad.

I woke up late feeling groggy and thickheaded. There was no time for breakfast, so I threw a banana in my beach bag and sent a quick text to my mom letting her know where I was going.

By the time I reached Java Café, I was drenched in sweat. I wiped a hand across my forehead. It was so hot it felt like the air was pressing on my lungs.

The place was packed with teenagers, all jabbering loudly. I looked up at the giant blackboard chalked in flowing cursive and eyed the fresh fruit stacked in shallow crates below.

Madison and I saw each other at the same time. She jumped up, waving her hands wildly in the air. Shoving her iPhone into her giant, black beach bag she ran over, throwing her arms around me.

'Livvie! It's sooo good to see you! It's been, like, forever, right? I mean, how has this whole summer passed and we've barely gotten to hang?'

I hugged her back. She was wearing white platform sandals, white cropped leggings, and a baggy black Van Halen T-shirt. One shoulder kept slipping down and exposing the edge of her black and white bikini top. Her hair was held off her forehead with a wide black headband. She looked very grown-up. My Adidas shorts, which felt unnecessarily snug, pink tank top, and flip-flops seemed very childish in comparison.

'I know. It's crazy, right?' I replied. 'You've been, like, super busy this summer. You must be excited about the play's opening night, though. Only a few weeks away.'

She rolled her eyes dramatically. 'Oh my God. I'm *so* nervous!'

'You'll be amazing. You always are.' I knew my own lines well.

She shrugged, mollified, and we walked to the cash register to place our orders.

Behind the counter, lush, rainbow-colored fruit gleamed from crates stacked on top of the cupboards. My mouth watered, but then I remembered the banana in my bag. What I really needed was a coffee to wake up.

'Oooh, kiwi,' Madison squealed, and pointed. 'My favorite! I'll have a strawberry kiwi smoothie, please.'

'I'll have an iced latte,' I told the girl at the register.

'A latte?' Madison teased archly. 'You never drink coffee.'

'Well, you know me,' I joked, flicking the end of my ponytail over my shoulder. 'I'm so grown-up now.'

She giggled and we took our drinks outside, crossing the street to the boardwalk. It was still early, but the sand was already packed with people. The beach was always mobbed the last week of August. All the families enjoying the last days before school started and the weather began to cool.

No sign of that now, though. It was blistering hot. I plucked at my sweaty tank top, trying to let in a bit of fresh air.

We made a beeline for two open sun loungers, plopping our towels and beach bags on top. The playful scent of sunscreen assaulted my nose, followed by the salty tang of the sea.

Heat wormed its way into my hair, lazy sweat prickling against my scalp. 'It's so hot,' I moaned.

Madison looked at me strangely. 'It isn't that hot.'

I took a sip of my latte. It tasted bitter and was so strong I cringed. I should've put sugar in it.

'So.' Madison straightened her beach towel, then sat down and started rubbing oil on her arms. She liked to let her skin marinate into that perfect shade of toffee. I got my sunscreen out, knowing I'd burn in a minute if I wasn't careful.

'You should take that bracelet off,' Madison said. 'You'll get tan lines.'

I hesitated. I knew Madison thought my bracelet was babyish. 'No thanks. Besides, I don't mind tan lines.'

She shrugged. 'So, how *are* you? Are you okay?'

'Yeah, I'm fine.' I smiled. But Madison kept looking at me like I was supposed to say something else.

'Really?'

'Yeah.'

She studied me for another moment, then focused her attention on rubbing oil on her legs. The smell of coconuts and sun rose from the bottle. I peeled my banana and took a bite, and the silence expanded between us. For the first time in my life, I felt a little awkward with my best friend. Maybe it was the lie that I knew sat between us, bulky and imposing.

A toddler streaked across the sand in front of us naked, his diaper clutched in a sandy fist. His face beamed with utter joy at the unexpected freedom. His frazzled mother ran after him, shouting in dismay.

Madison and I looked at each other and the awkwardness evaporated as we burst out laughing. 'How shitty would that be!' she spluttered.

'Ha! Literally!'

'It's weird, isn't it?' she said after a few minutes. 'Usually we spend, like, every day together, but I feel like I haven't seen you since school got out. What've you been up to?'

'Not much.' I forced a laugh. I didn't want to ruin the day by telling her I'd spent most of the summer with her brother. 'The days just slipped by, you know? I read outside in the hammock a lot. I swam, mowed the lawn, planted our garden. I prepped for the SATs.'

She slid a condescending look at me. 'I know, I know,' I rushed to add. 'I'm such a nerd. But I want to get into U-Dub. They have this international studies program that looks amazing. And, you know, I need to get a scholarship.'

'What classes did you sign up for?'

'Basically the same as last year. AP history, AP English, AP calculus.'

'Ughh. AP calculus? Why would you torture yourself like that?'

'Mom said it'll look good when I apply. That and volunteer work. So I'm gonna volunteer at the nursing home in town. I start in a few weeks.'

'Eww, gross!' She wrinkled her nose. 'Old people smell like pee.'

I laughed and pretended to hit her. 'Don't be mean! Besides, they have this therapeutic garden and greenhouse, so I'll be helping out there, not changing diapers or anything. Anyway, if it makes my mom happy –'

'–it'll keep her off your back.'

'No, I mean . . .'

It was what we always said, but I didn't feel like that anymore. I'd learned a lot this summer, and finding out who my dad was and the reason my mom had lied about him was a big one. I guess I understood now that sometimes worry and love and control could get all jumbled up so you couldn't really see the difference.

But I didn't know how to explain that to Madison. I wasn't sure I even wanted to.

'Madison!' A shout came from down the beach.

Madison lifted a hand to shade her eyes, and a few seconds later Peter jogged up to us, his pale face flushed red from the heat.

'Hey, gorgeous.' He leaned down and kissed Madison's glossy

lips. His loose tank top slipped down to show off his tan, muscled upper body.

'Hi, Olivia. How are *you*?' He said it in that same tone Madison had just used on me.

'I'm fine, thanks.' Irritation wedged in my throat.

'Just on my way to football practice and saw you lovely ladies.'

I'd forgotten that football practice started this week. That meant Tyler must be back in town. He hadn't even texted me, though, which was weird. But then, we hadn't spoken much all summer. Maybe it wasn't weird. Maybe growing apart like this was good. It meant that breaking up with him would be easier. Or maybe I wouldn't have to do it at all.

Peter turned to go, and at the last minute I shouted after him: 'Say hi to Tyler for me!'

He gave me an odd look, his eyes flicking to Madison's. They exchanged a fleeting glance before he turned and jogged away.

'What was that about?' I asked her.

'What?'

'You know. That look.'

'I don't know what you mean.'

My phone beeped an incoming text message. It was Derek, confirming I was coming over when Madison went to rehearsal in the afternoon. I typed a quick response.

'Who's that?' Madison asked playfully. 'You have a secret boyfriend?'

'What? No. Of course not.' My face blazed, going hot and itchy.

'You're blushing.'

'It's just . . . Tyler.'

Madison didn't reply for so long that I finally glanced up. Her brow was furrowed, the corner of her bottom lip tucked under her front teeth.

'What?' I asked.

'Just, I thought, you know . . .'

I set my phone down next to me on the sun lounger. 'Okay. What's going on?'

'I thought you guys broke up.'

I laughed awkwardly. 'Well, not that I know of. Why?'

Madison swept her hair up and fanned the back of her neck with one hand. 'Do you want to go for a walk? You're right. It's pretty hot.'

She stood and moved to walk away.

'Wait.' I swung my legs around to the side of the sun lounger and grabbed her hand. 'What's going on, Mad? What aren't you telling me?'

'I'm sorry, Olivia. I thought you were just too embarrassed to tell me.'

'Tell you what?'

'Tyler told Peter he was going to break up with you.'

'Oh.' I was speechless. A wave of nausea swept over me, and I pressed a hand to my stomach.

'I guess he hasn't yet?'

I shook my head and blew out a breath I didn't know I was holding. Her and Peter's funny looks now made sense. They knew something I didn't. Tyler had lied to me, too. Maybe not outright, but he'd held his plan to dump me close to his chest, the same way I had.

'I'm so, so, so sorry, Olivia. Please don't tell Tyler I told you! You know how weird he can get.'

I swallowed hard. 'Sure, of course. It's fine. I guess I need to talk to him. It's been a bizarre summer with him away and everything. We haven't really talked that much, to be honest. I mean, you know, he's in Seattle and I'm here, so . . .'

'Are you okay?'

'Yeah, fine,' I said vaguely. I inhaled through my nose, but the air was thick and soupy and I felt like my stomach was pitching about on the ocean.

'Are you sure you're okay? Because you look like –'

But her last word was lost in the space between us as I turned and vomited up the banana and the bitter latte.

34

ABI

november

I huddled in my freezing car the next morning, a tepid cup of coffee grasped in my gloved hands, my eyes fixed across the street on the Montgomerys' ornate black gate.

After a torrential dumping in the night, morning had dawned bright and clear, as had a fresh determination brewing inside of me. No matter what happened, I wanted to be able to tell Olivia's daughter that I'd done everything I could to find out what had happened to her mother.

Kendall hadn't told me everything. I was sure of it. I'd watched Gavin leave fifteen minutes ago, so whenever she left for school, I would be here waiting to talk to her.

My phone buzzed, and I glanced at it. It was my boss, Malcolm. He'd been bombarding me with calls and texts all morning. I knew I'd have to reply soon. I couldn't keep putting it off. Only a few days of my leave of absence were left, and Malcolm needed to know he could count on me.

But I was so close to finding the truth. I could feel it.

Just then the gates clanged open, and a second later Kendall's blue BMW Z4 soft-top nosed out of the drive. I shoved my door open and jumped out of my car.

'Kendall!' I waved to her, relief washing over me when she waved back and pulled her car up in front of mine.

She rolled down her window as I approached. 'Hiya. What's up?'

'There've been a few new developments about your dad in Olivia's case. Do you have a minute to talk?'

She nodded. 'Sure. Anything to help. You want to get in? It's freezing.'

I climbed in her car, and she adjusted the heating to maximum. She wasn't wearing a coat, just her Catholic schoolgirl uniform, which looked a little too naughty. The green tartan skirt was a little too short. Instead of tights she was wearing black knee-high socks paired with chunky ankle heels.

'Did he do it?' Kendall's eyes gleamed with a weird light, and I knew my bait had worked. The girl would throw her dad under a bus if she could.

'I'm not sure,' I hedged. 'That's what I'm trying to find out. Did you ever hear your dad threaten Olivia? Or did she tell you he did?'

'Not really. No.'

'But he knew who she was, right? They met before?'

'Yeah, like once.'

I watched her, assessed her face, looking for any cracks in the stories she was spinning me. And I was sure now they were stories. She was playing me, spinning her version of the truth. The question was why, and what *was* the truth? I needed to know if Kendall really thought Gavin had hurt Olivia, or if she was covering for herself, projecting her responsibility onto him.

I knew from accounting that sometimes you had to take a step back, look at the big picture, the full set of numbers, see it from a different angle, so it could all begin to make sense. That's what I needed to do now.

'What about when you followed them to the Black Cat Diner?' I said nonchalantly. 'That's at least twice they met. Did they meet besides that?'

Kendall's jaw clenched defensively. 'Who told you I followed them?'

'It doesn't matter,' I replied. 'What matters is whether you're telling me the truth or not. Was it your dad who threatened Olivia? Or you?'

'I didn't threaten her!' Her tone was defensive, snide as a spoiled child's. She crossed her arms over her chest.

I sighed, exasperated with her attitude, my patience wearing thin.

'See, I'm not sure if I believe you anymore, Kendall. You tricked Olivia into coming to your house when the press was there, which risked exposing who Olivia was in the middle of your dad's political campaign. You followed your dad and her when they met at the diner. Now you've told me they only met once, when I know for a fact they met at least twice. What else are you lying about?'

Kendall glared at me defiantly. 'I don't have to take this.'

'Did you have a score to settle with Olivia?'

'Of course not! I didn't hurt Olivia. I was trying to help her! I told you this already!'

'You didn't tell me you followed your dad and Olivia to that diner,' I countered.

'So?' Kendall snapped, her face a mottled pink. 'I didn't think it was important. Fine, you want to know what happened? Yes, I tricked Olivia into coming over so the media would find out about her. I wanted my dad to get caught.'

She reached up and ran her fingers through her shoulder-length blonde hair and continued, 'And yeah, I followed them to that scruffy diner. I heard my dad talking on the phone to Olivia that morning and I was mad, okay? I mean, my entire life he's either ignored me or totally fucked everything up. All he cares about is money and his career, in that order. It doesn't matter what I want, it has to fit in with his stupid career. That's why he always has me volunteering with him for his community shit. The only reason I go to this ridiculous Catholic school is because he thinks it looks good for his campaign.' She plucked at her tartan skirt.

'I told him no fucking way was I going there. I wanted to go to an alternative school to study music, so you want to know what he did? He planted a bottle of oxy in my room and told my mom he'd caught me about to down the whole thing. So off I went to a mental hospital. D'ya see what I mean? He's a fucking psycho.'

She flounced back against the seat, but she looked different now. Less the angry, defiant teenager and more like a victim. I knew what it felt like to be used as a pawn in Gavin's game.

'I know what you're saying, Kendall,' I said. 'I do. And I know exactly what he's capable of. But what does this have to do with why you followed Olivia? Nobody would blame you for being jealous.'

Kendall laughed, a harsh sound. 'Don't you get it? Yes, I was jealous, but not of her. I was jealous of *him*. For the first time in my life I had a sister, and she was on *my* side, not his. I didn't want him getting in the way of that and I didn't want them getting all chummy. I knew he'd turn Olivia against me the first chance he got. I wanted her to stay away from him so she would be mine, not his. He takes *everything* from me. I didn't want him taking Olivia too!'

'Did you hurt Olivia?' I asked softly.

'No! Olivia was nice to me. I was sad when she got hurt. That's why I've been calling you.'

'*You're* the one who's been calling?'

She looked away, ashamed. 'I'm sorry. I shouldn't have hung up. I just . . . I wanted to talk about her, but I didn't know what to say.'

'It's okay,' I said. I wrapped my hands around my stomach, feeling the ache deep within. 'Sometimes I want to talk about her too.'

We sat in silence for a long moment, staring out the car windows at a cluster of leaves that skittered across the pavement.

'Where was your dad the night Olivia fell?' I asked.

Kendall glanced at me, but her eyes slid quickly away. 'I don't know.'

Just then a loud revving sound came from behind us, and the gates clanked and opened. I twisted to look out the rear window and saw a silver Jag pull up behind us.

It was Gavin.

Kendall sat up straight. 'It's him,' she said.

And just like that, her eyes went flat and dead.

× × ×

Kendall and I scrambled out of her car. She came to stand next to me, and we huddled together like two guilty children.

Gavin stormed toward us, his shoes crunching on the gravel, his face like thunder.

'Abi, what are – Kendall, what's going on?'

'Why are you home?' Kendall snapped. She hunched her shoulders, rubbing her hands over her bare arms.

'I forgot my briefcase,' he growled.

Fear braided my stomach, a shimmer of nausea rolling in me. The paranoid side of my brain screamed at me to run away. But then he met my eyes, and there it was stamped unmistakably across his face: fear.

He was scared of *me*.

I laughed out loud as relief pulsed through me, strengthening my limbs.

'I was just asking Kendall where you both were the night Olivia fell,' I said.

'What the –?' He threw his hands up, looking incredulous. 'Are you *stalking* my daughter? You're pathetic!'

My face flushed and I clenched my hands into tight fists.

'Where were you that night?' I repeated.

Gavin shook his head, as if he were dealing with a toddler. 'We're doing this, are we?' He turned to Kendall. 'What were we doing that night, darling?'

Kendall glared at him, hatred radiating from her eyes. 'I don't know. I don't even know what night it was.'

'The first Saturday of October,' I said.

'It's not like I keep a diary of everything I do,' Kendall snapped. 'I'm not eight anymore.'

'A diary.' Gavin slapped a free hand on one knee with a faux jolly air. 'Excellent idea, darling.'

He pulled his phone out of his coat pocket and started scrolling. A breeze lifted his hair, and I noticed how thin it had gotten.

'Ahh. I remember.' He pointed at his phone and looked at Kendall. 'We were at a rather spectacular campaign dinner at the Fairmont Hotel. Do you remember, darling?' Kendall looked at him as if he'd grown four heads. 'Noah Harris. That executive from ComCore Tech. His company organized a dinner with the Republican Future Institute to raise funds for my campaign. His son took quite a shine to you, didn't he?' He slipped his phone back into his coat pocket.

Harris. Was the name familiar? I racked my brain but came up blank. It was a common name.

'What time was that?' I asked.

'Seven o'clock. But we were there late into the night, weren't we, sweetheart?' Gavin's father-of-the-year display made me sick. It looked like it was making Kendall sick too. She'd turned a disturbing shade of white.

'Yeah,' she mumbled.

I could feel Kendall slipping away, and Gavin was about to call the cops. But somehow I knew Kendall wasn't telling me everything. Gavin had disturbed her, made her flustered and uneasy.

Anger, hard as a pebble, swelled in my throat.

'Seven o'clock?' I exploded, whirling to face Kendall. 'Please! You had plenty of time to go to dinner, then drive to Olivia. Was it you, Kendall? Did you push her off that bridge?'

Her head jerked up. 'No! I told you –!'

Gavin took a step toward me. The air around us pulsed with tension, unspoken truths rattling through the decaying leaves.

'That's it.' Gavin fumbled for his cell phone. 'I'm calling my lawyer.'

'No!' Kendall bit the word off as if it were a foul-tasting piece of candy. 'I'll answer her.'

'Don't say another word, Kendall.'

Kendall whirled on him, eyes blazing. 'You're such an asshole,' she hissed. 'Pretending like you care about me. You don't give a shit. Not about me. Not about Olivia. She was just a problem you needed to get rid of. I know you pushed her. You didn't want anyone finding out you have a bastard daughter.'

She pinned me with her eyes, speaking fast so Gavin couldn't stop her. 'He left dinner early that night. Disappeared about nine o'clock.'

'That's enough!' Gavin roared. Kendall's eyes widened, and for the first time I saw her as a child, cowering in the face of his narcissistic bullying. 'Get in your car and go to school! That's an order, Kendall!'

Kendall's eyes narrowed to glittering slits, but she didn't argue. She threw herself in the direction of her car. A moment later, her tires squealed against the pavement as she raced away, leaving me alone with Gavin.

35

ABI

november

Gavin glared at me, furious, but after a minute, the strangest thing happened. His shoulders dropped, and he touched his fingers briefly to his forehead. He looked like he'd been leached of all vitality.

'Come inside, Abi,' he said, his voice resigned. 'You can ask me anything you like, but not out here where people can see.'

I hesitated, not sure I wanted to be alone with Gavin. I knew what he was capable of. But a small piece of me was curious about this new Gavin. This wasn't the blustering bully I remembered. And if he had some idea of what had happened to Olivia, I needed to know.

So I got in my car and followed him through the gates.

× × ×

Gavin led me into an impressive office tucked away at the back of the house. The furniture was dark masculine leather. An ornate mahogany desk with a green-shaded desk lamp was set in front of floor-to-ceiling bookshelves. He shut the door and peeled off his black knee-length wool coat, hanging it neatly on a hook on the back of the door before sitting in a plush leather chair behind the desk.

Seem like you're okay. Don't cry. Don't puke, I told myself harshly. I could control my mind, but not my body – the anxiety made my limbs shaky and my head light. The pit of my stomach felt ice cold with fear.

'Have a seat,' he said.

I stayed standing. I wouldn't let him have any power over me. Not anymore.

'What is it?' he asked. He leaned back in his leather seat and assessed me. 'Do you want more money? Because let's get one thing clear: that's not happening. You stole my money last time and never even got that abortion. I should press charges against you for theft.' He shook his head in exasperation, as if he were talking to a naughty child. 'You're just lucky my wife's out of the house today.'

The fear inside my belly caught fire and rose, white hot, until it rested on my tongue, pulsed in my neck. I walked to his desk and perched on the edge. I could tell it startled him, but he worked hard to cover it.

'So you *did* know Olivia,' I said.

'Yeah, I met her. In an extremely bizarre twist of fate, your daughter met my daughter and somehow they became pals. It wasn't hard to put the pieces together after that.'

'Were you sending Olivia death threats?'

He barked a short laugh. 'Do you hear yourself? I'm a grown man, Abi. A politician, not some jealous stalker or jilted lover.'

'Did you push Olivia off that bridge, Gavin?'

'Don't be ridiculous,' he snapped, his heavy brow folding into a V over his nose. 'Why would I do something like that? Especially right before an election!'

'To get rid of her. Obviously. You wouldn't want your wife, or your voters, to know about your illegitimate daughter.'

He threw his hands up in the air. 'Look, not that you'll believe me or anything, but I didn't hurt her. She seemed like a nice girl. I was sorry to hear about what happened.'

I pushed myself off the desk and slowly edged closer to him.

'I want to know what happened to my daughter. And I think you know. Don't forget, Gavin, I know you. I know what you're capable of, what you'll do for your own gain.' I leaned in, the intensity of my glare nuclear as I fixed it on his forest-green eyes, so much like Olivia's.

'I don't think . . .' He was calculating his next move, how to win this situation. But I had the upper hand now.

An intoxicating rush of power swept over me. How delicious it felt to turn the tables on him. The shy, insecure Abi he used to know was gone. I wasn't powerless like I used to be.

'You've made it so the detectives are doing fuck-all about her case,' I hissed. 'What I don't know is *why*. I think you pushed her, afraid she'd tell everybody you're her father. And now you've gotten Anthony in trouble for helping me look into it. Do you know what that makes you look like, Gavin?' I bent down so we were nose-to-nose. 'Guilty!'

I straightened up and pulled the letter Kendall had given me out of my purse, smoothed it against my chest, and held it out to him.

'Shall I tell you what it says?' I asked. 'It's from Seattle DNA Testing Services.' I tapped my finger against my chin and quoted: '"Based on the DNA analysis, the alleged father" – that's you, Gavin – "cannot be excluded as the biological father of the child Olivia Knight, because they share the same genetic markers. Probability percentage: 99.9942 percent."'

Gavin snatched the paper out of my hand and tore it into pieces, his jaw set, the cleft in his chin more prominent than ever.

I laughed, a hard, dry sound. 'I have copies upon copies of this document, including one in a safe deposit box, so if anything happens to me, all this information gets sent to the media. Oh, and speaking of the media, you'd better find a way to get Anthony out of trouble with the Seattle police chief or I'll make sure they get a copy of this.'

He stared at me, jaw hinging open. 'Are you *blackmailing* me?'

'Hell, yeah,' I said.

A muscle ticked in his jaw. 'You don't want to do this, Abi.'

'Oh, but you're wrong. I *do* want to do this.'

Gavin lifted hollow eyes to mine. The skin on his cheeks looked pale under his tan, and I could see a vein in his temple pulsing.

'I hear she's getting excellent care,' he said quietly. 'They've flown in a specialist to make sure she and the baby have the very best medical attention. It would be a shame to lose all of that.'

My stomach turned oily, and I gasped. 'What are you – how do you –?'

'Who do you think' – he leaned forward – 'is paying for her care?'

The anonymous donor.

I closed my eyes, feeling as if my brain were liquefying.

'But . . . wh –?'

'I couldn't let anybody know she was mine, but that doesn't mean I hurt her. In fact, I was going to set up a trust fund for her, but then I saw what had happened in the news. I wanted to do something to help.'

'You told me not to get in the way. You said you would kill us.'

'Come on, Abi. I was young, just breaking into politics. I didn't want you ruining my career. Not then and not now. I can't have anybody find out she's my daughter. But I'm not a monster. If you give that paper to the media, I won't pay for Olivia's care.'

I stared at him. For someone who saw herself as observant, detail-oriented, analytical, I'd been awfully stupid. I was such a fool. I'd thought I could beat him. But once again he had me. Check and mate.

I had to do what was right for Olivia and the baby. And I couldn't provide it on my own.

The agony of knowing that I would never learn the truth about what had happened to Olivia was like a kick to the stomach. I had to get away.

I turned and moved to leave, unable to speak.

Gavin's face flashed a look of smug triumph. He'd won and he knew it.

The loss was awful, a disorientating, panicky feeling sweeping over me in harsh waves.

Gavin stopped me when my hand touched the doorknob.

'Did you never stop to ask yourself why somebody from the Seattle Police Department would be working on a case in Portage Point?'

I turned around slowly.

'What?'

'Anthony Bryant. Why is he helping you? It isn't in his jurisdiction.'

'My sister – she asked him to help me. As a favor,' I stammered. 'He's being nice.'

'Don't be stupid, Abi,' he said, his mouth twisting in incredulity. 'Nobody's nice for no reason.'

× × ×

The sky had changed while I was inside. Dark clouds were heavy with rain, and wind sent flurries of damp leaves scuttling along the ground in angry little whirls. I shut Gavin's front door and dialed Sarah's number as I walked toward my car.

'Sarah,' I said when she answered. 'When you called Anthony and asked him to help me, did he ever say anything about jurisdiction? Or were you just asking him to help me as a personal favor?'

'Wait, hold on, I can't hear you,' Sarah said. The sound of children's laughter came through the phone. A second later it went quiet.

'Sorry,' she said, sounding breathless. 'I'm about to talk to someone about getting Dylan tested for dyslexia. What's up with Anthony?'

I started to repeat my question, but she cut me off.

'Wait, Abi. I never called Anthony.'

I froze, stunned. Rain started falling then, droplets soaking into my hair, so cold they stung my head. I thought back to our conversation in the hospital.

I know people at the Seattle Police Department through work. I'll call around.

She'd never actually told me she'd called anybody. I'd just assumed it.

'But – but, why? Why would he help me then?' My voice trembled.

'I don't know, Abi. I honestly don't. To be honest, I thought it was a bit of a coincidence he was assigned to you and I'd worked with him before. But it's Seattle. It isn't like it's a massive city. The police department and the psychologists work really closely. It wouldn't be unheard of for that to happen.'

'He wasn't assigned to me. He told me that from the beginning. He said . . .' I thought about the first time we spoke, his initial confusion when I said Sarah's name. We'd quickly segued into the missing information on the police report, so I hadn't pressed him for clarification.

I pounded my hand against my forehead. I'd been blinded by my desire to know what had happened to Olivia, who was responsible. I'd only heard what I wanted to hear.

'I *thought* he said he would help as a favor to you.'

'No, I never talked to him at all.' Sarah sounded worried. 'Why are you asking this? Is everything okay?'

I squeezed my eyes shut. 'I don't know,' I said. 'But if you didn't ask him to help me, who did?'

36

OLIVIA

september

I jumped off the school bus and glared angrily at the mustard-yellow rear, black exhaust belching from it as it chugged away. I'd gotten my license more than a month ago, but I still didn't have a car. I was the only seventeen-year-old in my class who had to take the bus. It was mortifying. Sometimes it seemed like I'd get one step closer to a sliver of independence, only to have it swiped away from me.

I was sure Mom had planned it that way. 'Sure, you can get your license,' she'd said, when really she was secretly scrubbing her hands together in glee. She'd let me win a tiny battle knowing she'd won the larger war.

I kicked a clot of dirt, then turned up the driveway to my house. The air was cool and cloudy, a warning that fall was on the way.

I sighed as I unlocked the door, letting myself into the quiet

311

house. It wasn't not having a car that was upsetting me. The small, rectangular box buried at the bottom of my book bag felt like it had been burning a hole there for the past three days.

I threw my bag on the couch and rifled through the mess of loose papers and books. I had to stop putting it off.

In the bathroom, I pulled the little white stick out of the box and read the directions. They were brief and simple. Even an idiot could understand them.

Remove the test stick from its individual foil wrapper and take off the cap.

Test directly in your urine stream, holding for five seconds only. Read your result after three minutes.

I held my breath and pushed the stick between my legs. After I'd peed, I set it on the back of the toilet and stared at it. How was it possible for time to slow down, like sap oozing from a tree? Every one of my senses was on full alert: I could hear the neighbor's dog barking across the street. I tasted salt on my upper lip. And my hands, when I looked down at them, felt like they weren't my own.

The air in the bathroom was too hot to breathe. I crossed to the window and struggled with its rusty lock. It finally opened with a raspy groan, and clear, cool air swept inside. I swallowed ragged gulps, trying to still my thudding heart.

When I turned around, it was there on the stick, clear as day. It didn't even take three minutes.

I shut my eyes, gripped my hands against the counter. The back of my throat filled with dread – coppery, dry, scratchy as sand.

When I opened my eyes, it was still there.

Two cheerful, bright pink lines.

I was pregnant.

× × ×

Amazingly enough, my body continued to function. I could breathe. I could talk. I could mow the lawn and do my homework.

But I couldn't think. I couldn't plan for the future. I felt frozen.

I avoided Derek. Avoided Madison and Tyler and the rest of my friends. Words dribbled out of me, mechanical and hollow. I kept my head down at school and ducked away at the end of each day. Going to Madison's play last week had turned out to be a tense, nauseating test of my own acting skills. Derek darted concerned looks at me all night. It was a job trying to avoid him. At least Madison hadn't noticed anything. She was too enthralled with herself to even realize when I turned down the invitation to have dinner with her family.

I dropped out of swimming, which I'd done every fall since junior high. I quit my volunteering job at the old folks' home before I even started.

I used homework as a shield so I wouldn't have to have an actual conversation with my mom. True to her promise, she'd stopped checking my homework and let me just get on with it. She didn't even make me show her my test grades, which was good, because I wasn't doing very well.

The problem was, all that studying got me nowhere. I couldn't focus to save my life. There was no point anyway. I'd be lucky to go to a community college now. Unless I got an abortion. But that wasn't an option. If my mom had gotten an abortion, I wouldn't even be alive, so I couldn't do that to this baby. Still, I couldn't go to school pregnant. It would be totally mortifying. I'd have to drop out.

I wanted to slap myself. How could this have happened to me? We'd been so careful. I thought about that ad they show in health class: it only takes one sperm. I was that stupid teenage girl who got pregnant in high school. Just like my mom.

Bile rose in my mouth and I rushed to the bathroom, slamming the toilet lid open just in time to vomit forcefully into the porcelain. I puked again and again, my stomach aching, tears streaming down my face.

Afterward, I went to my room and sat on the edge of my bed. I picked up my framed picture of Mom and me. In the picture we were sitting next to a wide, meandering river, ripe summer grass blurring in the camera's eye as it waved in a gentle wind. We were facing each other, our foreheads pressed together, joyful smiles cracking our faces open wide.

Looking at the picture, you couldn't see our eyes but you knew we were happy. Our blonde hair – mine pale like straw, hers gold like honey – whipped against our sunburned cheeks. Our cheeks were stretched wide with laughter. We were laughing because we knew each other and we were alive and because there was so much to look forward to. She was my mom and I was her daughter, and there was nothing more important than that.

I swallowed a rising bubble of tears. Now we were just familiar-looking strangers. I hated the distance that had grown between us. I hated that it was my fault. I'd lied about so many things, and now I missed her.

I couldn't tell her I was pregnant. She'd worked so hard to make sure I had a better life than she did, and now I'd ruined it all.

My phone rang, and I staggered down the stairs to where I'd left it on the kitchen counter.

'Hi, Mom,' I answered. My voice sounded a bit shaky, even in my ears.

'Hi, sweetie,' she said. 'Everything okay?'

'Yeah. I just . . . got busy on a calculus problem.'

'Okay, just wanted to make sure –'

'I'm fine,' I interrupted.

Mom didn't say anything, and I cringed, guilt sliding into my stomach.

'Liv . . .' She hesitated. 'Sweetie, is there anything you want to talk about?'

'I'm *fine*. I just have so many classes and tons of homework. I'm not trying to be mean, I'm just a bit stressed, okay? And I really need to get back to my homework.'

A long, awkward silence filled the line between us. And then a knock at the door made me jump.

'Honestly, I'm fine.' I wiped at tears that had started to cluster in the corners of my eyes.

'Should we get you into some different classes?' She sounded worried. 'Maybe it's all a bit too much.'

The knock came again.

'No, it's okay. Look, I've got to go. Calculus –'

'Olivia, you don't have to be perfect, all right? Sometimes good is good enough. You know that, right?'

I appreciated her saying it, whether she believed it or not. 'I know.'

'Whenever, whatever. I'm here forever. Remember that, okay?'

She hadn't said those words in so long. My eyes grew hot with tears, and I suddenly wished to be small so I could crawl into her lap and let her make everything better.

'Okay. Thanks, Mom.'

× × ×

When I opened the door, Derek was huddled on the porch. He wore cutoff jeans and black tennis shoes and a blue windbreaker that flapped against his chest in the brisk breeze. I'd never seen him in anything other than his black T-shirt and jeans and his leather jacket.

'You've been avoiding me,' he said.

'No, I . . .' I tried to deny it, but couldn't. I glanced vaguely toward the pile of homework on the dining room table, but couldn't bother coming up with empty lies. I was too freaking tired.

I moved out of the way so he could come inside.

'Are you breaking up with me?' he asked once I'd shut the door. 'Please tell me the truth.'

'What? No! I'm not –'

'Olivia, stop.' A spark of anger flashed in his eyes, the deep blue darkening. 'Why can't you just be honest? If you're still in love with Tyler, just tell me and get it over with.'

'Derek.' I laughed out loud at how wrong he was. 'I swear to you, I'm not in love with Tyler. It isn't that.'

I pressed my fingers into my eyes, trying to hold back the tears, but they came anyway, splattering hot against my icy hands.

He put his hands on my shoulders and turned me to face him. 'What's wrong, Olivia?' he pleaded. 'Tell me.'

I tried to speak but the truth stuck in my throat. My teeth were like bars that kept the words imprisoned in my mouth.

Derek took my hands in his. He understood that the more upset I was, the less I could talk about it. 'It's okay,' he said. 'Don't talk. Let's go for a walk on the beach. Does that sound okay?'

I nodded and dashed at my eyes, pulled in a ragged breath.

We drove to Laurelwood and strolled along the boardwalk past the farmer's market. Derek impulsively bought me a flame-colored scarf from a portly elderly man bent at the hip like a question mark. He wrapped the slip of silk around my neck and kissed me on the nose. It wasn't my usual style, the flamboyant red, but maybe that's what I needed.

'Thank you for this.' I fingered the material at my throat. It was so silky, cool against my tear-warmed cheeks.

We walked across the wet sand without saying a word, the red scarf caressing my throat like a promise. It was low tide, the sea lapping gently at the sand in the distance. The air was cool and damp, the way it gets when the clouds are full of water but it hasn't rained yet. Lethargic sunshine peeped shyly through racing clouds.

'I've been doing a lot of thinking –' Derek began.

'No, Derek,' I interrupted. 'I should talk first.'

He shook his head. 'Please. I need to tell you something.'

He stopped walking and turned to face me, taking both my hands in his.

'I love you. I love you so much. But you deserve more than a bum who hibernates in his parents' basement. I don't want to be that guy. So I started looking at classes at the University of Washington, and I've decided to study architecture. My dad said he'd pay for it, so I'm going to register for winter quarter.'

'Derek, that's amazing.' I smiled for the first time in what felt like weeks. 'I'm so happy for you.'

'I'm just so relieved, you know? Finally something my parents and I can agree on! Maybe if I go to school and get a good job, they'll respect me. It just, it feels good, you know?'

'Yeah, of course.'

'I mean, I know it'll be a bit annoying because we'll live so far apart. But I'll come home on the weekends, so we can still be close. And it won't be forever, just a year until you start college too.' His eyes glowed earnestly.

'I'm really happy for you,' I said again.

What else could I say? His parents' respect meant so much to him. It was what he'd always wanted. How could I tell him I was pregnant and ruin his chance at that? He'd want me to get an abortion. I knew that absolutely.

The implications of that realization crashed onto me, and my smile sagged. I stared out at the expanse of sea, speckled with white froth.

He cupped my face in his hand. It felt warm and scratchy against my skin. A wave crashed close to our feet, saltwater spraying our legs.

'Hey, look at me.' He pulled my face to his, leaned his forehead against mine. 'Whatever it is, Liv, it'll be okay. We'll be okay.'

I rested my cheek on his shoulder. The smooth material of his windbreaker rustled against my skin. Seagulls yelped and whirled above our heads. In the distance a couple was walking toward us, hands clasped, leaning against each other as the sea sprayed at their feet. A mountain of emotions sat on my chest, making it difficult to breathe.

He wound his arms around my shoulders, and I lifted my face, pressed my lips to his. I loved him so much. But I knew with a clarity I hadn't felt before that I loved our baby, too. I wouldn't sacrifice the baby to keep him. My mom had given up everything to have me, to give me the life I had. I would do the same for my baby.

Suddenly I was terrified, certain I'd lose him when the truth came out.

I kissed him frantically, my lips frenzied with fear of the unknown. I wound my hands through his hair and pulled him closer to me, but it wasn't close enough.

A familiar voice came from over Derek's shoulder, somebody calling my name. For a moment a split in the clouds made it impossible to see who it was, the bright glare casting a glow about the face. But then there she was: Madison. Peter was with her, and they both looked horrified, their faces stamped with a parade of emotions.

Madison's lovely face was hard, all sharp angles and rigid planes. Her eyes were colored with an intense, unmitigated fury, and her lips were drawn around her teeth in an animalistic sneer. Worse, her face was flamed with hurt, torn open by my colossal betrayal.

37

ABI

november

The clouds burst open and released sheets of water as I ran the short distance from Gavin's front door to my car. My heart clattered against my ribcage as I unlocked the door and jammed the key in the ignition. I turned the heating up to high and pressed the palms of my hands against my aching temples.

My hands shook as I massaged my skull. I thought about Gavin's smug face. Now that I was safe in my car, I felt a crushing sense of failure, a powerful regret at not standing up to him.

An unpleasant tightness squeezed my chest. The old Abi would've run away, spent the rest of her life avoiding Anthony. But I didn't want to be that person anymore. I didn't want to run. I didn't want to merely exist. I wanted to truly live.

My whole life I'd pushed people away because I thought I was better off on my own. But Anthony was different. He'd done more to help me than any other person besides my sister. He'd gotten under my skin and met me, the real me, and I couldn't imagine how or why he would betray me. There must be a reasonable explanation.

My phone rang, and I answered it immediately.

'Abi? Detective Samson here. Our tech team traced the addresses that those picture texts in Olivia's iCloud were sent from. Two were sent from the public computers at the Seattle Public Library, and a few more were sent from a proxy server, which we haven't finished tracking yet. But one was sent from 2652 Elliott Avenue, 39B, a Mr Noah Harris. Do you or Olivia know him?'

My mind jammed on her words. Noah Harris was the donor who'd had dinner with Gavin and Kendall the night of Olivia's fall. Somehow this was all connected.

'The name's familiar but I can't think where from. But I do know he's a donor to Gavin Montgomery's campaign.'

'Interesting,' Samson said slowly. 'I think I need to have a talk with Mr Harris.'

'Let me come!' I jumped in.

'Absolutely not,' Samson said vehemently. 'That would be against police policy. I'll call you after I've interviewed him.'

'Detec –'

But she'd already hung up.

I threw my phone down on the passenger seat, frustrated.

She'd said the address. What was it? Right, 2652 39B Elliott Avenue. If I hurried, I could beat her there.

I reversed and turned my car around, about to floor it down the gravel drive when I saw Gavin coming out the front door. I braked hard enough to skid, the gravel spraying my car like machine-gun fire. Gavin turned, startled. I stared at him in the rearview mirror.

For a minute, it felt like time had fallen away and I was a scared, pregnant teenager again. I'd made the wrong choice then. Not about the abortion – I'd made absolutely the right choice keeping Olivia – but taking Gavin's money.

I'd spent my life feeling like he had a claim ticket on us, afraid he'd come and collect on it. I wouldn't live the rest like that. I didn't know how I would pay for Olivia's medical costs. But I knew I could. I was older, stronger, better able to cope than when I got pregnant with Olivia.

And now I needed to fight for the truth – not only for myself, but for Olivia's daughter.

I pulled another copy of the DNA letter out of my purse and got out of my car. I crossed the distance between us swiftly, without breaking eye contact.

'Keep your money.' I handed him the letter. 'I will take care of *my* daughter, just like I always have. *Me.* But you, you have until midday tomorrow to get the detectives back on Olivia's case. I want answers, Gavin. And believe me, I'll do anything to get them.'

I turned on my heel and tossed over my shoulder, 'Otherwise this letter is going right to the media, with a copy e-mailed to your wife.'

× × ×

I drove fast toward downtown Seattle. I exited I-5, passing the Seattle Public Library and Westlake Center and threading my way along First Avenue toward Belltown.

I pulled up in front of a modern thirty-floor apartment building fronted by a rock garden, and jammed some coins into the parking meter. I climbed the steep steps and huddled in the doorway, the best spot to see any cars driving by. Before too long, Samson's unmarked police car pulled up and parked out front.

I flung myself down the stairs, words already spilling out of me: 'Detective, I need to be here.' Samson turned to me, eyes wide. She was dressed head to toe in black, with a police-issue jacket over the top. Her police badge was prominently displayed on a wide black belt at her waist, right next to her gun holster. 'Let me talk to . . .'

But my words trailed off as a familiar figure emerged from her car.

Anthony.

I froze just feet from the car.

'Anthony,' I said faintly. 'What are you doing here?'

Anthony and Samson exchanged glances. They looked like guilty children.

'What the *fuck* is going on!' I burst out. I turned to Anthony. 'Who *are* you?'

'Abi . . .' Anthony shoved a hand through his tousled hair. 'I'm so sorry, I should've told you the truth sooner.'

'Oh God!' I put my hands to my hot cheeks and felt a physical pain spreading through my chest, as if my ribs were cracking open. 'You work for Gavin.'

'What? No!' He blew out a long breath. 'I'm sorry. I tried to tell you, that night you were at my house. I just –'

'Tell me now.'

'All right. Last month Detective Samson called me asking for a favor. She was working on a case but was getting blocked every way she turned. She wasn't given the budget she needed; she found out her partner had left some significant details out of the investigating report; and then he lied about trying to find the victim's cell phone. Every time she got a lead, she was buried under more cases, so the only time she could work on the original case was during her own time. When she talked to the police chief, she was told in no uncertain terms to leave the case alone, to bury it. She knew something was going on.'

'What does this have to do with you?' I asked, frustrated.

'Detective Samson called me and asked if I'd get in touch with you, talk to you and find out if there was anything else you knew. She wanted to solve the case, but she was pretty sure somebody wanted it to play like an accident.'

'So you hired him to work for you?' I asked Samson.

She shook her ice-blonde head. 'No, of course not. I just needed some help, and Anthony said he'd get in touch with you. Off the record. I was working extra shifts, secretly interviewing witnesses, calling in a favor in the IT team to trace the texts. Anthony helped me find out what you knew.'

I shook my head, confused, and said to Samson, 'So the chief pressured you not to investigate Olivia's case? But why?'

'I'm sure there'll be an investigation. I spoke with the Seattle police chief about Anthony, and he now understands the scope of what's happened and has referred it for internal investigation. McNally will be put on administrative leave while they figure out whether he intentionally covered anything up.'

'I'm sorry –' Anthony began, but I whirled on him, anger frothing up inside of me, and cut him off.

'Was anything you told me the truth?'

He looked like I'd slapped him. 'All of it.'

'Your sister? Was she really murdered, or were you just making that up to get my sympathy?'

'I would never make that up, Abi.' His eyes had hardened, and I felt a moment of remorse. 'You know me at least better than that. Everything I told you is the truth. The only thing I left out was who I was helping. And why. Detective Samson closed my sister's case four years ago. I owe her a debt of gratitude that I'll never be able to fully repay. We stayed in touch after she moved to Portage Point, so when she asked for my help, I had no qualms about saying yes.'

He took a step closer to me, his eyes a bright winter green. 'You have every right to be angry. I should've told you sooner. But when was the right time? You've had so much to handle. I didn't want to add to it. I know that it matters how the pieces fit together. And once I met you, I *wanted* to help. It wasn't just a favor anymore. I couldn't let another person go through what I went through.'

He put one hand on my cheek. I closed my eyes and leaned against him, the truth flashing like fire along every nerve and into my brain. The hot anger I'd felt just a moment ago mutated into something softer: understanding. I knew how it felt to want to do the right thing while hiding the truth. I'd done it to Olivia her whole life.

'You can trust me,' Anthony said.

They were some of the last words my mom ever said to me before she killed herself. But Anthony wasn't the same as my mom. And I wasn't the same person I was before I met him.

Trust, I'd learned, was the greatest gift you could give, the greatest gift to receive. The belief that a person wouldn't betray you required a strength and confidence I was only just finding. Trusting someone else, having a partner, meant I was *living*.

My eyes snapped open and fastened on Anthony's. 'I do trust you,' I said.

Rain splashed onto my forehead, and I turned to Detective Samson.

'Thank you for trying to help me. Let me speak to this guy, though. Please. I deserve that much.'

She scanned my face, her mouth set in a hard line. I thought she'd say no, but after a minute she nodded briefly and said, 'Come on, then. Let's get inside.'

At the entrance, Samson lifted the intercom phone and pressed the button for 39B. A few seconds later the door buzzed open, and we entered a modern lobby decorated in neutral marble and bright chrome.

To the left was a gigantic wall of mirrors, to the right a row of mailboxes with tiny silver nameplates. As we crossed to the elevators, my eyes fixed on a name typed in block letters at the top:

HARRIS

And then everything froze, my body suspended between the seconds.

I flashed back to one of the first high school football games I'd gone to with Olivia. Tyler had scored a touchdown, and his name came up on the digital billboard in bright white lights: *TYLER HARRIS!*

Everything clicked into place.

Olivia had said Tyler was living with his dad for the summer.

Noah Harris was Tyler's dad. I remembered him now. I'd met him at that football game.

Tyler's dad lived at this address.

This was where one of the texts had come from.

I felt as if I'd been blundering along in the dark for weeks, and now, only now, had a spotlight finally been cast on the truth, illuminating it in all its gory detail.

Tyler must be the mystery boy who'd taken 'quite a shine' to Kendall at Gavin's campaign dinner – hardly surprising, given how much alike Olivia and Kendall looked.

All roads led back to Tyler.

My world spun and time sped up, as if trying to catch up with itself. I gasped, suddenly dizzy, the floor tilting.

'Abi?' Anthony lunged for me from the elevator, catching me just before I hit the ground.

'Tyler. It's Tyler *Harris*!' I babbled. The words spilled out of me, and there was nothing I could do to stop them. 'I knew I recognized the name! Noah Harris is Tyler's father!'

Samson looked at the elevator. 'Let's go.'

Anthony kept his arm around me as the elevator whisked us to Noah Harris's penthouse apartment. The doors opened to reveal polished oak floors and gorgeous floor-to-ceiling windows. An open-plan living room was decorated with warm tones accentuated by a stand-alone stone fireplace that separated it from an expensively adorned dining room.

The crisp clip of men's dress shoes smacked against the hardwood floor. Anthony dropped his arm from my shoulders, and

I turned to see Noah Harris approaching. The pointed nose and thick lips, the sandy blond hair and hazel eyes so like Tyler's. Noah's bulky frame was wrapped in a dark suit and tie, as if he'd just arrived home from work.

'Abi Knight?' A lopsided, questioning smile lit Noah's face. 'It's good to see you. How are you?'

Noah extended his hand to me, then to Samson and Anthony as I introduced them.

'Noah.' I faced him. 'Detective Samson is investigating Olivia's fall and has a few questions, if you don't mind.'

'Of course. I'm not sure how I can be of help, though.'

'Do you know Gavin Montgomery?' Samson asked, taking her notepad and pen from her coat pocket.

Noah seemed startled. 'The politician? Yes, my company organized a campaign dinner to raise funds for him. I met him there.'

'When was this?'

'The first weekend in October, if I remember correctly.'

'Where was your son the night of that campaign dinner?'

'Tyler? He came with me.'

'We need to speak with him,' Samson said. 'Is he here?'

Noah ran a hand through his hair. 'Is Tyler in trouble? Do I need to call a lawyer?'

'He was one of the last people to see Olivia before she fell, so we just need to ask him a few follow-up questions,' Samson said.

'Okay,' Noah said, looking troubled. 'Well, he's at his mother's in Portage Point.'

38

OLIVIA

october

I'm not usually a reckless person. What happened the day Derek and I slept together wasn't really about being reckless. It was about giving in to the moment, something I didn't do very often. Usually I lived so much in the future: go to a good college, get a job, be successful.

My mom taught me that: Look to the future and you won't stumble on the present. Stay in control. Never let go. I knew now why she was like that, and maybe it wasn't something you could unlearn, but I didn't want to be like that.

With Derek that day, the day we first slept together, it was about the moment. It was about living life, not letting it live you.

I gave up concentrating on my calculus homework and crossed the living room to stare out the sliding glass window. The yard needed mowing. A few dying brown maple leaves clung delicately to the tree; a handful of crunchy ones wheeled across the grass. An unexpected wind stirred the weeping willow at the back of the yard.

Outside, the air was starting to have that fall feeling. The last couple weeks had been damp and soggy, but today was clear and breezy, a new crispness in the air – that sense of things ending and others beginning at the same time.

I'd started to feel a little better lately. I was still sick some mornings, but not as often. And mentally I was stronger too. I hadn't told Derek about the baby, but I would tonight.

I'd put it off for too long. He was just so excited for this architecture course and the chance to prove to his parents he could be a success.

But I'd learned my lesson about telling the truth sooner rather than later with Madison. Since she'd caught Derek and me together at the beach, she'd made school pretty miserable for me.

At lunch, everybody squeezed together so my usual spot disappeared. Last week Dana called me a fat ho-bag as I walked past their table. Alicia stuck her foot out and I tripped over it, sending my milk carton crashing to the ground. The whole group had laughed and I hurried past, my face hot with shame.

It was like fourth grade all over again. Somehow Madison had turned all our friends against me. But this time I knew it wouldn't last forever. Angry Madison could be, like, lethal. But once she found out she had a niece or nephew on the way, she'd get over it.

I pressed the earbuds of my iPhone into my ears and turned up the volume on Bob Marley's 'Everything's Gonna Be Alright.' I grabbed the red scarf Derek got me and looped it around my neck, lifting my arms to the beat and singing along.

I was going to keep the baby. At first I'd worried Mom would be disappointed, but the more I thought about it, the more I realized she'd be totally awesome, just like Aunt Sarah had been when Mom got pregnant with me. Maybe I'd have to give up school for a while, but I could do it later. There was always later.

I'd tell her after I told Derek. After the barbecue tonight.

A soft touch on my shoulder startled me, and my eyes jumped open.

'Mom, hi!' I pulled out my earbuds. 'Sorry, I didn't hear you there.'

A wave of nausea rolled over me. All that spinning. I'd have to mark dancing off the list of things I could do for a while. I flopped onto my chair at the kitchen table and flipped open my history book.

'Are you feeling okay?' She looked worried and pressed the back of her hand to my forehead.

'I'm fine.' I pulled away, my shoulders rigid. 'Just studying.'

'I know it's Saturday, but I have to go into work for a bit.'

She paused, as if expecting me to argue. Inwardly, I perked up. She never worked on weekends. To be honest, I was looking forward to the time by myself.

I listened to her blathering on about me staying inside, locking the doors, not letting anyone in the house, not riding in my friends' cars.

My throat tightened with the effort of containing my impatience. She was leaving me on my own, but she still felt she had to control me. It wasn't like it wasn't safe here. The most exciting thing that had ever happened in our neighborhood was when old Mr Macy down the road died, but he was, like, ninety.

'Do you want me to stay?' she asked, a frown crumpling her forehead. 'You know you come first.'

'No!' I tried not to sound too eager for her to go. I took a deep breath and started again. 'Honestly, it's fine, Mom. I have to study for this calculus test anyway.'

I thought of the balls of crumpled homework assignments stuffed at the bottom of my book bag, all with red Cs and Ds splayed across the front. If Mom found out my grades were slipping, she'd go nuts. I reminded myself she only pushed me because she loved me and wanted what was best for me.

I stood and plucked up the scarf. 'I'm going to take a shower, Mom. See you at the barbecue later.'

It wasn't until she'd left that I remembered I'd forgotten to say thanks or good-bye or I love you, any of the things normal people say. My brain was all over the place lately. But maybe that was okay. Maybe recklessness and just a little bit of abandon were exactly what I needed.

× × ×

I tilted my chin left and right, looking at my new haircut in the mirror behind the cash register. I loved it! A totally new look for the totally new me. My scalp felt so light and free without all that hair to hide behind. My cheekbones were angular, my jaw sharp and defined. I looked older. Confident and bold, not uncertain and timid like my mom. Of course, the low cut of my new peasant top didn't hurt either. My boobs were *huge*!

I exited the hair salon and checked my phone. Five o'clock.

Time to head to Derek's. I strolled along the boardwalk, enjoying the fresh sea smell. The unexpected heat of the autumn day had warmed up the water, making it smell of salty, baked seaweed. Seagulls floated lazily in the sky, squawking and diving for food.

I cut inland from the boardwalk to the long, meandering road that led to the Stokeses' house.

Everywhere I looked the colors of the leaves were changing: fiery orange and red, burnt sienna, burnished gold. It was beautiful. Peaceful. My ballet flats clicked against the pavement, interrupted every so often by a soft carpet of pine needles that turned my steps to whispers.

My phone pinged with an incoming text. I thought it was from Derek, asking where I was, so when I saw the Photoshopped bloody picture of me with my head cut off, it was all the more upsetting. *Fuck you!* was scrawled where my head should've been.

A few seconds later, another message came through. It was a picture of me walking toward the school's track. Was it the day I'd sneaked away to meet Derek so we could find Kendall? My face had been scribbled over in hard, angry lines, a red noose drawn around my neck. *Kill!* was written in red at the bottom.

Then a text.

Fuck you!

And another.

Fuck you!

Then a series of texts started pinging *Die! Die! Die!* over and over and over.

A sob crawled up my throat and I frantically started deleting every hateful text and image I'd gotten, not wanting to see any of them.

'Stop!' I screamed, the air around me suddenly thick, poisoned with the energy of my fear. 'Stop! Why are you doing this?' I whirled around, my heart banging into my ribcage. 'Answer me, God damn it!'

The evergreen branches swayed in the gentle breeze. A squirrel chattered in the trees. Everything was quiet, but suddenly I was seized by a sense of dread. My limbs started quivering like a skeleton's. I knew the cold nausea edging up my throat was more than pregnancy. It was fear.

I launched myself across the bridge. My feet thudded hard against the wooden walkway as I ran up the hill to the Stokeses' house. I paused at the end of the driveway next to the house-shaped mailbox, my hands shaking, sucking in deep, gasping breaths of oxygen.

And then my phone rang, vibrating in the hand that clutched it.

For a second I was too scared to look. The phone rang and rang, my heart still wheeling around my chest. But then common sense washed over me. It might be my mom.

But it wasn't.

'Hi, Olivia.' I recognized Kendall's voice, and my heart sank. I liked her, but what Gavin had said about her being mentally unsteady made me a bit nervous. Plus, Derek had told me she'd followed Gavin and me to the diner. What a weirdo.

'Hey, Kendall.'

'It's been ages,' she chirped. 'How've you been?'

I walked up the curved pathway past trees strung with twinkling lights to the Stokeses' beautiful Tudor-style house, pausing under the arching brick entrance and sitting on the stone steps.

I resisted the urge to groan out loud. Talking on the phone

with Kendall was the last thing I wanted to do right now. I was already on edge about those creepy pictures, plus I had to face Madison, and then I needed to tell Derek I was pregnant.

'I'm good.' I glanced around to make sure nobody was listening. 'You?'

Three guys from my class walked toward me and exchanged glances, then waved awkwardly. I put my hand over the phone and smiled, then moved out of the way so they could go inside. I'd forgotten how many people came to this neighborhood barbecue every year.

'Good, good. So, I got the results back from that DNA test you had sent to me.'

I'd forgotten about that. It didn't matter now. I'd met Gavin and knew the truth, and a little piece of me wished I didn't.

'Yeah?' I replied, feigning interest. It had been nice of Kendall to let me have the results sent to her. I didn't want to hurt her feelings.

'Yeah. The letter says Gavin's your biological father. Probability percentage is 99.9942.' She laughed. 'I'd say that's pretty clear.'

'Yeah, no kidding.' A car pulled up and parked across the street. A man and a woman in matching khaki pants and white polo shirts got out and walked toward the house. They brushed past me as if I weren't even there.

'I guess that means we're sisters, right?'

She sounded delighted, but I knew the truth. It didn't matter at all. I wanted nothing to do with Gavin. My friendship with Kendall was just collateral damage.

I laughed awkwardly. 'Yeah, I guess it does.'

'Are you going to talk to him?'

'Definitely,' I lied. I didn't want to tell her I wouldn't. She seemed so pleased that we were sisters, like we'd end up hanging out and brushing each other's hair or something. 'I'll call him and try to meet up with him for sure.'

'Cool. Well, look. Just be careful, all right? He can be dangerous, and when he doesn't get his way, he's like a spoiled toddler with a gun.'

'Of course, yeah.'

I looked toward the house. Upstairs a curtain twitched. Madison was watching me.

'Uh, I have to go now,' I said. 'I'm at a friend's house. I'll talk to you later, okay?' And before she could protest, I hung up the phone.

39

OLIVIA

october

I shoved my phone into the pocket of my brown leather jacket and rang the doorbell. Dr Stokes threw open the door. She was dressed in a sleeveless, body-clinging red dress that showed off her cleavage. Who dressed like that for a barbecue? I glanced down at my leggings and loose-fitting peasant top feeling underdressed.

'Hello, Olivia, darling.' She air-kissed me on both cheeks like we were European royalty. She always did that, put on airs. Maybe it was where Madison got her snobbiness. 'My goodness! Look at your hair!'

I grinned and twirled like a ballerina. 'D'you like it?'

She tilted her head to the side and looked at me intently. 'I do. It suits your bone structure.'

I beamed, pleased. 'Thanks.'

I followed her into the house, shrugging out of my jacket and hanging it on the coat rack by the door.

Uniformed caterers and black-and-white-clad waiters carried giant trays of food from the kitchen to a linen-draped table in the backyard.

I peeked at one tray: fat wedges of cheese on pale crackers, a crystal bowl filled with suspicious-looking black balls, fire-engine-red chilies stuffed with cream cheese, massive green olives bloated with garlic wedges. And the smell . . . it was divine.

'Looks amazing, Dr Stokes,' I said. My stomach growled, and I crossed my hands over my middle and laughed, embarrassed.

'Madison!' she called down the hall.

I cringed, nerves fluttering in my stomach. Madison appeared like a wraith from the hallway a few seconds later.

'Oh, it's you.' Her inky eyes scraped across my face. I peeked at Dr Stokes, wondering if she could sense the tension between us, but she'd already wandered away, flapping her hands and saying something to the caterers. She was like that, though, totally self-absorbed.

Madison hitched one hip against the dining room table and leaned an arm on the chair while she looked at me.

'Your hair's short,' she said. I wasn't sure if it was a compliment or a criticism.

'Yeah.' I touched the strawberry-shortcake-pink tips self-consciously. 'I wanted a change.'

'Well, you got it.' A flash of sadness broke across the tight anger etched into her face.

'Mad –'

'Oh, hey, babe.' Derek appeared from the kitchen and grinned at me. A lock of hair hung over his eye and I wanted to brush it away, to feel the warm skin of his forehead. For a moment everyone else, including Madison, simply disappeared.

'Wow! Your hair looks amazing!' He fingered the tips of my hair. 'I really like the pink highlights. Very punk.'

Madison shoved away from the table and glared at us.

'Found a crowbar big enough to get the knife out of my back yet?' she snarled acidly. The comment was directed at both of us, but her eyes aimed at me. Derek stepped between us, catching the glare like a sword to the chest.

'For fuck's sake, Madison,' he said, eyes glowing fiercely. 'Just shut up, would you? Olivia hasn't done anything wrong.'

But I had. I'd betrayed my best friend and I had to fix that.

I reached past Derek for Madison's hand. 'Please don't be mad. I know –'

'Whatever,' she cut me off scathingly. 'You've told so many lies, I don't want to hear them anymore. I hope you smother on them.'

She huffed dramatically down the hallway. At the last second, she turned and smirked at us. 'Oh,' she said, all faux innocence. 'I invited Tyler here tonight. I figured it would be such a shame if he missed out this year. He is still *my* friend, after all.'

And with that parting shot, she flipped her hair over her shoulder and stormed back toward the hallway.

'But she hates Tyler!' I said to Derek, hurt mingling with incredulity.

'Ignore her. She's just trying to upset you. Don't worry, she'll get over it.' He grabbed my hand and pulled me toward the back door. 'I'm starving. Let's go get some food, and then I want to show you something.'

The backyard had been transformed. A canopy of lights arched over the deck; candles in delicate crystal holders were dotted around white-linen-draped tables. Next to a smoking barbecue was a sleek bar with a uniformed bartender already mixing colorful cocktails.

Derek made a beeline for the bar, but I tugged on his hand. 'Derek. Can we talk? I sorta need to tell you something.'

'Okay, but can we eat first? I'm starving, and my dad said I could have a drink.'

It was ages before we had another minute alone. I chatted to some kids from my school, and Derek had a few beers with his friends, so he disappeared for a while. Then my mom showed up and was predictably shocked about my hair. I could see her thoughts storming across her face, but she didn't say anything about it – she'd never tell me off in front of people.

A little bit later I got a text from her saying she'd gone home early, so I found Derek and tugged at his hand.

'Derek, can we go somewhere and talk?' I murmured.

'Oh yeah, sorry,' he said. His eyes were glassy, and I could tell he was buzzed from the beer. 'Hey, I have something for you. I made it and I think I want to give it to you now.'

'Okay, let's go to your room, yeah?' I said.

We sneaked around the side of the house to Derek's bedroom door. The party was in full swing now that night had descended, neighbors and friends around town streaming into the backyard, exclaiming over the beauty of the décor and debating whether it was warm enough to dive into the swimming pool. Uniformed waiters meandered through the thickening crowd with appetizers and tall, bubbling glasses of champagne.

Derek pulled me inside and shut the door, the thrum of the crowd immediately turning to a low murmur. He pulled me into his arms and kissed me full on the lips, his mouth tasting of beer and barbecue sauce.

'Here.' He pulled a blanket off his bed, spreading it on the floor like a picnic blanket.

'So, what'd you want to show me?' I asked.

'Ahhh. So the lady is curious.' The beer had made Derek extra goofy, and I debated for a second whether I should wait until he was sober to tell him about the baby.

'Very curious,' I said, smiling.

'Okay, but look, it's just something, I mean, if you don't like it, that is, you don't *have* to like it –'

'Derek, I'm sure I'll love it.' I hid a smile. He was so cute when he got nervous.

He nodded and disappeared down the dark hallway at the back of the room, emerging a moment later with a wooden ten-by-twelve picture frame. He flipped the frame to face me.

'I said one day I'd draw you,' he said quietly. 'I've been working on it the last few weeks.'

'Derek!' I gasped. The portrait was beautiful. He'd sketched me in black and white charcoal, the lines delicate yet flowing. My right hand was bent under my chin, my hair long, smoothed on either side of my face. My lips were dark, glistened with shadow, just a hint of a smile tugging at the corners. But it was my eyes he'd captured best.

They were pensive, wide and luminous, peeking at him through long lashes. He'd somehow exposed a vulnerability I'd never seen in myself before. At first glance I looked dreamy, wistful, an aura

341

of fragility about me. But on second glance, I could tell it was more specific than that. Derek had drawn me in love.

'It was that day, you know, our first time together in bed, and you looked at me, and the look you gave me, I've never forgotten it.'

I didn't say anything. I couldn't, I was so full of emotion. I reached for the frame and Derek started to babble in the lengthening silence. I traced a finger across the portrait.

'You don't have to put it up or anything, you know, if you don't like it or whatever.' He reached one hand over his head and rubbed his neck, looking uncomfortable.

I put my finger on his mouth and leaned in and kissed him.

'It's beautiful.' I looked again at the portrait. 'It's seriously, absolutely beautiful.'

I glanced at the darkened hallway. 'Is that what you do back there, then? Draw?'

'Yeah. It's sort of my art studio.' Derek shrugged, embarrassed.

'I love it.' I kissed him again. 'And I love you. Thank you.'

His shoulders lowered and he exhaled. 'So, what did you want to tell me?'

'Oh.' I shook my head, trying to change gear. 'Here, sit down.'

He leaned the frame against the foot of his bed and sat cross-legged in front of me.

'I don't know how to tell you. . .'

'There's nothing you can't tell me.'

As if it were that easy.

'Okay.' I exhaled through pursed lips, then inhaled deeply through my nose.

'I'm pregnant.'

× × ×

I don't know how long we sat there like mirror-image yogis. Derek had turned a disturbing shade of gray, not one syllable or drop of sound dribbling from him. Time ticked by at an excruciating pace.

Finally he spoke, his voice low and tight: 'What are you, we, what are we going to do about it?'

'What do you mean?'

'Well, I mean, I have some money saved. We could –'

I cut him off. 'I'm keeping the baby, Derek.'

'Olivia.' He shook his head, blotches of red rising to his cheeks. 'Fuck!' He shook his head again and rubbed both hands over his eyes. 'I'm starting college and . . . Fuck! My parents! I can't . . .'

Irritation slid up my spine, mingling with a nervous sweat that had broken out along the skin at my back. Upstairs, the doorbell gonged, then I heard a shout of laughter from Madison. A second later I recognized the low rumble of another voice. Tyler.

I jumped up, tears burning my eyes.

'I thought you'd be different, but you're just like Gavin,' I said quietly. Then I turned and ran up the stairs.

'Olivia!' he shouted behind me. But he didn't come after me, and that in itself was a slap in the face.

I threw open the door and burst into the living room. Madison, Peter, and Dan turned, surprised at the interruption. Madison narrowed her eyes at me. Peter shifted awkwardly from one foot to the other, while Dan openly leered at me.

'Is Tyler here?' I asked.

'Yeah, he's here,' Madison drawled. She folded her arms over her chest and jutted one hip out.

'Do you know where he went?'

She glanced at Peter, who shrugged and looked away. Finally Dan spoke: 'He probably went to find his girlfriend.'

I flushed, embarrassed. I could tell he'd slid the last part in to upset me.

'Oh.' I chewed a corner of my cheek. I needed to speak to Tyler. We'd never really broken up. Even after Madison told me he was going to break up with me, we just didn't talk about it.

But now I needed to tell him the truth. It was all going to come out anyway: Derek and me, the baby. It would be better if Tyler heard it from me. And I was sick of hiding everything.

'Excuse me,' I muttered. I grabbed my coat from the coat rack and let myself out.

I hustled down the driveway past Tyler's red Jeep Renegade, but I didn't see him, or his new girlfriend, whoever she was.

I shivered. The temperature had dropped. I walked down the incline to the bridge, the dark of night folding around me. It was so black I might have fallen into the sky, the only light the twinkling of peekaboo stars that flashed intermittently through the boughs of the evergreens.

I debated for an extra second whether or not to take the shortcut through the forest. Mom wouldn't like me walking that way in the dead of night. But I just wanted to be home, so I headed over the ZigZag Bridge toward the inclined shortcut that led to my house.

Beneath my feet the river roared angrily. I was gazing over the edge of the bridge at the turbulence of the muddy water, which was why I didn't see them until I got to the embankment on the far side. When I looked up, there was Tyler, clasped tightly in the arms of another girl.

It took me a second to realize who the other girl was, and when I did I gasped out loud.

'Kendall!'

They broke apart abruptly. Kendall stumbled a little to the side, and Tyler grasped her arm to keep her from falling over. She giggled, her head lolling back for a second before straightening. It took her a long moment to focus on my face. Was she wasted?

'Oh! Hi, Oliiiiiviiiaaa,' she slurred. 'My lllong-lllost sister!' Her eyebrows crinkled in sudden confusion. 'What are yooouuuu doing here?'

I looked at Tyler. A Cheshire cat grin was embossed on his face. I knew suddenly, with certainty, that he'd set this up to make me jealous. The idea of him going to such great lengths, using Kendall in this way, nauseated me.

'Tyler, why are you doing this?' I shook my head, disgusted.

'Doing what, Olivia?' Tyler asked innocently.

I sighed, exasperated with his games. 'You need to take Kendall home right now.'

'Whaaat? No way!' Kendall piped up. 'We're only juushhht starting. Tyler rescued me from my dad's reeeaaaalllly boring campaign dinner. Anyway, thisshh is way more fun!' She threw an arm around Tyler's shoulder and slurped messily at his neck. God, she was totally blackout!

'Kendall, Tyler was my boyfriend. Remember when you were

at my house, and I told you it was complicated?' I pointed at Tyler. 'He's why.'

It took Kendall a moment to grasp what I was saying. Then her arm fell from Tyler's neck and she stepped away from him, her eyes blazing.

'What the actual *fuck*? Were you jusssht using me to get at her? You fucking dick!' She shoved at him, but was too drunk to move him. He didn't take his eyes off mine.

'You are sshhheriously messed up.' She swayed on her feet. 'I'm going back to the car. You'd better take me home.' Kendall stormed unsteadily in the direction of the Stokeses' house.

The silence expanded between Tyler and me like a widening oil spill, but there was nothing else to say right now – I was too furious. I brushed past him and headed home.

'Olivia, we need to talk,' he called from behind me.

I sighed and turned around, pulled my phone out of my pocket to check the time. The battery icon flashed at me; it was about to die. And I only had five minutes before curfew.

I hesitated. He was right, we did need to talk. But it would have to wait. If I wasn't home before curfew my mom would send the cops out looking for me.

A wave of exhaustion crashed into me. I just wanted to go to bed.

'We can talk tomorrow, Tyler,' I said tiredly. 'Right now I just have to get home.'

And with that, I turned and walked away.

40

ABI

november

The rain had continued to fall while we were at Noah's. The pavement was slick and black, the orange orbs of the streetlights smeared against the darkening sky. The charcoal gray of evening descended quickly into the blackness of night as we drove north on I-5 toward Portage Point.

Samson had insisted we leave my car at Noah's.

'You're in no condition to drive,' she said. 'Parking's free overnight. We'll get your car in the morning.'

I wanted to argue, but something horrible buzzed deep in my head. Something like anger, only worse, like tar seeping into my head or a swarm of black flies feeding off my brain. My hands trembled and my breathing came fast and shallow. So I climbed in the front passenger seat.

Somehow I'd missed Tyler in all this. I'd been a fool. He'd

seemed so absolutely eviscerated by his loss. But I knew better than anyone that you could love someone and still hurt them.

I ran back through every moment of our conversations: when he'd come to my house a couple days after Olivia's fall, then again in the school parking lot. He'd said he was at the barbecue that night, and Madison had backed him up. But he must've slipped away when nobody was looking. The truth I'd missed flashed like fire at the back of my eyes.

The drive home seemed to last forever and go by in a blink at the same time.

We exited I-5 and wound along the sea. Night had pulled a black curtain over the sky, making the surf barely visible beyond the charcoal shoreline.

Samson's phone rang and she answered it, murmuring 'okay' a few times, throwing a glance at me, then hanging up.

'That was Gavin Montgomery,' she said. 'He said he left the campaign dinner early because he went upstairs to a hotel room with a waitress.'

'At his own campaign dinner? Jesus!' I exclaimed. 'How did his wife not notice?'

'He said he wasn't gone long. A half hour, tops. When he got back, Kendall was gone. So was Tyler.'

'They left together?'

'He told me to speak to his lawyer, but that's what I'm thinking.'

I chewed my lip. 'Do you believe him?'

'We'll question Tyler and Kendall. And we'll follow up on Gavin's whereabouts, speak to the waitress independently to verify it, but I'm sure he knows that.'

'You all right?' Anthony asked from the backseat.

'I'm fine,' I said. 'I just . . .' I glanced back at him. 'I'm not sure what Gavin has to do with all this.'

Anthony didn't reply, but I knew what he was thinking. Maybe he wasn't involved. Maybe I'd let myself be biased against Gavin from the start.

I thought hard, trying to make sense of what I knew so far, aligning the facts and making them into a coherent theory. The problem was, I had yet to piece together the facts of Olivia's fall.

Samson took the next turn, her headlights sweeping across the web of sharply bending roads that followed the contours of Portage Point toward Tyler's mom's house. After a few minutes we plunged down the steep hill that led to the ZigZag River. We careened around that last corner, and there it was, the intricate metal suspension of the ZigZag Bridge gleaming in the harsh yellow streetlights.

And there, sitting on the low cement wall at the edge of the bridge's pedestrian walkway, as if he knew we were coming, was Tyler.

× × ×

Tyler squinted as our headlights raked across his face. Gravel pinged the underbelly of the car as Samson whipped the steering wheel to the left and skidded onto the shoulder.

I heaved my door open and lunged toward the suspension bridge, vaguely aware that Anthony was right behind me. It was bitterly cold, a deep-down sort of cold that sliced into my skin.

The light drizzle picked up, hurled water into my eyes as I crossed the road.

Tyler was sitting on the low wall at the outermost edge of the bridge. His feet hung over the edge, but his upper body was twisted so he faced me. I stopped, suddenly cautious. I didn't know what he was capable of.

I glanced back at where Samson had parked and was calling for backup. A few feet behind me, Anthony waited.

Would Tyler jump? Did I want him to?

'Tyler?' I said.

'Hi, Miss Knight.'

His eyes were red-rimmed, inflamed, as if he'd been staring too long into the dark. His cheeks glistened damply in the glow of the streetlights.

'What are you doing there?' I asked, my voice taut and twisted, as if I had a fishhook jammed into my throat. My hands were stiff with cold. I pushed them deep into the pockets of my wool coat.

'My dad called. Told me you guys were coming.'

'Why don't you come over to this side?' I walked slowly, cautiously, toward him, my palm outstretched.

A gust of wind blew across the bridge, slicing through my coat. I shivered violently and stared into his hollow eyes. Up close he looked older, haunted. His eyes were shrunken in their sockets, his skin stretched over his cheekbones. His fair hair was plastered to his forehead in spiky little lines.

Tyler ignored my proffered hand. 'This is where she fell.'

A pulse of panic fluttered in my chest, and the world spun and tilted in a dizzying distortion of time. My head thumped and a wave of anger at my own stupidity washed over me.

It was Tyler.

Tyler looked out over the roiling water, and suddenly my anger turned outward. White-tipped and scorching, it launched away from me toward Tyler. *He* was the reason my daughter wasn't coming back to me.

The urge to understand the truth warred with a sudden, all-consuming urge to push him. I hated him viciously. I felt the anger, the same red anger I'd felt at Jen, grow inside me, a balloon about to burst. I moved toward him – but at the last second, I stopped.

If I pushed him, I'd never find out exactly what had happened to Olivia. I needed to know what had happened that night. I needed the truth more than I needed my version of justice.

'I know you loved her.' My voice was clear and calm, as if someone else were here in my place speaking for me; as if what he said now wouldn't crack the world in two.

In the distance, the caterwauling of police sirens wailed. Tyler's mouth gave a panicky spasm. He jumped up so he was standing on the low wall, his eyes glinting wildly. His nostrils flared. He was surrounded, with nowhere to go but over.

A sense of urgency seized me. My heart drummed a desperate beat. Despite the icy cold, sweat dampened my palms.

'You tried to tell me, didn't you?' The pounding of my chest launched the words from me. 'The first day when you came to see me.' I took a step closer to him. 'I'm sorry, Tyler. I'm listening now. Come down here and talk to me. Tell me what happened.'

His pupils dilated to pools of black. His mouth thinned.

'Please, Tyler,' I begged him. 'Talk to me. For Olivia's sake.'

And then the devastation and grief of our shared tragedy finally caught up with him. His face collapsed in on itself, sorrow a heavy weight that bore down on him. His shoulders hitched, and he dropped his head into his hands. A sob wrenched miserably from somewhere deep in his chest.

'She betrayed me!' The words sounded like they were pieces ripped out of his throat. 'She made me look like a fucking fool. But I swear I didn't mean to hurt her.' Tears streamed down Tyler's face.

'What happened that night?'

'She called me a psycho, and I was so pissed off. It was like I was in a dream, this big, red, cloudy dream. I wanted to stop myself, but it felt like my brain couldn't catch up to what I was doing, and before I knew it I'd hit her and it was too late to stop myself. I didn't know she'd die. I didn't know!'

His words faded into the wet, sucking sound of intense sobbing. The heaviness inside me became even more oppressive.

'Why didn't you call the police? Why didn't you get help?'

'She's a swimmer! I saw her in the water and she was swimming and I thought she'd be okay!' More sobbing. 'I didn't know she was pregnant until you told me. I think . . . I don't know . . . maybe she tried to tell me, but that's when I hit her and she was falling and I couldn't do anything about it.'

The branches of the evergreens shuddered in the wind, long, skeletal shadows skating across the dim streetlight. In my peripheral vision, I saw Anthony moving closer to me.

I took the last step and reached for Tyler's hand, gently tugging him down from the cement wall. A flicker of awareness washed over me, the power I had in that instant. But I knew that the price of my justice would never be enough. Or it would be too much, depending on how you looked at it.

He came easily, like a broken puppy, his shoulders slumped, his face a mess of snot and tears. He slid onto the damp walkway, his back against the cement wall, and I sat next to him.

Icy rain needled my scalp, plastering my hair to my head. The damp cold crept into my jeans, spreading up through my torso, cracking my ribs open wide and exposing my heart.

Samson stood within earshot, her hand on her gun holster. And a few steps closer to me, Anthony also was a witness to everything Tyler said now.

'Why did you send her those pictures?' I asked.

'My friend Dan, he saw her kissing some guy in Laurelwood.' Tyler's mouth twisted. 'I couldn't believe it. I mean, my mom cheated on my dad, and then my girlfriend cheated on me? It's like a fucking movie. I thought if I sent her those messages, she'd be scared and maybe she'd, you know, come running back to me? Like, tell me she was getting them. And maybe she'd . . . I don't know . . . stay with me.'

Awareness bloomed inside of me, a blaze of light shining on what should have been so obvious all along. He'd been afraid of losing her, so he'd tried to hold her tight, but in doing so he'd pushed her away.

The distant wail of police cars suddenly rushed forward. Four of them surrounded the bridge, two blocking off each end. The intermittent whirl of red and blue flashing turned the bridge to a scene of chaos.

'I'm sorry,' Tyler sobbed pathetically. 'I'm so, so sorry.'

I took his hand, my body shivering with cold. 'I know.'

He tilted his face to mine, his eyes hollow, rain pinging off his face.

'Why don't you tell me what happened that night, Tyler?'

41

OLIVIA

october

When I got home the house was completely quiet, the living room lamp producing a warm orange glow. A mostly empty bottle of red wine stood alone on the kitchen counter. I dumped the rest into the sink and threw the bottle in the recycling bin.

I'd bet my college tuition that Mom was asleep, and once she was asleep she was out for the night. So much for talking to her tonight. I hadn't even needed to rush home to make curfew.

I tiptoed up the stairs and peeked inside her room. Mom was completely conked out, her head slouched to the side and half buried under a pillow. I crossed the room and moved the pillow so I could kiss her on the forehead.

I thought about crawling into her bed and curling up next to her, the way I used to. When I was little, I did it almost every night, cuddling up to her while she snored softly. Especially if it was stormy or really cold. I think we both liked the feeling of having the other there.

'Love you,' I whispered as I switched off the lamp.

Back in my room, I sat on the edge of my bed. There was no way I'd be able to sleep with all this nervous energy in me. I grabbed my phone and texted Tyler. *You're right. We need to talk. You still at bbq? Meet in 15?*

A few seconds later my phone buzzed.

Tyler: *Yep. See you in a few.*

I wondered what Kendall was doing. It seemed like there would be a lot of questions from people who knew me if she was at the barbecue with him. I just didn't care anymore.

The battery icon on my phone flashed again. I reached for the cord at the side of my bed and plugged it in, leaving it on my bedside table. Might as well leave it here if it was going to die anyway.

I slid my coat back on and crept downstairs, shutting the door quietly behind me.

× × ×

The night air was chilly, a brisk breeze blowing. I pulled the collar of my leather jacket up to warm my neck and ducked into the copse of woods along the back of my house.

Despite the day's reprieve from rain, the ground was still slick and wet, rising unsteadily beneath my feet. I was only a few months pregnant, but my balance was totally off. I'd read online it was because all these wild hormones made my ligaments loose.

It was crazy how this tiny little bean could take over everything about me.

I placed my hand on my stomach and stroked it gently. There was a *baby* inside of me. Now that the shock had worn off, I felt . . . in *awe* of that fact. A baby I already loved and would do anything for.

A streetlight flickered over the ZigZag Bridge as I crossed it, reflecting against the metal suspension. My shoes echoed against the wooden pedestrian walkway as I moved across the bridge. Nearly on the other side, I stopped and peered over the cement barrier at the roaring river below.

My earlier inertia had subsided, burning away my fatigue and filling me with an uneasy anticipation. I had a plan now. First, I'd find Tyler at the barbecue and apologize for not being honest with him. I should've told him the truth from the beginning. I thought I was trying to save him from getting hurt, but if I was totally honest, I'd really wanted to save myself.

And after I spoke to Tyler, I'd find Derek. I'd been unfair to him too, dropping the p-bomb and running away. Not cool at all.

Of course it was a shock. What did I expect? It wasn't like he was going to dance for joy at being a nineteen-year-old daddy. But he'd come around. And if he didn't . . . well, at least now I knew it was better to have an absent father than a bad one.

'Hey.' A touch on my shoulder made me jump.

'Tyler!' I gasped. 'God, you scared me!'

'Sorry.' He stepped back and shoved his hands in his back pockets. 'Thought I'd meet you out here.'

I peered over his shoulder. In the distance, I could see his Jeep parked next to Derek's Mustang in front of the Stokeses' house. The irony didn't escape me.

'Where's Kendall?' I asked. 'Is she at the barbecue?'

'Naww, she passed out in my car.' He rolled his eyes. 'She won't even remember tonight. I'll take her home later. Fucking lightweight. She has serious daddy issues.'

'So . . .' I bit my lip and looked at the ground. 'I just wanted to say I'm sorry. For the way things have been. You're right, I haven't been entirely honest with you, and you don't deserve that.'

I looked up and caught his eye. His face looked very pale under the glow of the streetlight. The faint smattering of freckles across the bridge of his nose stood out sharply.

'Dan told me,' he said, his voice low and hard. 'He saw you in Laurelwood kissing some guy. But you wouldn't admit it. I followed you, but you were so sneaky. I never saw you go anywhere but over to Madison's. I knew Dan was telling the truth – I was just waiting to catch you.'

All those times I'd felt eyes burning into my back, I'd felt the hair rise on my arms – it was because I was being *watched*. Tyler hadn't realized I was going to the Stokeses' house to see Derek, not Madison.

'You *followed* me?' I whispered, my voice hoarse. A dark, inexplicable unease feathered inside me.

He didn't answer. I felt a thought crouching somewhere in the back of my mind. It leapt, and I caught up with the thread of possibility circling my brain.

'Tyler.' My stomach twisted painfully. 'Have *you* been sending me those scary picture messages?'

His nostrils flared and he cracked some tension out of his fingers, but he didn't answer. I backed away from him until my butt hit the bridge's low cement wall.

I pressed my fingers into my eyes until all I could see were white stars bursting in front of me. How could he do something so cruel?

'Tyler . . . why?'

'You were cheating on me all fucking summer!' he spat bitterly.

'Jesus.' My legs were unreliable, like new grass. I suddenly felt weak all over. 'You're such a creeper.'

He glared at me from under a brow thickened with anger, his mouth a narrow slit of fury.

'I'm a creeper? You're a fucking slut, Olivia!' His lip curled into a sneer of disgust. 'You lied to me the way my mom lied to my dad. You made me look like a fool!'

'I said I'm sorr –'

'Just stop! I don't want your fake apologies!'

Rage radiated out from him in waves. Adrenaline kicked hot and silent in my blood, and I leaned away, wanting to escape the vortex of his fury.

'Who is he?' he demanded, moving closer to me. 'Who'd you cheat on me with?'

'Look, I . . .' I hesitated, glanced over my shoulder at the river crashing wildly. The wind whistled through the trees, and I shivered.

'What?' He bristled, his lips pulled back in a snarl. 'What were you gonna say? You 'looove' him?' He spat out the word as if it had vile connotations.

I held his gaze. Madison was wrong. I wasn't vanilla, and I wouldn't be a doormat anymore. I could stand up for myself *and* the guy I loved. I lifted my chin and glared at Tyler.

'Yes, I do love him,' I said. 'I'm sorry I've hurt you, and I know I should've told you sooner. I've made a mess out of this, and I am sorry, but this is it for us. I need you to accept that and stop acting crazy.'

His mouth flapped open and fury rolled over his face like a tide; his eyes narrowed and glittered in the streetlight.

Like a snake he struck, caught both my wrists in his hands and squeezed, clasping me with fists of iron. I struggled, trying to wrench myself free, but he was stronger, his face twisted into an ugly mask.

'You stupid fucking bitch,' he hissed, spittle gathering in the corners of his mouth.

A cold edge of nausea slid from my belly into my throat and fear pinged metallic against my tongue. For the first time in my life, I was genuinely afraid of Tyler.

'Tyler, stop!'

I struggled against his viselike grip, twisting my hands left, then right. His fingers were like steel. I could feel the soft skin of my wrists bruising, smashed between my sharp bones and his hands. My mouth went dry and I forgot how to speak, how to scream. With one final heave I twisted my arms from him, and his hands snapped off mine with a sickening jerk.

'Stop! You're hurting me!'

'I'm hurting you?!' he shrieked. His eyes were black flecks of coal burning in his face. '*I'm* hurting *you*?!'

'You're a fucking psycho!' I spat. 'Fine! You want the truth? I'm –' My admission was cut off by a streak of blazing hot pain as something exploded against the side of my head. My brain barely registered the blow, my vision a dusky blur of red, pain searing into my skull and down my jaw. I felt my body spin with the force of it.

I reeled backward until my legs whacked against the low cement wall and I tumbled over, my body hurtling sideways across the ledge. A dark fog pressed against my outer vision, and before I knew it I was falling, plunging into empty space.

I hit the water on my back, my eyes fastened on the bridge's lacy arches illuminated by a flickering streetlamp.

Then the shadowy water tipped me under.

I kicked, clawed for the surface, but was tangled beneath the immense weight of the water. I didn't know which way was up, nor could I get my body to move to reach it. I tried to scream, but swallowed gulps of muddy river water instead. It burned as it slid down my throat.

Water shifted around me, twisting me this way and that. I kicked hard, my lungs desperate for air. My chest felt like it was being crushed between fiery jaws.

Suddenly the water thrust my body up and my head cracked against something hard. Pain seethed through my head, worse even than before. White light blazed behind my eyelids and a ringing crashed in my ears, like a giant elephant thundering down the stairs.

My baby, I thought, and it gave me the strength to give one last massive kick.

Fresh air burst into my lungs as I broke the surface, searing like fire across my chest. I sucked in another breath, and another, coughing and hacking as river water spewed out of me. And that air revitalized me just the ounce I needed.

I kicked again and moved one arm, just one, and threw it up and over my head. My fingers sank into pebbles lining the river's edge. I did it again, pulling my body up with every last bit of strength I had until only my lower half was submerged. My face pressed into the uneven gravel, hard and sharp.

I tried to lift my head, to call for help, but couldn't. A thick rushing sound pulsed in my skull, but I couldn't tell if it was the sound of the river or if it came from inside my head.

I spoke silently to my baby, the words my mom used to say to me when I was scared.

Whenever, whatever. I'm here forever.

I tried to stay awake, but my mind was trapped beneath the weight of my skull, diving into a thick, lethargic spin toward the dark mists of sleep.

It didn't hurt anymore. I was too tired to feel any pain. My eyelashes were so heavy, like sandbags were pressed against them. I wondered fleetingly if this was what it felt like when my mom slept so deeply, like the dead.

And I knew that, soon, I'd find out for sure.

42

ABI

february, 3 months later

I hurried from the edge of the hospital parking lot, cutting across the carpet of lawn that decorated the square in front of the hospital. Along the beach road between the hospital and Puget Sound, gigantic trees shivered in the bitter winter wind, their bare limbs clattering against each other.

Inside, the sudden quiet was unsettling. I rushed to the elevator, feeling as if something terrible was waiting.

Sarah was brushing Olivia's hair when I entered the room, long, languid strokes. In that moment, I loved my sister more than ever just because of how much she loved my daughter.

'How is she?' I dropped my purse in the chair next to the door.

'The baby's fine,' Sarah said. 'She's sleeping, actually. Dr Maddox just finished the ultrasound.'

I groaned, disappointed. I'd tried to make it to the hospital in time, but the court proceedings had taken longer than expected. Tyler's parents were fighting tooth and nail for their son. I understood. But I would fight back just as hard for my daughter. For justice.

The police had charged Tyler with assault causing bodily harm, a charge that would change to voluntary manslaughter when Olivia died. It wasn't a slam-dunk case, by any means – proving that he'd intended to kill her when he punched her and that the punch rather than the fall rendered Olivia brain-dead would be difficult. But his crime of passion meant a pregnant teenager was never coming back. He hadn't even tried to help her. Instead, he'd rushed in a blind panic back to the Stokeses' barbecue and pretended he'd been there all along.

He would be punished.

'Miss Knight?' A knock sounded at the door to Olivia's room, and I looked up.

'I thought I'd find you here,' Detective Samson said, smiling. Her expression wasn't warm exactly, but at least the blank slate was gone. I guessed everybody had their own way of coping with the ugliness in the world.

'Detective Samson,' I said, rising and shaking her hand. 'Has something happened?'

'We've pressed charges against Kendall Montgomery for obstruction of justice. We got access to her phone and found texts she'd sent to Tyler. She was blackmailing him. She suspected he'd hurt Olivia, so she threatened to tell the police if he said anything about her being there that night. They were each other's alibi. And each other's downfall.'

I was glad. Kendall bore some responsibility for what had happened. We would have known the truth sooner if she'd only told us about being with Tyler that night. She'd thought she could use the situation to frame her dad. I couldn't fathom how much hatred she must hold in her heart for him. In the end, it turned out she was just like him: selfish and manipulative to the core.

'And Gavin?' I asked.

After the media had caught wind of Tyler's arrest and the truth started to emerge, whispers began to swirl that Olivia was Gavin Montgomery's daughter. Once word leaked that he'd bribed the Portage Point police chief to bury Olivia's case, those whispers turned to a roar. He lost spectacularly in the election, and shortly afterward his wife had filed for divorce.

Samson nodded. 'We're charging him with bribery of a public official. The Portage Point chief flipped on him right away. Montgomery could get a year or more in prison, but he'll probably get a lot less. It's a first offense, and he's cooperating with the investigation. His political career, however, is almost certainly over.'

I couldn't even bring myself to be pleased about Gavin's disgrace. He was to blame for a lot of things, but in the end, not for what happened to my daughter. He wasn't exactly the bad guy I'd thought he was.

The FBI was now investigating the Portage Point police chief. They'd found out he'd taken bribes and improperly accepted gifts from numerous politicians and high-profile businessmen. He was facing charges of extortion, falsifying reports, and obstruction of justice, to name a few.

'What about McNally?' I asked.

Samson rolled her eyes, a complete break from her usual professionalism.

'He took the easy option the chief gave him and basically ignored Olivia's case, didn't ask any questions. I know it's no excuse, but he's going through a divorce right now, and I think he's burned out. He won't get any big cases for a while, but it doesn't look like he was actively malicious.'

'Thank you,' I said to Samson. 'I mean it. I appreciate you working so hard on this.'

'I'm glad we found the truth.'

She turned to go, but I called after her. 'Samson?'

She stopped in the doorway, waiting.

'Did you put that note through my door?'

'What note?' she said. Her face returned to that emotionless mask, but I saw a flicker of a smile twitch at the corner of her mouth before she pulled the door shut behind her.

I turned to Olivia and stroked her hair, full of gratitude. After a moment Sarah said what had been in the room all along: 'Olivia isn't doing very well.'

'I know.' I sighed and grasped Olivia's hand tightly in mine. 'Dr Maddox called me.'

I looked at my daughter. She'd changed so much in the past few months. She was pale, her skin thin, almost translucent, wrinkled as if she'd been sat in water for too long.

Olivia still had no corneal reflex and didn't respond to painful stimuli. She didn't smile, didn't grimace, didn't twitch. Even though her hand was still warm in my grasp, her chest rising and falling in time with the hissing of the oxygen machine, I could accept now that she wasn't coming back.

In the past few weeks, Olivia had been plagued by kidney infections caused by the catheter and recurrent bouts of pneumonia. The tube feeding her intestines to keep the baby growing had also become infected a number of times, leading to fears of septicemia. Dr Maddox was now giving her ultrasounds daily to make sure the baby continued to grow.

Tears leaked from my eyes. I watched as one splashed against Olivia's pillow. Sarah put her arms around me. I leaned my head on her shoulder and sobbed as she held me.

Even in the midst of my pain, I was grateful for one thing: I'd learned to take comfort from my sister. Grief, it turned out, was easier to bear when you had somebody to share the burden with. Knowing that I wasn't alone, that there was somebody to throw me a line if I needed it, was a huge comfort. It reminded me there was life and a normal world I would one day be able to return to.

'Hello, ladies,' Dr Maddox called as she bustled into the room.

Sarah and I pulled apart, eyes wet, as Dr Maddox pressed her stethoscope gently to Olivia's chest, then to the bump at her stomach. After a few minutes, she turned to me. She looked exhausted, blue half-moons standing starkly beneath her eyes. She'd worked tirelessly to keep both Olivia and the baby healthy throughout more than four months on life support, the longest on record. I trusted her implicitly, but I was terrified of what she was about to say.

'It's time, Abi.'

43

ABI

february

I heard Sarah's sharp intake of breath.

'Is the baby okay?' I asked.

Dr Maddox hesitated. 'She isn't thriving. She hasn't grown much the last few days. Olivia has pneumonia again, and her kidneys are shutting down. Also, her blood pressure is dipping very, very low, so she isn't getting enough blood to the baby.'

She sighed and flipped the stethoscope over her head. It settled like a black snake around her neck. She fixed me with a solemn look as an array of emotions flickered across her face: resignation, pity, sorrow.

'We need to deliver the baby, now.'

I exhaled hard, blowing air out of my mouth through the pursed circle of my lips. 'It's too early,' I argued weakly.

'She's over thirty-two weeks now. It's a better outcome than we'd hoped. We can be optimistic about this. And now, with Olivia having so many problems, the baby's safer outside Olivia's body than inside.'

Suddenly there wasn't enough air in the room, my lungs sucking through narrow straws.

I'd known all along that when the baby was born, Olivia would die. But somehow that knowledge didn't make this moment easier.

'I've given Olivia another round of steroids for the baby's lungs and I've called ahead to make sure the OR is ready for a cesarean,' Dr Maddox said. 'We were just waiting for you to get here.'

I looked out the window and chewed my lips. A swirl of leaves spun dizzyingly past the window. The trees along the edge of the parking lot bent submissively under the onslaught of wind, and rain galloped down the windows, thrashing against the roof.

I hadn't been able to keep my mother from leaving me, or my daughter, but I could hold the family I *did* have together. The baby had to come first now.

'Okay.' If Olivia had taught me anything, it was that I had to let go of control. I had to release my fears of the past in order to face the future. Sometimes the rest of your life arrived by simply saying good-bye.

'Let's do this.'

× × ×

Derek rushed into Olivia's room as Dr Maddox was handing me sterile blue scrubs and a cap. His hair was standing on end, his blue eyes wide and panicked.

'Derek!' I hugged him briefly, and he started to cry. 'It's okay. You made it in time.'

He accepted the scrubs and cap Dr Maddox handed him and pulled them on over his clothes. I sent Anthony a text letting him know what was happening. He was getting his mom settled into her new home at an Alzheimer's care facility today, but I knew he'd be here as soon as he could.

Sarah gently kissed Olivia's cheek, then gave me a quick, hard hug good-bye, blinking fiercely. Only Derek and I were allowed in the OR. It wasn't strictly allowed, but I'd fought hard for it. I wasn't there when Olivia found out she was pregnant. I wasn't there when Tyler pushed her off that bridge. The one person she should've been able to count on no matter what hadn't been there when she needed me most.

I wasn't leaving her side now. I wanted it to be the last thing I showed her: that she could count on me not to abandon her. And Derek deserved to see his daughter being born.

Derek and I followed Dr Maddox through the double doors to the operating room. When we got there, the surgical team transferred Olivia onto the hospital bed, started an IV in her hand, and adjusted the ventilator and pulse oximeter. Two chairs were set at Olivia's head, and Derek and I sat in them as a nurse pulled a wide screen above Olivia's shoulders, blocking off the rest of her body.

'Baby's heart rate is dropping,' one of the nurses called.

Will the baby be okay?

'Get these scrubs on me,' Dr Maddox barked. She held her arms out and one of the junior doctors pulled the blue scrubs on her, then a pair of gloves, and she disappeared behind the screen.

A few seconds later the NICU team came, walking fast, three doctors in scrubs flocking to Olivia's lower half.

Please, baby, I pleaded silently. *Please be okay.*

I pulled Olivia's hand to my mouth and kissed my daughter's limp fingers, struggling to catch my breath. Suddenly everything seemed to be moving in fast-forward.

A monitor clanged, and Dr Maddox cursed. Something splashed on the floor.

'Oh, my God,' Derek whispered, his face pale as he stared at the ground.

When I looked, a shiny ribbon of crimson liquid was splashing the floor. It sloshed across the papered feet of the surgeons, staining them red.

I stared at that blood in horror, and I couldn't help it, I stood up, gawking over the edge of the screen. My mind couldn't seem to piece together what I was seeing.

When my brain finally caught up, I saw that Olivia's stomach was a bloody, gaping hole, held open by silver clamps. Blood was everywhere: smeared across the doctors' face masks, soaked into the sheet draped across Olivia's chest, dripping from the hospital bed onto the floor and squelching under the surgeons' tennis shoes. Dr Maddox's arms were cut off at the elbow, and it took me a minute to understand they were buried in the cavity of my daughter's belly.

And then she pulled out the tiny body of a limp, blue baby girl covered in blood. Something thick and white and veiny was wrapped around her neck.

A nurse from the NICU team grabbed the baby as Dr Maddox untangled and cut the cord. The nurse rushed the baby to the warmer, rubbing her briskly with a white towel. She murmured unintelligible words, a lullaby, in the baby's ear.

The silence went on and on.

Come on, baby, I pleaded silently. *You have to live!*

Silence.

The only sounds were Derek sobbing, the thud of my heart pulsing in my ears, the occasional clang of metal on metal, the squelch of feet on blood.

And then, like a miracle, from the corner of the room came the thin, reedy cry of a baby.

44

ABI

february

The heart's electrical system can keep it beating for a short time, even after a person becomes brain-dead. It's an amazing organ, the heart. In fact, it can even beat outside the body. But without a ventilator to keep blood and oxygen moving, the beating stops very quickly.

The doctors were tying blood vessels, working to stop the blood, to sew her up. But I knew Olivia, my girl, wasn't here anymore.

'We have to let her go,' I murmured to Derek.

He knuckled his eyes, swiped at the tears cutting his face. 'I know,' he replied.

He took a long, ragged breath and bent over Olivia's still face. Then he did something that broke my heart. He covered my daughter's face in dozens of tiny, butterfly-soft kisses.

'Good-bye, my love,' he whispered.

He stood then, his face a map of pain, one I could trace from the agony in his eyes to the torment pulling at his mouth.

'I can't be here when they turn it off,' he said. 'I don't want that to be my last memory of her.'

A few seconds later, he was gone.

In a way, he was right. I didn't want this to be my last memory of Olivia either. I wanted to think of the sweet baby-powder smell of her pressed against my neck when she was a newborn. I wanted to think of her building sandcastles on the beach on a hot summer afternoon when she was a child, or smiling at me on Mother's Day when she was ten and brought me a breakfast of runny eggs and burnt toast in bed. I wanted to think of her dancing that last day, her crimson scarf twirling around her neck, her face softened by her secret.

I wanted to think of her happy and alive.

But I wouldn't leave now.

I stood up again so I could see Dr Maddox.

'We have to let her go,' I said.

Dr Maddox stared at me, her eyes pale-blue orbs above her white face mask. Finally she nodded and murmured something to one of the other surgeons.

A few minutes later a plump, creamy-faced nurse pushed a mobile incubator to me, Olivia's baby inside. I peered in at her from my seat next to Olivia's head. She was tiny but perfectly formed. A nasal cannula was fixed under her nose, a heart monitor attached to her chest, and two more orbs stuck to either side of her stomach.

She was beautiful: tiny and pink, with her little face all

scrunched up like a fist. Her movements were slow, as if she were swimming in gel. Her perfectly rounded head was soft, with fine wisps of blonde hair. Her tiny fists were curved under her chin, her petal-thin eyelids closed; her chest moved up and down with each breath.

Looking at her, I felt as if I were falling headlong in love. All the love and hope and optimism I'd tried to tamp down my whole life came flooding out. I loved her, this tiny magic bean. She'd floated at the center of everything, growing into something completely unexpected: hope for the future.

'Zoe.' I reached for Olivia's daughter, brushed my fingertip across her rose-petal cheek. It was Greek for 'life.' 'Her name's Zoe.'

'It's perfect,' Dr Maddox said. Her eyes behind her glasses were puffy and red. She cleared her throat and pulled her mask down, stripped her gloves off. 'Zoe's doing well, but we need to take her to the NICU.'

'Can I have a minute with her first?'

Dr Maddox glanced at Olivia and hesitated.

'Please. I need to . . .'

Dr Maddox held my eye for a long moment. Unspoken words passed between us. I needed to say good-bye, and to do that I needed Zoe to say good-bye.

'Okay,' she said finally. 'But only for a minute.'

The doctors detached the drape from Olivia's neck. They tossed towels onto the floor to soak up the blood. Then the room emptied, and it was just Dr Maddox and Zoe and me.

I looked around, feeling abruptly winded.

'Here,' Dr Maddox said. She carefully extricated Zoe from the incubator's tubes, nudging the white blanket up around her small head. Zoe woke briefly, her eyes flicking to see what had roused her. She yawned hugely, and the clear tube taped to the side of her face moved as her tiny mouth searched for something to suck. Dr Maddox gently placed her tiny body in my arms. I brushed my lips across her velvety cheek, breathing her in.

I held Zoe, feeling the warmth of her body curling into mine. She was so small, barely the weight of a breath.

Dr Maddox looked at me and I nodded. She bent and unplugged Olivia's ventilator from the wall.

Olivia's heart didn't stop right away. Her strong, beautiful heart, a heart that had loved me so well, that had struggled to stay beating to see her daughter alive, it kept beating; but it slowed.

I knew we were running out of time.

'I'll be back in a minute,' Dr Maddox said. She turned and left very quickly.

Before I knew it, I was alone with them: Olivia and my granddaughter.

'Olivia,' I whispered, wishing more than anything in the world that she could hear me. 'Your daughter's here.'

I carefully moved the tubes and lines off Olivia's body and clasped Zoe tight as I stood and laid the baby on her chest.

I slid onto the bed next to Olivia, positioned her in my arms so I could hold her and prop Zoe against her. I clasped Olivia to me, feeling the sharp ridges of her shoulders beneath the hospital gown, the prominent bones of her ribcage.

'We named her Zoe. I thought you'd like it.' I turned my face into Olivia's hair, hoping to catch the scent of her, but it wasn't there anymore. It, too, was gone.

I had a sudden memory of her then. She was standing on the beach, looking out to sea, her hair a long blonde flag behind her, her cheekbones sharp in profile. She turned to me and caught my gaze, trapped it for a fleeting moment in hers. Smiled. A soft smile, the kind you give somebody you know by heart.

Zoe mewled softly and nuzzled into the crook of Olivia's neck.

'She knows who you are,' I marveled.

Maybe it's possible to remember your mother from the womb. Just for those first few moments. Maybe you remember her smell or something less tangible, the sensation of swimming inside her, the familiar cadence of her heart pulsing against your ear, the sound of your shared blood powering its every beat.

I tightened my arms around them both. Zoe started making tiny baby noises, and I thought she would cry, but she didn't. Her lids bobbed closed, open, then closed again, and she drifted asleep, her mouth hanging open.

Olivia took a ragged breath, but it stuck somewhere in her chest. A sob wrenched out of my throat. I wished I could do it all over again, go back in time and be a better mother. But there are no redos in life. You can't go back and make things better. All you can do is live with it and move forward.

I looked at Zoe, asleep on Olivia's chest, and I was whisked back in time to the morning Olivia was born. I zoomed in on a memory of how my hands dwarfed Olivia's tiny body; how well she fit in my arms; the love that overwhelmed me just at the sight of her. They say time goes by fast, but really it was a blink, every single second between then and now just a blur.

I stroked a hand across Olivia's cheek. It didn't feel soft anymore. Instead it felt thin, papery.

'Whenever, whatever. I'm here forever,' I said.

And suddenly I understood what my mom was saying that last day. She was saying good-bye. And in her good-bye, she was promising she'd be here, inside of me.

Zoe opened her eyes. Her gaze collided with mine and she gazed at me seriously, the way only a baby can. I studied the smooth contours of her cheekbones, the delicate line of her brow, the slope of her tiny nose.

She looked so much like Olivia did as a newborn it hurt. But it was also kind of nice, like Olivia hadn't really gone, in a way. Or maybe just like Zoe was a piece of her she'd left behind.

From Olivia's bed, I stared out the hospital windows toward the sea and watched the sun set, a trickle of light receding in the distance. Suddenly the sun met the horizon, momentarily washing the room in a dazzling display of gold.

It reminded me that the first hour of every new day starts with darkness – and then the sunshine comes.

And right then, in my arms, pressed against the tiny, warm body of her daughter, Olivia took a ragged, uneven breath: her last.

I like to think she left on the wings of that sunbeam, dancing the way she did on that last day, flying away. Free.

45

ABI

A few months later, when the spring air was just starting to warm, Anthony, Sarah, Derek, and I took Zoe to the cemetery hill where we'd buried Olivia.

I could've come alone, but Olivia wouldn't have wanted that. Maybe I couldn't save Olivia, but I realized now that I could save myself. I could learn to open up to love and second chances. I could be better at that.

Zoe was strapped in a baby carrier across my chest as I walked. She wriggled and kicked, her whole body vibrating with happiness. You'd never guess she'd been born prematurely after her mother spent months on life support. She was the picture of health, perfect and whole.

The sky above us was a vivid blue with cotton-ball clouds floating lazily, the grass a carpet of vibrant emerald. In the distance, the sea was a shimmering expanse of blue, white swells cresting, then rolling in to crash against the rocks.

When we reached the granite headstone marking where Olivia slept for eternity, I unstrapped Zoe and propped her on her tummy on a waterproof pink blanket. I inhaled deeply, complex emotions braiding my stomach.

Anthony wrapped his arms around me from behind and held me tightly, took all of my sadness and fear and anxiety and held them so that, just for a moment, I wasn't the only one carrying their weight.

I looked up at him. He'd recently cut his hair into a short spiky do and shaved his face. When his bright eyes met mine, my heart gave a little skip. I smiled and lifted my face for a kiss.

He seemed a lot less frazzled since he'd moved his mom into the home. He had regular visiting hours where he'd take her for long walks or just to a café to sit and be together. And he didn't have to worry anymore about whether she'd set the house on fire or get lost roaming the streets.

I didn't know what our future held, but I did know I trusted him, was letting myself trust him, in a way I hadn't done in a long time.

I leaned my head back against Anthony's chest and remembered the day he'd shown up at my house with an espresso machine. Zoe had only just come home from the hospital a few days before, and I was exhausted.

I'd looked at the espresso machine and knew it was a gift with a meaning.

'I have a lot of baggage,' I warned him. He carried the box to the kitchen and put it next to the microwave.

'I'll help you carry it,' he replied.

He pulled the machine out of the box and plugged it in with a flourish.

'Voilà.' He smiled. 'Caffeine.'

'I have a baby.'

'I love babies.'

He crossed to me and took both my hands in his, smiling gently. His eyes were a vibrant pale green as they caressed my face. 'One step at a time, okay?'

We formed a loose semicircle around Zoe, facing Olivia's headstone. It was the first time we'd all come together to see Olivia. The first of many, I was sure. And next time, Madison would be here. That's what we were hoping, anyway. The poor girl still hadn't forgiven herself for her last words to Olivia being cruel ones.

'Why didn't you tell us?' I'd asked her later. 'If you knew Derek was the baby's father, if you knew they were together, why didn't you tell us?'

'He's my brother,' she said simply. 'Even when I hate him, I love him. I wanted to protect him.'

I sensed Olivia would've forgiven Madison. Family, after all, was the most important thing. Family was proof that love existed.

Zoe kicked gleefully and let loose a delighted baby shriek. Derek picked her up and nuzzled her nose. He was an excellent father, around as often as he could be despite being at the University of Washington throughout the week.

We'd decided Zoe would stay with me. After Derek graduated from college and had his own place, she'd spend weekends with him. For now Jen, Sarah, and I shared childcare.

Sometimes worry and anxiety slipped in like an old friend, fear that I'd lose her. But I pushed it away. To feel love was to feel fear – you just couldn't let it dictate your life. Love was a risk, but it opened up a world of possibility, one you would never experience without it. I'd never understood that before losing Olivia.

Olivia's daughter was loved. That was the most important thing.

I looked at Zoe in her father's arms. She was a miracle. Every night when I rocked her to sleep, feeling the weight of her little head resting gently in the crook of my neck; every morning when she saw me and her face broke into a gummy smile; every time I held her bottle in her rosebud mouth and she gazed at me with absolute trust and adoration, she helped push some of the grief aside. I took comfort in knowing that, although nothing would ever make up for losing Olivia, I had more than just a memory of her in Zoe.

We'd all brought something for Olivia, and one by one we set our tokens against her headstone. Me, Zoe's hospital baby bracelet; Anthony, a single white rose; Sarah, a stick of cinnamon gum; and finally, Derek stepped up.

'I didn't bring you anything, Liv,' he murmured softly. 'But I brought this for our daughter.'

His voice was thick, gravelly, as if it hadn't been used in many months. He was different now, thin as a rake in his skinny blue jeans, his face almost as white as his T-shirt. His eyes were hollowed out by grief. I thought about the future he'd now face without Olivia in it – the future we'd all face.

He settled Zoe in my arms, then reached inside a large plastic bag and pulled out a framed picture, setting it on the ground in front of Zoe and me.

It was a charcoal sketch of Olivia. In it my daughter came to life: the tilt of her chin, the spark in her eye, the tug of a smile on her lips. She was looking at the artist, and I could see what she'd been feeling in that moment cracked open wide and on display for all to see: love.

I moved Zoe to my hip and knelt to trace my fingers across the portrait. 'Did you draw this?'

He nodded. 'I thought Zoe . . .' He stopped, raw heartache playing across his face.

'It's beautiful. I'll hang it in Zoe's room.'

On the horizon, the sun burst out from behind a collection of clouds, painting the sky gold. I looked around at my family. Never in a million years had I thought it would turn out this way.

I closed my eyes and let the grief wash over me, let the bitter sting of loss clutch at my bones. What followed was a release, not just of grief, but of gratitude too. Of what Olivia had given me, both in life and in death.

One of my tears splashed onto Zoe's cheek. She blinked, startled, and reached for my chest.

I pulled Zoe close, breathed in her scent, and whispered in her ear: 'Whenever, whatever. I'm here forever.'

ACKNOWLEDGEMENTS

Publishing a book is a team sport, and there have been so many amazing people along the way who have made this book a reality. First, thank you to my super-agent, Carly Watters at P.S. Literary Agency, for picking me out of the slush pile and making my dreams come true. You guided a novice writer to a debut author and believed in me every step of the way. I'm forever grateful for that.

Thank you also to my fabulous editor, Kate Dresser. Your insight and enthusiasm turned this novel into a polished piece of work, and truly inspired me. Thank you so much for taking a chance on me and being a champion for this book.

I am so grateful to the team at Simon & Schuster and Gallery Books who've worked so passionately on this novel: Molly Gregory, editorial assistant; Chelsea Cohen, production editor; Jen Bergstrom, publisher; the marketing team, Liz Psaltis, Abby Zidle, Mackenzie Hickey, and Sade Oyalowo; and publicist Michelle Podberezniak. Thank you also to HarperCollins UK, especially to editorial director Manpreet Grewal, who brought my book to the UK; editorial assistant Cara Chimirri; and the marketing and sales team, JP Hunting and Georgina Green. And thank you to my publicists Crystal and Taylor at BookSparks for giving my book the reach I hoped for.

I'm also grateful to Richard, my husband, my best friend, and my biggest champion, who not only let me disappear to write whenever I needed to but actively encouraged me every step of the way; and my boys, Adam and Aidan, who inspire and delight me every single day. Thank you for teaching me about love: the unconditional type. Also my wonderful friends who've listened to me talk about writing over coffee, wine, or basically any other time: Aimee, Anna, Annemarie, Danika, Natalie, Laura, Sarah, Nick, and Shareef. Thank you! And thank you to Lisa and Michael, who patiently answered my endless questions about police and detective procedures.

I am indebted to my mom, who encouraged me to reach for my dreams; my dad, who in life taught me to laugh and in death taught me to say good-bye; and my siblings, Kimberly, Sheri, and Daniel.

I would never have finished this book if it weren't for the insightful and inspiring teachings on story, plot, and character by John Truby in his London masterclass. Thank you for taking the time to answer all my questions.

Finally, thank you to all my readers and every single reviewer and book blogger who's taken the time to talk about my book. You are the reason I write. Thank you.

READERS GROUP GUIDE

This readers group guide for The Night Olivia Fell *includes an intro-duction, discussion questions, ideas for enhancing your book club, and a Q&A with author Christina McDonald. The suggested questions are intended to help your reading group find new and interesting angles and topics for your discussion. We hope that these ideas will enrich your conversation and increase your enjoyment of the book.*

Introduction

In the small hours of the morning, Abi Knight is startled awake by the phone call no mother ever wants to get: her teenage daughter, Olivia, has fallen off a bridge. Not only is Olivia brain-dead, she's pregnant and must remain on life support to keep her baby alive. And then Abi sees the angry bruises circling Olivia's wrists.

When the police unexpectedly rule Olivia's fall an accident, Abi decides to find out what really happened that night. Heartbroken and grieving, she unravels the threads of her daughter's life. Was Olivia's fall an accident? Or something far more sinister?

Christina McDonald weaves a suspenseful and heartwrenching tale of hidden relationships, devastating lies, and the power of a mother's love. With flashbacks of Olivia's own resolve to uncover family secrets, this taut and emotional novel asks: How well do you know your children? And how well do they know you?

Topics and Questions
for Discussion

1. Consider the novel's structure of Abi's and Olivia's alternating viewpoints and time periods. How do you think the reading experience might have been different if the story had been told chronologically? What about if it had been told by either one narrator or from a third-person point of view?

2. Compare and contrast Abi's and Olivia's perceptions of each other from what we learn about each woman through their own words in their designated chapters. Discuss the discrepancies between who they are and who the other person thinks they are.

3. It's clear that Abi and Olivia love each other deeply, but as with any mother-daughter relationship, they sometimes misunderstand each other. Are there any moments in the novel in which you feel they could have communicated better? Do any of these scenes remind you of moments in your own life with your mother or daughter? If you feel comfortable doing so, consider sharing them with your book club.

4. 'Mom told me I should stand up to her. Tyler said I always saw the best in people. The truth was, neither of them was right. I was just scared of not being liked' (p. 20). Discuss this statement of Olivia's and compare it to Abi's statement of 'I was really more of an observer than a participator. I was better at standing on the sidelines' (p. 53). While Olivia may seem more social on the outside, how do both women isolate themselves from others?

5. When Anthony tells Abi that he's 'just grateful I have [my mother] at all,' Abi thinks, 'It was a funny answer, so different from how I would look at it. But he was right' (p. 130). What else does Abi learn from Anthony about coping with grief?

6. Sarah tells Olivia about an experiment from her college psychology class where the teacher asked the class if they would prefer happiness or truth. Sarah's class chose happiness, but Olivia says she would choose truth, and claims that it brings happiness in itself. Consider these two statements. Do you think truth and happiness are mutually exclusive? Which would you choose?

7. 'I was scared. Of rejection. Of loss. Of hurt. Of being anything other than Olivia's mom' (p. 163). Why do you think Abi uses being a mother – the most vulnerable occupation of all – as a crutch to protect herself from the world?

8. When Kendall pretends she doesn't know Olivia, Olivia is deeply hurt, and says that 'the rejection was like acid in my stomach. I didn't know what I'd done wrong' (p. 175). Compare Olivia's feelings of rejection from Kendall, her half-sister, to Abi's feelings of rejection from Gavin, Olivia's father, years ago.

9. 'Being a mother wasn't something you just "handled" . . . her death didn't have anything to do with me at all' (p. 216). How do you think reading her mother's suicide note and learning more about her mother's death helped Abi cope with losing Olivia?

10. Mother-daughter relationships form the core of *The Night Olivia Fell*. Compare and contrast the relationships between Abi and Olivia, Abi and her mother, Olivia and her baby, as well as the relationship between Abi and Sarah, who plays a maternal role in Abi's life, the relationship between Madison and Jen, and any others you can think of!

11. When Kendall and Olivia spend time together, Olivia eventually realizes she's fond of her. 'It was cool that she might be my sister. I'd always wanted siblings' (p. 195). Compare Kendall and Olivia's relationship as half-sisters to Abi's relationship with Sarah.

12. 'If my mom had gotten an abortion, I wouldn't even be alive, so I couldn't do that to this baby' (p. 314). Compare Olivia's

reaction to her pregnancy to Abi's reaction to her pregnancy with Olivia years before.

13. Olivia says, 'My mom taught me that: Look to the future and you won't stumble on the present . . . I knew now why she was like that, and maybe it wasn't something you could unlearn, but I didn't want to be like that' (p. 329). Discuss the merits of living in the present versus planning with the future with your book club. Is there a way to balance both in our lives?

14. Author Christina McDonald keeps us guessing throughout the novel on who was ultimately to blame for Olivia's tragic death. When the guilty party is revealed, was it the person you suspected? Why or why not? If not, who else did you suspect, and why?

15. Throughout the novel in the present day, Olivia is kept on life support so she can carry her unborn child to term. Is it morally or ethically right to keep a woman, let alone a teenager, on life support to keep a baby alive? Respectfully discuss your views with your book club.

16. 'I let myself stand on that cliff and peer over the edge into the future, at the happiness that I could have one day if I would only allow it' (p. 148). Do you think Abi finally allows happiness to come to her at the end of the novel? How else does she grow as a character at the end of the novel?

A Conversation with
Christina McDonald

Q: **What inspired you to write *The Night Olivia Fell*? How did you visualize the cast of rich and varied characters and their emotions?**

A: Back in 2013 I was rocking my new baby to sleep while reading the news on my phone. I came across a story about a teenager in California, Jahi McMath, who had been declared brain-dead after a routine tonsillectomy went wrong. My first thought was for the girl's mother and how utterly heartbreaking it would be to lose your child. I think this is every mother's biggest fear – it's certainly mine!

After reading that story, I looked down at my new baby and imagined myself in Jahi's mom's position, and I started asking myself, 'What if?' What if her daughter was pregnant? Would that be a comfort or a curse? What if she'd suffered her own tragedies in her past? What if she were a single parent? What if she thought her daughter had been murdered, but nobody believed her? And thus was born *The Night Olivia Fell*.

Q: **How does your experience as a journalist and copywriter inform your fiction writing? Do you find any connections between writing news and writing thrillers?**

A: I started as a journalist, so obviously I've seen some crazy stories. I think a lot of these stories cemented in my head and they've given me a great launching point. But to write a novel you have to connect with your characters and the journey they go through. I learned that in copywriting. As a digital copywriter I had to guide a reader through different steps to get to the resolution I wanted them to reach, much the way an author has to when writing a book.

Being a copywriter and journalist gave me a huge appreciation for emotion, mostly because you have to take it all out when writing a piece. I like feeling things; I like the emotion I feel when I read, so this is the aspect where I feel most free when writing a book. Using sensory words that are vivid and evoke a taste or a smell – those things get lost a little in news (less so for copywriting), but I love words and how rich and varied they are.

Q: **You were born in the Seattle area, where the novel takes place, and you render the area's atmosphere so vividly throughout the novel. Can you talk about why you chose Seattle as the book's setting?**

A: I chose Seattle and the Puget Sound area literally because I was born there and have such a great history of experiences there. It was an easy place to use as a setting because it is so beautiful and varied. And I figure if you know it, write it. So I did!

Q: Besides Seattle, you've also lived in Ireland and London. Can you talk a bit about how each place informed your worldview, and subsequently, your writing?

A: I think each place I've lived has given me a rich perspective in seeing how people live, gathering more details about location, and meeting a variety of wonderful people. I've seen so many different people living different lives and having different experiences than what I would've done just by living in one place.

It's (I hope!) also made me far more open-minded, so I can now see that the way one person does things, or the way one country does things, may be different from another, but they're simply doing what's right for them in their particular set of circumstances. This ability to see both sides of the same coin has helped me create better characters, I think, who are more like real people: a mix of good and bad, right and wrong.

Q: On your website, you say that choosing to go to graduate school in Ireland 'wasn't part of the master plan,' but the result of a spontaneous trip. Can you tell that story a bit more in detail? Did you have another plan in mind?

A: I graduated from the University of Washington in 2001, and there were just no jobs in media or journalism. So I decided to work as a waitress for a year and save up to go traveling. I bought a ticket to London and headed off on my grand adventure, vaguely aware I wanted to go to Europe, but with no hard plans, accommodations, or bookings. Now I wonder what I was thinking, but then I guess I just wanted to be open to do whatever came up.

So I landed at London's Heathrow very early in the morning and was completely disoriented and jet lagged. I gathered my backpack and stumbled out of baggage claim and the first desk I came across was Aer Lingus. Completely on a whim, I bought a seat on the next flight to Ireland. I spent an absolutely amazing month traveling around Ireland, meeting some of the most incredible people and having the best time of my life.

At some point I ended up in Galway, and one night I was at the King's Head on Shop Street. Over a pint (Bulmers Cider for me!) a guy told me about a great master's in journalism program they had at the university in Galway. After I returned to Seattle I promptly applied, got accepted, sold all my stuff, and moved to Ireland, where I met my future husband.

It's one of those pivotal moments that completely changed the course of my life. I often wonder what would've happened to me if I hadn't seen that Aer Lingus desk!

Q: **How do you deal with writer's block? What drives you to keep going when you figuratively 'hit a wall' while writing?**

A: I sleep on it! Our minds subconsciously untangle problems when we're sleeping, so a lot of the time I'll have figured out the problem in my sleep and it will pop into my conscious thoughts at some point in the day. If this doesn't work, I talk it out. I tell my husband or my friends what I'm thinking, and usually I've sorted it out by the end of my monologue. Hearing things out loud or getting another's perspective really helps.

Q: **What are some of your favorite novels or authors? If you had to pick one that you think has inspired you the most, who or what would it be?**

A: One of my favorite authors of all time is Jodi Picoult. Her book *My Sister's Keeper* impacted me so much, in terms of emotion and structure, characters' POV, and the evocative use of words. Ditto John Green's *The Fault In Our Stars*. I'm not a crier, so if an author can make me cry, I know they've done something right. I also really love thrillers by authors like Heather Gudenkauf, Mary Kubica, and Clare Mackintosh.

Q: **What do you like to do in your spare time other than writing?**

A: I have two young boys, so I don't have a lot of free time. But when I do I'm a huge bookworm, so I like to read. I also love going to the gym and walking my dog in the park.

Q: **Are you working on anything now that you'd like to share with us?**

A: I'm working on a new domestic suspense novel set in Whidbey Island and London, in which a woman wakes in the hospital after being struck by lightning and can't remember if she killed her mother.

Q: **What do you most want readers to take away from *The Night Olivia Fell*? What emotion do you hope lingers in their minds when they close the book?**

A: Well, *The Night Olivia Fell* is a suspense novel, so I hope I keep readers flipping pages as they're trying to guess whodunit. But I also hope readers fall in love with Abi and Olivia and the world they inhabit. I want readers to have tears in their eyes and hope in their hearts, and I hope they really feel and understand the whole theme of the novel, which is that a mother's loyalty to her child is undying, even in the face of death.